A Stopping Place

A. G. MOJTABAI

Simon and Schuster
New York

1/1980
Gen'l

Designed by Elizabeth Woll
Manufactured in the United States of America

1   2   3   4   5   6   7   8   9   10

Library of Congress Cataloging in Publication Data

Mojtabai, A. G. date.
A stopping place.

I. Title.
PZ4.M715St   [PS3563.O374]   813'.5'4   79-18796

ISBN 0-671-23083-2

Acknowledgments

Two years of support from the Radcliffe Institute for Independent Study (now the Mary Ingraham Bunting Institute of Radcliffe College) and the Joan Carberg Memorial Fund have made this book possible. The Institute gave me more than financial support, important as this was: it provided time, faith, a community. A. Alvarez, Monroe Engel, Sidney Morgenbesser, Barbara Mueenuddin, and Nan Talese read the manuscript in its draft stages and raised searching questions. Ethel Held told me all about floaters. Conversations with John Haffenden, E. N. Mangat Rai, Carol Booth Olson, and Nayantara Sahgal have been generally helpful.

In order to refresh my memory with details of background and atmosphere, I consulted innumerable books, periodicals, and newspapers, then set all the facts aside to improvise and to dream, for A *Stopping Place* is a work of fiction. Readers familiar with the area will realize that I have scrambled many of the landmarks, directions, and dates. Even where the maps seem to be faithful, I have meddled, adding streets that never were to cities that emphatically are. And my meddling has not ended there.

Nevertheless, I have leaned heavily on a few factual books and documents; they are:

A *Stopping Place*

Ahmad, Jamil-ud-Din, *Historic Documents of the Muslim Freedom Movement*, Lahore, Publishers United Ltd., 1970.

Ali, Chaudri Muhammad, *The Emergence of Pakistan*, New York, Columbia University Press, 1967.

Baqir, Muhammad, *Lahore Past and Present*, Lahore, Punjab University Press, 1952.

Bolitho, Hector, *Jinnah*, London, John Murray, 1954.

Ispahani, M. A. H., *Qaid-e-Azam Jinnah as I Knew Him*, Karachi, Forward Publications Trust, 1967.

Mangat Rai, E. N., *Commitment My Style: Career in the Indian Civil Service*, Delhi, Vikas Publishing House, 1973.

Mehta, Ved, *Portrait of India*, New York, Farrar, Straus and Giroux, 1970.

Mullik, B. N., *My Years With Nehru: Kashmir*, Bombay, Allied Publishers, 1971.

Outlook: A Journal of Opinion, Karachi, Publishers Combine Ltd., 1963–64.

Report of the Court of Inquiry Constituted under the Punjab Act II of 1954 to Enquire into the Punjab Disturbances of 1953. (Munir Report) Lahore, Superintendent, Government Printing, Punjab, 1954.

I have cited directly John Berryman's "Dream Song #54," with permission from Farrar, Straus and Giroux, and Richard Wilbur's "Potato," with permission from Harcourt, Brace, Jovanovich. The brief translation of Asadullah Khan Ghalib is by Ahmed Ali, of C. P. Cavafy by Rae Dalven. I have consulted A. J. Arberry's, M. M. Pickthall's, and N. J. Dawood's translations of the Quran, and freely tampered with all of them.

None of the foregoing is responsible for my limitations or excesses, or the strange uses I have put them to in the service of my particular preoccupations.

A. G. M.
Cambridge—New York,
August 1978

To
CAROLYN HEILBRUN
and to the memory of
BETTY SEIFERT

Contents

PART II

PART III

Contents

Note to the Reader

While writing this book, I was haunted by an image—an image of parallel roads unfolding, nowhere converging . . .

The Place,
by Way of Introduction

Before Partition, the city of Alminar was large, bustling, and prosperous. For generations, Hindus, Muslims, Christians, Sikhs, and Parsis lived together, if not in peace, at least in a state of mutual accommodation. In 1947, this ended. Alminar was divided in half along the east and west banks of the Hafsa river and a shifting of populations took place.

In ironic deference to Sir Cyril Radcliffe, the man who, with a stroke of his pen, made two nations of one, the two halves of Alminar were called Cyrilabad and Radpur. Thus was a man's name torn asunder and what was unitary divided against itself.

In time, the fortunes of the two cities diverged. Both towns shared the same small industries, chiefly factories for the production of dyes and agricultural implements. Both shared the same terrain, the same weather. But the city of Cyrilabad, Pakistan, prospered as though blessed, while Radpur, India, fell into decline.

Cyrilabad had one unique asset—a holy relic, a hair of the prophet Muhammad, which brought thousands of visitors yearly and substantial wealth to the city and its ancient shrine.

Ten times a year, the relic was exhibited to the public, and pilgrims from many miles around flocked to view the sight, as beneficial to the faithful as a vision of the Prophet himself.

One thing leads to another. Due to the influx of visitors to Cyrilabad, the tourist trade and the merchandising of charms and prayer beads was brisk. The town railroad station with its nearby guest house became an imposing affair, and the road between Cyrilabad and its neighboring cities all the way to Lahore was paved and wide. But Radpur had no train station, and the road that led from Radpur to the nearest railroad town on the Indian side was unpaved, rutted, and narrow.

Still the river Hafsa flowed indifferently between the two towns, parching, flooding each in season. The two cities were close enough for the early risers of Radpur to wake to the first Muslim call to prayer, the *azan* for the setting of the stars. Habits die hard and, in the first days after Partition, old friends would shout across the river, but as time went on there were fewer old friends.

In March of 1964, the relic was stolen.

The book opens a few days before that theft, and moves toward it and around it. My story is less concerned with the theft than with the passions surrounding it and with the reverberations of those passions.

Whatever else it may be, my story is not as improbable as it sounds. There was such a relic and such a theft: it took place in Srinagar, Kashmir, at the end of December, 1963, and it very nearly precipitated a war between India and

The Place, by Way of Introduction

Pakistan. But I am writing fiction and have taken every liberty with this incident. As far as I know, there is no river named Hafsa. In any case, it cannot divide the cities of Cyrilabad and Radpur, for these cities do not exist.

A Stopping Place

A. G. MOJTABAI

Part I

—Of mightiest empire, from the destined walls
Of Cambalu, seat of Cathaian Can,
And Samarchand by Oxus, Temir's throne,
To Paquin, of Sinaean kings; and thence
To Agra and Lahor, of Great Mogul . . .

—Milton,
Paradise Lost, XI

1
In a Far Country

Lahore, Monday

It was so quiet, he could hear his heart open and shut, boom softly in expectation. Yet he was expecting no one. And was surely dressed to receive no one, bare to his barest briefs, cheeks grey with stubble, hair—what there was left of it—all straggles.

Tom Melus crossed the room to his only window and leaned out, but he might have been peering down a mine shaft, there was nothing to see. The night outside was warm, impenetrable, black as bell metal. There wasn't a sound.

Only . . . heartsteps . . . tumbling, slow . . .

It's crossing the border, he thought, always unnerving. Always a delay, a doubt—some difficulty, never named.

Today's trouble had started at the customs desk in Delhi. "Visiting poet, U. S. Information Service," Tom introduced himself, slapping down passport and State Department affidavits, "cultural ambassador, you might say . . ."

The clerk, a Sikh in a magnificent red headpiece, seemed unimpressed; he'd lifted one document after another to the lamp, and of course he'd managed to find some slight irregularity.

Was money supposed to change hands? Tom had hesitated. Maybe not. Weren't the Sikhs famed for their probity? Tom couldn't remember. Or was it their martial arts? Better not. The official made out a form in triplicate, then dispatched Tom to his supervisor, a certain K. Singh, a meticulous man in a still higher turban, with a beard so full he wore it in a hairnet, much compressed, the strings fastened over his ears.

A busy man, K. Singh. He received Tom's papers with his fingertips, without looking up. Tom sat quietly, heavily, trying his best not to look too hopeful, not to stare, not to stare at the hairnet. Finally, after a wait of more than an hour, K. Singh referred Tom back to the first official, who announced that everything was now in order as far as India was concerned, a clear intimation that Tom could expect trouble from the Pakistani officials on the other side. But there'd been no difficulties on the other side.

Which was just as well, for Tom's nerves were frayed, his temper close to flash point. Arriving in Lahore, he'd taken a taxi straight to the hotel.

Traffic was heavy: cars, bicycles, motor scooters, bullock carts, pedestrians, all swarming, and they moved slowly. The sun was setting. Tom caught a few glimpses of exotica on the way: a white dome, some minarets, small tent-towers that moved—women, he supposed, a boy brandishing stumps for limbs, beggars, gibbering shapes like scraps of paper blown about—a moving decor with human features. All distant still. As if he'd not yet touched down, but remained airborne in an unmapped space.

At the hotel, Tom had gone directly to his room. Even here, the sensation of weightlessness persisted. Tonight, he unpacked and settled in; in a very little time, he'd pack up and go. It hardly seemed worth the effort.

He opened his suitcase and took out only the immediate things, then disrobed, began pacing, staking out his new territory. It wasn't much: the walls were cream-colored, blank, the bed—modern, low and wide, with a thin cotton spread over it. Along its border, a procession of green camels marched round and round bearing gifts. Standing next to the bed was a brown armchair with a browning antimacassar. The only other chair was a wooden one that went with the desk against the far wall. A telephone, lamp, pitcher and water glass cluttered the small surface of the desk. The lamp was strange, squat and clumsy, with a painted leather shade and a red leather bulb for a base.

Except for the lamp, he might have been anywhere; the room resembled a hundred others from Akron to Calcutta. But the light, in its cone of leather, had a tinge to it, faintly bloodied. And now, in this light, nothing was familiar.

Tom wasn't sure where he was in the week, either. It might have been Sunday, he had that Sunday feeling, the desolation of the Sabbath. The empty, filching sadness. Nothing doing, no one around . . .

He located his engagement book and rummaged for the date. It was Monday. "Monday," he said it over to himself. And—wait, he squinted, there seemed to be something on for tonight. "Wick" . . . Howard Wick? Must be. A dinner set for nine. Sheffield Road. At nine . . . Plenty of time. He could make it if he wanted.

Well? It was something anyway to do.

Tom sang in the shower, his voice wobbling on the tiles. Drying off with vigorous swipes and pats, he felt better, braced. Oh, much better. Back into the same jockey shorts —not so good. No help for it, though, they were the cleanest to be had.

There was a big amber bottle on the shelf above the sink. Tom brought the bottle to his lips, took a short snootful— ah . . . And gagged. One more, lip to lip, a long slow pull . . . Easy does it. He flashed his gums at the mirror.

Then groped along the shelf, toppling things: blue pills for bad water, aspirin, cornplasters, suppositories, toothbrush with limp bristles, until he reached his razor. Another reinforcement from the big bottle. He whipped up a lather and began to shave. The mirror was a friendly one, dim with steam, his face came through bloated and kindly, softened through mist.

The mist was kindly but treacherous. Tom felt—sharp and tingling and clear—the tiny cuts mount up. With his palm, he swept the mirror clean, then stood, his hand pressed to the glass, wondering. Thought he heard—

"Who's there?" he called.

Some sort of commotion in the hall.

"WHO IS IT?" Tom shouted. "I don't want anything!" he added for good measure. The noise grew louder. He lurched to the door—

—unlocked! Someone must have leaned against it, the door cuffed Tom as it swung open.

A small crowd was waiting.

Mistaking Tom's presence at the door for an invitation, the men entered. Jostling, in twos and threes, they kept coming until the room was full. Tom was swept up in the confusion; he came to rest standing in the middle of it, arms crossed over his next-to-nakedness, ears flaming, blood loud within him. Someone had brought a garden into the room.

"Most esteemed Professor Sahib, sir—*Salaam aleikum!*" came a voice from the crowd. Mayhem followed: a tower of arms, a swirl of petals, a lasso, and looking down at his bare chest with its few sad grey hairs, Tom found himself harnessed in hoops of marigold and jasmine, among the flowers, bejewelled, enlaced.

Tom glanced desperately for cover and, finding none, had no choice but to brazen it out. The crowd drew back a little, and a man in white, a tiny man with a short forked beard, introduced himself as a spokesman for the Bulbul Academy, a literary society; these—his hand swept the room—were its members. After welcoming Tom to Lahore in perfectly plain English ("It is my pleasant duty to welcome you . . ."), he unfolded a page of notes and began to deliver a literary oration.

"Who is Thomas Melus, poet?" the prongs of his beard lifted in query. Then dipped, pointing, for the answer was written down. "A degree-holder of far repute, a critic of the utmost uncommon acumen, a bouquet of profuse particularities, of gifted talents numberless . . ."

The speaker drew a deep breath and continued. "His poetry shall live on, unparallel, the simplicity and multiplicity, loftiness and lowness, fragrance and flagrance, unflinchingness, promptness, ripeness, rareness, noncompliance, all so melodious and harmonious. I have read it all —all—and ensozzled myself. Such is my captivation, *such* my heart's fond adhesion!"

"And now I welcome the distinguished sahib and beg leave of the intellectuals . . ."

"Hear! Hear!" and "Wah! Wah!" abounded on all sides. Hearty applause followed; the spokesman stepped back, flushed and gratified. It seemed to be Tom's turn. He felt quite numb.

Decked out in garlands above, jockey shorts below, Tom felt his image somewhat short of ambassadorial. *Clearly* short of ambassadorial, for the welcoming speaker kept his eyes glued to Tom's head and neck, never once straying below. The strain of the man's effort showed, giving his face an aspect of frantic fixity.

Under the circumstances, Tom's reply was halting and monosyllabic. He thanked the group for the warmth and exuberance of their welcome. He thanked the spokesman for his eloquence and generosity. He proclaimed the growing closeness of East and West, the necessity of mastering both great cultural heritages in tomorrow's world. Once Tom warmed up to it, there was no hitch; he'd made this speech before.

If they were disappointed, they had the grace not to show it; if they had wanted something from him, they never betrayed it. There was much embracing, pressing of garlands, a confetti of hands, then they shuffled out quietly as though a full day's work had been accomplished. The spokesman was the last to leave; he took Tom's hand in both his small ones and said: "Someday, God willing, I shall translate you."

Tom said what had to be said: that he was honored, that he was not worthy, and the spokesman went his way. Tom waited until the last footstep had faded, locking the door carefully, this time, drawing the bolt. He took a long, deep breath.

Then Tom Melus, man of "gifted talents numberless," fell soddenly across the bed. He lay there with arms and legs flung out, heaped with flowers as though for the ultimate bed. Too weary to begin disentangling the garlands, his right hand brushed the floor and rested there, beyond retrieval. The flowers weighed upon him, their scent heavy, rank.

Ensozzled . . .

For some minutes he slept and saw nothing but unbroken darkness. He floated. It was so restful . . . He was at a party; the lights had just dimmed. Everyone was lying down. He moved on all fours, groping, struck something soft, caressed it. It was a woman's hip; she sighed deeply. The wrong woman: the hip was too full. "Sorry," he said, "I made a mistake." She clutched his hand and cried out: "You schmuck—don't stop now!"

Tom woke in a cramp: the garlands were strangling him. Unable to sit up and lift them over his head, he snapped the strings. He shifted to his side and was about to fall off again when the phone started. He rose, tottering to the desk, his eyes only half open.

"Hey—" the voice was American, "you all right?"

It was Howard Wick. He mumbled a bit, then said: "It's about our shindig tonight . . ."

"Tonight?" Tom tried to recollect. There was a dinner

party tonight, yes. At nine, he remembered, and this single isolated clarity amazed him, for he could not at this moment name what country this was, or the city he was in, the most basic things. Nevertheless, he would not panic. He *would* not. It would come to him, by and by. And if it didn't, he would ask someone.

"I'm about to send my car around. Think you'll be ready?"

Tom fingered his chin uncertainly, discovered to his surprise that he'd already shaved, and assured Howard that he would be.

2
A Gathering

"If we're going to talk about boundaries, we might as well begin by dividing up the lawn," said the man on Tom's left. The group moved down the steps and reassembled on the grass.

"Let this be the Hafsa River," he continued, indicating a border of marigolds with his right hand. "And this—" his left hand traced a wandering curve, "this is the ill-fated Sialkot-Jhelum line."

Tom Melus wavered on the ill-fated Sialkot-Jhelum line; the man in grey moved swiftly down the garden, his listeners in train.

"Tom!" A voice from the porch.

Howard Wick, cultural attaché and host of the evening, stood with arms out, smiling broadly. Tom mounted the steps and joined him on the verandah. They gripped hands vigorously and greeted each other like the old friends they scarcely were. They'd both taught at Fordham extension at one time, sharing an office. That was nearly twenty years ago, and they hadn't met since.

He's gone a bit slack, Tom thought. Not much, though.

Each stood back a little to gauge the ravages of time, each scanning the other to guess at himself. The years had not been unkind to Howard, they'd only honed a little here, blurred a little there. Pin stripes minimized, but did not mask, the thickening torso. His hair seemed closer to the bone than before, and soft pouches narrowed his still-brilliant blue eyes. Howard had been excessively handsome when Tom first met him; he'd lost a certain surplus now, but he was handsome even so. "I'd know you anywhere," said Tom. "You, too—you look just the same," said Howard, "well *almost* just the same." They both laughed. "Good to see you, Tom. Wasn't interrupting anything, was I?"

"Not a thing."

"Just run along—don't let me keep you if I was. Anderson's an old Asia hand and quite a performer. Fascinating business."

"Too political for me," said Tom. "I'm not in the least political. Never was."

"Quite right," said Howard affably. "Can be an awful bore, really. Take Anderson here. He goes to a party and never stops working. Always talking shop—he puts us all to shame. Sometimes I think that's what he means to do."

"Hon, how could you? Here's a guest with nothing in his hand!" Howard's wife—she could only have been Howard's wife—wedged a place for herself between the men. "Nan," she said, extending a cool hand. "I don't expect you'd remember me, no way you could. I came into Howie's life a year or two after Fordham." Tom noticed that the couple wore matching colors: Howard's tie and breast-pocket handkerchief had been cut from the same tawny silk as his wife's dress.

She was a stunning woman—sleek, sharp-chinned, vibrant. Her gold hair, riffled by invisible winds, was lacquered stiff and frozen in motion. Gesturing rapidly with her hands, her eyes flashed as she spoke, yet her face re-

35

mained carefully composed. She must be Howard's age, Tom decided, but fighting every inch.

"So . . . it's your first visit," said Nan. "How do you like it?"

"Give him a chance," said Howard, "he's hardly arrived."

"Only sampled the air so far," said Tom. "Seems balmy enough."

"Oh, this isn't the usual," Nan assured him. "It's crazy —we just skipped a month. The *rath-ki-rani* is out already. Everything blooming like April. Means summer will be blazes." She turned to her husband: "Hon—do get the man a drink."

"What'll it be?" said Howard.

"Scotch and water would be fine."

"Where were we?" said Nan.

"Just in from Delhi," said Tom. "Oh, say—" he called after Howard, "the less water the better."

"That's marvellous." Nan smiled. When she said "marvellous," her voice deepened and dipped. Like a mating call.

"What is?" Tom asked. "Whiskey and water?"

"Oh *come*," said Nan. "I mean India."

"That all depends." Tom did not elaborate. "Tell me about yourself—you and Howard—how long you've lived here. Fill me in."

Nan began to fill him in, then stopped. "Here comes your drink," she said.

"Your drink," said Howard.

"Your guest," said Nan, handing Tom over. "Must be off to the ladies now."

"Let me take you round," said Howard, "now that you're armed. Let's go in." He slipped his hand under Tom's elbow and they went forward through the vestibule into the parlor. The air was close inside. Tom balanced his glass in the other hand, sipping noisily as he went. The glass was none too steady, so the quicker he emptied it, the better off he'd be. They skirted a dense cluster in the middle of the room. "There's Alavi, the Iranian ambassador," said Howard. "Oh," said Tom, "where?" He looked back over his shoulder. "There—in the middle," said Howard, "the hole in the doughnut. He's at least a head shorter than anyone else. You'll forgive me if I don't introduce you right now. It's too jammed to get an elbow in."

"Seems very popular," said Tom.

"Brazenly so, if you ask me. Dreams of empire."

"How's that?"

"Well, the court language of the Mughals was Persian, you know. That was the golden age of culture here. Way he tells it—Alavi, I mean—nothing much has happened since."

"Could be," said Tom.

"Now he wants to bring back the Persian language as a solution to the local language question."

"Local what?" said Tom, who was having difficulty following any one voice above the din.

"You know—whether Pakistanis should speak Urdu or Punjabi or Sindi or Pashto, or you name it. Locals will *kill* for the mother tongue, and there's God's own abundance here, a hundred mothers, so you can just imagine."

"Nothing wrong with English," said Tom, "it's already here."

"Tainted by association."

"Were the Mughals so benevolent?" Tom wondered.

"Of course it's a pipe dream—Alavi's off his rocker. No one's turning the clock back . . . John Gore, British Council—I'd like you to meet Tom Melus. You two have a lot in common. Tom—John . . ." The introductions began, a rapid succession of faces and hands—a CENTO representative, a rather haughty Iranian press attaché, an editor from the local branch of Oxford University Press, a burly American military attaché in a crew cut with the improbable name of Fred Flower, and a man named Kenny, who seemed to be an American, but whose title and affiliation Tom failed to grasp. A fellow named Sam Curtis joined them: he called himself "a used-car dealer," but Kenny introduced him as "a business consultant." It couldn't have mattered less to Tom, either way.

Tom was not adept at circulating. Standing in one place as the crowd shifted, he seemed to get around. He watched people come and go. They call this "meeting people," he marvelled. Around him, people jostled and stood still, bumped and recoiled. The faces changed, although the questions were the same; even the points at which these conversations were broken off had a certain sameness, and they always were broken off. Howard had unobtrusively removed himself during the second shift, leaving Tom on his own.

Tom looked on, as though from a great distance. Around him, voices rose and fell, hands zigzagged in their wake, like birds caught in a confusion of currents. Then someone caught his attention—a dark, tall man with startling white hair—the only native in the room. He was standing near the sofa with his back to Tom, haranguing one of the Americans Tom had just met. The American, whose name Tom could not remember, was listening patiently with his head inclined at a graceful angle; he had just conceded a point, but the native was still pressing his argument home: "Once upon a time, Westerners came to rule. Now they come East wanting to *be ruled*, tired of too much freedom, they come seeking order and submission. It's quite a stunning reversal when you think of it."

"Oh, you mean the hippies," said the American. "They've gotten far too much attention for their numbers. They're really quite a small group—in comparison."

"In comparison with what?" asked the native.

"Why, with the rest of us," said the American.

"Who's that?" said Tom, turning to his neighbor.

"Which one? You mean Kenny?"

"No, no—the dark one. With the white hair. Over there —standing with his back to us. I thought Asians were a passive lot."

"Must be Nirmal Roy—I recognize the voice. An old ICS man. He's such a hermit these days—it's rare to see him being social."

"Can't say I'd call that being social."

"For Roy it is. I'm amazed to see him going through the motions."

Tom continued eavesdropping, intrigued by the native's intransigence; Roy was now holding forth to a small crowd, and seemed to be quarrelling with Gore, the British Council man. "You paid no attention to Edmund Burke, you see, and the consequence was—you lost America."

"Well now, *I* never lost America. I never had it," said Gore soothingly.

Too many voices after that for Tom to follow the rest of the conversation. He scanned the room for other diversions, noticed a shock of red hair, and then the women's enclave in a quiet corner. Tom had seen this happening all over India; there was a steep, but not impassable, divide between the men and women's sides of the room. Here goes—into the breach, he said to himself, plunging forward. His eye had chosen and his feet followed.

"You look like a rose among thorns," he said, "no fooling." She smiled doubtfully, a mousy-looking girl in a dress too long for her. "That's *some* dress," said Tom. "You like it?" she said. "Do *you?*" he answered. She looked down at herself, pinching the fabric of the skirt: "I don't know . . ."

Who's she trying to impersonate? Tom wondered. And why? It was an old-lady dress of sensible grey flowers on a mauve ground. How old was she? Twenty-three? Twenty-five? Could easily pass for twenty. Her face was prim and pale, with a spray of freckles over high cheekbones and a pert nose. Young, but nothing special. She had a bad habit of squinting. It was her hair that had struck him, clear across the room, like a shout. Hair the color of burnished copper, curly and so full that it had worked free of its restraining pins and fell in wandering spirals over her forehead and ears. Hair of Lilith, it blazed.

"My name's Tom—Tom Melus."

"I know," she said, "you're the visiting poet. USIS tour, right? Howard told me. I'm Kate Nazar."

"Nazar? Don't think I've ever heard a name like that before."

"It was Conway before I married. Nothing unusual in that. You know—it's funny—I heard you give a reading once, years ago at one of the libraries in New York. I like poetry—I like to listen to it, not just read it with my eyes."

"Small world," said Tom. "You're from New York, then?"

"Oh, no, from Chicago. Not even Chicago—the sticks."

"And you came to the Big City seeking glamour, romance—"

"I wanted to be an actress. Isn't that corny? Just what every girl from the sticks wants to be? Anyhow, I never made it. So I took a job—clerk-typist, only thing I could find, and was bored to death. Then I met Firuz."

Tom waited for more.

"And now you know the story of my life," she concluded.

An exceedingly short story, Tom thought. "So Firuz is the happy ending?" he asked.

"Firuz is my husband. Here he comes now—I'll introduce you."

"No need," said Tom, turning in time to see an intense young man with a moustache bearing down upon them. "We've already met." This was the rather imperious Iranian, the press attaché, to whom Howard had introduced him earlier. His appearance was nothing short of princely. He was wearing a dark grey suit with a pearl grey silk tie and a silver clasp. He said: "I see you are enjoying my wife."

"Give me time," said Tom.

Firuz, innocent of the idiom, did not see the humor of
this, and the conversation soon flagged. Tom sensed that it
was time for him to move on, excused himself, and turned
to the neighboring ladies. He was sad to leave Kate behind
with her husband, but it was clearly indicated. By now, he
was curious to know what brought her from Chicago to
Lahore via Iran—it seemed a tortuous route to a dubious
destination.

He moved on, and into a circle dominated by Mrs.
Kenny, a stout, elderly woman with a fan. It was a
hatchet-shaped fan of woven straw and Mrs. Kenny moved
it abruptly up and down as she spoke, although the evening
had grown cool. Chop: "She's fifty if she's a day." Chop:
"Only her hairdresser knows for sure." Chop: "It's no secret, dear, she's slippery as an eel at bedtime, simply packed
in lotion. She never uses soap . . . her little secret . . .
don't ask me why . . ."

It took Tom a full moment to realize that the lotion story
referred to Nan Wick. With each chop of the fan, a repu-
tation suffered, an illusion died.

"You've met the international couple?" she said to Tom.

"Who?" said Tom.

"The Persian-American pair?"

Tom nodded.

"Siamese twins, practically," she observed, "joined at the
shoulder. Never saw such a close couple."

Tom glanced over to where Mrs. Kenny was looking and
saw Firuz squeeze Kate's shoulder. It did not seem a wholly
loving gesture to him, and he did not miss Kate's slight
recoil.

Mrs. Kenny was a shrewd woman, and lively at first; her
cool, merciless eye roamed the room, and stabbed where it
rested. "He's a doll, all four feet of him, a living doll," she
said of the Iranian ambassador, "God's gift to woman . . ."
There was a brief silence as she picked up her glass and
drained it. "You'll have another?" someone said. "No, no,

I never really drink," she replied, "no more than a nightingale's tear, as they say here . . ."

Two people drifted off, others filled in, and the group took on a new shape. Mrs. Kenny was beginning to repeat herself, however; she was back at Nan Wick and her revelations were no news the second time round.

Tom was bored again. In Delhi, he'd met some adventuresome women—there'd been one from the Midwest who was making her way around the world as a call girl. That took spunk. But here all the women seemed virtuous. And the men were no better, or worse—stuffed. Crashing bores. Tom excused himself and walked on into another room. This was much better, emptier, and he noticed at once the warm corner where the bottles stood.

Unfortunately, the bottles were not unattended; a bearer stood over them. "What'll it be, sir?"

"How about scotch and water?" said Tom. "The less water the better," he added.

Tom pulled the glass away quickly to avoid the offending water. Too quickly, he saw. The gesture was not lost on Nan, who was making her rounds. "Well, Tom," she congratulated him, "I see you've found a place close to the bar. How'd you manage that?"

"Native intelligence," he answered, smiling. For an instant, his eyes sparked and he looked quite intelligent. The scotch was in him now, steady comfort, like a banked fire. He studied the half-empty glasses littering the table, their upturned mouths inviting him. Contrast and compare, they seemed to say. And he was game. Another finger of, a peg, a belt, no more. When Nan and the bearer had stepped away, he lifted first one glass, then another, quite calmly and experimentally, as though he were conducting a highly responsible survey, a taste test. But he tasted nothing; slack, indifferent, numb, he craved only the burning. Sometimes, Tom thought his thirst and his aching to express were one and the same—his lips moved when he strained to write, his poems welled up out of his throat.

Used to well up . . .

The bearer returned, and with a slight adjustment of the same motions, Tom was able to change his act completely, gathering the glasses together, going through a charade of helping the man clean up. "Take 'er away, Brevelli," he said. "My name is not Brevelli, sir," said the bearer with pained dignity.

Tom decided he'd overstayed his welcome in this corner and left to find himself another. Not much later, soup was served. Cream of something—celery, perhaps. The same bearer who'd been acting as bartender brought the soup round in large teacups and saucers. It was an awkward way of serving and especially so for Tom. "Is this the usual custom?" he asked his neighbor. But got no answer. The man was so busy blowing and sipping, he seemed not to have heard.

Teacups made Tom nervous, whatever their size. The cup rocked unsteadily in its saucer. He stashed the thing on the nearest shelf and busied himself with his pipe. The other guests stood in clusters and spooned their soup slowly, with delicacy.

After soup, the guests gathered in the dining room for the buffet supper. Everyone commented on the magnificent spread. There was an array of cold meats and salads in the American fashion, a hill of white rice, a hill of yellow, two steaming tureens of curry on each corner, one hot, one mild, and bowls of curd everywhere in between, some sweet, some salted.

Tom approached the formidable buffet and began heaping his plate. A dab of everything was his policy—that kept the hostesses at bay. The plate full of leftovers could always be tucked away between the knicknacks somewhere. He wanted to eat in peace and not have to chatter.

He was busy dabbling in the curry when he spotted a woman headed in his direction; he ducked his head down low to his plate and took a full mouthful, hoping she'd made some mistake.

No mistake—she had her sights fixed on him, she kept on coming; he could hear the glass bangles chiming on her wrists.

"Kate's told me all about you. I'm Sue," she began at once.

"Tom Mel—" he whispered, his mouth afire.

"Curd," she answered, recognizing his symptoms at once. "Only thing that helps. Whatever you do, don't drink water. Water only makes things worse."

"Pleased to meet you, Sue Curd," he said when the burning subsided.

She opened her mouth to correct him, then smiled. "Actually, it's close—it's Sue Curtis. But you couldn't of known that." Gold hearts, little ones, danced in her earlobes. For an instant, they distracted Tom from her plainness, her long face, long teeth, and ubiquitous gums. She smiled continually, and never to her advantage. She was a small-town girl from Missouri, she told Tom, and before she married she'd never been out of the state. "You'd never know it," Tom said graciously. "You're putting me on," said Sue. "No, no," said Tom, "I mean it," already weary of the gallantry. Tom thought she said her husband was a used-car dealer, and that they travelled a great deal in his line of business.

"Kate says you're a *fantastic* poet."

He snickered unpleasantly.

She pretended not to notice. "I write poetry," she confessed. "Well, verse—I guess you'd call it. Anyhow, I try. Just to amuse myself, something to do. I don't fool myself that it's great stuff or anything."

Tom continued to make an effort: "I suppose you find a lot to write about here?"

"Sure. I love the East, don't you?"

"Like I love Coney Island," said Tom. "Look, let's talk about something pleasant. How about Kate? Tell me about Kate."

"There isn't much to tell," said Sue. "I mean, there *may* be, but I just met her tonight. You talked to her husband?"

Tom made a gesture that might have meant yes or no.

"I see you have." Sue went on to tell him what little she knew about the couple.

"I can't figure out what girls like Kate and you see in this kind of life," said Tom. "You really like it?"

Sue insisted that she did. She was a social person, loved parties and crowds, gracious living, *adored* travel—it broadened the mind, didn't he think so? "New experiences. One is bound to grow . . ."

"You say 'one' is bound to grow—do *you* grow?"

She nodded vigorously.

"Really? You're lucky, then. It never happens to me," said Tom. "I always hope it will. I float, the old ties loosen, that's all. I feel like a voyeur sometimes." She stared. "That's right, Peeping Tom. But most of the time—like now—I don't see anything new. I see people from home, the same sort of people. Here I am, moving down this sanitized corridor the embassy has made for itself—"

He could hear her stiff intake of breath, the little click of the glottis that said "cut." Like a telephone disconnection. But why? Tom wondered. Just when he'd started saying what he thought. Sue stared at him blankly.

Tom was alone in the silence. He glanced nervously from left to right; suddenly there was too much space around him, as though he'd found himself playing tennis in the wrong court or driving down the wrong side of the road. Finally, Sue spoke: "No need to be rude."

"I'm not rude, I'm candid," said Tom, smiling benignly. "I'm all candor."

Sue did not return the smile. "Must get some more of this," she said, pointing to a smudge of something on her plate. "Nice meeting you."

"Charmed."

Tom moved on to a crowded, laughing cluster. People in

this group were enjoying themselves so much they'd never notice him, and that would be restful.

It was quite restful, for a while. The bland agreeable words went back and forth like singing rounds. Tom pretended to be listening, turning his head from side to side, from volley to volley, but the words conveyed nothing distinct. He'd lost sight of Kate. Whenever he focused on someone's face, he saw loose threads, wisps of shadow blowing past, giving the face, the scene before him, the texture of an old film.

Words and rounds. His floaters were back with a vengeance—rifts in the fabric of things. They were slight and insubstantial enough when Tom's attention was fully engaged, but devastating otherwise.

Floaters, little feathered wisps, aptly named "*muscae volitantes*"—flitting flies—they'd come along, keeping Tom company all the way from New York to Delhi to Lahore. Sometimes he saw past them, and crossing the border, Tom had hoped wildly as he did the first time and every time: now I'll be free of them: clean, clear sight ahead. He'd hoped—fully knowing it couldn't be: the floaters were part of him, casked and sealed, minute hemorrhages drifting into the vitreous chamber of the eye. "You'll simply have to think beyond your eyeballs," the doctor advised. "You could go easier on the alcohol, that never hurts." Ah, but it did, it did hurt.

"Overheats the blood," someone said, "better not."

The unreality was strong now. Tom could not believe that he was part of the charade, standing here in white collar, black shoes, bored, screamingly bored, not letting a sound out. He tried his pipe; it had a bitter taste. Bitter equals real, he told himself, and was momentarily calmed.

Dessert was served: rice pudding flavored with rosewater and almonds. The pudding was crisscrossed with thin gold and silver strips, hammered to an almost transparent thinness. "Custom of the country," one man said, spooning up

silver. "Good for the heart, they tell me." He sounded none
too sure. "Thought it was the liver—good for the liver,"
said another. "My dears, it's nothing of the kind. It's con-
spicuous consumption, plain and simple," said Mrs. Kenny,
who'd been eavesdropping in her travels to and from the
buffet. "It's the famed spirituality of the East—that's what,"
she pronounced, and continued on her way.

Liver or heart—or show, it made no difference to Tom;
the precious metals, though tasteless, soured the delicate
pudding for him, and he abandoned the dish half-eaten.
He made one further attempt at conversation, then let it
go.

He'd lost the knack, he'd lost the knack of the most ordinary things, of knowing how much pressure to exert in a
handshake, when to let go the hand, when to stare a man
down, when not to stare. He couldn't keep his pipe alight
for more than a minute at a time. His right forefinger had
gone dead from tamping the bowl; it was so thickly cal-
loused that, though he touched fire, he felt nothing.

There was no clock. The voices of the guests were thick
with eating. Tom edged back the cuff of his shirt to glance
at his watch. Nearly ten: the second hand went round and
round, mouths gaped open, snapped shut. Americans
tended to open their mouths wide, to curl their tongues and
display their fine dentistry; the British were close-lipped.
Tom might have drawn significant social generalizations
from these facts had he been energetic and interested; but
he was not energetic, he hadn't the slightest interest. He
badly needed a change of scene.

Tom asked his way to the lavatory, found it without mis-
hap, but lost his way in returning. The house was huge and
rambling. He stumbled into a room where the coats and
shawls of the guests lay heaped on a bed. A short, stubby
man in an overcoat and lavender ascot was primping before
the mirror; he had just licked his finger and, with it, was
carefully guiding his few remaining strands of top hair

across a shining bald pate. He seemed to have some sort of part in mind, but what it divided was a mystery. "Sorry," said Tom, feeling he'd stumbled into something intimate. The little man glanced up—a moon face distinguished only by sideburns and heavy eyebrows—then back to the mirror, without comment.

Could that be the little ambassador? Looks harmless enough, Tom thought, and went on.

Tom walked on to the end of the hall and found himself out on a verandah overlooking the back garden. It was smaller, yet more luxuriant and wild than the garden in front of the house. The borders here were tangled with dark vine and shrubbery and laced with jasmine creeper, a thin, shimmering trail of phosphorescence. He breathed in deeply.

Then he heard voices behind him, a door slammed; he stepped back, away from the railing, into the cover of shadow. A couple brushed past him, crossed the verandah and tottered down the steps leading to the garden, the woman wobbly on very high heels. The man and the woman were both strangers to Tom; he hadn't encountered either of them in the course of the evening. Tom wished he had met the woman, at least. Her voice was slow and languishing, it pleased him. "Full moon . . ." she said.

"What?" said the man.

"Nothing."

"Sorry. I didn't catch—"

"Nothing to be sorry for. I said nothing." She sighed deeply. "It's gotten chilly. Let's go back."

They opened the door and voices tumbled out—a man's laughter, in short, sharp spurts. Then other voices, fainter, muted . . . pipings from the bottom of a well.

Tom stepped out to the edge of the verandah again. He inhaled deeply. Spring . . . he could smell it, a touch of swamp, a touch of jasmine. He leaned over the balustrade, hoping to ease the load on his heart. It was too much—the mixed drinks, the stifling party, that pathetic girl with the untamed hair. He moved down the length of the verandah and leaned out again. Worse here. Here, the air was thick and oppressive, clotted, cloying with sweetness. It was that infernal bush, Queen of the Night, maddening the air around it. When Tom was really drunk, sick drunk, the liquor poured out of his nose sometimes. The nearness of the Queen bush felt much the same way; it streamed and seemed to stream from him, so deep an invasion of privacy.

He walked away, out from the hedge and the shelter of the verandah into the moonlit open space. This was much better. He could breathe easily now. The lights from the house did not reach beyond the verandah, only the moonlight, clear, even and mild. Tom took a slow circuit of the garden. He was feeling steadier now.

The lawn was bounded by a garage on the right and what looked to be an outhouse on the left. On closer inspection, the outhouse turned out to be a kitchen. The cook emerged and stood in the lighted doorway, stirring a tin bowl. His clothes, once white, were covered with soot; his hands were black to the elbows. He traced a wide arc with his hand, flinging outward from his chest, the gesture of a man throwing seed to chickens or dispersing a flock of crows. Tom heard scratching and scuttling in response, but saw no birds; he stood at a fair distance and fixed his gaze on the clumped shadows at the cook's feet. It was puzzling. The clumps seemed to be laundry sacks. Then the sacks began to heave; small rakes on sticks, or brooms of twigs— *hands*—reached out. And then Tom saw and understood: a family of scavengers, humped low to the ground, moved in a closed circle, their fingers scraping: they, too, were dining.

It was high time to make his way back into the house.

"Thought we lost you," Howard greeted him. The party had thinned out. The remaining guests were sipping brandy and benedictine. Howard made a space for Tom beside him. This time, Tom recognized most of the guests: the Kennys, Fred Flower, Nan, Sue, Sam Curtis. Howard was complaining about Mahmoud, his bearer, who had a mind of his own and had all but ruined the evening with his stubbornness. When giving out soup, Mahmoud had served the Iranian ambassador last, since he was the shortest man in the room, and he'd served some Turkish nonentity first, because the Turk was tall and looked imposing. The implications were not lost on the parties concerned, and the Iranian ambassador had left early, taking his entourage with him. "What, gone?" said Tom. "The wife, too?" He glanced round the room with baleful eyes.

"Whose wife?" said Howard. "Ambassador Alavi isn't married."

"You know . . ." Tom said softly. "She isn't even Iranian."

Everyone smiled a little indulgently at that. Howard ignored the interruption: "It would make an interesting article, don't you think?" he went on. "I can see the title now: 'Soup and Precedence: Critical Issues.' Somebody ought to write it up." The conversation drifted into politics.

Tom scanned the room again. The few interesting people seemed to have left. Kate was gone, the woman with the languishing voice had disappeared, and there was no sign of the native who'd been arguing so vehemently earlier in the evening. Instead, Sam Curtis was holding forth. He was just back from someplace or other and full of news. Trouble was brewing all along the Indian border, he reported, and in Jammu-Kashmir events were moving to a head. The Pakistanis were forcing the issue of a plebiscite by stirring up Muslim discontent wherever they could. Curtis spoke with the authority of an eyewitness: he'd been caught in the middle of a riot, set off by a group of Hindus playing music outside a mosque. One of the bystanders, an old man, kept wringing his hands and wailing: "If only Gandhiji were here to help us!"

"As if Gandhi would be of any use!" Fred Flower cut in. "Let's face it—Gandhi's usefulness ended long before he was assassinated. His politics—bullock-carts! Living in villages, spinning by hand . . . Indians don't need more cottage industries; they need *real* industry. And they want it. Don't they want it? Here's a man just over from India—" He pointed to Tom.

"Well, I just—"

"Well, they do," Flower resumed. "They want television, transistor radios, and fast cars. Who doesn't? And as for nonviolence—who ever believed it? Try that number on a Hitler or a Stalin, see where it gets you. It's a fact—Gandhi was out of touch long before he died. *He* knew it—he called himself 'a lone voice.' People were tired of him, they were tired of all that Mahatmic obstinacy— You laugh . . ." He turned to Sue Curtis; she had, in fact, laughed. "It's a funny expression," she said, and fell into a glum silence.

"You shouldn't laugh. 'Mahatmic obstinacy' was the assassin's phrase, and a good one. People got sick and tired of all the theatrics—that immaculate coolie dress and expensive poverty, all those hunger strikes and penitential beds . . ."

"I don't know about penitential beds," Sam Curtis said. "It was the other kind that made people wonder." Knowing looks were cast about, smiles. "That Ma-Bapu business of sleeping beside virgins. In a motherly way, of course, and only to test himself, of course. Things like that made even the faithful wonder."

"Oh, but now look—" Howard protested. "Gandhi was a great man, one of the great men of our time. Of any time. None of you can deny it. What you've got to realize is that a man isn't uniformly great. He was a great man, so people magnified everything—his foolishness, too, his merely-humanness."

"No," said Flower, "that's not what I mean. I'm telling you Gandhi was *mistaken*. Mistaken in the most important things. He left nothing behind but bitterness, far as I can see. He failed. It's that simple. Look what happened. Partition—you call that success? How many million lives? And the score isn't even yet. You can't change human nature."

"Well, of course, coming from a military advisor . . ." Howard began.

"You can't change human nature," Flower repeated. "Nonviolence just isn't natural."

"Maybe not, but why does it get people so flaming mad?" Nan gave a mock growl.

"That's easy," said Flower, who had clearly worked it out long before. "It's because revenge is only natural—it's a moral law as compelling as any law of nature. Think about it. Would you deny the pendulum half of its arc? Same principle here. Retribution is as natural as action and reaction. It restores equilibrium, moral equilibrium."

"Maybe that's why all the apostles of nonviolence meet with such violent deaths," Mrs. Kenny speculated.

"But they haven't!" her husband said sharply. "I can think of three exceptions right off the bat—Jaya Prakash Narayan, Abdul Ghaffar Khan, and Muste."

"Badshah Khan is in trouble, last I heard. And as for J. P.—there were demands to arrest him in Parliament," said Sam Curtis.

"I'm afraid," said Flower, "J. P.'s time may come."

"Whatever happened to that lovely Ahimsa feeling?" Nan turned to Tom.

Tom Melus did not know.

Only minutes after Tom and the last guests had left, the American staff sat down to post-mortem the party. As was their custom, they left the litter to the servants and withdrew to the verandah, men at one end, wives at the other. They turned off the overhead lights and sat in near-darkness. The wives refreshed themselves with a crock of iced lemonade, sipped and gossiped, relieved of the restrictions of politeness now, relieved, too, of the shoes with the narrow spike heels and dagger-pointed toes that were in fashion that year.

It was a splendid night, cool, with a clear moon. In the pauses, the women were able to hear small voices in the grass, or a cluster of night creatures in a nearby tree, breathing hard and rhythmically with the noise of ratchets going around. The moon cast a violet-white scrim over the lawn, a wintry light over faces, mottling the soft pulp of their cheeks, stencilling without compassion each droop and fold of flesh, while doting on ice, glass, silver, gold, the frozen stones on fingers and throats. In such a light, only minerals bloomed.

"Melus—Melus, what sort of name is that?"

"God knows. He ought to have come in huaraches and colored beads, you know what I mean? You know the type?"

"Do I! What he really needed was a poncho or a cape. I shouldn't say this but—"

"Say it—say it!" one of the women cried out.

The thing, whatever it was, was said: there were splintery bursts of laughter, cold gleams, in the shadows.

The men, for their part, sat around a small table, loosened their ties, and set to work. As a rule, the wives took no part in shop talk although, afterward, bits and pieces would filter down to them, if only in the form of admonitions—the rice overdone, an important guest slighted, the wrong dress, or an indiscreet remark . . .

Neither Howard Wick nor Sam Curtis thought the party had been a success, although it had been far from a disaster. The incident of the Iranian ambassador and the soup was noted again, and Wick was urged to change his bearer. "I'll see if I can prevail upon Nan," Wick offered, "she's awfully fond of that young man. Anything else?"

"Some matters of interest have come to light," said Curtis.

"Oh?" said Wick.

"Tom Melus—for a starter. And then those other two. You know—Nazar and company."

"Am I blind? I didn't see a thing."

"Firuz Nazar is a press attaché—right? Must have his finger on a lot of information, wouldn't you say?"

"They all do. So? They're not all political agents, if that's what you're driving at. Look—you know all their people . . . How come you know nothing about him?"

"That's what makes me wonder," Curtis said darkly.

"Could be there's nothing to know."

"I wouldn't bet on that. Nazar *does* know something about Melus, that's pretty clear. And Melus knows something about Kate Nazar . . ."

"Like what?"

"He sure was upset by her leaving early."

"What does *that* prove?"

"Nothing," said Curtis, "nothing yet." Here, Fred Flower took over. Perfect synchronization, Wick thought, as if rehearsed. Flower had a question or two of his own. About Kate Nazar, for one—how much did she know about Iranian operations? What sort of passport was she carrying? "And as for Tom Melus," Flower continued, "he's of the rosiest political coloration."

"Pink as a rose," said Curtis, "stewed—even before he got here."

"That's hardly a political offense," said Wick.

"No . . . well, we have a report on his tour so far," Curtis amplified. "Just came to us from Si Morton in Delhi. If you'd care to look at his assigned itinerary on the map and then at the tour he's managed to create for himself, you'd begin to wonder, too."

"I imagine he's wobbled some," Wick sighed. "He's the sort of man who likes to see things for himself."

"Wobbling is putting it mildly," said Curtis.

"Mazy motion, then," said Wick.

"*What* kind of motion?"

"Some poet's expression. One of those echoes I can't locate . . . So he wandered a bit—so?"

"There's more . . . ," said Curtis. "I happen to know he toured the Taj Mahal with a Marxist."

"A *student* Marxist?" Wick wanted to know.

The others ignored his question.

"I'm talking about Tom Melus," said Curtis. "Whether sober or stewed, he certainly needs a lot of mothering."

"Mothering!" Wick shouted. "That what you call it?"

3
Dreaming Out

"Literature is man's rendering of praise to God, grateful for all the beauty which surrounds him, grateful, too, for his own endowment," the Chancellor of Municipal College began.

A shout from the abyss, rather, Tom amended for himself.

"Inspiring and ennobling, or else a waste of breath . . ." The Chancellor lifted the long sleeves of his gown in the gestures of pulpit oratory. The pieties went up and up.

Only Tom and the custodial help were ungowned. Tom felt rather unfrocked, but he always did, a little. All zippered and buttoned up? All those treacherous, slippery buttons? He glanced down: yes, all joined and holding still. His hands were steady now, but earlier, they'd trembled uncontrollably.

Hangover did not begin to describe the state of Tom's head and heart. Sleep had soured his mouth. Dawn was a yellow stain that tarnished where it touched. To add to the desolation, Tom's floaters had started up as soon as he rose from the bed. The floaters were with him now: a fine litter of particles and wisps drifted lazily across his field of vision.

Here I am, a sort of live exhibit, he thought.

"But for all that, literature is not religion. Literature cannot be above human life . . ." the Chancellor went on.

You do lay on the butter so, Tom moved his lips soundlessly. *Enough,* already. At a loss for something to occupy him, he studied the backs of his hands, noticed, and not for the first time, white hairs and speckles, faint, liverish spots. Time—there wasn't a whole lot more of it. Unforgivable, this wasting of it. He'd forgotten his wristwatch and there was no clock in sight. No windows. No air. The auditorium, with its dark walls, motionless fans and pallid lights, seemed under a spell of sleep, and here and there in the audience, an ebony head nodded, flashed dully, sinking down. The suggestion was contagious: Tom found his head sinking as well; he drew himself up sharply with a little snap of the neck. Must stop this. *Must.* Suppressing a yawn, he swallowed fiercely; he blinked and stared.

It was a curious assembly. Some of the women were both gowned and veiled, faces cancelled by dark gauzy curtains, only the whites of their eyes shining through, headlamps in a deep mist. *Most* unnerving . . .

As if these little curtains weren't provocative enough, the hands of many of the veiled women had crimson nails, and were loaded with rings and glass bangles. Jingling ornaments—Tom knew why the Quran had forbidden them. A shapely bare foot, adorned with ankle bracelets, darted out into the aisle and scooped up a dropped sandal with its toes, toes as long and prehensile as the fingers of a hand. The foot belonged to one of the faceless number. The sole was red with henna, as though from a ritual trampling in blood.

Segregation of the sexes seemed to be the rule. Tom noticed that even the unveiled women kept to the right half of the room. Now and then, a glance would fly across the aisle from the men to the women, and one bold woman glanced back in return, but these exchanges were few, furtive, and swift. Under the circumstances, Tom reminded himself to carefully monitor his jokes.

"I venture to predict . . ." said the Chancellor. Better watch it.

After the Chancellor had finished speaking, and the Provost said a few words, and the heads of the Punjabi and Urdu departments had debated the "artful artlessness" of Bulleh Shah and Ghalib, whether Farid or Amir Khusrau were the finer poet, whether Punjabi or Urdu was closer to the people, which language had the greater brilliance, the deeper resonance, the problems of Sufi imagery, Persian influence, Hindu influence, after Professor Abdullah of the Urdu department had declared in ringing tones that American poetry was utterly lacking in spirituality, sublimity, and beauty, that America was a backward nation, a nation close to barbarism still, full of young, brash energies, untempered by history, after innumerable sips of water, shufflings of paper, after the Vice-Chancellor's frail attempts to smooth over and muffle Professor Abdullah's frontal assault, after coughs, sighs, protestations, honorifics and submissives, *finally* Professor Manto, chairman of the English department, rose to introduce the principal speaker.

Professor Manto was a slight fellow with a narrow face and eyebrows that soared to a peak over his nose, giving him an expression of permanent perplexity. He was in high disarray: his spectacles were foggy, his gown awry, the sleeves grey with chalk. "A few words, please," he began, unfolding his notes and blowing on them, releasing a fine cascade of crumbs. His mild and befuddled appearance soon proved to be most deceptive.

Like Abdullah, Manto was no mincer of words, and he disagreed with his learned colleague on only one essential point. Manto, for his part, found American poetry to be prematurely old, not young—"burnt-out, in fact, like a dissolute life."

Manto's introduction was brief but trenchant, and much to Tom's surprise, not altogether undeserved. His first task was to place Tom within a tradition—The Wasteland tradition, at its numb, furthermost end. "The Wasteland," he repeated, "where all ends in barrenness, death, and dissolution, instead of love, renewal, and growth. A line or two from the poetry of Thomas Melus will illustrate my meaning. Listen—I quote:

> *The stars are setting and in the east a glow*
> *rumors of some far fever or contagion . . .*

"I repeat: 'some far fever or contagion.' That's all that remains of the sun.

"Take another poem:

> *Winter has stamped the world;*
> *rebuked; arrested; condemned.*

"Hmm? How about that? Or, here again, from still another poem . . ." Manto read slowly. Tom was forced to listen to his own lines:

> *. . . where wind shreds tundra, ice splints stone. Far and low*
> *over the moraine, the gulls, the dark gulls, come.*

"Notice, please, the dim vowels, the off-rhyme of 'stone' and 'come,' the dissonance. And take a good look at the landscape itself—the polar waste, the waning air, the oncoming darkness. This is entropy, this is terminal vision—make no mistake. And here is the contemporary poet of the West in his characteristic stance. The landscape *withers* before him. He sings of the debilitation of the human spirit, the death of love.

"Did I say love? How is love possible in such a world? His lovers come together only to fall away, or they never come together—they pass through the same rooms and they never speak—the smallest distance is unbridgeable. 'This silence, an ocean in its tracklessness . . .' Melus is, in his own phrase: 'shoaled-in, dreaming out.' The few saving words, the words of ransom, remain unspoken, his tongue, as he puts it, 'so locked in salt.'

"Need I say more?" Professor Manto paused, leaning his elbows on the lectern with the air of a lawyer resting his case. "You see my point. I think I can say without exaggeration," he smiled benevolently in Tom's direction, "that Thomas Melus is the contemporary poet of the West *par excellence*. The poet of lost meanings, of missed connections. The poet of emptiness, transience, attrition of energy. He is *the* poet of entropy, I would say. I trust we all know—that even literature students know—what entropy is . . ." In the event they didn't, Professor Manto droned on in explanation.

Damn the man, Tom swore silently, damn the entire academic breed. So he'd been *placed*, had he? Categorized, swallowed up—

There was applause, a silence. Professor Manto relinquished the podium, nodding complacently: Tom's turn had come. Was he ready? No, but he would never be readier. What could he say? He grasped the lectern squarely with two damp palms; the wood squeaked faintly. He paused for smiles or relaxed faces in welcome. There were none. Dull homage instead: everyone looked serious, intent, pens poised over open notepads.

How to begin? Tom fingered the bristles of his chin—he'd shaved badly—and tried to direct his thoughts to the task at hand. He had no prepared notes, and they would have been useless in any case, since he had not anticipated an attack. He remembered his State Department instructions. They were the same as the Salvation Army gave to its street-corner Santas: Don't stand in front of your chimney. Ring your bell forcefully. Be sure not to have liquor on your breath.

He took a deep breath; he rang his bell forcefully, starting out with a direct challenge to Professor Abdullah. This removed it from the personal plane: Manto had fixed on Tom, one particular poet, but Abdullah had indicted American poetry itself, and Tom would answer the larger challenge. It was also easier to answer, since he could do so in the same sweeping terms.

"We Americans say what we see," Tom began. "We try to, anyway." And in a mood of deepening conviction, which only strong opposition could induce, Tom went on to declare American literature, and especially American poetry, alive and well, spiritually honest—"not puffed up. Beautiful without adornment or cosmetic beauty."

Professor Abdullah rose to say that he wished to make an exception of William Cullen Bryant.

Tom replied that he did not take kindly to this exception. "Furthermore," Tom insisted, "contrary to all reports, I consider myself a conservative, a conservative in the sense of Tennyson, who said:

> *That man's the true Conservative,*
> *Who lops the mouldered branch away."*

Full of conviction now, Tom confessed that the words "spiritual" and "sublime," like the word "infinite," conveyed nothing to him but unease, a sense of blurred edges and vague, shadowy forms. "Approximate magic," he called it, and he reminded them that an approximate magic was no magic at all.

"I don't suppose you've read Richard Wilbur." Tom saw from the students' faces that they hadn't. "Richard Wilbur —a young poet you'll be hearing from. Let me introduce him to you." And quilting the air with his hands, Tom began to recite:

> . . . *Oh, it will not bear polish, the ancient potato,*
> *Needn't be nourished by Caesars, will blow anywhere,*
> *Hidden by nature, counted-on, stubborn and blind.*

> *You may have noticed the bush that it pushes to air,*
> *Comical-delicate, sometimes with second-rate flowers*
> *Awkward and milky and beautiful only to hunger.*

There was a dreadful pall. No one walked out, but Professor Abdullah muttered to his neighbor the single word "tasteless!" in a voice so sharp it could be made out in the last rows of the hall. The other dignitaries on the platform remained in place, despite Tom's considerable provocation. He thought he could hear their lips moving, though. Eternity, transcendence, nobleness, remembrance, they seemed to whisper behind his back.

Tom felt the students' attention riveted to him now, innocent eyes wide open for the first time that morning. Potatoes? He knew he had startled them. Here was life in its drabness, faithfully, lovingly, rendered, nothing exalted—no chiming, no chanting—how could this be poetry? Tom knew enough of the poetry they were taught to cherish, a poetry of mystic aspiration, of pathos and nostalgia, thwarted longing, streaming sighs—an emotional range of a fraction of an octave, its narrowness cunningly disguised. Like a needle seen through a waterfall . . .

The image of a needle prompted his next recollection. John Berryman, this time:

> *Nitid. They are shooting me full of sings.*
> *I give no rules. Write as short as you can, in order,*
> *of what matters.*

They listened.

Growing bolder still, Tom ventured a local poet, Faiz Ahmad Faiz. A tactical error, he realized at once, because the students were more familiar with Faiz than Tom was, and he had a vague recollection of a State Department briefing on avoiding local mentions, a proscribed list; he'd made a special effort to acquaint himself with the work of the writers named on it.

A profound stillness reigned.

He went on in spite of it, spouting lines and naming names—Emily Dickinson, Roethke, Stevens, Williams, Lowell, and Crane. A pen dropped, another, and then another in rapid sequence.

Enough. Tom signalled to Professor Manto that it was time to open up the floor to questions. Well past the time, Tom thought to himself.

The questions were the usual, expected ones, starting with Tom's writing habits—a touchy question since Tom had no habits and he was not writing at present. Tom wished deeply for a purifying silence. The irony of his speaking tour was this: it came at a time in his life when he was drawn to silence. More—it seemed especially fraudulent coming now, for he was in the midst of a long dry spell, and had written nothing for months.

He could, of course, remember other times. Days when creation was so explosive in him, he could not contain it, he thought his heart would give. Time was, when a day with nothing written seemed a day unlived. It still seemed so. No help for it.

There were more questions from the floor when Professor Manto rose and adjourned the meeting. The applause was polite, if bewildered and faltering. It was time for refreshments.

The reception that followed was uneventful and largely painless. Tom had put in a full morning's work and was hungry. He tried not to think of what was lacking in the fruit punch, devoting most of his energy to eating and seeming to listen.

Their food was not very filling, though, and the effort to make something adequate of it kept Tom's hands very busy. There were *samosas*, chilies and crispies, tiny tea sandwiches, arrowroot biscuits; there were even, heaven help them, cucumber sandwiches, and the familiar fried sweets Tom had learned to avoid in India. "*Gulab jaman* . . . digestive biscuits," Professor Manto pointed proudly.

Some of the sweets had decorative silver strips. "It's quite edible," said Manto. "Gossamer thin. Have no fear."

"Thanks," said Tom, avoiding them. "It's one of those things I can't get used to."

"You probably wonder about this eating of silver."

"I do," said Tom, "I do wonder."

"Actually, it has a long history," said Professor Manto.

"I *bet* it does," said Tom.

"The Queen of Sheba used to send Solomon sweets wrapped in thin strips of beaten gold and silver. And the Mughals had the same custom. It's quite pleasant," Manto's lean jaws rippled. "It has no taste, no taste at all. You see —" Manto dispatched another of the silver sweets in three swift bites by way of demonstration. "QED—Quite Easily Done!"

"Please, if you please—" Someone was trying to break through the close faculty ranks surrounding Tom. The line fell back a little.

"Ah . . ." said the student as he arrived face to face with Tom. "I only thought of getting through. Now that I'm here . . ." It was as though he had tossed a stone over a wall, just to see what would happen. The boy glanced from side to side in confusion.

"Take a deep breath," said Tom.

Much to Tom's amusement, the boy did so. A slow, deep, audible breath.

"Melus here," Tom extended his hand. He was all smiles, genuinely grateful for the interruption; he'd had quite enough of the faculty by now.

"Aleem Khan," said the student, and seemed to lose his voice again. He had a doe-eyed, innocent, rather unformed face with a very new moustache, which looked pencilled on. He kept fingering it, as if to make sure it was still there.

"Anything I can do for you?"

"I would like some advices, please."

"You write poetry?"

"I write—" the student hesitated, "in English."

"English?" said Tom. "Why? Why not Urdu?"

The boy looked somewhat stung; he said in a burst: "I write in English, Urdu, and Farsi. Some Punjabi, too—not so much . . ."

"Well, I can tell you're bright. Recite me something, then. Let's hear."

"Oh, I have nothing. Only some scribbles."

"So let's see one of your 'scribbles.' "

As Aleem withdrew a sheet of paper from his pocket, and smoothed out the folds with trembling fingers, the last remaining academic fled.

The boy began to read, but in a voice that was scarcely audible. Tom cupped his ear, without effect, then suggested they move into the alcove where it would be quieter and more private. He was genuinely curious, though not at all hopeful, expecting nothing more than the usual pastiche, or the characteristic whining note of pathos that Asians seemed to find so eloquent.

But even in the alcove, little came through. "Maybe it would be better if I read it through to myself," Tom suggested gently. Aleem reluctantly surrendered the page. This, clearly, was no casual verse, but a thing of deep personal import. Tom braced himself for the worst.

He read the poem twice through, then asked for another, and read that too, stalling, trying to think of something to say. He didn't know what he thought—only that these were better than he expected. The boy's voice was thin but clear, with none of the drenched sonorities, the muddy booms, of a man gone beyond his depth. None of the tired thematic conventions, either—the cruelty of the beloved, the ruby brightness of her lips or blackness of her hair, the indifference of fate, the fickleness of the nightingale, the transience of the rose, the immolation of the moth, nothing of Job's patience, Suleikha's lust. There was strength and virtue in these exclusions. But Tom knew he had to say more than this.

"Is it so bad?" said Aleem mournfully.

"Not *too* bad," said Tom, but, noticing Aleem's face fall, he said: "Listen here, a 'not bad' from me is not lightly given. When I say 'not bad,' that means 'not bad at all,' or, in the language of your friends, 'wah, wah, wonderful!' Believe you me!"

"Oh, it is very bad!" wailed Aleem.

"No, it's not bad at all," Tom said emphatically. "And it's quite different from the sort of thing I'm used to seeing from people your age. In fact," he added, "I suspect it's a good deal better than what most of your teachers could do." So as not to overdo it, he said: "That last bit, the ending—those 'tired pennies, the rain'—they're a little tired, though. They remind me of someone—Spender or George Barker, maybe. I don't know if you've read any of these people . . ." Tom had not raised a full question and Aleem did not answer, for he was uncertain whether it was better to have read these poets or not—in fact, he had not read them. "Got anything else to show me?" Tom asked bravely.

Aleem made his next offering with a steadier hand. This he explained, was a series of variations on a theme of Salman of Salveh.

> *I am passed from hand to hand as a cup,*
> *I am spun, spun, spun again as a wheel . . .*

Which was more along the lines Tom had been expecting: impotence glorified, made sublime, mystical. "Mmmm, interesting," he said, "not as good as the first, but still— Have you tried sending these out?"

Aleem dove into his notebook by way of reply, and produced a ragged, bursting envelope.

"Rejections?" said Tom. "Let me see."

"Do you think they ever read the poems?"

"Sometimes," said Tom, taking out one after another. They all seemed to be form letters. He added: "But they don't read very carefully or sympathetically when you're young and your name isn't well known."

"But how do I get to be well known if they won't read my work?"

It was a fair question. "Accident, luck, persistence," said Tom, repeating what had been said to him as a young man, and Aleem's reaction was the same as Tom's had been. He heard the older man out in silence, his face clouded with sullenness. Tom shuffled through the sad collection, the familiar litany of: "so sorry," "truly sorry," "I *am* sorry," of thank yous and regrets. There was one "exceptional mention," whatever that meant.

"Oh, well," said Tom, "this is no news. I've gotten the same letters myself in my time."

"The same?" said Aleem, brightening.

"There is nothing to do but to push on with it. In time, the acceptances will come."

"Do you really think so?"

"I do—more's the pity. Take my advice: study banking or engineering. I'm sure you've heard this before, from your father or uncle, but it happens to be true. You can't earn a living by writing poetry. And being a poet isn't a life. One of these days you'll thank me for this advice." My God, he was being kind.

"Then I have no talent at all?" said Aleem, crestfallen.

"I didn't say that."

"Too little talent."

"That remains to be seen. It would be better, I think, if you had no talent at all. Take it from one who knows."

The boy had become tiresome. Tom feared he was in for an endless discussion. Time for a final, useful, word of advice: "Study banking, you hear?" And, tapping his wrist where his watch was supposed to be, he excused himself. "Banking!" he repeated. "Lotsa luck." And walked away.

Tom flew the length of the corridor, down three steps, and found himself out in the sun, free of the dim, stale air

of the classroom, out of school at last. The light was dazzling: it was a brilliant March day. The trees bordering the
college grounds were in their first feathery leafage.

A pinwheel vendor came up the street, balancing his
wares like a headdress. Red and orange, tiny whirling suns
. . . The breeze was up, full of shifts and turns; the wheels
spun, stalled, and reversed themselves.

Tom did not know which way to turn, but this sense of
directionlessness, ordinarily irksome, pleased him now. He
might go in any direction. His obligations were over for the
day; there was no need to return to the hotel; he was free to
be a tourist, free as air.

"Oh, sir!"

The call gave Tom a sense of direction; he continued
briskly down the street. But soon knew he was outpaced.

"*Oh, Professor Melus!*" It was Aleem, running now in hot
pursuit. He was still gowned, and his sleeves flapped awk-
wardly.

"Now see here!" said Tom. "I am *not* a professor. And
I'd appreciate—"

"But my papers!"

Papers? The boy's precious rejections—had he? He had.
There was no denying it: he was still clutching the packet,
the boy's only link with the world of letters. "Ah, sorry,"
said Tom sheepishly, handing them over. "Really sorry—I
didn't realize. That was careless of me."

"Are we going the same way?" Aleem asked.

"I'm sure not," said Tom. "It's been nice meeting you."

"I could show you Shalimar garden, Zamzama, the museum, the fort—since you are new . . ."

"I'll let you know," said Tom. "At the moment, I have a
very important appointment."

"You won't forget? I'll give you my phone number and
address." Aleem whipped out a pen and a memo book.
"There—it is all written." He tore out the leaf.

"Well now, I've got everything I need," said Tom. "If I

ever find the time, I'll give you a ring. Scout's honor." He shook hands for a final time, once again wished Aleem all the best, and started off with long, purposeful strides. The day was heating up, and, gradually, the paper became limp and began to cling to his skin.

At the Happy Haven Bar and Grill, he reached for some salted nuts. The blonde on the next stool pointed and said: "Bit of serviette sticking to your fingers there."

"Bit of who?" he said. Bits of things, scraps, were always attaching themselves to Tom in his travels. He shook the paper loose and laid it on the counter to dry; the ink was smudged, but it was still legible.

"Been here long?" said the girl. She turned to face him, one arm twisted back, her full breasts canted upward and out.

"Long enough," said Tom.

"My name's Fiona."

"Tom," said Tom. "You're British, aren't you?" She smiled and nodded. "What are you having?"

"Anything but tea," she said, folding her arms on the counter. She leaned forward, resting her breasts on her forearms.

Tom ordered two gins, because they were cheaper than other things, and it was too early to tell whether he liked the girl or not. He liked her tits, the way she used them. The girl played with her side curls and sipped slowly. "You're all green and gold," he noticed. "Look like you're going to a party." She wore a dress made of sari cloth, a green oiled silk with wide gold borders; her glass bangles were also green and flecked with gold paint.

"Wherever I am, it's a party," she said.

Tom ordered seconds to make it a real celebration.

"Where you from?" she asked, and the game was on. Tom named a few of the many places; she said she was from Chelmsford.

"Chelmsford to Lahore? How did that happen?"

"That's a long story," she sighed. It was, Tom imagined, one of the usual stories. She'd fallen in love with a student from Lahore. He'd promised to come back and marry her, and when he failed to return, she'd gone after him—only to learn that he was already married.

"No problem here," said Tom, "you could be the second wife."

"Oh, but I wouldn't," she said, "I want to be Number One. Soon as I find the right man."

"Don't look at me," said Tom.

"Don't worry. I knew you were married right off. Meanwhile, till the right one comes along, no harm having a little fun, is there?"

"No harm at all," said Tom graciously, "sounds very sensible to me. So I look married, do I?"

"You have that look."

"What look is that?"

"Umm . . . hard to say. Caged, I guess. Wee bit frantic."

"So that's how I look . . . ," he said. Barbara would be pleased. He wasn't married at the moment, not technically. He'd been with Barbara for six years, though, and chafed a little from time to time, as though it were a real marriage. His two marriages, stood end to end, hadn't lasted as long. Except for his son from the first, they might never have been. *His* son . . . it was hard to believe. He hadn't seen Steve in a decade—the boy was only four then. Sylvia had told him it was for the best: Tom, she'd explained, would only make difficult the boy's adjustment to his new father. And Tom had accepted that. He'd never felt much like a father. The relationship was too little visceral, too abstract. He'd never wanted a successor, couldn't afford an heir, and the idea of leaving any replica of himself appalled him.

He stared at the bottom of his glass for a moment.

"Forget I said anything," Fiona closed the subject. "Say —know what the big event in this town is?"

"Haven't the foggiest."

"The annual horse show! Isn't that a gas?"

They were on to bourbon next. And Tom had a scotch, neat, after that. He was about to order another round when Fiona took his hand gently and led him away. She teetered a bit on her spindly heels, but was quite decisive about direction.

Tom came along quietly. He didn't mind, he had nothing to lose.

Her room was small and bare—except for a huge almirah that took up most of one wall. There were two beds: one, a bare cot, the other—a couch for sitting, draped with brightly colored shawls, throw pillows, and two large stuffed animals, ancient cuddly toys. A pig and a bear, as near as Tom could make out; it was hard to tell—both had fat snouts and limbs, imbecile faces; their pelts were matted and grey with age.

What followed was perhaps predictable: a long, fruitless grappling on the sweaty bed, soft suction, amorous friction, over, under, over—out—

Nothing cohered.

Tom left the cot and sat down on the edge of the couch, sagging in his damp skin. Tom Melus, poet of missed connections . . . Who'd called him that?

He crossed his legs and folded his hands primly over his private parts. "Bodies are such fun," he said. The bolus stirred listlessly beneath his fingers.

"Hey—hey—," Fiona called from the bed. "None of that. It doesn't matter. *Really*. It happens sometimes." She smiled and stretched.

Now the thing was definitely, perversely, stirring, nuzzling his fingers. Worm! Pitiful, pitiful creature, this—a snail unhoused, slinking, slipping away . . . When most needed, most away.

Normally, the slightest glance in the direction of his belt buckle was summons enough. And here was flesh, warm, palpitating, moist. The girl was no girl, but comely, ripe.

71

"Guess I'm all tuckered out," he said.

Fiona yawned. She lifted her wristwatch off the bedside table, then turned it face down, sighed, and drew the crumpled sheet up to her shoulders. "In a minute, I'm going to take a bath," she announced.

Time to be off. Tom stood up, dropping his hands. Fiona —Fiasco—studied him carefully. He followed the line of her squint and saw what she saw—plumped and red and hot. Now, of course, it would be now, the rest of him exhausted.

Grunting, he lunged for her.

"Oh, no!" she cried, shot up in alarm and ran. Tom fell, bursting, face down, belly down, onto the empty bed—

He lay in the wetness, all force spent. Fizzled out. It wasn't the first time, it seemed to be his way with the world now—too early or too late. There was no give-and-take, no sense of unforced rhythm. He'd missed a beat somewhere.

He emerged from Fiona's hotel, damper than ever. The glare and din of the street dazed him, and he stood for a moment, waiting to gain his bearings, patting his pockets, back and front. Keys, wallet, matches, pipe—all in order. As much order as before. He was reassured.

Reassured, too, to find the traffic bustling all around him, the afternoon unspent with hours yet to go, the town still new. Shop around, shop around, the unknown streets beckoned: all pleasure, no consequences. No consequences —he would be gone before the month was up.

He took to the sunny side of the street to start. The shops he passed were modern and prosperous. Local handicrafts filled display shelves of plate glass and chrome; the sign read *Pakistan Cottage Industries*. Spectacles in the latest frames: *Eastern Optical Company, House of Quality*. A window full of plaids and winter tweeds: *Hamidul's Fancy Cloth Store—Stockists—Caravan Fabrics—Selections to Suit All Pockets—Insist on Hamidul* . . .

Tom walked on and, gradually, the streets changed character. The signs were unreadable to him now, written in some other script, which looked to him like Arabic, but was probably Urdu. He began to favor the shady side of the street. His pace was even and purposeful, although he hadn't the faintest idea where he was heading. At the first major crossroad, he came to a dead halt, unsure which way to turn. He decided to follow the street on his left, the one with the dim arcades and tumbledown housefronts. It looked authentic.

He inhaled. Yes, this was it, the true East, authentic, unmistakable: a rich compost of many things, of turmeric and ginger, curry, rotting fruit, attar of roses and open drains.

As Tom walked on, the beggars followed. He gave out a few coins as toll for passage, small coins first, then larger ones, whose worth he did not know. But the more he gave, the harder it became to move. He was besieged by tattered hands. This is the last, Tom swore, the very last. Well, only this last.

Word must have travelled up the street—RICH AMER-ICAN—LOADED—WILL SPEND—for Tom was attracting a crowd. He badly needed a guide, a native. He pushed forward, hands pressed to his pockets. "No—sorry—no—no—" One man followed relentlessly; he was all but legless, without feet or shins, a three-quarter man with wooden cups for knees. He rattled after Tom, making a ferocious clatter. "God bless," he whined.

Tom threw him a coin, but missed. The beggar scraped it up from the ground, dusted it off, and regarded it disdainfully. "It's better than nothing," said Tom.

He crossed rapidly to the other side of the street. Onward! He passed a row of men sitting cross-legged on the pavement, low desks in front of them. "Change money here. Give me your money!" they cried. Tom hurried on. At the corner, a tout in Western dress offered him a "nice memsahib—discount, very, very nice," then a "nice boy massage—only two rupees," then Johnny Walker at cost. He continued trailing after Tom, repeating his wares, and it was some minutes before he became discouraged, slipped a card into Tom's hand, and turned away. When he was quite gone, Tom glanced at the card:

ANWAR DIL—MY FORTUNES ARE RELIABLE
I warn gravely, suggest wisely, explain fully . . .

He tucked the card in his pocket and turned down a street of cinemas with red and yellow pennants and lurid posters; it was crowded here, and Tom was jostled, fondled, his pockets lightly grazed. He turned down another street; here, the merchants did not specialize, they were selling zippers, inflatable balls, plastic sandals, paper suitcases, pipes, cigarettes, chewing gum, scissors, razors, pocket knives, faucet handles, watchstraps, transistor radios, batteries, brass buttons and medals from assorted wars. Tom paused to take it all in. A young boy had spread a blanket in front of him with exotic treasures: a pencil sharpener without a handle, a thermos without a cork, an ancient fountain pen, a key ring full of keys, a limp, faded cardboard box of *Trojans*, which looked as though it had been dragged up from the bottom of the sea. Tom wondered whether the child who sold these things had even the faintest notion of their use.

Another turning. Tom passed through a narrow alleyway where the buildings locked out the light. The houses were not really leaning, as they looked to be, but each storey projected out over the one below until, at the very top, the facing houses were only inches apart. Tom felt very lost, but plunged on into the darkness. It was a dismal street, made infernal by the din of the copper beaters whose shops lined the pavement. They hammered without letup, flattening old pots and rounding new ones; the finished pots were stacked in graceful arrays, tapering upward, tiny ones on top.

The darkness, the din, began to seem insupportable to

Tom as he went along. He was about to turn back when he saw an opening like the mouth of a tunnel. He moved quickly toward it, and soon found himself out on a wide, sunny street.

For an instant, everything here seemed blessedly humdrum, just an ordinary street of vendors displaying their wares and sunning themselves. But their wares were strange, very strange. For here, down the length of this street, they seemed to be selling nothing but secondhand teeth. There were some complete sets in wax, others were heaped in glass bowls like penny candy. Some seemed to be human teeth; most, plainly, were not; they might have been extracted from sheep for all Tom could tell, so oddly shaped, full of strange ridges and indentations. As Tom lingered over the glass bowls, a vendor smiled and gestured to him. He hovered over Tom and put his finest samples forward. "Discount," he urged, "best quality. You buy, yes?"

When Tom waved his hand dismissively, the vendor smiled wide and pointed to his own mouth, a mouth crammed with splendors. *"Beautiful,"* said Tom, trying to count rapidly, for the old man's mouth seemed to have twice the normal allotment of teeth. "You like, yes?" said the vendor. "Yes, yes!" said Tom, hoping he would open his mouth again. "Here," said the vendor, *"accha* for you, sahib—" and dropped a gleaming tooth with a long root into Tom's palm.

"No, no—" said Tom, tossing it back in alarm. "I have all I need. You see?" And he stretched his lips to prove his point.

4

The Wells of Lahore

Lahore, Wednesday

"Serving time is over, sir."

At Tom's hotel, the Luxe, they were stacking the chairs on the dining-room tables. Tom was unceremoniously ushered out after the last couple left. They always have patience for couples, he observed.

"On my way—" he grumbled. One of the waiters looked up and asked: "Anything wrong, sir?"

Tom settled his bill, stuffing the change in his breast pocket without counting it, where it made quite a bulge. He was greatly annoyed; he'd only begun to sip in earnest and a long thirst was upon him. What to do? He had no desire to return to his room, although there was still something to spare on his bathroom shelf. "It's only a little after nine," he protested to the headwaiter, "bedtime for children, but not for us . . ."

The headwaiter referred Tom to the cabaret, through the lobby at the other end of the hallway. There, he promised, business was just starting. "Ah, I know *that* business," said Tom, "that's an old business." Still, a drink was a drink. He was old enough to handle the hustlers.

There was a small crowd at the end of the hallway, girls of every size and hue, and some old girls, too. Most were fair-skinned, though, and only one or two seemed to be natives. They were chattering and powdering their noses; from the distance, they seemed to be dismantling a luminous flower, petal by petal. The illusion was caused by their open compact mirrors, reflecting a cluster of overhead lights.

One by one, they pocketed their mirrors and entered the cabaret.

As the corridor emptied, Tom noticed one of the girls waiting. Couldn't be . . . He came to a dead halt, unsure. Stared. This was the very Kate who . . .

A Kate much subdued, dressed in another of those mission school numbers. It was a frock of unrelieved dullness, solid brown. On anyone else, it would have been a disaster, but on Kate, it only served to highlight her hair. She sat close to the doorway, lips primly set, stiff-backed, in a narrow chair.

Tom lingered a little distance away and fiddled with his pipe and pouch, trying to make sense of what he saw.

She sat with her hands on her lap, left hand uppermost; there was no missing that little gold band on her second finger.

Whatever he did, sure to be a blunder. He moved toward her. "Kate!" he called out, as if just noticing. "What a pleasant surprise!"

"Oh, Mr. Melus."

"My name's Tom."

"Tom," she said indifferently. Then, with a quaver: "You haven't, by any chance, seen Firuz?" Tom shook his head emphatically. "He told me to wait here until he came back. Said he'd only be a minute. He still hasn't come—it's been more than half an hour. I don't know what to do."

"Look—don't look so worried. He'll be back in no time. Why not wait for him inside? It's pleasanter and, really, a lot safer. This is the kind of place where the sight of a woman waiting by herself can only mean one thing. I'm surprised at your husband."

"Oh, I'm sure he meant—" she said, and faltered. She was not at all sure what her husband meant. "Come on," said Tom. He took her firmly by the elbow and propelled her through the doorway.

In the center of the room, a single couple was dipping and scraping to a waltz tune no one was playing. Tom settled Kate at a corner table and went up to the bar to order one gin, one Orange Smash. A girl with long fair hair propositioned him as he waited. He looked her over: in the dimness, young and promising—God knew what in the light. "Been here long?" she drawled. It was hard to place the accent, although he guessed it was well south and west of New York.

"I told you before," he said.

She shrugged at the rudeness of that, and passed by. Tom made his way back to Kate with their drinks. "Cheers!" he said. "Here's to— You tell me what."

"Just cheers," said Kate.

"Nothing to cheer about?"

"I guess there is. We've been looking for a house. Today, I think we found it."

"Here's to the new house, then," said Tom. They touched glasses. "I bet that's what your husband is up to— he went to a telephone to clinch the deal. He wants to surprise you."

She looked skeptical.

"Tell me about it," said Tom, "your new house, your old house—anything. Just talk. Talk to me."

"Seems like I've forgotten how," said Kate.

"Try."

"Well . . ." she sighed, "let's see. We came here from Karachi—we live in Karachi, you know. We may be moving to Lahore. Then again, we may not. It depends on— I don't know what it depends on. Or who. Emiri, maybe."

"Who's Emiri?"

"He's my husband's boss. They really do the same thing, I guess that's the trouble. I don't know what they do most of the time, but it's the same. Am I making any sense?"

She wasn't, much, but Tom nodded and said: "Sure. Go on."

"Maybe Alavi's the one who wants us to move—Ambassador Alavi. You met him?"

Tom made an ambiguous gesture. He hadn't really *met* the ambassador.

"He was at that party the other night. You wouldn't think much to look at him. He's a dwarf, practically . . . a little squirt. Alavi goes back and forth from Karachi to Lahore. Don't ask me why—the embassy's in Karachi. There's nothing but a consulate here. I don't know what he does in Lahore."

"Smuggling, probably," said Tom. "With all that diplomatic immunity."

"Am I boring you?"

"No—but I don't see what this has to do with you."

She took a sip of her Orange Smash and asked: "Where was I?"

"It's a little complicated," said Tom.

"Not complicated—but . . . *obscure*," she laughed a little, without mirth. Then paused. "We came here from Karachi, looking for a house . . . I told you that already?" Tom nodded. "My husband's a press attaché, you know?" Tom nodded at that, too. "I don't really know what that means," she confessed. "I don't know what he really does."

"Why don't you ask him?" Tom suggested.

"You don't understand . . ." her lip quivered. In an instant, her eyes were brimming. Not knowing how to handle this, Tom reached over and patted her shoulder, then took her hand in his own. She made no motion to withdraw her hand and gazed up at him gratefully.

Firuz stood in the entrance to the cabaret, a look of utter desolation on his face. He'd been disconcerted not to find

Kate where he'd left her, but never, never, until this moment, had he suspected her of outright shamelessness. So brash, so blatant. Kate, *his* Kate, his *wife*, was sitting in a dark corner tête-à-tête with a strange man. The stranger had his back to Firuz, but Firuz could see that he had taken Kate's hand in his own, and Kate was gazing up at him, misty-eyed.

Kate had not yet noticed Firuz. To gain time, he moved first to the bar. He ordered bourbon and ginger ale. An English girl in a Spanish shawl asked him to buy her a drink; he turned to the bartender and ordered a Fanta for her; she sneered and dismissed the order. In all this time, Kate and the strange man had not looked in his direction.

Tom heard, but did not see, Firuz bearing down upon them, ice cubes quaking in his glass.

"It's time, Kate—" Firuz said.

Tom turned round. Firuz recognized Melus at once, but gave no sign of ever having met him before. Tom rose and extended his hand, saying: "We met at the party the other night, remember?" Firuz set down his drink but did not take the hand offered. "I'll remember you now," he answered coldly, then turned to his wife. "Are you coming, Kate?"

"Look," said Tom, "let's not make an international incident of this—whatever it is. You left your wife on the doorstep here. Not a very nice doorstep, either."

Firuz said nothing, but continued to glare at his wife. Kate rose from her chair. "Thanks for keeping me company," she said. "Bye." And followed her husband out as though leashed.

"Hey, you've forgotten your drink!" Tom called after Firuz. Heads turned, but neither Firuz nor Kate seemed to hear. "Untouched," he added in a softer voice.

Tom moved up to the bar after Kate left. He'd lost count of how many glasses ago that had been. Quite a few, he supposed. By now, he was not so much drinking as mulling over his glass.

He continued sitting; there was some sort of entertainment in the offing. The few couples who'd been dancing left the floor; three spotlights, one white, one yellow, one blue, made a slow pavanne in their absence, then a single white light came to focus in the center of the room. It made a cone of dusty brightness. And a silence. All faces turned toward it.

What followed was a pastiche of nightclub and cabaret around the world. After the jazz instrumentalists, came a torch singer, then a belly dancer, then a local singer—the woman's voice sounded like mosquitoes to Tom, it was so high and nervous and small. Then came a comic talk routine in Vegas dialect, a magician in turban and tuxedo, and, finally, some dances from Kazakistan. A man in rooster red—what looked like a version of Cossack dress—kept smacking his heels and thighs, the woman alternately wrapping herself in paisley shawls, spreading them wide like wings, and shaking her titties. There was a lot of stamping.

After this, the floor was opened to the guests once again; the business of the evening resumed. Breasts rustled Tom's shoulder, a voice pried his ear: "All alone?" He didn't bother to answer, but the warm, breathy voice persisted: "Don't I know you from someplace?"

"Tell me," said Tom, "I forget."

"Ah," said the girl. "Someplace. Around."

"A woman," Tom declaimed, wagging his pedagogic forefinger, "should be palpable and mute . . . as a globed fruit . . ."

"You're fruity yourself," said the girl evenly. "Bats. Definitely mental," she pronounced, and passed by.

Tom turned to the bartender and asked to borrow a cigarette. The bartender offered Tom a Players, then whipped out a lighter, holding it low to the counter and a little to the side, so that it revealed the face of the girl on the next stool.

Tom took the light, studying the gold points of the bartender's teeth as he did so. He ordered a fresh gin and lime, although he hadn't entirely finished with the glass before him, he had so little patience. "Nice?" said the bartender. He meant the girl. Tom glanced at her. She was pretty, yes —ivory-skinned with lustrous black hair, but she paid no attention at all to Tom. She was too busy smiling at herself in the mirror over the bar, smiling and patting her hair. "What I want is—" said Tom, turning back to the bartender. He paused. He did not know what he wanted. He said the first thing that came into his head: "What I want is someone who will press my feet. Whatever that means," for he'd only read that such things were done.

"All that can be arranged," said the bartender, "a wifely type. You want a local girl."

"Yes, maybe," said Tom, "but not tonight." He had absolutely no desire for a woman. He downed his glass quickly.

Tom left the cabaret and found his way out into the open air. It was a clear night and cool. He was still thirsty, eager to plumb the wells of Lahore. There was no sign of any other bar, though, and he walked through the quiet streets. His footsteps echoed: free, unfree.

It was late, too late for prudence. A veiled woman approached Tom and lifted the flap that covered her face, then the folds of the veil parted: Tom stood and stared, too stunned to move or glance away, his gaze clamped on the stranger, as shocked as if he'd spotted an eye opening in the middle of the man's chest. For it was a man, and he had nothing on. He had the furtive look of a shopkeeper, tampering with his scales, and he *was* diddling with his scales: two soft weights and a quivering beam. "Faggot!" cried Tom. "Help—faggot!" But few people were about, none close by, and no one turned. The faggot closed his veil modestly. "*Wuh . . . hogi,*" he said, and passed by quietly, slowly, taking small steps, moving with the utmost decorum. Such decorum that Tom wondered whether he had only imagined the encounter. *Really*, he thought, I must pull myself together. He said aloud: "Must." And then to himself: Mustn't talk aloud. He needed something to sober him up.

Tom turned left at the corner. And walked smack into the arms of a beggar with no visible deformity save a cast in one eye. He tossed a few coins at the beggar's feet and fled from the man's blessing as though from a malediction— into the path of a moving car.

Brakes shrieked, someone shouted—words he did not understand. Shutters on the balcony overhead flew open, slammed shut. Shaken, he crossed to the other side.

He felt thoroughly sober now. The moon cast a cold light on the narrow thoroughfare; many of the shops were boarded up or covered with sheet-metal hoardings. It was chilly out. Bed would have been cosier, but Tom was too excited to sleep; bed would have been far safer, Tom knew, but he continued to move on away from the hotel, away from his first and best impulse. His life was structured so, if you could call it structure. Whim upon whim, a whole life long—it looked like freedom, but it spelled irrevocable. Same as the other way.

All things same in end.

He heard footsteps behind him; he slowed down to make sure, then halted; they kept coming, so they weren't echoes.

Perhaps he had better turn at the next corner and head back. This search for a nonexistent well seemed to be a fool's errand, the Islamic ban on alcohol everywhere in force.

Short of breath, he was forced to stop. The shadowing steps gained upon him, and the voice, when it came, was oddly familiar. "It is only I—Aleem Khan."

Tom turned to greet him. "Oh, it's only you," he said with relief. It was the student from Municipal College again. "We keep running into each other . . ." Tom observed.

"It is Fate," said Aleem majestically.

"I don't believe in it," said Tom. They walked on together for a few blocks, making small conversation. Then Tom said: "Time to turn back," half afraid that the boy would turn with him. But no, the boy simply shook Tom's hand and wished him a good night. "I think we shall meet again," he prophesied. "It is written in the cards, as you say."

"Maybe . . ." said Tom. "Who knows? I might take you up on your offer to show me round, after all. I got a little lost today. Could have used you, then."

"I've lived in Lahore all my life," said Aleem.

"Well," said Tom, "we'll see. Wouldn't you be missing some of your lectures?"

"I wouldn't miss anything. I'm clever, too clever. I'll write down my number for you—"

"But you've already given it to me. Look—I'll show you," Tom said, pulling ANWAR DIL—MY FORTUNES ARE RELIABLE out of his jacket pocket. Rats! He ransacked his other pockets to prove his word was sound—nothing. His word was not sound. The scrap was lost in his travels somewhere. Probably slipped through his fingers at the Happy Haven Bar and Grill . . . First he'd walked off with Aleem's letters, and now this. This was the second time he'd let the boy down. By way of reparation, Tom made a sudden proposition: "I've got nothing on for tomorrow. How about tomorrow?" And Aleem said that would be fine.

The hotel lobby was deserted by the time Tom returned, the desk clerk nodding over his ledger. But upstairs, in the room next to Tom's, people seemed to be wide awake. A party was in progress, the laughter fairly continuous, punctuated only by the shattering of glasses, which everyone seemed to find hilarious.

It didn't sound at all amusing to Tom. He was tired now. Hungry, too. He'd eaten nothing since supper at the hotel. Already, it seemed the night before. He remembered something about a cabaret, and Kate, who'd been on the edge of tears. He didn't think he'd done anything to cause those tears, but he couldn't remember, he wasn't sure.

"Puss puss—here, puss . . ." There were loud cat sounds: hisses and meows. Tom rapped on the wall for quiet. "For cripes sake!" he called. Someone knocked back, giggling— a woman's laugh, without much body. Chairs toppled, one, two, one. The laughter rose to a crescendo.

Too tired to sleep, anyhow. Tom got down on all fours and groped under the bed until he found his portable typewriter. There was something he'd been putting off; it would help him pass the time. Clearing the desk of everything but the lamp, he set the typewriter squarely down, fetched paper from his briefcase and, in a burst of energy, began:

Dear little fox,

Why did he call her that? Why "little"? Barbara was tall for a woman, and he wanted her that way; he liked his women large. And why "fox"? Her hair was dark brown, closer to black than red. Nor had she the cunning of a fox. Far from it—he'd seduced her easily with a trumped-up tale. It was winter . . . he'd been wearing his khaki long johns, saved from his army days in France; he wanted to tell her about his war exploits and knew these would give him a plausible start. Softly, reverently, she'd run her fingers over the moldy cloth and asked him about moth holes —were they from bullets? He hadn't the heart to let her down and fabricated wildly. She'd hung on every word.

He'd remind her of that:

K dzouy yqmd—

He glanced up, startled. One space off, and everything changed to this crazy Cyrillic. He returned his fingers to base position, but by now, had forgotten what he wanted to say.

Why not go to bed and start over in the morning?

85

But no, he sat on, waiting for some sort of dictation. His fingers tugged, rayed out over the keys. Any minute—

It wasn't a letter he had in mind.

He fetched another sheet of paper and wrote, without pausing to think about it, the single word *advent*. His typing made brittle sounds, stiff little fractures; nothing flowed. Nothing further came, and he studied the wood surface of the desk, traced the grain-markings—saw river prints, fire fringes, aureoles of flame. Then only his fingers, idling. He ran his fingers lightly and expertly over the keys of the typewriter, testing the alphabet. Stalled. Looked up. Only a subdued murmuring next door now, a faint choral humming. Start again. He withdrew the sheet marked *advent*, set it carefully aside, and inserted another sheet of paper. He rapped out: *malocclusion*. Waited. The word was interesting, seemed apt, but brought nothing in train. He marked the stresses. Double-spaced, indented, rattled the keys once more. The words formed:

drowning in the shallows

How true.

He examined the phrase carefully: it looked oddly settled and familiar. The words poised themselves as if hoisted on little placards, ready-made. He realized, with a sickening lurch, that he'd written this sometime ago; he was quoting himself.

He couldn't remember what came before or after.

Still, he could go on with it differently from here. He'd needed a break for a long time; although he denied it hotly with his lips, he'd counted on that from his tour—fresh sights, sounds, encounters, fresh shocks to the system—presto: new themes, new rhythms, a transformation! It wasn't happening.

"You will find no new lands, you will find no other seas . . ." It had all been said before. He sat forward and rocked a little—it didn't help. Silence now on all sides. The paper white, so white; words stained it, he was tired of words. He was tired.

His critics were right.

5
A Lesson

Lahore, Wednesday

Everything about Firuz annoyed her, and the sounds he made undressing seemed unnaturally loud, magnified by the silence in the room. Kate listened with distaste to the rattle of his belt buckle, the dry scraping of his zipper, the whisper of cloth and skin.

Kate and Firuz undressed in silence, their faces averted. Only once did Firuz look directly at her, and then only at a segment of her neck, near the collarbone, at the gold chain he had put there on their first anniversary; he saw nothing above or below this, all else blotted out by his anger.

Kate felt the brutal narrowing of her husband's gaze, and at the same time, felt the chain around her neck, equally cold.

Loosening the covers of the bed, they climbed in from either side. They lay back, stiffly parallel, with a wide corridor between them, a passage like a buffer zone. Minutes passed.

It was Kate who broke the silence. "What about the house?"

"What *about* the house?" he echoed.

"You going to take it?"

"I'll let you know when it's decided," he said. "Alavi leaves for Karachi tomorrow. Friday morning, we'll go back."

"Don't you have to say something to the renting agent before that?"

"When I'm ready."

"But you know—"

"What?"

"Nothing," said Kate.

They lapsed into silence again.

It was almost peaceful until Firuz started up: "Do you have the faintest idea why I left you where I did?"

Kate had a very good idea. She didn't bother to answer.

"Did you find those ladies a pretty sight? Did you get a good look at them? Western women. Americans—very advanced! Keep up the way you're going . . ."

Kate had heard this cautionary tale before. She said nothing, but retreated further, to the very edge of the bed, widening the space between Firuz's body and her own.

Her time at the cabaret, all told, had been most instructive, although not along the lines that Firuz had intended. She'd gotten a good look at the ladies and, no, she hadn't liked what she saw. She'd seen the false eyelashes, the painted cheeks, the tawdry satins and paste jewels. It was no trick to see that much. She'd kept her ears open, too, and found their conversation no better, and surely no worse, than conversations usually were wherever women gathered. If anything, there'd been a little more spunk to it.

"I don't ever want to be shut in. I want to be where the music is," one of them had said. (Who didn't want that?) "Falling in love is the biggest mistake." (Well, wasn't it?) And one of the women, sensing Kate's newness and discomfiture, a woman with a magenta mouth like a gash, had come to Kate's side and tried to console her. "It's like working in a candy store, honey, or a restaurant, or any other damn thing. You get used to it, we all do. It's better than typing, or turning tricks in the office closet, you take it from me. Every night I say I'm from another town. It's like theater, you know. Hell, it's the closest I'll ever get to being on stage . . ."

"I wanted to teach you a lesson," said Firuz, "for your own good."

Firuz's lesson had come as a conclusion to a day that had begun normally enough, pleasantly enough. That morning, he'd taken Kate out house-hunting. They'd decided to have a look at Gulberg, a prosperous suburb of Lahore.

The day was bright and clear. The poplars along the canal had light, fluttering leaves. They sped past the small cottages. Soon the streets had opened up into wide boulevards bordered by gracious lawns. Most of the houses were grand, many were mansions, and a few were almost palatial. The agent persisted in calling them all "bungalows." He dropped names continually. "That bungalow belongs to Hasina Hamid . . . the famous singer. And that, on your left . . ." The names were unfamiliar to Kate. They passed the houses of government officials and diplomatic personnel, the estate of a rising film star, the mansion of a foreign manufacturer. Along the canal, Kate spotted a flaxen-haired child in a riding habit, complete in miniature from boot to cap. The child was mounted on a full-sized horse, although she looked to be no more than three or four years old. A servant in white walked a few steps ahead of the horse, solemnly bearing the reins.

Finally, they came to a low but sprawling white stucco bungalow; it had a long front verandah and grass on all sides.

"It's lovely!" Kate exclaimed at once.

After walking through the house twice, and around the grounds many times, both Kate and Firuz agreed that the house was perfect, the price negotiable, and anyway, an embassy expense—not Firuz's headache. There were seven rooms, although some were very small, and one—no bigger than a closet.

Firuz and Kate were in the mood for celebration after that, and when they got back, they dined at their hotel, taking the full meal, skimping on nothing. Firuz was quite cheerful before the main course, but by dessert, his mood changed. The old fretfulness returned. He banged on the table with his ring to catch the attention of the waiter. "What's the hurry?" said Kate. "You've got the whole day." Firuz went on banging. The waiter turned his back and refused to be rushed. "And anyway, what's the use?" Kate added. Firuz didn't answer, he was totally preoccupied with the waiter now; his eye never left the man's back. The more impatience Firuz displayed, the more leisurely the motions of the waiter became. It's like a ballet, Kate thought.

Firuz left the dining room in an angry, sour mood, but seemed much calmer after he'd napped for an hour. When the heat of the day had subsided, they stepped out for a stroll along the Mall. Firuz loved to compare and price things, but Kate soon tired of shopping and not buying— things blurred for her. Every now and then, she'd be attracted by something, a bangle or a reticule, and give her husband a nudge, but Firuz refused even to begin to bargain, insisting that, whatever the price, it was too much, and explaining, as he always did, how Kate's mere presence, so obviously foreign, caused the prices to double.

Business was shady here, and time and time again Firuz would tell Kate how the vendors of single items got their wares: a man bought or stole a pair of sunglasses, say, then walked as far away as he could to sell it; this was his entire day's work.

Nearing Anarkali Bazaar, they were pursued by beggars. One man walked alongside Kate, opening his mouth and grunting, pointing to the dark cavern within. Finally, Kate looked. His tongue had been cut out at the stump. She'd seen this sort of thing before, yet the horror, when it came, was always fresh—from the pit of her stomach to her scalp. She fumbled in her purse and gave the man three annas to remove himself from her sight. "What are you doing?" said Firuz, whose attention had been distracted elsewhere. "What have you done?" For no sooner had the first beggar disappeared, when a man with no hands had taken his place. "Look what you've done!" The beggar extended his arms so that Kate could appreciate the knobby ends where the hands ought to have been; the skin was puckered over the knobs, and shiny, like gathered satin. It wasn't leprosy. His hands must have been cut off for the exact repayment of some petty crime. Double theft, by strict equivalence. "Do you see what you've done?" Firuz cried. Kate saw, but didn't know how to end it. Firuz stepped in front of her, stamped, and made a threatening gesture at the beggar, as though he were shooing a cat. The beggar scuttled away, clacking, waving his stumps.

"Keep your hands away from your purse," Firuz warned.

Entering the bazaar, they were stopped by a native in Western dress. He must have been sizing them up from a distance, since he launched into a little speech the moment they came close. "I see an auspicious beginning," he said, "an important decision."

"Who are you to see such things?" Firuz challenged.

With a slight bow, he introduced himself: "Anwar Dil, fortune-teller. My fortunes are reliable."

This time it was Kate who gave the signal that she wanted none of it. But Firuz, who put great faith in random oracular utterance, the falling open of the pages of Hafiz at a moment of decision or crisis, was eager to see what time had in store for him, for his new house and for his marriage.

They haggled over the price, then an agreement was reached whereby Firuz and Kate would both have their palms read for what, the man swore, was the price of a single reading.

Kate's fortune first. Firuz regretted it at once. He should have sent the man packing immediately. Those large mournful eyes, the eyes of a holy man or profligate, those long sensitive fingers, flat and tapered at the tips, nervous fingers in constant, tremulous motion, the fingers of a musician or pickpocket, none of this boded well. Firuz was filled with uneasiness from the moment Dil took possession of Kate's hand. The man continued to hold it as he pondered, or pretended to ponder, taking his time. "This is quite interesting. I see the line of the fish here." He traced a lozenge in the base of Kate's palm. "A line of great destiny. You see? Catherine the Great had such a mark as that. Goethe, too. Even that way . . ."

Firuz, peering over the fortune-teller's shoulder, saw nothing remarkable at all, nothing but the encroaching fingers of the native, dark, against the whiteness of Kate's skin.

The intensity of the husband's gaze was not lost on the fortune-teller, who amended: "Your son will be a great man." He glanced up swiftly to see how Firuz was taking this.

Not well, not at all well. This sudden revision had not been lost on Firuz. He had not expected much, although secretly, he had hoped for something, a falling into place, a subtle, unsuspected connection between disconnected things. Instead, he'd found an oracle who changed with the wind, adjustable wisdom, Firuz was far from pleased and interrupted to cry fraud. The charlatan was now stroking the line of the heart across Kate's palm, measuring it with mock precision, thumb and forefinger moving like caliper points. Firuz seized Kate's hand, and insisted that Dil stop at once. "You're not getting a single *anna* from me. I don't want it. I changed my mind—"

"You pay!" said Dil.

"I won't be cheated!" said Firuz.

"You cheat me!" said Dil. And each man retreated to his

own language, their voices grown so loud that a small crowd was forming around them. Kate was elbowed back to the sidelines; she pushed and cried out, but it was useless. All she could see from where she stood were heads and backs, a milling and shoving. Firuz had started the shoving.

A constable battered his way through to the center of the crowd, switching his stick from side to side like a broom. Kate could hear Firuz shouting in Farsi: "Son of a burnt father! Snake poison! . . . Oh, excellent animal!" Then his voice grew small and the voice of the constable came through; they were speaking in English and, to Kate, it sounded like civility itself. Firuz spoke with quiet insistence: "I have a diplomatic passport. I'm a diplomat. I'll show you my passport." He must have done so, for there was a hush, the crowd was rapidly dispersed, and Dil, sniffing trouble, disappeared with the rest.

As the crowd cleared and Firuz came forward to claim Kate, an old man who'd been standing on the sidelines spat at her. His mouth had been full of betel juice, and Kate's dress was spattered with blood-colored stains. This was the final insult. Firuz swung out blindly, both hands open—

But the constable, coming between the men, gently turned Firuz and steered him away; he signalled Kate to follow and stood waiting with them at the curb until they had safely boarded a taxi. They rode away in silence, Firuz sullen and brooding, Kate stunned, too mortified to speak.

Firuz had done a lot of this lately, Kate noticed, brandishing his diplomatic passport, pulling rank, and insisting on privileges over and above those of ordinary men. And it seemed clear to her that their life together had taken a turn, not a happy one, with the awarding of a special passport. Now assured of special rights, Firuz had become less sure of the rights he shared in common with other men.

"Look," said Kate, when the silence had become unbearable, "look at you. In your own country, you'd call it cleverness."

"In my own country, it *is* cleverness," he said, "with my own people . . . But *these*—are not people."

And now he slept, the untroubled sleep of the just, and Kate lay propped up on an elbow alongside, fist on her ear, watchful, unable to sleep. Firuz lay with his free arm flung across his neck, his hand resting on the opposite shoulder blade, as though embracing himself, consoling himself. Although his eyes were his best feature, large and soulful, even now, with his eyes shut, he was impossibly handsome. His eyebrows met in the middle, giving him an expression of pain and puzzlement. His mouth, half-open, pouted a little. He *was* vulnerable; it always came to Kate as a fresh surprise—the surprise she felt in touching the soles of his feet, where the skin was so silken, so unlike her own peasant roughness. For Firuz was a rich landowner's only son and had never walked barefoot.

Late in the night, Firuz woke and could not fall off again. He began to cough. Pretending to be asleep, Kate listened without comment. She recognized the cough as a query: Are you there? Are you awake, too? People who woke alone in the night didn't cough like that.

But she didn't answer.

Later, it was her turn to sleep, while Firuz turned, wakeful and restless at her side. It seemed to him unjust that she could slumber so peacefully.

"See how she sleeps!" he cried aloud to the wall for a witness.

The wall did not answer, the room was silent. Nothing answered. Kate only stirred a little and shifted the position of an arm.

"When did your lies begin?" he whispered low to her ear.

She smiled faintly by way of reply and remained deep in her dream. Her heavy hair lay flung out over the pillow, rippling with irrepressible energies. Her hair had no color in this light, but even so, seemed to crackle with dim, malevolent, animal heat.

6
Thirty Birds

"Let me tell you a little about what you are going to see," said Aleem. He carried two little books.

"By all means," said Tom, tamping down his live pipe with the numb yellow forefinger he used for that purpose. "Tell away—I'm listening." He was in a genial mood, having risen after seven, breakfasted on two Gibsons, an orange, and a plate of salt crackers. All tanked up and raring to go. He'd even done some homework beforehand, leafing through one of the hotel brochures. He knew what to expect—Mughal architecture, Mughal splendor and spoilage.

It wouldn't be his first taste of the Mughals. He'd been to Fatehpur Sikri and, of course, to the Taj Mahal. He'd seen the Taj twice, in fact. The first time was with a student as guide. Gopu had made such a racket, stirred up such a haze of anger, that Tom had scarcely known what he was seeing. "The waste! The shameless waste!" the boy had cried at every turn. "We are a poor country—who needs this?" Tom had tried his best to be conciliatory: "But this is a sort of riches, you know." An odd business, for it wasn't Tom's place to justify Gopu's own heritage to him. "There's tourism, for one thing," said Tom. "Tourism!" Gopu spat the word out. "As if that could make up for what it cost us!" And he went on to tell Tom what it cost. Did Tom realize that the architect of the Taj had been blinded afterward so that he could create nothing to surpass what he had done? Tom hadn't realized—was that a fact? Blinded, or his hand cut off, Gopu wasn't quite sure which. A gentle fate, comparatively, for the workmen had been thrown from the roof. So that here, enshrined in alabaster, stood the loftiest monument to the exploitation of the worker ever built!

Tom had wanted to admire the fine inlays of graveyard flowers, the irises of amethyst and carnelian, but didn't dare. After ten minutes, he wanted only to be quickly gone. A few days later, Tom had returned to the Taj, alone this time, prepared to judge the building on its own terms. He'd found it as magnificent as everyone said it would be, but alembic, cold; it left him strangely unmoved. The great dome loomed over him, white, inviolable, remote. Moon-bright by full day, burning without heat. *Dry*—to a man whose passions were always moist . . .

"There's a proverb about Lahore in its prime," said Aleem, "that Isfahan and Shiraz united would not equal half of Lahore."

"And when was that? Its prime, I mean."

"Ah . . ." Aleem's voice dropped, "that was long ago."

They spent their morning branching out from Charing Cross and the Mall and, by evening, everything—mosques, towers, tombs, all seemed to merge. Tom had seen the same pattern repeated wherever they went. The distinctive Mughal style of scalloped archway and lace of stone was, Tom conceded, a thing of beauty and consummate craftsmanship. Consummate, but stultifying, he thought to himself, inflexible in conception as a cobweb is. One could look at just so many cobwebs. It was the busy traffic junction where Charing Cross met the Mall that would outlast all the other memories. Of all the tombs, only those of Anarkali and Maharaja Ranjit Singh remained distinct in Tom's mind.

He'd been especially taken with the Maharaja's tomb, a mixture of Hindu and Muslim architecture. The front of the doorway was adorned with images of Ganesha, Devi, and Brahma. Inside, the ceiling glittered with tiny convex mirrors. A marble lotus flower contained the ashes of the great man, and, forming a ring around that, were four identical but smaller flowers, the ashes of his wives. These were surrounded in turn by seven still smaller flowers, the ashes of seven slave girls who had immolated themselves on the pyre of their lord. Two pigeons, caught in the great mass of flames and immolated by accident had been given the benefit of doubt, and the honor of self-sacrifice had been conferred upon them, too; they were commemorated in a pair of marble knobs.

And the story of Anarkali had touched Tom. Aleem insisted that the story was legendary and that no one knew for sure who the lady in the tomb was or what she had done. But the legend, if legend it was, remained memorable. Anarkali—a great beauty and one of the favorite wives of Akbar—had been bricked up alive for smiling at the Emperor's son, Prince Salim, the future Jehangir. It had been a costly smile.

Aleem read aloud from a guidebook. Together they noted that the tomb was hexagonal in plan, with a domed octagonal tower at each corner, crowned by a central dome and supported inside by eight arches, "a masterpiece of solid masonry work of the early Mughal period, neatly and prettily fitted up." In the confusions of history, this structure had become a residence for the Sikh rulers, a church for the British, and a record office for the Civil Service.

But the abundance of Mughal architecture had a wearying sameness for Tom, as did Aleem's rhetoric, prompted by the guidebook he was carrying to be sure they weren't missing anything: there, love was "touching," sacrifice was "noble," betrayal was "cruel." Poverty was "sad," fine work-manship was "chaste." "Chaste workmanship" was a favorite phrase and endlessly repeated. Tom's thirst, never chaste, was beginning to rage; he tasted dust on his lips; his eyelids were inflamed; dust touched the naked whites of his eyes. He put on his sunglasses: that altered the color of the day but helped a little. As the morning drew on into noon and past noon, Tom was not in a generous mood. Had the boy not been with him, he'd have sought remedy long ago. Early on, he'd relinquished his pipe, which only made things worse.

They lunched finally in an imitation English restaurant. It was a long dim room, more hall than room, with a faded green and brown deer-hunting mural along the walls and dark wainscotting, a preponderance of brown.

"It's safer here," Aleem explained. "Our food takes some getting used to, you know." Tom knew.

It was a relief to be out of the sun's way. Here, everything was unhurried, restful, easy on the eyes.

They dined on boiled mutton, boiled potatoes, and boiled cabbage. "Don't suppose *you* ever drink . . ." said Tom. "Oh, yes," said Aleem, "my family is very progressive." Tom ordered a beer for Aleem. "You drink that down now," he urged, "it'll put hair on your chest."

"Hair?" said Aleem.

"Good for you," said Tom. "Attaboy—down the hatch! That's the way—" Aleem swallowed and coughed. "And don't hold your nose." Aleem was about to protest that he never did that. "I mean figuratively," said Tom.

Tom ate ravenously and randomly; he never could eat food in proper sequence, and so hopped from cabbage to beer to mutton, drowning it all in Worcestershire sauce and ketchup—and would have mixed this with dessert, had dessert been on the table, out of sheer boredom with orderly sequences and progressions. He washed down the half-chewed with the unchewed, swallowed noisily. It was tiresome, tiring, lining the old flue with solids; it required patience, a sense of balance and proportion. Lacking these, he ate badly and his digestion was terrible; the old pipes whined and muttered of their abuse. Tom simply could not be bothered.

That was bad enough, but when Tom bashed out a cigarette in his cabbage, it was too much, Aleem winced and glanced away. This was not a country where food was wasted or desecrated. From childhood, Aleem had been taught never to throw food away. Whatever was left he was to give to beggars, and if he found a scrap of bread in the street, Aleem's father told him he was to pick it up and place it in a hole in a wall, where some hungry soul would find it and be solaced.

Two blonde girls at a nearby table were laughing loudly. Aleem turned and stared disapprovingly. "Peace Corps," he said to Tom, "I know them. They can't marry in their own country, so they come here."

"Now, now . . ." said Tom.

There were tiny colored tea cakes for dessert. Tom ate two of them, one yellow, one pink, before he realized just how evil they were. Abruptly, he excused himself, scraping back his chair noisily. He felt seasick. "Delhi belly," he explained. Since that was the wrong side of the border, he added: "Teheran tummy, Karachi cramps. A little green about the gills, as we say." Hugging his midriff, he made his way to the lavatory.

He lost most of his lunch, but felt immensely improved afterward.

A glance in the mirror, however, failed to confirm his improvement. His face remained distinctly off-color, lips pale and puckered, and his eyes were very red. Too much sun, probably. He'd have to slow Aleem down.

The dining room was quite empty when he returned; it was too early for dinner or tiffin, and well past the usual lunch hour. Aleem was resting his elbows on the table, reading one of his books. "Mind sitting a little longer?" Tom asked.

"Oh, no," he clapped the book shut. "I like it here."

"Me, too," said Tom. "What's that you were reading?"

"I wasn't really reading. I can almost recite it. It's Attar."

"At Tar?"

"Farid-ud-din Attar . . . a long poem called *Manteq-ut-Tair—The Language of the Birds*. '*Manteq*' isn't exactly 'language,'—"

Tom ordered a glass of Hennessy, neat. Then he said: "About *birds?*"

"Ah, but it is and it isn't about birds," said Aleem.

"Tell me about it," said Tom. Talk, talk at length, talk for at least two glasses. A few sips of the Hennessy had begun to revive him.

Aleem began to babble on happily; he was so eager to educate Tom, he fairly shone with it, and for the moment, Tom was quite as willing to be educated. "The birds are very much like people, you see—the nightingale wants love, the parrot wants sugar; the peacock lives to be admired, and the duck thinks he is purer than any other bird, since ducks are always in water. The hawk is ambitious and wants only the company of kings; the owl doesn't want to leave his home in the ruin, and the sparrow is too weak to do anything but shake with fear—but the hoopoe is brave. The hoopoe was King Solomon's bird . . ."

"And the Queen of Sheba's, too, I believe," Tom put in, trying to sound alert.

"But here, in this poem, the hoopoe wants to find the Simorgh and to bring the other birds along. They all give their excuses why they can't go. They all know that no one who has made this journey has ever come back."

"Who, may I ask, is the Seemore?"

"The Simorgh is the king of birds. 'Simorgh'—the name —means 'thirty birds' in Persian. The hoopoe tells them that all the birds in the world taken together are only a shadow of the Simorgh. He is their true king and he lives behind the mountains. The hoopoe says: 'He is near to us, very near, but we are far from him.' "

Aleem paused to make sure Tom understood.

"Ah . . ." said Tom appreciatively, his eyes a little unfocused and misty. He sniffed theology in it somewhere.

Encouraged, Aleem went on. "The first appearance of the Simorgh was in China. It was the middle of the night. A feather fell on China and the fame of the Simorgh went everywhere. Everyone drew a picture of the feather and, from it, formed a picture of the king of birds. The pictures were all different."

"*Ahhh* . . ." said Tom.

"When the hoopoe persuaded all the birds to set off in search of the Simorgh, they made a cloud so large it covered the sun. They flew over seven oceans of light, seven of fire, seven valleys . . . the Valley of Love, the Valley of Understanding, the Valley of Detachment . . . some I forget, but then comes the Valley of Astonishment and, after that, Nothingness.

"One by one, the birds fell. Some of them drowned in the ocean, some died of thirst. Some were eaten by tigers and wolves. Some of them died of heat, some—of cold. Some fought and killed each other over a grain of wheat. Some were so tired they forgot where they were going and stopped and rested and never remembered again. So, from thousands and thousands of birds, only thirty reached the palace of the Simorgh. And when the last door opened to them, they went in and found only themselves inside. They saw themselves—dusty, their wings broken, their feathers torn away. They saw themselves—thirty birds . . ."

Aleem's voice trailed away. He glanced at Tom expectantly.

"I see . . ." said Tom, seeing nothing but the glass in front of him, and even that imperfectly. "You tell that very well, Aleem," he added, and, when he saw that wasn't

enough, said even more forcefully, "Very subtle. It takes
some time to see."

The heat was a little abated when they resumed their
tour: Zamzama—Kim's gun, the museum, Punjab University, the Christian burial ground, the Masonic Lodge, Jinnah Gardens . . .

They were back at Tom's hotel before sunset; their plans
were for an early rising the next day, when they would
begin a trip to some of the villages around Lahore. Aleem
would be skipping some lectures, but Tom had taken him
at his word that he could easily make up whatever he had
missed from the notes of his friends—he would do the same
for them. Besides, Aleem assured Tom, he could always
purchase bazaar notes for a few annas.

Tom was utterly done in. He wanted nothing more than
a long soak in Epsom salts, and a long glass of something
cool. And bed. Most of all, he longed for bed. Tomorrow,
they would be up before dawn. Now they made their final
plans. "What I want to see most," Tom said, "are streets
and people—real life. Even more than tombs and monuments."

"There's no way of not seeing that," said Aleem. "There
are streets and people everywhere we go." Tom was certain
that Aleem saw his point and deliberately missed it. "We
have such a history . . ." he'd say. A sense, half-confessed,
of not being up to the present.

But the boy was so quick and sensitive that Tom made a
special effort not to offend him. Now he seemed to want to
linger on the hotel terrace, and although Tom was wilting
with fatigue, he did his best not to show it.

There was a breeze stirring, the air was cooler than before. The sky was beginning to lose color. As poets, Aleem
felt it only fitting that they say something memorable and
poetic to one another. There was a blare of static from
some public building close by; then a voice, as if in pain,
rent the air. "Do you hear that?" said Aleem. "That's the
azan, the call to prayer."

"There's no way for me not to hear it," said Tom. Rasped, strident, it set his teeth on edge. Someone crying in the wilderness . . . Hagar's voice, clotted with tears.

Aleem was silent, listening to the *azan*.

It's all reproach, Tom thought. Once again, Tom felt he was expected to say something more. "It's very worrying," he observed, and when Aleem looked up and asked, "What is?" he could only add: "That public address system—it's so full of static. You people seem very fond of electronic gadgetry and things."

To Aleem, it was the most disappointing response imaginable. "You people" was a phrase almost insolently familiar, a casual, careless lumping. And to have noticed only the public address system, not the artistry of the voice, might have been understandable in a tradesman or engineer. But, from a poet, a poet at sunset—unforgivable!

Now there was nothing but silence.

"Well, that's that . . ." Tom held out his hand. "Early start in the morning."

Aleem walked homeward slowly. He was deeply, deeply disappointed. His irritation with Melus was general: it extended to the smallest things, to the style of his sunglasses, even—metallic mirrors from the outside, so you couldn't see the expression of his eyes but he could see yours; it included the slug-white color of his skin. Why bother, then? Because . . . Because that wasn't all, there was more. Aleem couldn't say exactly what that something more might be. The man was a puzzle. His walk, for one thing, was so odd. None of that brisk, headlong, obstacle-crushing stride of other Americans. Nothing like that: Melus seemed bowed somehow, his chest curved in; he didn't carry himself with any degree of pride, but walked with a step so shambling and shuffling, he seemed to move forward and backward at the same time, as though he were struggling through sand.

What was one to make of him?

7
The Red Gate

Lahore–Karachi, Friday

Even the sky was dust-colored. They travelled south and west from Lahore to Multan. The trip would take at least fourteen hours by car; leaving Lahore before dawn, they wouldn't reach Karachi until nightfall. A long morning on the road, and now all the boiled water was gone. In Multan, they'd pick up some bottled soft drinks, but there would be nothing before then.

Twice, they lost their way. The first time they asked for directions, the man had taken one glance inside the car, noticed Kate, and walked abruptly away. Whenever they stopped after that, Kate had wrapped her head in a towel and cast her face down so as to become as nearly invisible as possible. She was learning all the time.

Kate and Firuz sat in the back of the car. Charles, the driver, was alone in front; every now and then, he stretched out his fingers to ease his grip, leaving only his thumbs on the wheel.

Kate strained her eyes for landmarks. There were none. Unless the tree up ahead counted. A tamarisk stood in the middle of nothing, like an upended broom. The patches of green that had come before seemed fugitive and illusory with the shimmer of long ago, all vanished or imagined things.

For Firuz, the monotony of the landscape was fitting; it matched the arid repetition of his thoughts. There was no accumulation. The land was flat, all but featureless, with only little rills and heaps and hollows to mark the passage of the wind. Here, nothing but sage and scrub seemed to take root; a land of blight, habitations, cities, monuments lay lightly on its surface for a moment, then were gone.

Firuz kept his profile turned to Kate. Even so, she could make out the long pull of his lip. He was aggrieved; Kate, too, was aggrieved; to speak the first word would be to yield, to admit that one was the lesser wronged, and neither Kate nor Firuz was ready to do this. So they went forward through the still landscape, their lips parched and sealed. Only when Charles lurched to avoid a bevy of chickens did they stir, lurching forward, their heads knocking together with the sound of wooden mallets. Charles, whose real name was Chandrashekhar, had swerved repeatedly in the course of the journey, once, to avoid a donkey, and again, because a dog was sitting in the middle of the road, and still again, because a single sparrow was too busy worrying a speck of grain to see them.

Charles was a convert to Christianity, but it was easy to see that his old faith still had a powerful hold on him. The sparrow had almost caused them to collide with a tree, and Firuz made some bitter remarks about people who were so wrapped up in their concern for the lower incarnations that they sacrificed the higher. Frightened as she had been, and absorbed in her continuing anger as she was, Kate couldn't help remembering the old school ditty, the funny one—the one which went:

> Be kind to your four-footed friends,
> 'Cause a dog may be somebody's mother . . .

The dog had, indeed, looked like somebody's mother—
soft belly, bulging paps, crossed paws in idleness, and such
sorrowing eyes.

But Kate's amusement didn't last long. Her head ached
from the collision with Firuz. Her throat ached from thirst,
from silence. The horizon mocked her, watery and wavering in the strong light. The sun washed over it, as Kate's
anger washed over her afresh, wave upon wave.

She had reason to be angry; she'd been misunderstood
and wronged. A tiny seed of doubt, once planted in prepared ground, had burgeoned so swiftly that it now surrounded her completely, choking off light and air.

It had sprung up so suddenly, without warning, only a
few weeks before. A stray, passing remark of Ambassador
Alavi had been sufficient. A remark cryptic enough to have
meant anything, peculiar enough never to have been repeated. Twisted enough, Kate thought, to have been mis-
heard.

Alavi had taken Firuz aside and said: "Your wife is a good
woman, I'm sure. But that hair . . . there ought to be some
way to tone it down. There ought to be something she
could do . . ."

"I don't understand," said Firuz.

"Oh, don't you?" said Alavi, and he recited the familiar
lines from Sa'adi:

> *Who gives his heart to the ravisher of hearts,*
> *Has his beard in another's hand . . .*

Firuz had been too stunned to answer and had simply
turned away, full of shame. It had been no light insult to
one for whom honor and respectability were quite literally
"the water of the soul," and all week long, he had silently
nursed his sense of injury, a sense of persistent humiliation,
impossible to ignore, impossible to define.

Finally, more than a week after the event, he'd told Kate

about it, reporting only Alavi's first remark, omitting to mention the warning verse from Sa'adi. "You're sure he said nothing more?" Kate asked.

"Why do you ask? *Is* there something more?"

"Of course not," Kate was quick to answer, "but it makes no sense otherwise." Then she'd begun to laugh, it seemed so impertinent, so patently ridiculous. Kate would soon rue her laughter, but at the time she could not guess how serious the matter would become.

Well, and what did the remark mean? Nothing—anything—Kate hadn't the faintest idea. Persians were fond of indirection, loved speaking in allusions—so that Alavi's reference to hair might have nothing to do with hair at all . . .

It could be that Alavi was simply drunk at the time. For a Muslim, he was very fond of his cognac. A dwarfed, spiteful man, who could not hold his liquor, Kate told Firuz so in so many words. Firuz answered that Alavi was perfectly capable of holding his drink, and he'd been clearly sober at the time; there was cool purpose in all he said and did.

Kate had to agree that Alavi was a scheming man. She'd watched him often enough at public gatherings. Even the manner in which he greeted women was full of calculation: the way he kissed their hands, doling out kisses according to rank. If the woman's husband were very high, Alavi bowed deeply and placed the full print of his lips upon her hand; if only middling high—the wife of an attaché or deputy counselor—he lifted up the woman's hand and merely brushed it with his lips; for the lower ranks, he made a token effort of raising a woman's hand and ducking his head down a little, as if the intention were there, had circumstances not prevented . . . In between high, medium, and low, there were fine gradations of inclinations of the head and intensities of effort, precision in every gesture. No, it had not escaped Kate that Alavi was a purposeful man. But what was the purpose here?

It was a warning, Firuz told her. "It was pure spite,"

Kate said. "People don't say a thing unless there is something . . ." Firuz insisted. He racked his memory for possible slights to Alavi, real or imagined. The tiny ambassador had, in fact, suffered an indignity at Firuz's hands. They'd been visiting some historic gravesites and had come to a wall; everyone else in the group had jumped clear of the wall, but Alavi seemed to be hesitating, so Firuz had quietly lifted him and deposited him on the ground. It was all over in an instant and the event was never mentioned between the two men, but it made quite a picture, and in private, Firuz and Kate had laughed themselves silly over it. And, come to think of it, that wasn't all.

There'd been another incident, some months ago, when Alavi had just arrived at his post. The ambassador had asked Kate to give him a few refresher lessons in English, claiming that his English was weaker than his French. Firuz had told Kate to refuse. "All the man wants is a new mistress," he explained.

So Alavi had reason to be less than cordial to Firuz. Still, there were other ways of showing his displeasure than by picking on Kate. Why *Kate?* There had to be something, Firuz thought. In retrospect, each word seemed heavy with innuendo. Of course, Alavi might simply have been trying to warn Firuz that Kate was attracting too much attention —a word to the wise before anything actually happened. Or Alavi might have been trying to tell Firuz that Kate was considered a security risk, that she'd been noticed and perhaps certain suspicions had been aired, but it wasn't yet too late to do something, to tone it down. He *might* have meant that, but the true explanation might have been simpler, and much more shattering. Suppose the ambassador were trying to tell him that his wife was a loose woman, trying to break the news to him in as delicate way as he knew how . . .

At the very minimum, Alavi's remark was a warning. Firuz's projected move to Lahore might also be a probationary measure: Firuz would be on his own, separated from Emiri and the intense professional rivalry that had so hampered both of them. There was no embassy in Lahore: Firuz would be isolated, yet responsible. The remark about Kate's hair meant, at the very least, an admonition to be careful.

For Kate, nothing was clear. Someone was out to do her in—who? Why? Why should anyone? She had done nothing wrong; she had tried her best to fit in. Her hair tended to be a little wild, it was true, and she had pinned it back by way of correction. She had also, finally, taken Firuz's advice about her conversation and dress, toning them both down. It wasn't worth making an issue. But she was adamant that she had done nothing to deserve the past few weeks, this nightmare of suspicion and reproach.

And she couldn't help noticing how shapeless Firuz's suspicion was, how it spilled out in all directions until it touched everyone he met. Even their household servants had begun to move furtively, as people will do when they know they are being watched. When Kate lost a ring, Firuz had called in the local police at once, overruling all her objections with silence and implacable will. When polite methods brought no results, he hadn't hesitated to demand the services of Ibrahimi, a specialist in interrogation. Everyone remotely connected with the household was called in and questioned—the *dhobi* who picked up the laundry once a week, the *mali* who came to tend the garden on Mondays and Thursdays. Hours of harassment—and why? Because Alavi had made a remark. What was the result? Nothing turned up; Kate had undoubtedly misplaced the ring as she'd told Firuz from the start.

The ring was no heirloom: the setting was plain silver, the stone wasn't particularly precious. It was a dull blue stone in a silver mount, topaz or sapphire, Kate could never remember which. It had no facets and no brilliance in any light. There was a blurry star in the center with a milky film over its surface, like a once-clear blue eye clouded with cataract. The ring had been a birthday gift from Firuz, that was its only distinction. It was a little too large and the odds were she'd simply dropped it.

Ibrahimi, too, had said in the end that he thought there was no case. Firuz continued to fume, and Kate had not made it easier for him by asking: "Aren't you going to apologize for all the trouble they've been put to? The humiliation—"

"Apologize? *To servants?*" To Firuz, the question was incredible and typical of Kate. He pitied her simplicity and was reminded once again of how easily she could be deceived. Nothing easier, a child could do it. "Take my word for it, they're all guilty of one thing or another. Of filching on the accounts, if nothing else." He spoke from long and bitter experience. "Guilty—every last one of them."

Firuz was plainly tired, his nerves frayed. Overwork, simple exhaustion, Kate explained to herself, that's all it was. Everyone in the embassy was worn out, socialized to a frazzle, unable to see straight. It had been too crowded a winter. There'd been a military delegation, a trade delegation, then a team of wrestlers, followed by librarians, followed by poets, followed by cyclists. Firuz and his supervisor clashed repeatedly over each arrival, for their press and publicity functions overlapped. Firuz had originally been first choice for Emiri's job, but after some discussion, it was decided that he was too young, and Emiri, who had seniority in the service, was given the ranking position. Emiri was a counselor, Firuz only an attaché. From the beginning, Emiri had found fault with Firuz's work, and at social functions, the two men bristled with politeness and hostility. It occurred to Kate that Emiri might be behind her troubles —damage to Kate would be mere mischief to him, for he was a notorious libertine.

It might well be Emiri, Kate thought. And then again, it might not . . .

They were nearing Multan. Kate asked: "Is the city famous for anything?" She directed her question to the air, and Charles answered.

"Dust, heat, beggars, tombs."

"Anything else?"

"Coming into the city by this road, we pass through a red gate."

At the red gate, they were stopped by a constable.

"How many passengers in the car?" he asked.

Firuz didn't bother to answer directly, for the number was obvious. "What's the problem?" he asked. "This isn't an international border."

"A little emergency," the constable explained. "There's been an outbreak of smallpox here. Nothing much yet—but we don't want it spreading. We can't let you through unless you've been vaccinated."

"We've all been vaccinated," Firuz assured him. He was unsure of Charles, though, so he said: "I'm a diplomat, travelling on a diplomatic passport."

"We'll need proof of your vaccinations. This is a health alert, an emergency," the officer repeated. "It's for your own good. To the smallpox, it makes no difference—the passport."

"I'll look after my own good," said Firuz. "Drive on, Charles, will you?"

"Firuz! You're not going to do this!" Kate reached out and touched his sleeve. He drew his arm back sharply. Kate turned to the driver: "Don't start! Please—"

"Drive on, I say!"

"Firuz, stop it—please stop!" Kate was begging now. "Before it's too late—" But Charles had already started up.

They drove on with mounting speed. Kate, twisting to look back, saw the constable run inside the guard station and stoop to dial. Then he was too far off to see. They made good time, cutting across town. No one followed. Kate held her breath, but no one came after them. She began to weep. She wept clear across Multan, from one end of the city to the other, and their passage was winding, but smooth. There was no gate and no patrol on the other side; soon they were out on the Grand Trunk Road, crossing the desert of Sind. Kate's voice was a rasp now, and still she did not stop. Firuz wanted to shut out the sound. He closed his eyes with disgust. Let her weep, he thought, women always weep.

8
Taxis

The house was in darkness as they approached. It was early in the evening but Abdul Ghani was already asleep on a mat on the front verandah. The old man stirred and cried out: *"Toba!"* as they mounted the steps, then turned over.

"And this is our night watchman!" said Firuz.

Except for a few unavoidable words, Kate and Firuz did not speak to one another that evening. Kate was calm now, outwardly calm, her tears long since dried by the desiccating air of the desert of Sind; she remained composed as Firuz gathered up his pajamas and shaving things and prepared to move out of their bedroom. She supposed he would sleep in the guest room next door or in the parlor, wherever—it did not concern her.

It did not concern her, but it took her an inordinate length of time to get ready for bed. She could not remember why she was here, why she had followed a man she scarcely knew to the ends of the earth. She sat at her dressing table, staring at the mirror, at the expressionless oval of her face, and then, beyond it, to the wall behind her. Two lizards were chasing each other over the ceiling and down the wall; when she rose and went after them, they flashed their tails and disappeared into some crevice she could not see. From the neighboring guest room, she could hear Firuz approaching the bed and turning back the bedcovers, she could hear the abrasion of sheets, it was that still.

She confronted the mirror. "Help!" she called into its depths. "Help me." The mouth in the mirror said "help me" back again. "Tell him you'll do what he wants," a voice prompted her. But another voice questioned: "What if he wants you not to breathe?"

She remembered what the fortune-teller had said about her unusual destiny, the mark of the fish that she shared with Goethe and Catherine the Great. That was nonsense, of course, but whatever it meant, the mark was there. With her forefinger, she followed the outline of the fish on the base of her right palm. How strange that she had never noticed it before . . . The mark was less clear on her left hand. Her hands, left and right, were very different, she saw. She studied the palms closely: the left hand had clear, firm lines, without any breaks or forks or tassels: the right was full of twists and turns, intersections and fissures. The right was her "made" hand, for the life she shaped; the left was her natural hand, for the life she'd been given. Turning the palms down, the backs looked more alike. She coughed and cleared her throat, which seemed to be full of sand; she could hardly breathe. Suddenly, her right hand seized her left, lifted it—and slammed it down hard against the table. Again—so sharply, her wrist and forearm ached. And again. She sat there terrified, watching her hands in severed motion.

Her hands fell heavily. Apart. Red and slack, yet all alive, pulsing with pain. She felt violated and betrayed. But betrayed by whom? She was quite alone now.

Nothing stirred in the neighboring room.

What I need is someone to talk to, she thought, a friend. As a couple, Firuz and Kate had a full circle of acquaintances, but among them all was protocol and good form; if Kate went to them in desperation now, they would thoroughly enjoy her loss of face. Kate could think of only one warm acquaintance—Sylvia; she was almost a friend. They'd met five or six times. Sylvia had no connection with the embassies and was only occasionally invited to functions; but even if she had been invited more often, they'd never be close friends. Firuz didn't like her. He called her "*Khanum Modir*"—Mistress Manager—for she was efficient and forceful, and had her own opinions on everything.

It was so hard to breathe. Her left hand ached and her right, too—in remorse or sympathy. There was so little air. She walked over to the window and opened it wide as Firuz had warned her not to do. End of winter—she could smell the richness. The last of the roses . . .

The night air swept in, redolent of jasmine, the sickly sweetness of mango blossoms, and something more, fainter, vaster, a marshy rot coming from farther away, perhaps from the mudflats off Clifton. She leaned her elbows on the windowsill and looked out. Nothing. Murk from pole to pole. There would be rain before long, everything cried for it.

Waiting for rain, she stretched out on the bed. In the shadows, she could make out another lizard, zigzagging lazily across the ceiling.

When the lizard moved beyond her line of sight, there was nothing to focus on but the gradations of dimness. Close by, the crickets chattered with a rainy sound, she could hear the metal sidings of a truck rumbling dully in the distance, the muffled, dimmed roar from the highway beyond the garden. But there was nothing to be heard from the other side of the wall where Firuz was sleeping.

Kate touched her face; the skin was unpleasantly damp and warm. Numb, too, as though she'd been given novocaine. Strange . . . how she felt her own touch more from the outside than the inside. Perhaps it was fever. She recalled the sentry's warning. She had all the symptoms of fever: the tight head, the clutch of fear in her throat, the restlessness in her legs, in her knees.

But, no, it couldn't be fever, not *that* fever. They'd passed through Multan only hours ago; the incubation period had to be longer. Some other fever, then. It was a rage too long held in, under compression. She wanted to shout, to make a scene. She wouldn't, though. She wouldn't give Firuz the satisfaction. The only sound she made was a sharp hiss with each intake of breath as though she were breathing through a straw.

She slept for half an hour, then woke abruptly in a sitting position, her arms stretched out to the empty air. Someone had grabbed her wrists, yanked her awake, and withdrawn. She thought she heard sounds, light, muffled footfalls, the snapping of twigs, the sound of long skirts grazing, of cloth burnishing a wall. Night creatures, lizards and small insects, most likely, but ominous in the surrounding silence. She remained sitting, then, when she heard nothing further, lay back on the bed once more. As soon as she'd stretched out, the sounds struck up again, more innuendos than sounds, the shadows of sounds, the whispers of a ghostly encirclement. It occurred to her, not for the first time, but with the first full realization of what it meant, that she was utterly in Firuz's power. She had surrendered her life to a stranger. She'd become strange to herself.

The air was dense and oppressive. Breathing out and in, she hissed again. She tried resting for the better part of an hour, then gave it up for good, rose and dressed. She gathered her keys and purse and shut the windows softly behind her. I can't go out at this hour, she said to herself, it must be close on midnight. And I certainly can't go out alone. Nevertheless, she was leaving. She did not pause to ask herself why she was doing this, nor what she was doing. She did not know. She had no choice. She knew only that it was time to go.

As she stepped softly out of the house, skirting clear of

Abdul Ghani's pallet on the verandah, cutting across the lawn, she moved decisively, as though she had a plan. Yet she knew of no plan. Madness, she thought, this is clear madness, and quickened her steps.

Strange, the cant of the ground beneath her feet, she had never noticed it before, this easy downward slope. I must be dreaming, she said to herself, this will come to no good. She moved swiftly, over and down.

It amazed her that she could summon her resolve, that her legs obeyed her, that the ground was solid beneath her feet, that distance was accomplished and that nothing, nothing yet, had struck her down. And standing alone at night on the edge of the road (forbidden, unwise), she waited to be struck down.

But, somehow, was not. Nor did she have long to wait. "Bunder Road," she said to the taxi driver. Her voice was small, unsure; she did not know beforehand what she would say. I'll go to the center of town and then I'll see, she told herself.

They came to the Municipal Corporation Building; she recognized the four big corner domes with the central watchtower. This was Bunder Road. Now she would have to decide.

"Luxury Hotel," she said. "Quickly!" she added, for the slightest hesitation would have brought her full circle home.

"Right here, Miss!" The bartender leaned across the counter and patted the empty stool.

"What'll you have?"

Kate surveyed the near shelf: Seagram's, Cutty Sark, Vat 69 . . . what did it matter? Her hand was trembling—did it show?

"Lime rickey, please."

"That's not a drink," said the bartender, "not for a big girl like you." He was in shirtsleeves and Kate found herself staring at his arms; she'd noticed a strange tattoo on his elbow. "You like that?" he asked. She couldn't take her eyes away. "I see you do," he stretched out his arm to show her the full beauty of it. The tattoo was a hinge; as he flexed his arm, it opened and shut just as a door hinge would.

"I've never seen anything like it," Kate said admiringly. She kept her eye on the hinge and felt calmer. "Make that a gin and lime," she amended.

"That's better," he said, "gin and lime it is." When he stepped away, her jitters started up again. She opened her purse and began to rattle things inside.

"Here you go, lady," said the bartender, putting down the glass. "My name's Malcolm." He waited for hers, but all she said was: "Thanks" and "How much?" She downed half the glass the minute he turned his back to get the change. For courage or thirst? he wondered. Then he said: "I don't believe I know your name."

"You don't," she said, "you definitely don't."

"Later, maybe?"

"Maybe."

"Anyone ever tell you your eyes were sad?"

"Oh, lots and lots," she said, and swung round on her stool. She knew enough to know where that question was leading.

The room was packed, swarming with "girls"—women of indefinite age and definite experience. There were only a few natives. There was dance music playing but no one was dancing, no one seemed to be listening. She swung back round again and faced the bar.

"Everything all right?" said Malcolm. "Want me to liven up that drink for you?"

"I'll be taking it slower now," she said, "no need."

"Want me to fix you up with a date?"

"Does it look like I need help?"

"Some are nicer than others," he warned.

"I'll let you know," she said. She felt quite masterful sitting there in her usual dowdy dress. She was breathing now. Breathing without permission. She was aware that her hair was loose and that the way she was sitting, elbows on the counter, head thrown defiantly back, accentuated her breasts and upper arms. So be it, she was shameless and exulted in it. If this was exultation . . . Dry, silent laughter rippled through her throat and chest; she felt utterly joyless. She was so high up. So high: she peered down from the top of the tallest barstool in the world; leaning over, the depths were dizzying, drew her downward to drink, like nectar.

The dance music ended to no flourishes. And now a vocal began.

> *Have ya evah*
> *Evah evah*
> *Evah nevah*
> *Nevah evah*
> *Woo woo woo . . .*

When the vocal ended, the dance music started up again, something lively, Latin this time, a rumba. "Want to dance?" A hand came to rest between Kate's shoulder blades, and paused there, a light, tentative pressure, not unpleasant. Not pleasant, either, and rather intrusive. "C'mon . . . give it a whirl." As Kate did not turn round, the hand retreated and the man hoisted himself onto the stool beside her. "Same here," he said, filling in her silence, "I'd rather talk." He wore glasses in colorless plastic frames and his narrow face was creased and folded, pale as a priest. His accent was hard to place—Canadian, maybe.

"I'd rather not," she said.

"Rather not what?"

"Either. Talk or dance."

"No? Why are you here, then? I see you're wearing a ring . . ."

Kate had forgotten about that.

"Look, it's none of my business—"

"That's right—it isn't."

"So you want to be left alone . . ." he said. "You don't expect me to believe that, do you? You're giving off signals, love. Signals that say just the opposite—hold me, comfort me, talk to me. I study things like that."

"I don't care what you study."

"No? Well, no bother—" he said. He paused a moment to give her a chance to reconsider. She remained expressionless, staring at her glass, and did not watch him move off. When she looked up next, she had entirely forgotten him, her eyes full of a new sight, her face mottled with alarm. Firuz's boss, Emir Emiri, had just entered the room! For an instant, she stared at him in disbelief. I'll pay for this, she thought, and then: it can't be. I'm imagining things. It couldn't be!

The resemblance was so very cunning, though. A trick. Yet if it *were* a trick—if the man were a stranger in the mask of Emiri, why did he blanch so? Why did Kate and he stare at one another in such shock and recoil? Unless the man's face simply mirrored Kate's own . . . Maybe that was it.

He seemed to hesitate.

Then Emiri—or the semblance of Emiri—veered away, across the room and out by the opposite door, moving quickly past Kate, without the faintest show of recognition. It was over in a flash, whatever the damage—done.

When he was quite gone, her sick feeling subsided. What was done was done. The worst had likely happened, Kate felt, and the rest would be easier now. She looked up and round the room again. The light had changed: faces were cast in blue, green, violet, the colors of corrosion. It was a light that hollowed out the eyepits and blackened the mouth, made a sooted mask of every face. The mirrors on the far wall were dim and smoked.

A new man approached her. Not so new, actually. He looked to have been through at least one heavy night already; his collar was undone and there was a slash of lipstick on his left cheek. "Mind if I?" he seated himself alongside. "You don't look like the others . . ."

They all said that; Kate smiled to show that she recognized the ritual; he took the smile as encouragement. He was very blonde, fair and handsome. And evidently well known here, for the bartender was hovering near, regarding him with a steady, wary eye. "Lo, Malcolm," said Carl. "Hello, Carl," said Malcolm, "for the tenth time this evening—hello." Carl pointed to Kate with a hand that was none too steady. "I'll drink whatever she's drinking," he said. "I wouldn't call that drinking," said Malcolm. "Want it anyhow," said Carl, and turned his attention back to Kate.

"You're not happy—I can tell," he said.

"How?"

"Ways. Got my ways. I'll tell you if you come closer. C'mon bend an ear. That's it—it won't hurt." Kate tilted her ear in his direction but looked away. "Entry new . . ." he whispered, leaning closer; his lips nibbled the outer rim of her ear, his breath was hot and moist. "Please get it over with," she said, "you're tickling me." Explaining further, he shot the tip of his tongue into the well of her ear. She stiffened, jolted away. "Got you all aroused, huh?" he said triumphantly. "Get out!" she cried. "Leave me alone!"

"Muzzn't," he leered, "muzzn't touch—thinks she's special!"

If he wouldn't move, she would. Kate stood up and rushed to the powder room, her face burning. She felt queasy suddenly, swirling with liquids, unsteady on her feet. She coughed into the basin but nothing came. "Are you all right?" someone asked. Kate glanced up; it was a woman in a tight sari; she was dabbing a bright vermillion *tikka* spot between her eyebrows, where it stood out like a third eye. "Fine," Kate answered, "just great." But she was far from fine. Leaving the house, she'd been filled with the amazement of speed, of unimpeded motion; all that had vanished now, and in its place had come doubt, motion sickness, profound distrust. She was free, wasn't she? Yes, free. Yet, somehow, moving out on her own with the wide ambit of the world to choose a path from, she'd chosen the path Firuz had set for her, she'd remained strictly within the terms set for her kind. Revenge by prescription, almost. And where Firuz had nothing definite before, she was giving him precise ammunition, precisely the ammunition he desired.

Even so, it was better this way. At least *she* was choosing. Having given Firuz something definite, Kate would set both their minds at rest. He would no longer have to guess, chasing every innuendo, every shadow. And Kate would know what she had done. This was better, it would ease them both.

She returned to her post.

A new man entered the room. White flannels, white shoes. He flashed his Masonic ring as he made his way to the bar, and winked at Kate. She smiled, gave the come-on salute, everything was under control, *her* control. Now he approached, he spoke his name; it might have been a street name for all she cared. When she felt like it, she'd send him packing.

She lost count of the others. There was only one she couldn't handle—a friendly, older man, who simply, truly, wanted to talk. But he was the hardest of all to bear. Kate couldn't cope with kindness right now. She excused herself and returned to the powder room, taking her time there. When she emerged, he was gone.

The others came and went: she told them when to go. She had control, that was all she knew, and sufficient marvel in that.

As the latest man approached, Malcolm leaned close:

123

"Don't fall for this one," he breathed. "A sharp talker—but he's got problems. Watch out."

Kate felt quite solid now and well able to take care of herself. She was into her second gin and on her way up. In her mind's eye, she saw the red gate of Multan; she saw it in a hard light, part sun, part anger.

"I think you're a tease," the man began. "I've been watching you. I know your type. This is some kind of test for you, isn't it? We fail—you pass."

"Might be," said Kate.

The man addressed Malcolm: "Wants to kick us in the balls, she does," he said.

Malcolm, who was busy arranging glasses, grunted non-committally. The man turned back to Kate. "Been in this country long?" he asked.

"Long enough," said Kate.

"Then you know what these girls are called?"

"I guess."

"No, you don't. They're called 'taxis'—because they're for any man's hire. We don't think much of them, but I think even less of you. At least they're what they seem to be. While girls like you—"

"Think of me what you like," said Kate. How many times had she said that tonight? Said it and meant it.

A few more thrusts and he was off, murmuring "bitch" to himself. Gone as fast as she could hope. Kate wanted to laugh out loud with her surprising secret: she did not have to say yes, she was not at the mercy of anyone.

The mirrors whitened as they moved into the morning. The room emptied out. Kate listened to the tarrarram of her heart, a bold and exultant beat. No one would bother her now.

Those who remained were leftovers, unwanted. There were four women, not counting Kate, and one man, the one Malcolm had warned her against, the sharp talker with "problems." Two of the women were dancing; they moved in a parody of a proper married pair, stiff steering arms pumping away, taking elaborate box steps, squaring every corner, and laughing uproariously.

The young man with problems sat at a corner table with two women. He held the younger of the two on his lap; she had put her arms around his neck. She was wearing a sleeveless blouse and Kate could see the stubble of her armpits, streaked with white powder. The man was absently fondling the woman's breasts while staring pointedly at Kate. The other woman at the table was slapping down cards and turning them over. She seemed to be playing solitaire; though her cards were grouped in some curious design of squads and straggles, there wasn't an orderly row in sight. Perhaps she was telling fortunes.

"Was that a Bentley I saw parked outside?" she asked.

No one answered. She turned over a new card: jack of diamonds. "What a farce!" she said to no one in particular.

A silt, a weariness had settled over everything; it was visible, grainy, palpable. "Long night," said Malcolm. Kate nodded. Strange customer, he thought to himself. Malcolm couldn't make any sense of what she was after, but, then, he was too tired to make sense of anything; he wanted only to clean up and clear out. He began swabbing down the counter.

Kate knew her time was up. She felt like Cinderella on the morning after, an evil Cinderella. Back to the ashes . . . In a very little while, she would have to leave. As soon as she figured out where to go.

9
The Road

Aleem had made arrangements for the car and the driver; Tom was paying. They left town before dawn, the *azan* for the setting of the stars reverberating in the dark streets. The cry was repeated, now faint, now full, one *muezzin*, then—far out—another, then another, closer in. A sort of reveille, Tom thought, hallooings from pike to pike.

They were heading north and east. As they went on into the sun, they watched the buildings grow sharp against a whitening sky. Already a few shopkeepers were sprinkling water in front of their doors, damping down the dust.

Soon the domes of the Badshahi mosque could be seen, glistening against the sky, then the turrets of the great fort. They approached the Ravi River. There was a mango grove, the branches of the trees were thick with green blossoms. Above them, Tom could see the minarets of the great tomb of Jehangir and over on the facing bank, submerged by the trees, the modest tomb of his wife, Nur Jehan— Light of the World.

Now they had left the city behind. They passed a hydro-electric station, and then, on an eminence, a strange, squat tower, shaped something like a water tank. Huge birds roosted on its edge and others darkened the sky above it. "Thirty birds . . ." said Tom absently. "No," said Aleem, "not these. These are filthy, evil birds—" Tom kept his eye on the tower. The birds perched on its rim seemed to be vultures. But the birds high overhead, circling the tower with slow wheeling glides, were strange to Tom. They floated with such easy grace, a flight that seemed effortless, all repose; they did not seem to rise or sink, or ever flex a wing. "Birds of prey, aren't they?" Tom persisted. Aleem admitted that was so. "What do you call them—those high gliders?"

"Kites," said Aleem.

"Kites? Like paper kites?"

Aleem changed the subject. Tom continued to wonder what the tower meant and why Aleem wouldn't say, but did not ask again.

The day was warming up.

For once, Tom had awakened with a clear head. He'd supped alone after Aleem had left, taking only a glass of seltzer with the meal, and a small brandy afterward. There'd been two phone calls later that evening. The first was from an American consular official on a matter of business, a question of getting papers "squared away," a form updated. It would take only a few minutes, he promised, if Tom would simply drop in sometime before noon the next day. The other call was from Howard Wick, reminding him of a publisher's reception scheduled to take place that afternoon. Tom was now in flight from both men and mightily pleased with himself. He felt very well indeed as they left the hotel, better still, as they left the city limits behind, superb as they hit the open plain, triumphant with a sense of shedding his pursuers.

"You're sure you don't want to see the Lever Brothers' Soap Factory?"

"I'm sure," said Tom. "We'll skip that one."

"You said you wanted to see real life, remember?"

"I'll grant you that's real. But let's just skip that one. Tell me again what we're planning to see."

"From here on—circles!" said Aleem, smiling. "I warn you—there's a much shorter way from here to Cyrilabad —we won't be taking it.

"Never have taken the straight path," said Tom, undeterred. "So tell me."

"Ralu Station first. Then Iskanderabad, and the monument to Iskander—you know, Alexander the Great. Three cities were built there—you can see the ruins of all three, one over another." Aleem went on: "Then, tonight— Tajpur. Tomorrow—Naral, Durran. You said you wanted to go slowly." Tom nodded again; he couldn't remember saying so, but he trusted Aleem's memory. "Then back on the straight road—Kamran, Wilford, Cyrilabad. Saturday evening in Cyrilabad and Sunday morning—the Mehab shrine. On Sunday afternoon, back to Lahore without stopping, by the straight road."

"Then you to your studies and I to my—" Tom didn't finish. I to my whoring round the world, he thought. "Cyrilabad . . ." he mused aloud. "Sounds a bit British . . ."

"The name came after the British. It's a long story," said Aleem gravely.

Here he goes again, thought Tom, on and on like a heavy tome. "Tell me the shortest version of it," he said.

"I have to go back many years," Aleem began. "Up till Partition, the city was called Alminar. A river ran through the middle of it—the river Hafsa . . ."

Green land, then dry land. The road ahead continued to be well paved, even though the land seemed forsaken on both sides, yellow earth and raw bush. Then a few plowed fields. There was a graveyard and, beyond that, a barren field pitted with small holes. "What are those?" Tom asked, and Aleem explained how the villagers patched their mud walls after the rain.

"Well, it's pretty strange," said Tom, after a long pause.
"Strange? How strange?"

"Your dividing a man's name in half like that."

"Just so," said Aleem. "And dividing a city in half—you don't find that strange?"

"Mmm . . ." said Tom. "Tell me again what we're going to see there. In the shrine, I mean."

And so Aleem began telling the story of the holy hair, how it began its travels from Medina and its adventures along the way. Tom was only half-listening now. He took out his pipe and caressed the cold stem, put it to his lips, then returned the pipe to his pocket. He had no desire for a smoke. A terrible thirst was upon him. He took out his handkerchief, spat into it and moistened his mouth. His lips were rimmed with a thin, bitter crust. Leaning out the window did nothing for him; the air rushed past, abrading where it touched.

There was little to see now: only a low, bare horizon, thorny scrub, the yellow dust rising, drifting, and falling back, the land lying supine beneath a sky that overwhelmed it. Only shadows moved.

Aleem offered Tom an orange from the bag at his feet; Tom accepted hopefully; the inside was red, parched, burning with sweetness—no help.

They passed a hill split by a glaring white crack, the scar of subsidence from an old earthquake that ran on for nearly a mile. They passed a boiling spring.

Aleem had begun to recite from Ghalib.

> *Come, let us reverse*
> *The whole order of the sky!*

The morning wore on.

Part II

Listen, I have wept patiently.

IMRU AL-QAYZ,
Mu'Allaqat (A. Howell version)

10
Unpurchasable

Lahore, Friday

The car was waiting: a long black Chrysler with an empty flagpost on the hood. Scarcely had Nirmal Roy settled himself in the back seat when the driver uttered a fervent *"Bismillah!"* and they were off. Downstream, it felt: the motion of the car was so smooth that houses and streets seemed to flow past him.

It was chilly, late, the sky densely overcast. Nearly all the houses they passed were shuttered, dark. Nirmal leaned forward to check his watch with the clock on the dashboard —two minutes difference. It was nearly midnight and well past his bedtime on any account. He felt dull and irritable. What was it that couldn't be discussed on the phone or wait until morning? And what business could he possibly have now with the Chief Secretary of the Punjab, friendship aside?

They passed a guard station and entered the government compound. The car moved more slowly now, up a gravelled slope, between lawns drenched in darkness. In the huddled bordering hedge, there were thin fizzles of light: jasmine creeper. Not yet spring and halfway into summer

. . . Nirmal put down his window to catch a breath of the garden. A soft breeze rustled his ear. They passed a flowering bush of an immodest brilliance—Queen of the Night —spilling out fragrance like an unstoppered fountain. Rich air. Nirmal drank it in thirstily. Drink—*drown*, he warned himself, there is no limit.

But there was. The car came to an abrupt halt: they had arrived.

Two sentries flanking the front entrance of the building snapped to attention; one stepped forward. "This way, excellency," he said, leading the way on inside. His pace was swift: down a deserted hallway, turn left, turn right; Nirmal followed breathlessly. There were only four lights burning in a long corridor. Their footsteps echoed in the surrounding silence.

"That you, Nirmal?" Husamuddin stepped out of his office to greet him. "*As-Salaam Aleikum!*" The men embraced. "It's been too long—too long—there's no excuse!" Husamuddin grumbled cheerfully.

"I'm here. Come—have a seat. No, no—over here," Husamuddin guided his guest to the armchair closest to his desk, a soft wing chair covered in worn blue velvet. Nirmal eyed it distrustfully; he didn't like soft chairs. "*Please*," Husamuddin insisted, "there should be no ceremony between friends." The chair was as Nirmal had feared; he sank deeply into it.

Nirmal glanced quickly round: it was a huge office with tall doors, a high ceiling, blue carpet and curtains. Husamuddin's desk was imposing, its surface strikingly uncluttered. The desks of his undersecretaries would be cluttered and heaped, but here, clearly, decisions were made, and papers did not linger. Yet for all the stateliness of the room, the air inside it was bad, thick and musty—close. The windows must have been shut fast: the curtains did not stir. Nirmal thought with regret of the banished garden.

With his visitor captive, Husamuddin began the ritual

exchange of courtesies. Since Nirmal was a bachelor, living with his unmarried sister, the ritual was soon dispatched. But the Chief Secretary had an ailing mother and three young children, and each of these took time. And then two older sons at Oxford. Here, Husamuddin waxed expansive: "How it brings back the old days!" he murmured. But it didn't—not for Nirmal. He'd never gone to Oxford, or Cambridge. He, too, had crossed the dark waters to take a degree in England, but at the wrong school, the redbrick college of Keeton, an institution famed only for its first-rate rugby.

Nirmal couldn't help staring at his friend: Husamuddin did not look himself, he thought. Lusterless, somehow. It was nothing Nirmal could pinpoint, nothing so consistent as a flush or a pallor, or loss of flesh—if anything, his friend had put on weight. Yet there was *something*. Even when speaking of his sons, Husamuddin's eyes wandered.

"How is it with you? You're feeling well?" Nirmal asked for a second time.

"I breathe," said Husamuddin, "I breathe. Thank God for that."

The phone rang. Husamuddin smiled at Nirmal, shrugged and stretched out an arm for it. "Be a moment—" he promised; he picked up a tiny paper knife with his free hand. "Take your time," said Nirmal, for there was nothing else he could say. "Mind if I walk around?"

Husamuddin did not answer, did not seem to hear. Nirmal was anxious to know whether he would be able to rise from the chair.

He was, but the maneuver required both arms.

Left to his own devices, Nirmal wandered over to the far wall where a great many framed certificates and photographs were on display. Actually, he hobbled across. His left foot was asleep; he stamped on it twice. Husamuddin glanced up at the sound, then down again. Nirmal busied himself in reading the citations . . . The *Nishan-i-Khidmat* for meritorious civil service, *West Pakistan Lawn Tennis Association Membership, University of Aligarh Old Boys Association* . . . a certificate of distinction from the Lahore High Court. "Has he given you a reply?" Husamuddin asked, tapping his teeth with the paper knife. He glared into the mouthpiece of the phone.

Nirmal moved on to the photographs—nearly all were of Jinnah. One, top center, had pride of place; it was only a profile, but fully life-sized, taken close up. The Great Leader had been caught off guard. Fragility in every feature, and no hiding it: temple and cheekbone were hollowed out and smudged with shadow. In these concavities and in the pits of the eyes, Nirmal could see the actual thumbprints of death. Clear, too, in the transparency of the lips, in the vent of the nostril, hungry, like a mouth, in the eye itself, collyrium-bright or fever-bright, afloat in its pool of shadow. Frail as Jinnah was, racked and dishevelled and wasted within, his outer garments were still immaculate. This was Jinnah before the birth of Pakistan, in faultless Western dress: dark tie, white jacket and shirt; no doubt his trousers were white; his shoes, very likely, were white as well; the collar of his shirt was high, white, and smooth, his neck so thin that cloth and flesh did not touch. He was dabbing his lips with a spotless white handkerchief; his fingernails were neat and oddly flat, like coins.

The portrait alongside was smaller but more detailed. It must have been taken only months before Jinnah's death; he was standing at attention, reviewing a military parade: he'd just become the first Governor-General of the new nation of Pakistan. Hardly a military figure himself, only a matchstick of a man—all eyes, bones and hollows, so thin that, between waist and shoulder, his coat seemed uninhabited. Native dress in this one: the neat black caracul cap that was to be called a "Jinnah cap" in years to come, a long dark sherwani jacket, loose white shalwar, gleaming black pumps, and around his neck, worn like an order of merit—a monocle on a thin ribbon, inspired by the sight of Joseph Chamberlain in the House of Commons.

Nirmal had met with Jinnah alone only once, about the time this picture was taken. The experience had not been a happy one; it might have been a public meeting; he'd found Jinnah cold, quite simply, needlessly, cold. Lord Mountbatten had once described Jinnah as "crisp" at his warmest, and Nirmal could not help but feel the description apt. Nirmal had extended his hand only to meet with air, for Jinnah was too busy counting off his points of argument on his fingers to shake hands.

And here was the Great Leader in full face. The eyes were keen and penetrating—and cold. The lips, on first glance, seemed full and sensual—strangely sensual for so astringent a man. Yet, looking closer, something about the set of his lips contradicted their fullness, the way upper and lower met and rested together, as though locked, sealed in refusal. "Unpurchasable," people called him.

Unyielding always . . . "No, I am not," Jinnah said to the doctor who assured him that he was going to live. The last words from a man of his word: he was dead in thirty minutes.

"Needs time to think about it, does he?" said Husamuddin, a distinct rumble of threat in his voice. Nirmal moved on to the next portrait.

It was a rare shot of Gandhi and Jinnah together; Nirmal wondered whether it was quite politic for Husamuddin to display it. It must have been taken at the time of Jinnah's resignation from the Home Rule League. That would be 1920. Gandhi had appealed in vain for Jinnah's return. The two men were stepping through a doorway and smiling, though not at each other. Gandhi was in coolie dress, Jinnah in a dark double-breasted suit with pin stripes, wide lapels, a rich tie, and two-toned shoes; he was wearing a white carnation in his buttonhole. Gandhi's arm was resting on Jinnah's shoulder; there was no reciprocal gesture from Jinnah. Both leaders smiled into the camera; reporters and photographers were pressing in on all sides. Nirmal recalled the incident: both men were delighted with the publicity, and the press had made much of the exchange. Gandhi had just turned to Jinnah and said: "You like this, don't you?"—Jinnah's reply: "Not as much as you do."

A youthful portrait of Jinnah next to this: the new barrister in wig and gown. There was only a remote family resemblance to the man he was to become here, only in the quickness of his eyes . . . Husamuddin put down the phone noisily. "And now, my friend," he said, gesturing to the chair Nirmal had vacated. "Another time I'll show you my collection. It's grown since. Some other time. Now let's sit and talk."

Nirmal returned to the soft armchair and, once again, sank reluctantly down.

"I can't help noticing you've been keeping to yourself lately, Nirmal. Why?"

Nirmal didn't feel inclined to go into it. "I've been busy," was all he said.

"You're right," Husamuddin corrected himself. "I didn't call you in here at this hour to catch up on personal news. We'll do that some other time. Soon, I hope. Now I've a favor to ask you, a job I'd like you to take on. I need someone who can't be bought." Husamuddin rose and swiftly crossed the room; he opened the tall doors outward, only enough to scan the hallway in both directions; then he shut the doors carefully, testing the knobs. "I'd offer you some tea," he said, "but everyone seems to have gone home to bed. We'd best get down to it." He leaned forward, and said in a voice that was little above a whisper: "What's your position on relics?"

"Position?" said Nirmal. "I don't understand. I have no position."

"I'm looking for a man to do a job. Not an easy one. It's an emergency. I wouldn't have called you in at midnight otherwise, Nirmal, be sure of that. In simple decency I ought to have given you a night's sleep and some time to think it over. But the situation is too serious—critical, maybe. I *hope* I'm wrong."

"What does the job call for?"

"Nothing much—endless patience, limitless tolerance, farsightedness, *and* practicality."

"In other words, an impossible job."

"Just barely possible, perhaps."

"But I don't want a job, certainly not that kind. Retirement agrees with me—I'm quite happy. Don't you believe that?"

"Mmm . . ." said Husamuddin.

"Well, I am."

"Retired and happy? A contradiction in terms," said Husamuddin.

"For *you*, maybe."

"You're too young to be writing your memoirs, Nirmal."

"Sixty-two is hardly the flush of youth," said Nirmal. "It may not be as old as it once seemed, but—" Husamuddin would not hear him through. "I'm nearing sixty, myself," he confessed, "and I've only now come into my maturity. I know my limitations. But I know my powers, too, and I've finally found the position which gives them full scope."

"That's very fortunate," Nirmal agreed, "to be used to the full, the best of fates, I think."

"Which is why I find it so particularly unfortunate," said Husamuddin, not relinquishing his point for an instant, "that *your* talents have not been allowed full scope." Nirmal raised his hand to object, but Husamuddin ignored him. "I know your talents. I've seen you in action, remember. You've a real gift for practical administration, a rare gift. Most of us are pure theorists, good on paper, but all thumbs when it comes to the test. Twenty-three years in the civil service is nothing to squander in any case, and your record is outstanding—Finance, Transport, Famine—all of it first-rate. First-rate! No, my friend, you may *not* interrupt—" Nirmal had, in fact, only shifted uncomfortably in his chair; his foot was beginning to fall asleep again. "I'm going to say what I think," Husamuddin persisted. "You were let go at an unconscionably early age. Why? Partly your own choice. Oh, I know—according to you—entirely your own choice. Well, let's be honest—it *wasn't* entirely so. Partition was a time of great simplification. Your views were a little too complicated for most people at that time."

"No—no backward glances," Nirmal protested, "I've never allowed myself that. I have no regrets. And I'm not idling, as you seem to think. You know I'm teaching—two classes in public administration. I'm writing, too—articles and things."

Husamuddin waved the defense away. "Those who can —do," he recited. "Leave teaching and writing to the other ones. Let me tell you what's happening. Much as I can." He looked up, around the room—quick, measuring glances, then began to speak softly and rapidly. "Sorry about all this fussiness—these precautions. There's a news blackout on. So far it's holding. You're familiar with the Cyrilabad-Radpur area?"

"Yes . . ."

"Been to the Mehab shrine?"

"Oh, yes."

"Good. So you must have seen it—the *mu-e-muqaddas* —the holy hair?"

"Not really—I'd hardly call that seeing. It was much too crowded. Too far off."

"Always is. I've never been to a *deedar*, myself, not much my sort of thing, but my mother went, and she has never been able to tell me whether the holy hair was black or red or grey. Her eyes, she said, were so full of tears."

"You're keeping me in suspense, Husamuddin. What exactly . . . ? What about the relic?"

"It seems to be missing."

"Missing?" Nirmal tested the word. "You mean stolen?"

Husamuddin simply spread his hands.

"I'm very sorry to hear that," said Nirmal, "but I don't see—"

"You will: I need someone to recover the relic. I'd like it to be you."

"I have no background in police work," Nirmal was quick to answer, "that should rule me out."

"Nothing along those lines," Husamuddin assured him. "Looks to me more a political than a police matter. I know you're the right man for it."

"You'll have to convince me of that," said Nirmal.

"I can only tell you the barest minimum. The holy hair was reported lost early this morning. The town is in an uproar as you might expect. Tomorrow will be a day of protest and demonstration—they've scheduled a general strike for Monday. They might as well keep up the strike indefinitely once they've begun. Shut down the city while they're at it. Economically, the city depends upon the relic, so there's nothing more to lose. That's bad enough, but there's worse. I'll spare you none of it if you decide to take on the job. It's a bad border. But I'm sure you see all the implications . . ."

"Some . . . Radcliffe was especially uneasy about this one," Nirmal recalled.

"And with reason," said Husamuddin. "Nowhere else did he divide up a city."

"A botch," Nirmal said sadly. Neither spoke for a moment; the two men sat on, silent, face to face, yet gazing past one another. Nirmal thought of his retirement, how quiet and clear his days had been. Quiet and clear and numb, he thought, a vacancy somehow, a great slackness, a sleep. "A border like a wound," he said softly, so softly he might have been thinking aloud. Then he collected himself and said in his public voice: "The damage was done seventeen years ago. So why should trouble start now?"

Why now? They worked over the question. There was, of course, a fresh crisis in the Vale, both men seized upon the word "Kashmir" at once; seized blindly, for the precise connection was not at all clear.

The new trouble had begun less than two weeks ago; there'd been rioting in Srinagar and in some of the surrounding villages—the heavy Muslim majority in Kashmir demanding self-determination, a plebiscite—India furious at what she called "Pakistani agitation," foreign meddling in her internal affairs. There'd been shouts and threats in the Security Council, although the Indian delegate had begun quite calmly by "telling what the whole world knows" —that the Kashmiri Muslims were happier in a secular state than they ever would be in Pakistan. The accession of Kashmir to India was "full, final, irrevocable—as everlasting as the snow on the mountaintops." Kashmir was "thoroughly absorbed, by law and fact." The Pakistani delegate had foamed at that: Alsace-Lorraine, too, had been "absorbed," absorbed by Bismarck, absorbed again by Hitler —but it was justly French today . . . The debates were still going on.

Something to do with Kashmir, then? But what? Distraction, Nirmal guessed. Yes, surely this was the easiest and timeliest explanation: the theft of the holy hair an Indian plot, a diversionary maneuver to keep Pakistan out of Kashmir, tied up at a distant point. And the Cyrilabad-Radpur border would be a natural place. There were ample grounds for resentment in Radpur—old rivalries, economic jealousy of its more prosperous neighbor—resentments waiting to be put to work.

As soon as they'd put the thought into words, Nirmal decided it was too easy; it was always easier to look across the border for blame. The trouble was as likely to be internal, the theft a sabotage from within, some Pakistani factional intrigue, political or religious. A Muslim splinter group, perhaps: a resurgence of the Ahmadiya movement was not unthinkable, or a Shi'a plot . . .

"I am sure . . ." Nirmal said. Of what? He wasn't sure.

"Only one certainty," said Husamuddin, "the situation isn't good."

"Not good"—that was putting it mildly. Each knew what the other was thinking: it could be war. A war over a hair, thought Nirmal, that would be the limit. "How exactly does that boundary go?" he said. "You'll take it on, then?" said Husamuddin quickly. Too eagerly—Nirmal did not reply. Instead Nirmal asked: "Does the river take a loop north or south of Muhsan?"

"You don't expect me to remember," said Husamuddin. "Let's have a look." He crossed the room and stooped to a low corner cabinet. "I've a good map here . . . somewhere . . ."

They pored over the map in silence at first: West Pakistan —green, East Pakistan—yellow, India—blue—in the middle. Impossible country, Nirmal said to himself, two severed, lopsided wings with an alien body between them. Here was the Punjab—province of five rivers. Nirmal traced the meander of the Hafsa River and repeated the motion several times, as if seeking to store the memory of its shape in his forefinger. He paused where the Hafsa neared the fifth river. Long ago, Alexander the Great had passed this way. And here, not far east of Muhsan, was where Alexander's troops mutinied and forced him to turn back, close, he imagined to the outer rim of the habitable world.

The rim of the habitable world . . . Well, sometimes.

"What are you thinking about?" Husamuddin asked suddenly. "What?" Nirmal gave a little start. "Me? Nothing . . . it isn't marked." He'd been daydreaming again— there'd been altogether too much of that lately. "Look here—" he jabbed the map decisively at a spot just north of Muhsan. "You see the gap?"

Nirmal continued following his finger. "There's a dip in the river here—and here. And around Muhsan there's a loop. And here's what I was looking for . . . see it? Here the border runs over land." He tapped the paper: five black squares stood for boundary pillars. "See how widely spaced they are? It would be easy enough to cross the border between any two of these points and close enough to Cyrilabad for the thieves to have come that way. Assuming the river is under efficient surveillance and difficult to cross at Radpur. And assuming the thieves came from the Radpur side of the border, none of which we know . . ." Nirmal's voice trailed off. There was nothing he did know.

"Muhsan won't be your worry. We're already alert to it. Your problem is Cyrilabad. It should keep you sufficiently busy."

"Ah, but you're forgetting—"

"I'm not forgetting. You haven't yet agreed to take on the job. Would you, Nirmal?"

Nirmal looked down at his hands and spread his fingers. He was free still. At his age, he was entitled to a little peace; he had the right to say no. He sighed deeply.

"May I take that as assent?" Husamuddin asked.

"I'll do what I can," said Nirmal. He spoke very low.

"Wonderful," said Husamuddin, beaming warmly, "I'm so glad." He caught a glimpse of his wristwatch; his face changed. "You'll need all the sleep you can manage. It's later than I thought—I'm sorry. Let me tell you all I can as quickly as I can. Your mission will be twofold. First, to recover the holy relic and apprehend the thieves. Yusuf Waheed is Superintendent of Police there. He's first-rate, as efficient as they come. You're fortunate in that. The second task—and this is equally important—is to contain the local disturbances. Mansur Latif—he's Deputy Commissioner—should help you there."

"What should I know about him?"

"Well . . . he's served a long time. Durable; he'll do. Not very versatile, I expect. He's near retirement, but wants his increment, so he's holding on for another year or so. Does that give you any idea?"

"Some."

"Where were we?"

"Second prong: containing the local situation."

"That's right. Try to keep up the news blackout as long as possible. We want the situation in Cyrilabad kept under wraps until we know what's what—who's doing what to whom. *If* the theft is an Indian plot—once it's more than a guess—then we won't keep quiet any longer."

"And the town officials?" Nirmal wondered. "What should I expect?"

"The usual mix: inept, corrupt, competent. You'll find no *lal kitab* to give you the facts you need to know about them. All I can do is supply you with a list of names and titles; it's a poor second best. I only wish . . . Well, what's the use of wishing? I'll send over authorizations, maps, briefing papers —everything I can think of—with the car in the morning. You're to be sent in as Special Assistant for National Security Affairs. This should give you sufficient authority to move as you see fit. What else? Anything? Yes . . . I should tell you that we've had our first border violation already— our first *known* violation, that is—not far from where you were pointing. Your instinct was exactly right."

"What's the story?"

"Six Indian students—they called themselves students. They managed to sneak over in broad daylight. We caught up with them a few miles into our territory. They said they were hunting butterflies."

"Doesn't sound that serious to me," said Nirmal.

"Hunting butterflies with knives and chains!"

"Ah," said Nirmal.

"And that's only a beginning, I'm afraid," said Husamuddin.

11
The Public Servant

When Nirmal returned home from his meeting with Husa-muddin, it was a little after two in the morning. His sleep that night was short and not at all sweet. He was troubled by a bad dream.

He was dictating an urgent message to his stenographer, a young man with a full black beard. The stenographer held a notepad in his left hand, positioned for taking dictation; he peered intently into Nirmal's face, his neck at full stretch, so as not to miss a single word, but there was no pencil in his right hand. "Are you ready?" asked Nirmal. "All ready, jenab." Nirmal began with the date and saluta-tion; the right hand of the stenographer began to fondle his beard. "Have you got that?" asked Nirmal. "Yes, jenab," said the stenographer; but his answer was entirely equivo-cal: his voice said "yes" while his hand continued to play with his beard. "Read it back!" Nirmal demanded, and by way of answer, the stenographer took his beard between three fingers and lifted it until it touched his nose. *"Is the worm in you satisfied?"* Nirmal cried out. His shouting woke Meena in the next room.

A silly dream, more cause for amusement than anger or

alarm. But Nirmal had been unable to fall back to sleep afterward. He'd listened to the bursts of static preceding the first call to prayer from the nearby mosque. In the still night, it sounded like gunfire. Each time the defective loud-speakers brayed, prowling dogs and cats would join the chant, and one demented bird, thinking it was dawn, took up the cockcrow, his perch not distant, not half distant enough, from Nirmal's ear.

Morning had always been a hallowed part of the day for Nirmal, a time spent at his writing desk on the verandah, overlooking the garden, a quiet time, sweetened by a lei-surely pipe and cup after cup of white tea. This morning was different: he didn't allow himself to linger.

It was a fine day, cool and clear, the sun mild, a light breeze riffling the small branches of the trees, a fine down, faint tremulous hairs on everything. Yet Nirmal remained tense and irritable; no question was innocent as Meena soon discovered, and any attempt at conversation was haz-ardous, like placing a finger on a very taut drum.

Eight forty-five. Nirmal was ready minutes ahead of time. He studied the government car as it moved down the driveway. It was the same car as last night: a long black Chrysler with an empty flagpost on the hood.

The bearer helped him to load; when Nirmal turned around, Meena had vanished. "I'm going now!" he called through the vestibule. No answer. He ran back to the sit-ting room, and found Meena absently dusting a table with her hand. "I'll be home soon, you'll see."

"Hmmm . . ." she said, "you'll ring me up, Nirmal, won't you?"

"If I can."

"When you can. I'll be waiting."

She kissed him, avoiding his eyes.

They followed the canal out of the city. It was better to be finally underway, better to move than to wait. The canal flowed past, then the rifle range and the hydroelectric sta-

tion. Ahead—the Parsi graveyard, marking the outer perimeter of the city; it loomed upward to a great height on
the horizon, for it stood on rising ground. They approached the tower of silence where the dead were laid:
from close up, it looked like an oil tank open to the sky, or
a high well. But the sky overhead was darkened with vultures and kites. The kites floated above the other birds on
stiff, unbending wings.

"They don't seem to be very interested—those kites,"
said Nirmal.

"Oh, they're interested, believe me," said the driver, and
he invoked the name of Allah as protection. "In an hour, it
will all be over. The bones into the pit at the center. Those
birds will be so stuffed they won't be able to lift their wings.
Infidels—animals! Those people have the customs of animals."

On the contrary, thought Nirmal, this is quite civilized.
Fire seems cleaner still—but that's the old Hindu coming
out in me. This makes good sense. Better than the grave,
the rich still proud in their tall stone huts, the engraving of
names and honors in the general dust, the slow dissolution
in darkness . . . *Far* better, he thought. But he kept his
thoughts to himself.

They left the tower behind and joined a broad highway.
Settling himself, Nirmal noticed a thin portfolio on the seat
beside him. Clipped to the first sheet was a personal note
from the Chief Secretary. It was written in a minute callig-
rapher's hand; Nirmal brought it close to his eyes and read:
"All my sympathy, Husamuddin." Underneath this, were
briefing papers. The top page was a script of a news bulletin
to be released within the hour. It bore the imprimatur of
the Prime Minister, and was marked for limited distribution, strictly within the confines of Cyrilabad. Elsewhere,
the paper reminded him, a news blackout was in force. The
bulletin was an appeal to the citizens of Cyrilabad to keep
calm and to cooperate with the official now in charge of

the area—James Nirmal Roy—a civil servant with an un-
matched record in the resolution of difficult disputes. No
mention of his long retirement from all disputes.

James . . . It was a name he never used, but marked him
clearly as a Christian, a man above the fray. This was
shrewd.

And here were the highlights of his career: famine duty
in Bihar, Chief Transport Officer in the Punjab during Partition . . . Anything to build up an image. No mention of
the heaps of paper work, the real heroics.

What else?

The hopes of the nation go with him, so said the bulletin.

God goes with him.

It was nice to think so.

Nirmal had never been on particularly intimate terms
with God. His father had been, suffering the stigma of
castelessness for his conversion. Nirmal, free to be a Christian without stigma or strain, found his conviction pale,
where his father's blazed. He was a Methodist by habit and
custom, but he might have been a Baptist or a Buddhist; if
he belonged at all, it was more from a sense of family loyalty than conviction. To Nirmal, the question of religion
was exactly like the local language question, the passion of
regionalism: which language is truer? richer? more expressive? Your own, of course, whatever it is.

The vegetation thinned out as they left the river behind.
Here the dusty plain began; it had been a dry winter and
the soil glittered with thin traces of white alkali. The towns
were smaller as they went on. The richer houses were of
baked clay brick and had windows with wooden shutters,
though without glass, but most of the houses were blind, no
windows at all, tombs made of mud with a few timber sup-
ports. To an eye blurred by motion and distance, they
might have been natural outcroppings of the soil, the work
of wind, erosion, and drift.

At Kamran, they stopped for tea.

Nirmal moved up front beside the driver for the next stage of the journey; he wanted to see as fully as possible.

"It's a pleasure, such a smooth ride," he said, anxious to put the man at ease.

"Good suspension," said the driver, but the conversation went no further.

From Kamran to the town of Wilford, the highway ran parallel to the railroad tracks. Buses, motorcycles, trucks, bullock carts, tongas, and men travelling on foot, all moved along this highway, and traffic was slow. A working day, nothing out of the usual. Stalled at a crossroad, they were besieged by vendors selling tea, fried sweets, nuts, and popcorn with sharp spices.

More fields, then a large town. Allanabad was a railroad junction; from here, tracks branched off to Suraj and Banarsi. Another village: some clumps of mud. Soon the road was lined with tall poplars, too high and narrow for shade. Traffic had thinned out. The sun shone hard in Nirmal's eyes as they entered the city.

A policeman stopped them at the first intersection; he exchanged a few words with the driver, then attached a scrap of black cloth to the flagpost of the car. He nodded to Nirmal and touched his fingers to his forehead as the car passed by.

The driver began to accelerate, as if the usual rules were suspended; Nirmal wanted to hunch forward, but forced himself to lean back. The hood of the car gave off shuddering reflections.

As they came through the first roundabout, the car was again flagged to a stop. Three officials stood waiting for Nirmal; the news of his arrival had preceded him. "*Shahbash!* Well done!" they cried. Nirmal stepped out of the car to greet the officials. There was a mingled chorus of congratulation on the wisdom of the Prime Minister's appointment, and the men introduced themselves. Ali Rahman, the District Magistrate, said that he felt like an old friend:

"My father spoke of you often. He was in the ICS with you —border transport—1947."

"Your father . . . let me see . . ." Nirmal scanned the young man's face for clues. He was thin, shorter than average, with skin of a shiny mahogany cast, wistful eyes, and an exuberant smile.

Nirmal racked his memory for an image of the young man's father, but nothing came; there had been quite a number of Rahmans in his life, and the name brought a flurry of impressions to mind. By now, the year of Partition was a vast turbulence—dense, still painful, unsiftable. Ali Rahman sensed Nirmal's difficulty and said: "His name was Mir Rahman—peace to his memory. A simple man—you wouldn't remember him. He sat in a back office and made out train schedules. But *you*—how my father's friends looked up to you! They talked of you all the time. The way you took it upon yourself to guarantee safe passage to the villagers who were being evacuated, riding over the border with them on those trains, those death traps—"

"Oh, only once or twice," Nirmal said, brightening in spite of himself. "Young blood . . . Not any more." It was good to find a friend here, impossible for Nirmal to disguise his pleasure.

The other officials were less enthusiastic, and noticeably so. Masud Munim, a young police constable, whose exact title Nirmal did not catch, would be Nirmal's "personal assistant"—whatever that meant. Since Nirmal had been promised a complete crisis management team, the full panoply of civilian, police, and military staff assistants, he did not see where Munim fit in. They mean "bodyguard," Nirmal thought, only no one has the courage to say so. As a man who valued his privacy, Nirmal wanted none of it; he'd have to find something useful to occupy Munim. Useful and distant, yes. Munim's appearance did not inspire confidence, in any case: doe-eyed, with a slumped sedentary build, he seemed strangely miscast in any active profession.

Mansur Latif, the Deputy Commissioner, looked to be past Nirmal's age. His hair was scant and white, his hands heavily veined. Latif never once smiled, but Nirmal thought that might be because his teeth were so bad, solid gold, some of them, the rest—grey and yellow. But, of course, Latif had other reasons not to smile; as senior official, it was natural to think that he should have been placed in charge of the investigation.

They entered the car, all of them. Everyone was uncomfortable, hot, cramped, confined. The car started up. Latif and Nirmal sat in uneasy proximity, side by side, in back. Under the circumstances, Nirmal decided, humility was the best policy. Breaking his silence only to ask a question or two, offering no opinions, Nirmal let it be known that he was eager to listen and be instructed.

"What a year!" said Latif, spreading his hands.

"A busy year?" said Nirmal.

"Busy! I won't survive another like it. Gales and cyclones, a cut in the railway budget, the Martyr's Day debacle . . ."

"Oh, yes, I remember hearing about Martyr's Day," said Nirmal.

"And then the deputations! Islamic Ideology Advisory Council, Salinity Control Board, telecommunications research . . . Never an idle moment—"

"You had some important visitors this year," Nirmal suggested.

"Visitors! Afghani, Chinese, Lebanese, Polish, Iranian . . . Yugoslavian . . . And then Chou En-lai on an 'informal' tour—you can imagine how informal that was! And now this . . ." Latif sighed again. "Now this," he lifted his hand to the window. Staring through the window at the passing streets, he resumed a morose silence.

Nirmal, too, looked out in silence. Ullah Street, Kohlu Park, Mochi Roundabout, Lohari Road, Jamil Bazaar, Nawaz Produce Yard, Jinnah Square, Municipal Corporation Centre . . . It was the same wherever they went. All the shops they passed were closed, their ripplefront shields drawn down, as though it were late night. The smaller booths and stalls were boarded up solid. Even the Sultana Cinema was shut fast; the yellow and red banners strung across the marquee seemed tawdry and faded in the strong light, an empty gaiety, the jubilee celebration for "Blood on the Mountain" in its hundredth day cancelled now.

The main streets were clogged with long processions. They turned down side streets heading for the north end of the city. Shah Abdul Latif Street, Circuit Road, Gymkhana Road, McLeod Street . . . It was a drab town, drabber than Nirmal remembered, a city of flat facades and single entrances, the houses built back to back as protection against thieves.

First stop: Government Rest House, Nirmal's official residence. He dropped off his luggage, though he doubted he'd be spending much time here. He'd been given a room with a verandah overlooking a garden and fish pond—altogether too peaceful and removed.

The Civil Lines Police Headquarters was next. Nirmal looked over the control room, noted with satisfaction the large desks and tables, all cleared for action, and the cot laid out for him. There was a *charpoi* in the corner for Munim. Telephone, telegraph, wireless, maps of the twin cities and outlying districts on the wall—everything seemed to be in order.

In the conference room next door, Nirmal was briefed by the Superintendent of Police, Yusuf Waheed. Waheed jabbed a large street map with a pencil as he spoke: a shower of scattered points, the gesture was impressive but not informative. The police were nowhere in their search.

"To be honest, we haven't a clue," said Waheed.

They did have a number of theories. First—that it was an Indian conspiracy, plotted from Radpur. Most people believed this.

"On what evidence?" Nirmal asked.

"Evidence?" Waheed paused.

"Evidence: threats, suspicious movements on the other side of the river . . ."

"No, no threats," Waheed replied, "nothing so simple. There's been some sniping from across the river, though. More than usual. Radpur went into receivership this year, while Cyrilabad, by the grace of God—We aren't hurting certainly, and they are. There are motives—wouldn't you say? Old grudges. Tensions everywhere, disputed borders heating up wherever you look. I don't need to tell you. Kashmir, for a start . . ."

None of this was new to Nirmal. They went on to discuss other possibilities. "No one's mentioned municipal intrigue," said Nirmal, "how about it?" No takers. Nirmal persisted: "There's someone missing, isn't there? Where's the man in charge of this city?" Deep silence. An indelicate question. "Well?" He glanced round the table. Munim poked his ear with a key; it was not his place to answer. Rahman coughed. Finally, Latif spoke up: "You mean Qureshi—the Chairman of the Municipal Corporation?" Nirmal stared blankly, there was no other meaning.

"Rumor has it that Qureshi's mother is ill. Taken very suddenly, I'm afraid."

"Very suddenly," echoed Waheed.

"So Qureshi rushed to her bedside," Latif went on. "It's most inconvenient, of course, just now . . ."

"You mean to tell me that the man in charge of the city has chosen this moment to disappear!" Nirmal found his voice rising a little. "That's interesting. And the Vice-Chairman?"

"Emir Kabir? He's with the custodian of the relic, as far as we know. They've formed an Action Committee."

"Ah," said Nirmal, "that's interesting, too. It all bears thinking about, doesn't it? What else? Any other theories?"

"Spring, for one," Latif proposed, "every year it happens, some craziness—men become strange to themselves . . .

Then again, it could be the work of professional thieves. Or hoodlums. A bad joke."

The problem was that no one of these theories was more compelling than another. At the moment, only one thing was certain: the police were keeping very busy. Reporters and foreign visitors were being rounded up and detained at Hotel Metropole. The news blackout was holding, but the secrecy couldn't be kept up indefinitely. "We don't know where to start," said Waheed, "so we're starting everywhere. You may not recognize our men, but they'll be watching *you*." By all reports, the Holy Relic Action Committee, a group formed to meet the emergency, little more than a day old, was now in charge of the city. Nirmal was told that the crowds were calm, but he wanted to see for himself.

A quick midafternoon lunch and they set off, leaving Waheed behind at headquarters.

Nirmal had never seen so many women out in the open. Where did they come from? He had not known there were so many. Most were veiled in black or white, but a group of young women with colored *dupattas* were chattering as they walked along; were it not for their black armbands and bare feet, they looked as though they might be going to a party.

It was painfully slow going. The entire city seemed to be on the move, and all the children were out, underfoot. Each family carried a scrap of dark cloth, and most were barefoot in mourning. Some of the marchers were carrying mats, bedding, and charcoal braziers for the night ahead. Some—most—Latif explained, were headed for the court-yard of the mosque, others to the railroad station waiting room. A group of the well-to-do were already gathered at the Field Club. There would be speeches in all three places.

As they neared the center of town, it would have been impossible to move at all if it were not for the official car and Nirmal's name and title made familiar by the Prime

Minister's bulletin. Six men, three holding on to each of the front fenders, insisted on escorting the car through the crowd. The throng divided before the nose of the car as water before the prow of a ship.

Nirmal had seen nothing like this, ever. Everything was shut down. Eating stalls had been set up at every third crossroad. They parked in front of one of these and stepped outside for a minute. Weak tea in clay tumblers was being given out; Nirmal was offered a cup; milk clotted on the surface; he took the merest sip—it was bad. *Chapattis* were stacked high for the evening and huge vats of *dahl* had been placed over a fire, the cauldrons sooted and seething. It looked like the preparation for a wedding party, enough for hundreds. But thousands—could they handle thousands? What would happen when they ran out?

A few questions. The answers were as expected. The Holy Relic Action Committee had set up the stalls. The committee had urged all citizens to douse their cooking fires, leave their homes, and come mourn for the city, the relic, the Faith. The committee was also in the business of supplying the marchers with flags.

It was twilight as they made their circuit of the outer districts, and evening when they started for the river. They passed the double barricades and headed down. Here the soldiers wore flak-jackets and security precautions were especially strict, for the first reaction of the townspeople to news of the theft had been to stone the border guards.

Nothing like that now: the bridge and both embankments were brilliantly illuminated by electric arc lamps. Nirmal examined the sentry box where the first officer was wounded: there was nothing to see.

All calm. The river gleamed like still mercury under the blinding arc lamps, the moon dim by comparison. A heavy guard stood on both banks behind loops of barbed wire and sandbags. The soldiers rose above the Radpur embankment like the palings of a picket fence. Then one moved out of alignment, momentarily resting the butt of his gun. Surely the line left off somewhere and could be breached—*had* been breached, if the thieves came from the other side. The guard had been doubled since then. Even so—

They headed back out. "And now what?" asked Nirmal.

"Nothing else on the agenda tonight."

"How about the shrine?"

"Oh, not tonight," Latif and Rahman opposed it in one voice. "Better in the morning, *enshallah.*" Nirmal did not argue. He agreed to return to Rest House, secretly determined to visit the shrine within the next few hours—just as soon as he could shed his advisors.

At Rest House, they had tea and went over the same ground. Rahman, and Rahman alone, had faith that a solution would drop out of the sky. "He who gives teeth shall give bread," he assured them.

Munim remained after the others had left. "Why don't you go home?" Nirmal suggested.

"No home to go home to, sir. Besides, I was told to stay with you."

"And now I'm telling you differently," Nirmal said patiently. When that made no impression, he ordered Munim to leave; it was an assignment: to try and locate his parents and wife. Chances were, they had more information than the officials. "I'll expect you back at police headquarters first thing in the morning. Not before."

"If this is your will then . . ."

"It is."

Munim hesitated, then, tapping his forehead with the fingers of one hand, rapidly salaamed and left.

With everyone official out of the way, Nirmal lay down for a brief rest. He intended to give himself no more than half an hour, only enough time to make sure his advisors were really gone.

He had so little time, and already he was tired. The city

was strange to him; the officials were men he did not know. Latif was counting on him to fail—Latif and Munim both. Nirmal did not know how he knew this; it was something he sensed, a sort of mutual bristling. Nirmal knew what they'd say: "He's not a Muslim, so why should he care?"

In the past few hours, he had learned very little. The city was under control for the moment, under the control of the Holy Relic Action Committee. Scant comfort in that, since no one knew the real aims of its members. If something were not done quickly, the crowd would push through the barricades leading to the waterfront and storm the river. And then the matter would be out of his hands; it would be the opening stage of a war.

So little time . . . Reclining, he did not rest. His thoughts kept circling, like those carrion birds round the tower.

It was nearly eleven when Nirmal ordered the car brought round and slipped out of Rest House. He rode to the middle of the city, then ordered the driver to wait and proceeded the rest of the way on foot. Nirmal had only to utter his name and the crowd made way for him. An old man tried to kiss his hand: "My heart is just breaking. You will find the holy hair?" he pleaded. "You are our mother and father!"

Here and there people were chanting: "God is great, God is true!" but without much feeling, as if simply to punctuate their walking. As Nirmal neared the courtyard of the Mehab shrine, the chanting grew more rhythmical and pronounced.

Nirmal had hoped to enter the mosque unobtrusively, but this was not to be. At the sound of his name, he was again jostled by well-wishers, and anxious to avoid attention, he rushed through the dim passageway to a floodlit area, an anteroom, ringed with police, which led to the heart of the shrine. He passed through a succession of doors, one of silver, one of glass panels, one of wood. The last door hung on twisted hinges; it was the only one which showed signs of forced entry.

The custodian, Naseem Shah, was not around. "Busy elsewhere," Nirmal was told; he had a good idea where. Tomorrow morning, first thing, Nirmal resolved to reach the Action Committee on his own. The custodian's younger brother, Aslam Shah, was available and willing to talk; he would have to do.

Nirmal was ushered into a tiny space eight or nine feet square. "So this is it . . ." he glanced around, disappointed; the room was nothing more than a large cupboard. It was sparsely furnished and unadorned, except for an ornate box on a table of bare planks. Nirmal noticed that the box was finely inlaid with ivory and gold. "And this—" he pointed, but did not touch, "this—enclosed the holy relic?"

"The reticule, yes," said Aslam Shah.

"The thief forgot this . . ." It wasn't a question; Nirmal was simply thinking aloud. The box was clearly valuable, no ordinary thief would have left it behind. Nirmal pressed for a description of the safety precautions used to protect the relic. Aslam Shah had difficulty finding the right words and resorted to sketching the air with his hands.

The available facts were none too solid: keys to the silver, glass, and wooden doors were kept by separate individuals. A single individual might or might not, upon occasion, open all doors. The relic might or might not be shown to private visitors of importance. There might or might not have been private viewings for a fee. Aslam Shah could not speak for his brother. Nirmal studied the man carefully as he improvised. Aslam Shah's face revealed nothing, his explanations helped not at all, and Nirmal, losing all sense of relevance, found himself concentrating on the man's ears, which struck him as remarkable, although he could not have said why. They were exceedingly small ears, unformed, without lobes.

There was more to be explored in the question of private

viewings. Nirmal would pursue it later, with Naseem Shah himself.

Pacing, he explored the entrance hall. There were two points of access: he had entered through the three front doors, but there was a single side door he hadn't noticed before, through which, he was told, the women entered. The women's door was light and ramshackle; it could be forced open with very little effort. The flimsiness of this door, the fact that the table with its relic display had never been roped off, puzzled Nirmal: "Why is the holy hair, so precious to you, left so unprotected? Anyone could stretch out his hand and touch it."

"We like to think," said Aslam Shah, "that it protects itself."

It was well past one when Nirmal reclaimed his shoes. The crowd in the courtyard was undiminished. Some figures were huddled and wrapped, sleeping through the noise; others were still milling about. *"Bismillah Rahman ir Rahim* . . . Down with Qureshi! Expose the plot!" the cries continued, antiphonal, hoarse. Close by, an old woman was gently and persistently butting her forehead against the wall, as though in conversation with it. It was a scene of frenzy, but of frenzy muted and contained.

Out into the street and more of the same. Nirmal pressed through the crowd, fighting the current; his name and title did not precede him now; his progress was slow, and people were often rude.

"Sah'b . . . Sah'b!" a young man beckoned him to the side. He touched his brow with the fingertips of his right hand and bowed slightly in salutation. The light was wretched and it was hard to make out the man's features, except that he was young—his face smooth, his hair heavily oiled, and his eyes, round, impudent, and lustrous, rimmed with a black line. Smartly dressed in white trousers and a plaid sportshirt, he seemed part of another crowd, a bigger city—Karachi or Lahore.

"What do you want?"

"Something, ah, private, Sah'b." Nirmal did not like the looks of the young man, but at this point, he could hardly afford to be choosy; on the long chance that he knew something useful, Nirmal motioned the man to come along.

"Not here. Follow me."

"Not yet," said Nirmal, spotting the car on the other side of the street.

They crossed over: "Get inside."

The driver was wary: "Should I start up, sir?"

"Yes, drive around, will you? Get us out of this."

They drove a short while in silence. Nirmal put up the windows.

"Now," said Nirmal, "tell me what you have in mind," for here the streets had emptied out.

The young man was smiling; it occurred to Nirmal that he had been smiling all along. His lips were moist.

"Well?"

He spoke in a small voice, not much above a whisper: ". . . a little sweetheart?"

"What?" Nirmal was stunned. Had he *heard* correctly? Was this a message in code? He waited for more.

"We have some very nice ladies, Sah'b. Very respectable. A widow from Lucknow—she knows all the ways. Absolutely sixteen annas to the rupee. How about a British Airlines hostess? White lady . . . No? A boy, if you prefer—"

"Get out! *Fast*—" Nirmal began to shout, for now there was no mistake.

The driver brought down the brakes hard and the young man leaped from the car, fleeing with quick, crooked steps.

The door rocked on its hinges; Nirmal drew it back to him with effort.

"No good," the driver nodded his head sagely, "I knew it the minute I saw him. Back to Rest House now, jenab?"

"Yes, let's go home," said Nirmal. Home? He stared at the window and fumbled for his pipe and pouch. He packed the bowl; his hand shook, spilling tobacco. He struck a match and a nimbus surrounded it. It was a face, faint with dark pockets, the white lake of an eye—his own, estranged in the glass.

He has not had a woman in years.

His trousers were spotted with grains of tobacco and ash; he cast them off roughly with both hands.

Is it as late as it feels?

First to Rest House to gather a change of underwear and his shaving things, then on to the control room at police headquarters. From headquarters, he tried to telephone Husamuddin but the lines were down, so he sent a wireless report as agreed. He mentioned the Holy Relic Action Committee, the little he'd managed to hear about it; in his exhaustion, he called it the Holy Action Committee. He reported that the municipal structure had collapsed. He described the crowds and asked for army support as a precautionary measure.

That was all. He was going to try and sleep. He stretched out on the cot fully clothed. Only this morning, he'd been sipping tea on the verandah . . . it seemed so far away now, a pastoral, untroubled and unreal. He could still hear the chanting from the streets, rasping but regular, a "white noise," like a moderately ruffled sea. Now he would sleep. Three—four hours—if he were lucky.

12

The Chase

Karachi–Cyrilabad, Saturday

Firuz woke, shaved, dressed, and entered the dining room early to find no one there. Last night, he'd fallen asleep at once, but he'd awakened well before dawn, and now that he thought back, it had been strangely quiet next door.

He was feeling much better this morning, despite the early rising. The trip back from Lahore had been trying, and the last lap, from Multan to Karachi, with Kate's sobs rasping on his ears, especially so. By the time they'd arrived home, his nerves were shattered. He'd been harsh with Kate. Life wasn't easy for her here, he knew.

But not unnecessarily harsh. Kate was hiding something, had been for weeks now. Her slightest motions looked furtive. Often, she shuddered when he spoke to her, and shrank from his touch, his gaze. She avoided his eyes, a sure sign of guilt.

The only question was when her deceptions began.

It was all so clear to him. Yet . . . what if he were wrong? The supposition was hideous. He couldn't be wrong, Kate *had* been acting strangely of late. Firuz wasn't imagining this. Emiri had been the first to mention it, and then the ambassador had made those remarks. Firuz didn't know what Alavi's remarks meant; it was sufficient to know that people were watching Kate. Alavi and Emiri—they *knew*. The husband was always the last to find out.

Trouble was, he had no footholds, no mislaid letter or handkerchief, not a shred of tangible evidence. He couldn't be sure. He thought he'd seen someone lurking round the house one afternoon when he returned from the office early. But that was hardly conclusive evidence.

Firuz had always been unlucky in love and his love affairs before his marriage had been stormy, poisoned with jealousy. But then of course, the women involved had all been untrustworthy. In his country, marriageable women did not have love affairs; they came to their husbands unsoiled.

Still, even that wasn't quite true, not these days. Nice marriageable girls were no longer what they seemed. There were doctors who specialized in patch-up jobs, and one famous case where the restoration was so successful, that the groom found himself unable to consummate the marriage. That would have been the worst choice of all—an intractable virgin, stoppered in plastic. Firuz had preferred the company of frankly unmarriageable women, and quietly sabotaged his family's plans for an arranged marriage.

But what kind of woman had he chosen to marry? He'd never met a girl with so few connections. They'd married in New York, a civil ceremony, and Kate had given herself away without a relative present. Only weeks afterward had Firuz met her father, cousins, and aunts, a single, brief meeting in Chicago. Firuz had mixed feelings about this: Kate brought no debts with her; at the same time, she'd come to him without a dowry. On the whole, he preferred it this way; she'd come to him free of encumbrances, and Firuz had hoped to take her under his protection, to shape a new life for her, to possess her completely.

What sort of girl gives herself away? Without a price? The question haunted Firuz. He could not say what kind of woman Kate was; she was the only one of her kind he'd ever known. At least, she was not a patched virgin; she had not deceived him on that.

The stubborn fact remained that Kate had not been intact when Firuz married her. Although he'd known and accepted this beforehand, it had not been easy for him. Another country, he told himself, the customs are different. He had never condemned Kate; he considered her slate wiped clean. But trust was another matter. Try as he might, his trust in Kate could never be restful or complete.

Never complete and, somehow, he'd suspected all along that their marriage would never work. He'd foreseen from the beginning what form her betrayal would take. He'd been here before, trembling, wavering between faith and doubt, exactly so, and it seemed as though he were about to enter the future by an act of remembrance.

There was no answer when he knocked on the bedroom door. He was certain now that he'd dreamed this moment before, that he'd been standing before a shut door exactly as he was standing now, that he called out a woman's name as he was calling now—he did not know whether he was the dreamer or the dreamed. His hands were shaking, his heart loud with fear; he hurled himself against the door. There was no resistance, the door gave at once: that, too, was in the dream.

But the rest was not.

The room was empty, the bed unmade. The windows were closed. He went over to the bed and circled it slowly, twice. No sign of struggle or escape. He scoured her dressing table for a note. Not a clue. Then he shouted for Abdul Ghani.

"When did she leave?" Firuz demanded the minute the old man hobbled into view.

Abdul Ghani opened his mouth moistly, made a swift, inaudible notation with his tongue.

"You didn't know she left the house? You haven't yet

noticed that she's gone? You lie out on the verandah like a turd, when people come and go, they just step over you, that's fine with you!" And when Abdul Ghani still did not answer, Firuz continued in Farsi, pouring out abuse.

The invective cooled Firuz somewhat, eased him. When the master had finished, Abdul Ghani tried to explain that he had been up since dawn and heard nothing, which could only mean that the memsahib had left before then. Firuz didn't know whether to believe him or not.

What to do now? Firuz was at a loss. He hadn't the faintest idea where Kate might have gone. She had no real friends among the Iranians, she had not warmed to the wives of his colleagues, nor they to her, and the American embassy people had always held her at some distance, as though Kate had defected by marrying him.

There was no one he could easily ask. People loved scandals, Iranians most of all, so there was no one Firuz could call without starting rumors. Only one possibility—that Khanum Modir friend of hers—Sylvia, the pilot's wife.

He picked up the phone with many misgivings. Sylvia's bearer answered: the sahib and the memsahib had gone away for a short holiday. Firuz was back where he'd started. He stood for a moment, receiver in hand, lost in thought.

Suppose Abdul Ghani were telling the truth . . . Suppose Kate had left before dawn . . . Then she could be miles off by now. Miles in any direction. He wouldn't know where to start.

Where does a woman go who has once been bitten by a snake? Into the garden, into the lair, to be bitten once again. Firuz recalled the cabaret in Lahore. Kate had been easy there, and shameless afterward. There were a number of places like that in Karachi, clubs and bars frequented by foreigners. A limited number—Firuz could check them out. At least that would give him a sense of doing something. Inaction, doubt, these were the unbearables; any certainty, however painful, would be better.

His mind made up, Firuz rehearsed the questions he

would ask. He sent Abdul Ghani out to the highway to summon a taxi.

Entering the hotel, he spoke first to the desk clerk. The story was the same everywhere: no single woman had checked in after ten P.M. Of course, this told him nothing, did nothing to rule out the possibility that Kate had entered with someone else. Had there been any red-haired ladies checking in with their husbands?

No, none.

Firuz's next stop was the bar, where he went through the same business again.

At the Luxury Hotel bar, Firuz learned that there had been a customer answering his description. The bartender was too tired to say more. "Got to close up now," he said. "Sorry." Firuz stuffed the man's hand with bills and they sat down together.

"That red hair," said the bartender, "it's hard to forget." He didn't recognize her as one of his regular customers. She'd sat on at the bar over two drinks all night. Hadn't changed her seat. Hadn't taken up with anyone. Wouldn't even tell him her name. "She was waiting for someone who didn't show . . . that's my guess. Seven o'clock when I start mopping up, she splits. She was dead sober, I'll tell you that. Seemed to know where she was going."

"She didn't say where?"

"Not a pip. There's one lady who knows her own mind. I got the feeling she was going away for a long time."

Firuz moved quickly after this. If Kate left at seven, she couldn't be that far away yet. Another taxi: the expense was not light. His next stop was the airport: international departures were listed, but Kate's name was on none of the lists. What was he thinking of? There was no way she could leave the country without his knowing, for they shared a passport. Unless Kate had reactivated her American passport on the sly . . . Would she have been that cunning?

Possessed of a fierce, but futile, thoroughness, Firuz made inquiries at the local flight desk: no one seemed to remember a red-haired woman of medium height. It was a useless line of inquiry, anyway; it would have been easy enough for Kate to cover her hair.

There was only one place to go after the airport—the American embassy. It was distasteful to Firuz, but he had no choice. Arriving in a rush, full of determination, Firuz found the building shut tight. It was Saturday—he'd forgotten. He was lucky, though, and crossed paths with an official he recognized. It was John Beal and he was just "dashing in and out," as he explained, to retrieve a file. "Perhaps you will be able to speak with me a moment," said Firuz. "In private," he added. Beal was about to tell him to come back on Monday, when he registered the expression on Firuz's face. Impending catastrophe was written all over it. "All right," said Beal and took Firuz on inside.

"Sit down, sit down," he said, shifting a few things on his desk.

Beal's preliminary courtesies were of the briefest, and although Firuz had no time to lose, he could not help resenting this. How utterly lacking in breeding Americans were—no civilization, no culture, no history! How apt the phrase "the wild West!"

"What can I do for you?" said Beal, picking up a pencil and holding it so that it balanced on its point.

Firuz read the gesture as a request to come to the point.

But that proved to be extremely difficult for him. Try as he might, Firuz could not bring himself to mention his wife's name. He was a man, after all, and had his pride. By indirection, he hoped, he'd get the information he was seeking.

"I'd like to know where we can reach Professor Melus."

"Any special reason?"

"I think you call it 'cultural diplomacy,' " Firuz improvised rapidly; he hadn't known beforehand what he would say. "My embassy is interested in a poet's exchange. Nothing official yet—I'm simply 'probing,' as you say. You see, His Excellency Ambassador Alavi is a poet."

"That so?" said Beal.

"Oh, he wouldn't want it known."

Beal picked up a piece of paper, shifting it to a stack on his right, then hesitated, and returned it to the place it had been. He stared at Firuz obliquely for a moment, then said: "It's a bit odd you should ask today."

"Is it? Why?"

"Well, I don't know . . ." Coyly.

"There's something you *do* know," said Firuz.

Beal leaned forward a little. "Whatever I tell you is in absolute confidence."

"I understand . . . I think you can take that risk."

"Then I must tell you that we've a report on the man you're asking about. It's just come in. Mr. Melus has left Lahore. We don't know what he's up to, but we mean to find out. Frankly, I'd suggest you have as little to do with him as possible. He's unreliable."

"Unreliable? You mean—with women?"

"I mean much more than that. I can tell you this much: he's a known security risk. Puts on the most fantastic act of political innocence. Don't you believe it!"

"He's left Lahore, you say?"

"We'll be putting someone on his trail shortly. We'll use as many men as we need, as facts warrant. From first reports, we've reason to believe he's not alone."

"Not alone?" said Firuz.

"I really can't tell you more than that. I've said more than I should."

"Can't you tell me when he left Lahore?"

"Is that a nice question, now? I said I can't say. I really can't. Melus had a scheduled engagement yesterday afternoon and didn't show. Our cultural attaché in Lahore was concerned about him and called his hotel. He might have left the day before. We've no way of knowing."

Firuz made some gesture of lip and hand preliminary to asking another question.

"Want my advice?" said Beal.

"Please."

"My advice to you and your colleagues, and to His Excellency your ambassador, is not to mess with the man."

"Mess?"

"Stay as far away as possible."

"Yes, I see that," said Firuz, aware that he was betraying too much interest. He tried to smile and failed. "Perhaps some of our people could be of use to you in locating Melus. We have—how shall I say?—'friends?' Friends in many cities."

Beal paused to consider this. "Thanks," he said, "for offering. We'll get in touch if we ever do need your help. Right now, Melus is our concern. It's too early to know where he's heading. Of course, we'll alert the border patrols."

"The border?"

"It's a possibility," said Beal.

"The shortest route over the border is the Cyrilabad-Radpur bridge, isn't it?" Firuz persisted.

"That may be the shortest," Beal conceded, "but we have no reason to believe he's headed that way." He picked up the pencil again.

Firuz realized that the interview had gone on too long. He'd astounded himself by speaking of the border—why the border? Out of how many square meters of possibility? That was why. Because a border was something definite. Otherwise he was left with a vast desert of Sind and endless stretches on every side.

Beal rose from his chair and extended his hand. "I've spoken to you in the strictest confidence," he said, retaining Firuz's hand beyond the customary handshake. "We'll be in touch."

After Firuz left, Beal went to the window and stood there, musing. He watched Firuz go down the steps and board a taxi. Then he turned his back on the window and picked up the phone. "Sam Curtis, please. I'm holding," he told the operator.

The connection to Lahore was crystal clear, and the men talked for some minutes about Firuz's visit. Beal did most of the talking. Curtis kept saying: "You read my mind."

"If the Iranians are so keen on finding him, then God only knows what he's up to."

"Iran's the next stop on his tour," Curtis reminded him.

"What do they know that we don't, I wonder? One thing —Nazar did mention the border. The Cyrilabad-Radpur line."

"I see . . ."

"You do? Wish *I* did."

"Listen, maybe it's time I start to work on this, myself."

"I'd like that, Sam. Let me consult with Fuller at this end and get back to you. Meantime—you call Fred Flower and see what he thinks. But wait for me before deciding anything. I'll get back to you."

Beal was about to hang up, but Curtis had more on his mind.

"I knew that man was trouble from the minute I laid eyes on him," he said. "We've got a dossier on him as long as his travels—Burma through India. Not once—not *once—* has he stayed with his itinerary. Mixes with troublemakers —finds them first thing wherever he's at. A little boozing and brothel-hopping, that's understandable, but the rest— He's in Lahore not two days and I hear he's spouting Faiz from the lecture platform! How did he come to learn of Faiz so quickly, I ask you?"

"One of our lists, I expect," said Beal. "Look, let me consult here and I'll get back to you."

"Better make it soon," said Curtis, "he's got time on his side."

"Within the hour," Beal promised. "Stick around."

Firuz first stopped off at home. He had to get to Lahore on the earliest flight, so he kept the taxi waiting outside. It was past noon, and Kate had not returned. Had he found her at home, Firuz would have been shocked, for his picture of what had happened was now very clear.

Abdul Ghani was nowhere to be seen. Just as well.

He phoned the office: only the clerk was in. Firuz asked him to take a message, explaining that he had to be out of town for several days, giving "family illness" as a reason. Then he packed an overnight bag, locked up everything in sight, and returned to the taxi with its escalating meter. "Airport," he said, settling his bag. She'll pay, he thought, I'll make her pay. He sat well forward, not allowing himself to lean back: if he didn't keep his eye on the driver and the meter, there was no saying where they'd end up. They passed the *maidan* and the military hospital, then the Imperial War Graves Cemetery for British Officers.

They passed the new golf course. "Bitch . . ." Firuz murmured. The driver glanced back, startled.

The sun was bright, steadfast, the horizon sharp, and the land stretched before them without dip, pleat, or elevation, all open to plain view, yet dark, dark, tangled to Firuz now. Along Drigh Road, a small city was springing up. Firuz stared glassily at the new construction and continued moving his lips. "The whore!" he said to himself, "Oh, the whore!" His lips moved: no sound came out. The driver, watching Firuz through the rearview mirror, thought he might be praying.

At the airport, Firuz bought a sandwich and a soft drink and a one-way ticket to Lahore. The waste! He'd only just come from there—his own motions mocked him, cancelled themselves out.

Soon afterward, he was strapped in, awaiting takeoff. "We'll be arriving in Lahore at 14 hours," said the pilot over the intercom, *"Enshallah."*

"Enshallah," Firuz breathed to himself. Normally stringent where money was concerned, he had surprised himself by purchasing the more expensive one-way ticket—why?

Because, one way or another, he could never return to the same life.

It had been a day full of fate.

Kate left the bar early in the morning, when the mopping up began. By that time, the hotel restaurant was open; she was the first customer and she sat on for nearly an hour over an elaborate breakfast of porridge, eggs, kidneys, and toast, forcing herself to eat everything—for strength, she told herself. The long breakfast was a postponement, she knew, a way of not facing the question before her.

Where to go now? Anywhere but home. She needed a friend, and Sylvia was the only person who came close. Kate hadn't enough money for a full cab, so she summoned a "rickshaw," one of the many motor-scooter cabs that lined the curb. It was a long trip and an expensive one, way out past the polo grounds on the outskirts of the city; Kate was crushed to learn that Sylvia and her husband were away. She felt foolish and impulsive, as Firuz so often said she was, not to have phoned first. Only the bearer at home, and when Kate asked him how long the Newmans would be away, he said: "To Friday or Saturday." "Sunday or Monday, maybe?" she tested. "It may be," he answered, in the same voice.

Michael, Sylvia's husband, was an airline pilot, and since they'd left in a small private plane, there was no telling where they'd gone or when they might be back. Nothing to do now but to leave a note: "Please come visit. Soon." Then, as an afterthought: "Please. Kate." If it sounded frightened, it couldn't be helped: she *was* frightened.

Where now? Not home. Not yet.

It was strange when the rickshaw went past her house;

she looked out at her own home as though it had nothing to do with her, just another bungalow on a shady boulevard. Kate was on her way to the only other place of refuge she could think of: the British Council Library. Here at least she was assured of a place to sit in peace.

It was peaceful inside, all but deserted: a librarian fussing with papers behind the counter, two or three readers rustling faintly in the corners, one—somewhere between the ranges of shelves. The lamps were all on, the place was puddled with lights. Kate picked up a stack of illustrated magazines and took a chair under a lamp with a green shade. She didn't feel her long night of sleeplessness yet, but she knew it would catch up with her. Her sense of triumph had quite faded, though.

She riffled through the glossy pages of the magazines without great interest. They might have been travel brochures with their snapshots of life in impossibly exotic cities —New York, London, Liverpool. The women in the ads all looked like streetwalkers. There was a photograph of a woman eating an apple as she walked along. In the open! How impossible that seemed now, what outrageous provocation! How distant that life . . .

Books next, a few slim volumes of poetry, Melus among them. She liked the poem called "Dreaming Out," it seemed to speak to her. By midafternoon, she was ravenous, but the feeling soon subsided; her hunger was nothing to her fear of going home to Firuz. Her ankles were swollen from her long night of sitting on the barstool, but that, too, was nothing. It was so peaceful here she scarcely looked up until closing time.

She left at five, dreading the return home, but now there was nowhere else to go.

13
Morning in Cyrilabad

Who rises early owns the day.

Nirmal did not. It was nearly nine; he'd overslept. He surveyed the room irritably through the fringe of his lashes, his eyes half closed.

The blinds were shut, but the sun managed to seep through; the light cast a broad stripe across the rough planks of the floor. Down the hall, someone was frying eggs with onions and chilies; he could hear the hissing of *ghee* on the fire.

What was Munim up to? He was sitting quietly at Nirmal's cluttered desk, staring into space as though listening to something, and delicately circling one wrist with the fingers of the other hand.

"Munim?"

No answer.

"MASUD!"

"Yes, sir?"

"What are you doing?"

"Taking my pulse, sir. Sorry, sir."

He wasn't a bit sorry. "What's the matter with your pulse?"

"Stops and stumbles, sir." He spoke in the fewest words possible, so as not to lose count.

Nirmal sat up abruptly: "I'll give you stops and stumbles to remember if you don't stop this at once! What are you *thinking* of? A war might break out while you sit there taking your pulse! Every moment counts."

Munim dropped his wrist and smiled wanly: "You were sleeping, sir."

Ah, how true. Nirmal felt his small authority diminished. "Pass me those newspapers," he said gruffly. "And have breakfast sent in. A light breakfast—no eggs—biscuits and tea would be fine."

It was clear that Munim would not be very useful. Again, Nirmal ordered him out of the way, this time to find the headquarters of the Holy Relic Action Committee and to stay there.

With Munim gone, Nirmal surveyed the news. There were papers from Rawalpindi, Lahore, Karachi, and Multan. He lined them up to compare their front pages at a glance. The central government's censorship seemed well in force. In each, the format was regular and the headlines spotlighted news from other places. Nothing out of the usual: a temporary power failure in Rawalpindi, three more cases of smallpox in Multan. Ismail Shamsuddin, Minister of Food, Agriculture, and Undeveloped Areas, was stepping down. There was speculation as to who his successor would be.

He picked up the troublesome weekly *Outlook*, the latest issue, just out. What have we here?

> The new ban on brothels has not yet been enforced in Lahore as the civil authorities have not yet received any written instructions. Meanwhile, in Lahore, the affected prostitutes have joined forces with such film stars

as Khurshid and Miss Parveen Khan and formed an action committee. They issued a statement to the press which makes very pathetic reading: "We are the sewers of the city," it began, "vital to the health of the town."

Meanwhile in Karachi—

An advertisement below:

WE SERVE YOU WELL
TRUST BURMAH SHELL

One more paper, then on to serious work. Ah, happy news . . .

With echoes of jubilant calypsos—sung at the end of the recent Oval Test by the deliriously happy West Indian spectators still ringing in our ears, we welcome the Commonwealth Cricket Team, who are here to play six matches, including three five-day tests . . .

Enough of this—

He still had time. It would be a day of rounding up suspects and looking for leads, even the most far-fetched.

It was bright out, though windy, an unsteady, shifting wind. The wind blew dust in Nirmal's eyes; stray scraps of paper scuttled past.

"Give, in the name of God, and may your children live long!" An arm with a stick barred Nirmal's progress.

"I have no children," said Nirmal, and was at once angry with himself—why did he feel obliged to answer such people?

He took a good look at the man with the stick: he was blind: his stick said so, the yards of soiled cloth wrapped crookedly around his head, his white unmoving stare, a cloud over the countenance which couldn't be simulated. Rummaging in his pocket for a few annas, Nirmal reflected that the blind man might be useful to him: it was a very long chance. "Listen closely," he said, "there'll be more for you later, depending. I have a job for you—I need your keen ears."

Another beggar emerged from behind the wall; this one limped. "Cherisher of the poor," he whined in anticipation, rattling a tin bowl. "All right, you, too," said Nirmal, "but that's all." He quickly explained that they were to listen for every rumor, to report all and to prejudge none. He would send a messenger to them at five.

That done, he hurried away, before others came trooping.

With helpers like these, how could he fail?

He returned to the shrine. A few banners, which yesterday were held high, were now drooping. The chanting was still fairly continuous, a little thinner and hoarser than before, but people took turns, so there was no break. Today there was a new slogan: "No progress!" This one, Nirmal took personally.

Naseem Shah was still out. Nirmal hoped to catch up with him by afternoon at latest, on his visit to the Holy Relic Action Committee.

Shoes Lost and Missing Notices were tacked to the outer wall of the courtyard. Nirmal read them all—*avidly*. Nothing there.

"My God, Helen, you're not supposed to do that!"

Someone was speaking English. Nirmal turned abruptly; it was a man in sunglasses and a sport shirt.

"Says who?" A woman, American by dress and accent, was taking snapshots of two veiled figures, who were crouched in immemorial squatting postures against the wall. They were completely veiled in black *burqas*, a thick mesh over the eyes.

"Hell, Marty, those things are like tents—they don't *see* anything."

"I'm telling you, Helen. It's forbidden by their religion. It's making graven images or something."

"That's *God*. Making graven images, that's God. Jeez, don't you know *anything?*"

"Their husbands won't like it. Maybe their husbands are looking now. They have such big feet, Helen—I'm *telling* you—"

The veiled figures rose in unison. The feet were large and approaching; the tourists were quickly surrounded. One figure relieved Helen of her camera, the other withdrew a warrant from the folds of his veil. For Nirmal, it was a heartening sight. The tourists were probably innocent enough, but they'd be better off out of harm's way. It was good to see Waheed's men on the job.

The rest of Nirmal's morning wandering was aimless and revealed nothing. He returned to the control room before lunch. Already his desk was stacked with memos and reports. He plunged into the heap, hoping desperately for a ransom note, but found nothing of the kind. There were two letters addressed to him personally; he scanned them rapidly, with mounting impatience.

The first was from an angry Christian, asking: "Brother, are you *saved?*" then supplying the answer by calling him "an unfaithful steward (Luke 12:45)," and "savorless salt (Matthew 5:13)," and commanding him "to leave the wretched hair alone." Next, was a very similar letter from an angry Muslim also directing him, though not in the very words, to leave the wretched hair alone, denouncing its cult as idolatrous and anti-Islamic. Nirmal tossed the letters aside; no answer required; he expected more of the same in the next batch.

There were a number of reports on arson attempts. A student had been nabbed trying to set the Municipal Corporation Building on fire. Before dawn, a crowd with torches broke into the lobby of the Sultana Cinema; the cinema was owned by a relative of Qureshi. Least damaging, but most alarming, was an attack on the Cyrilabad-Radpur bridge—the original structure was of wood, although re-

cently reinforced with steel. Torches and homemade fire
bombs had been hurled from the embankment—the result-
ing destruction was minimal, but what disturbed Nirmal
was that the border guards had been powerless to prevent
the attack. He was chagrined, too, at the fact that he had
slept through all this activity.

Elsewhere, the reports noted, there had been a continuing rash of small fires at scattered points in the city; none
were serious, all were under control.

The phone rang: an assistant subinspector with an account of the roundup of newspaper reporters and foreign
visitors. The American woman with the camera had been
questioned and returned to her hotel, along with her husband; the couple would remain there indefinitely. Only one
American had not been returned to the hotel, an abusive
customer, found loitering in the courtyard of the shrine,
who'd resisted arrest. He'd been taking notes. The notes
were strange, they seemed to be in code. Would Nirmal
like to question him?

Nirmal wasn't sure; he thought it best to first look in and
then make up his mind. It was hard to stand behind the
one-way mirror, though, to watch and make no sound; Nirmal kept wanting to cough.

The man the police had taken into custody was big, un-
kempt, very red in the face. The officer was gently rolling
the man's thumb over an inkpad, the American shouting
all the while, as if the people around him were half deaf. A
foot constable stood in the corner, motionless and atten-
tive, ready for trouble. The officer said quietly: "So you'd
like to speak to the mayor? But we don't have a mayor."

"Whatever you call him!"

"You mean the Municipal Chairman?" The officer took
the man's middle finger and pressed it to the inkpad.

"Him! I want to speak to him."

"Qureshi's his name, and we'd also like to speak to him.
He's quite vanished."

"Listen, you got the wrong man—how wrong can you be?"

"That so? You didn't attack Fazal here—a constable in uniform?"

"He took away my notebook."

"What was your business inside the shrine?"

"I wasn't the only one, you know."

"Mr. Melus—that *is* your name? You were picked up with a notebook in your hand. You were writing in it—why?"

"I've got a terrible headache, do you mind?"

"I'm going to read to you, Mr. Melus, from your own notes. Refresh your memory, please."

"I'm a poet, see. That's the reason."

"You call this poetry?" The officer picked a page at random and read: " 'Unable to sort out the law by which I live.' —Is that a poem?"

"That's a self-observation, aptly put—if I may say so."

"What do you mean by 'law'?"

"It's no use, you wouldn't understand. I'm not talking about anything on the statute books."

"And what does this mean: 'the mind incendiaries'?"

"I don't have to put up with this!"

"I'm afraid you do. Would you care to explain this: 'Mayday.' Hmmm? Or this," he paused significantly, " 'hair of Lilith, sizzle of fire'? That's the second mention of fire, I believe. No comment?"

"Do you happen to have an aspirin?"

"What does this mean: 'nullities'?"

"We are now exchanging them."

"You're not being very cooperative, Mr. Melus."

"You bet I'm not. That's *my* notebook and I want it back. *My notebook!* I'll bring down the American Embassy on your heads, you'll see. I'm here for the USIS—know what *that* means? United States Information Service—CIA, you understand?"

"Sorry, we'll have to detain you while we check up on what you say. Slight emergency here, we have our reasons. You may give him an aspirin, Fazal. And show him to the yellow room, please."

"The yellow room? Oh, yes, yes . . . the yellow room . . ."

"You can't do this to me—*I'm an American!*"

"Give him an aspirin, Fazal. Show him the room."

Nirmal decided not to intervene. The American could do with some calming down. He left for lunch, then for the headquarters of the Holy Relic Action Committee.

14

The Holy Relic
Action Committee

Cyrilabad, Sunday

By Sunday afternoon, the city looked like an armed camp; there were jeeps and police, soldiers everywhere. The sun's glare was unremitting, the heat—almost palpable.

The Holy Relic Action Committee headquarters turned out to be a large godown on a street called Khem Karan, which ran parallel to the river. Two young men stood at attention on either side of the wide entranceway; they seemed to be sentries, although they had neither uniforms nor visible weapons.

"I have no appointment," Nirmal began. He introduced himself, then asked to see Nassem Shah. The two men regarded him warily. One went inside to make inquiries.

"A little rain would be a fine thing," said Nirmal, passing time.

"When Allah wills," the man answered.

The door opened and Nirmal was allowed to enter the shed. Twilight within: dim and smoky; a row of neon tubes on the ceiling made faint sputtering noises, but little headway against the gloom. There were a few chinks in the walls for windows, but they were placed high up, above eye level. Sheets were stretched over the concrete floor, with scattered bolsters here and there. The floor was dotted with empty cups, signs of a long encampment, and a haze hung low, acrid and resinous, in the bottled air. It must have been quite a crowd before, but only a few scant clusters now—no more than thirty in all. Most of the men were sitting and murmuring quietly; they had unwound their turbans and the long strips of cloth dangled round their necks and between their legs. A few sleepers lay about, as if thrown.

Munim was nowhere in sight.

Nirmal went forward. At the far end of the room, five men sat together at a long table, working in silence. They were very busy with their hands and did not glance up as Nirmal approached. Merchants, Nirmal thought, from the looks of it.

The youngest of the merchants was clearly Naseem Shah; Nirmal recognized him at once, for the resemblance to his brother was striking—the same eyes, mouth, the beard blunt as a shovel. The same ears: tiny crescents, barely sketched in, joined close to the head. The eyes were more widely spaced, that was the only marked difference.

Naseem Shah glanced up briefly as Nirmal cleared his throat; he signalled his awareness of Nirmal's presence with a nod, but his hands continued to move in an unbroken rhythm. He was busy transferring money and metal objects from a tray to a bowl, and making some sort of tally in the process. The tray was heaped with brass and silver rings and bangles. There was a glass jar full of coins in front of him.

Nirmal waited until Naseem Shah paused in his work, then introduced himself and asked if there was some quiet place to talk. Naseem Shah indicated a small side room with a door of slatted boards. Noticing the wide chinks between the slats, Nirmal couldn't help but remark: "That isn't very private."

"There's nowhere else—it will have to do. Besides . . . we have no secrets here."

The room was a cubicle, no bigger than a closet. There wasn't even space enough for a table, only two folding chairs close together. There was a small air inlet high up, but no window. The only fixture in the room was a light-bulb in a wire cage, suspended from a long cord. Naseem Shah closed the door, such as it was. The men took seats facing one another.

"You realize that at this moment you are the most pow-erful man in the city," Nirmal began.

"You think so?" Naseem Shah doubted.

"Don't you?"

"Not at all. You think so because you're new here. The divines—the maulanas and, of course, the Pir—are far more powerful than I. I'm a simple man, only a custodian."

"I'm not talking about the Pir's kind of power. For a simple man, your administrative skills are very impressive, I must say. To have mobilized this committee, the entire town, within hours of the theft—"

"Emir Kabir is the skill behind it."

"How's that? Kabir—you say?" Nirmal was all slowness and clumsy diligence. He'd heard of Kabir at his first brief-ing. Still, there was no harm in learning all over again. But Naseem Shah told him little beyond the fact that Kabir was Vice-Chairman of the Municipal Corporation and a prac-ticed administrator.

"What do you think of Qureshi?" Nirmal ventured at last.

"What should I think? He's a coward, and that's the least of it."

"You know him well?"

"Well enough."

"Tell me something about him. Is he married?"

"Not he—a spoiler of marriages. He's the sort that gets his legs kneaded by a certain kind of woman, and spends his nights drinking. Siddiqi here once gave him a shoe-beating—after Qureshi made remarks to his wife."

"Not a very nice fellow?"

"Nice! Fornicator! Blasphemer, pig, traitor, thief!"

"Thief?"

"He took bribes—everyone knows it."

"And Emir Kabir is a leader of your committee . . ." Nirmal added in the tone of one thinking aloud.

"What has that to do with anything?"

"Nothing, I'm sure. Qureshi was top man, and Kabir was his second on the municipal committee . . . Were they friendly to one another?"

Naseem Shah stroked his beard thoughtfully in silence. "No," he said finally, "they were not. What of it?"

"I don't know yet," Nirmal confessed.

They went on to discuss the Holy Relic Action Committee. Finances, first. Nirmal was told that money was given freely. Those who had little money often gave ornaments. Those who had nothing to give, gave nothing. Until the money ran out, food would be distributed free. After that —at cost. The committee hoped there would be no "after that," that the thief or thieves would be quickly apprehended and punished, the holy hair restored and life return to normal. "Nothing will please me more than when that hour comes," said Naseem Shah. He explained matters to Nirmal slowly and patiently, as though to a foreigner: "We Muslims have the same regard for the holy hair that we have for the Prophet himself—may peace be upon him. Since the holy hair was part of his body, whenever we see it we feel we are seeing the Prophet himself . . ."

"It's been in your family for generations, hasn't it?" said Nirmal.

"It has been our great blessing," said Naseem Shah.

Nirmal hesitated before asking the next question.

"Did you—did you—ever permit private viewings?"

"Myself? No, never," said Naseem Shah.

There was a pause.

"No more questions, then?" said Naseem Shah brightly.

"Only one. What are the chances of Qureshi's having taken the holy relic?"

"Why would he do that?"

"It's only a supposition."

"Yes, I understand that. But even so—"

"Suppose Qureshi had planned to restore the holy relic after mobilizing the city? To show of his administrative skills and strengthen his image of political prowess, maybe. I gather he's not much respected here. I don't know what his political ambitions might be—the Constituent Assembly, perhaps . . ."

"Could anyone be as cynical as that?" said Naseem Shah.

"I don't know," said Nirmal, "you tell me."

Both men fell into silence, a silence of deep, mutual attention. Nirmal let the question hang between them for a long moment. Then Naseem Shah said mildly: "Not a very good plan, if respect was what he wanted."

Nirmal agreed: "No, not a good plan. It misfired almost at once. Your Action Committee mobilized more quickly than anyone could have ever dreamed—and it happened to be led by one of Qureshi's rivals—"

Naseem Shah listened without comment, his lips compressed.

Back in the main room, Nirmal was relieved at its vastness. He took a deep breath. Munim was back, and that, too, was reassuring. Nirmal and Munim stepped to one side for a minute and conferred. "Your instructions were to remain here," said Nirmal. "What took you away?"

"More trouble at the river," Munim explained, and described another assault on the bridge.

"The bridge patrol will handle that. I want you here. Mix with these people—" Nirmal's hand swept round the half-deserted shed. "Mix and listen, as far as your uniform allows. Have some tea. And a smoke of whatever it is they're smoking." Munim hardly needed these instructions; he smiled, vacant as a cat, exposing the rosy roof of his mouth and many betel-stained teeth.

Then Nirmal returned to Naseem Shah's side and asked to be introduced to Emir Kabir. Nirmal was almost certain that Kabir was one of the merchants at the long table, and said as much. He was too direct, he knew. Even good friends were apt to say to him: "He is England-returned and has forgotten the ways of his people . . . Too long in the West, a pity." Long before Nirmal had ever gone to the West, they said this, and long after he was England-returned. It was a frankness and impatience to get things done, an unwillingness to wait on ceremony.

Emir Kabir was the austere figure at the head of the table. He was tightly buttoned up in a white sherwani jacket; he wore a Jinnah cap. Nirmal mumbled some preliminary politenesses, then said: "You're a banker, aren't you?"

"It's no crime," Kabir answered.

"I never said it was. I'm not here to prosecute anyone. I'm here to learn."

"We're very busy. As you can see . . ." said Kabir. "Details, so many details. I've been working on food distribution and, let me tell you, it isn't simple."

"Good practice for an aspiring municipal chairman, don't you think?"

"Perhaps," Kabir said mildly.

Nirmal changed the subject. "As a banker, how long do you think the funding can hold out?"

"We have enough for at least another day of free food—provided there are no abuses."

"And after that?"

"After that? God willing, with a little fasting, we could go on for a very long time, indeed."

The news was depressing indeed to Nirmal, and shortly afterward, he turned to go. "I hope you find what you're looking for," said Kabir.

"What we're *all* looking for," Nirmal corrected him.

He left the godown without ceremony and started back for police headquarters. Then, abruptly, he reversed himself and headed for the Municipal Corporation Building.

A military guard had been placed around the building, but once Nirmal introduced himself, he had little difficulty in gaining access to Qureshi's office. Only the file cabinets remained sealed to him—no one could locate the key. It was just as well; scanning the files would take days and, at the moment, Nirmal had no idea whether Qureshi or his files had the slightest bearing on his search.

The Municipal Chairman's desk was full of the expected clutter. The draft of a letter; it looked routine:

> Dear Sir,
> In reference to your demi-official letter No. 1000019–37/471 . . .

A rough memorandum:

> Existing policy will meet the situation. All that is needed is strict and impartial

What situation? Impossible for Nirmal to make out. The memorandum broke off in dithering over the last phrase, whether strict and impartial "application" or "implementation" was in order. And something in pencil, very faint, that seemed to read "by deed and directive."

Nirmal found an unfinished proposal for the development of a circular railroad around the perimeter of the city as a tourist attraction, and a sketch of two of the railway cars, the engine and the caboose. Tucked away underneath the telephone was half of a requisition form for office supplies; on the back of it—an intricate design of ripples and slashes, interspersed with a few words:

A *Stopping Place*

       If by evening Hafsa
       sorry to say that
                        not responsible for
           PIA   or?

It made no sense at all to Nirmal. He opened the drawers of the desk and found nothing of consequence, only paperclips, stamps and inkpads, pencil stubs, a bottle of imported brilliantine for the hair, a bottle of scent; well to the back of the bottom drawer, he discovered two worn paperbacks—an English mystery, and a manual of erotic arts in Urdu, without illustrations. It did not strike Nirmal as the desk of a man with any sustained political ambition. A man susceptible to impulse, rather, and perhaps to quick money-making schemes. Private viewings of the relic might have been among these schemes, although, Nirmal reflected, they couldn't have been carried out without the knowledge of Naseem Shah . . . His thoughts had come full circle. He gave a quick glance to the shelves above the desk: the usual gazetteers, inspection manuals, rules-and-procedures guides, population surveys, lists of one kind or another, a book of homeopathic medicine. All rather humdrum.

The sun was already low in the sky by the time Nirmal left the building. All day long and for several days past, there'd been dust gathering in the air, a parching that cried out for relief. But the commotion in the street continued undiminished, without regard to thirst. A young man with a massive voice rode the shoulders of his companions. He was shouting hate slogans, the sun was setting, and in its going down, Nirmal saw flames touch and ravage the city, the river run fire.

Then the sun touched the horizon, went over the rim. Nothing caught; the fire faded. The sky and the river had the same ashen, bled-out color.

Hour by hour, deeper and deeper, Nirmal thought, and

not the faintest glimmer of sense. And later, as he listened to the wireless tuned in to the bridge patrol, he could hear the familiar calls to crush, avenge, destroy—*"Murdabad"* slogans clashing across the river. Between nations, Nirmal reflected, yet the voices on either embankment sounded just the same, only a little fainter from the Radpur side.

15
The Yellow Room

Tom Melus had been locked up for nearly seven hours now. For supper he was given curry, rice, and curd. Only the rice was bearable, he washed it down with a bottle of warm Pepsi.

His notebook had not been returned to him. The authorities had been gracious enough to let him keep his wristwatch, but nothing else. His clothes had been taken away, and he was wearing pajamas of some coarse white material which didn't even have buttons, nothing but little pieces of cloth tape which he knotted together. He wore plastic bathroom flippers for shoes, the kind children called "flipflops"; they were several sizes too small, but latched over his big toe, so he could manage. Besides, he wasn't going anywhere.

His headache had not abated. He'd tried resting, pacing, then resting in darkness. The narrow bed was far too short for him. Lying down, his feet remained homeless, suspended in midair.

He rose and walked over to the small window; it was slightly above ground level and covered with a thick grid.

The patch of street before him was all but deserted. Only a solitary figure up against a painted wall. The moon shone full upon him; his skin was dark, but his clothes were white. He seemed to be fishing with a willowy wand: a frail silvery arc went out from his hand to the pavement. The whispering ghost of a fountain.

Same gesture world over. It took Tom home, if he could call it home, to the subways of New York and the predawn streets.

Now there was only the night and the painted wall which read:

HABIB MATCHES ARE NONFAILING

Nonfailing . . . He didn't understand why the embassy was so slow in claiming its own. *If* anyone tried to contact the embassy . . . there was no way of telling.

What was Aleem up to? he wondered. The poor boy was probably frantic.

Tom could still hear the commotion in the surrounding streets; outside, the barbarous chanting continued. What was it all about? Why didn't everyone go home?

Again, he surveyed the room. Those bars on the window were not for decoration. They called it "the yellow room." The walls must have been white once; now they were dingy, the color of aging paper. No Gideon Bible, no souvenir ashtrays, no friendly little packets of soap—he missed the amenities. This was a room through which many transients had passed, leaving not a trace of passage.

"Like birds whose paths are traced in air, home after home they abandon and go," he intoned. The words were resonant. "Home after home, they abandon and go"—that applied to him, but the rest did not. His path *could* be traced; he'd left a wake of unpaid bills, wives, a child, mortgages, one woman after another. Which reminded him.

Nope, no hotel stationery either.

A Stopping Place

Tom rattled the door until the guard came. He demanded paper, envelopes, and a pen. He was given three sheets of brown wrapping paper and the stub of a pencil. There was no table, so he sat cross-legged and used the floor.

At least this would keep him busy. What could he say? "Here I am chafing, like a pledge in pawn?" No, better not. What was the date? It hardly mattered. He began to write:

> Dear little fox,
>
> Hope this finds you bright and glistening as I wish I were. I need ink and more besides. I keep waiting for your billy dues.
>
> Where am I? Somewhere, somehow, barely west of India. Near a border, barbed wire, guards. All borders look the same. Exotic isn't a place, it's a state of mind; it lasts six weeks at most, and I am well beyond it. Was lit'rally met at the door of my hotel room in Lahore by a delegation of the local Browning Society and haven't been alone since.
>
> Yes, a little hung-over. Not very. Not to worry. Yes, I took my vitamins, iron, yes, love. Balanced meal as directed: tedious lean meat, tedious green and yellow vegetables, tedious salad. All for you.
>
> There's a poem about you I've written on my eyelid, pouch side, not to be published.
>
> How's things? Friends? Eve and Claude are nice, sure. Nice to know they looked you up. But leave it there. Eve's sweet but you like men, dear (you know you do), and Claude does too.
>
> Write soon, soon. Direct to consulate in Lahore is best. Talk to me, I

Tom worried the pencil stub with his teeth and read over what he had written. At once overcome, with memory, or incantation, or fear, or weariness (no telling which), he bent and wept—my dear my dear

my dear   my dear—

16
Strangers

Cyrilabad, Sunday

Night. The news blackout was still holding. At the Hotel Metropole, the bar was doing record business. A man named Stanley stood at the counter, holding Sam Curtis captive:

"I had a good job, you know. Used to work for the best company in the world. Know what that was?"

"The United States Government."

"*Right!* Let me shake your hand. You said it! Best company in the world. Nuclear power—shit, man—shit power. They can send their shit all over the world—"

"What did you say your name was?" said Curtis. "Stanley what?"

"None of your fucking business," said Stanley, and he zigzagged off, thick arms sawing the air. He settled at the nearest empty table.

Sam Curtis had located a telephone near the men's room, miraculously overlooked, intact and functioning. He tried not to attract attention to it, making calls at half-hour intervals, pleading an erratic bladder to Jeff, the UPI correspondent, who'd joined him on the next bar stool. "Call of nature," Sam explained.

"I understand," said Jeff, "it's old age, man." He had a notepad in front of him and was busy scribbling, getting his phrases in shape for riot or invasion. He showed the list to Sam, asking for suggestions:

> deploy/defile
> fired at point blank range/reprisal
> military intervention
> salvoes (sp?)
> border violation/incursion
> ambush   bridgehead
> skirmish/snipers/direct hit/strafing
> forward positions
> artillery and mortar fire
> sally

"There's a word that escapes me," said Jeff.

"How about 'lathi-charge'?" Sam suggested. "For a little local color." Jeff duly noted it down.

> Lathi—long bamboo staff—often
> weighted with lead

"More in five minutes," said Sam. "Right now, I'm off . . ."

"When you gotta go, you gotta go," said Jeff. He continued writing:

> detonated/fusillade . . .

Sam's timing was exact. The corridor was patrolled at fifteen minute intervals, and the guard had just passed through. Sam slipped quietly into the telephone booth and made three calls in rapid succession. But it was the same story this time, and every time. Whenever he attempted to contact his sources of information in the city, he was connected with the same desk clerk at police headquarters. And the clerk's answer was always the same: "State of emergency. Sorry, sir. I'm not authorized to answer any questions."

One more try. Sam dialed the operator and said: "I'd like to make a long-distance call." The operator lifted the receiver, Sam could hear it, but not a word was said; as soon as Sam asked for an outside number, there was a faint click: the receiver was replaced.

Then Sam heard the sound of steps. Someone was pacing the corridor, had been for some time. Sam glanced at his watch: according to his calculations, he had a clear interval before the next patrol, at least seven minutes. Something was out of phase. Hunched, unable to move, he sat on in the tiny booth until the pacing figure passed by.

But it was only Stanley, the drunk. Sam extricated himself from the booth and proceeded down the hall to the washroom. There he soaked his wrists and dabbed his face. When he came out, he found Stanley still pacing, like a blind man trapped in a cul-de-sac.

"Where's the *road?*" he called out.

"What road?" said Sam.

"How do I get out of this dump? Want to get the fuck out of here. Where's the fucking *road?*"

"This here's the main road," said Sam. He took Stanley by the elbow and led him to the lobby. Stanley balked on the threshold. "Why don't you sit down with the rest of the guests?" Sam urged.

"Guests? That bunch of turds! Poop, man—that's all I see. Gotta get outa here!"

"There's a bar and a lobby," said Sam patiently, "take your pick. You've had plenty of bar already. If I were you—"

"You aren't," Stanley said reasonably.

They returned to the bar, and Stanley to his table, where he soon put his head on his arms and collapsed quietly. Sam returned to the counter, where his wakefulness increased. He ordered a club soda—neat; he would need his wits tonight. Jeff had a full page of phrases by now, enough for any contingency. After the guard made another patrol of the corridor, Sam excused himself again. "See a doctor," Jeff advised, "doesn't pay to wait."

Each round of telephone inquiries brought the same results: the desk clerk at police headquarters, and the same silent long-distance operator.

Before midnight, the telephone went dead. When this happened, Sam left the bar for good and joined the others in the lobby.

Jeff had preceded him, settling himself in the last of the comfortable armchairs. The notepad rested open on his knees; he was waiting now for events to actually break.

Sam recognized Firuz from the party at the Wicks, but Firuz did not seem to recognize him. Just as well, Sam said to himself, if I mean to get to Melus first. He found himself a place distant from Firuz and took the only chair to be had there, a wooden contrivance with a carved back and no arms. Actually, it suited Sam's purpose very well: he had no choice but to remain wakeful and watchful.

None of the guests had been allowed to stay in their rooms, and the lobby, after many hours of occupation, had a camped-in look: sandwich crusts and crumpled paper, teacups underfoot, ash on the carpet. The floor was strewn with tourist trophies—brass bowls, bookstands, leather lamps, hashish pipes, postcards. On one of the coffee tables, cluttered with curls of exposed film, cameras lay in a heap.

In the middle of the room, a blackboard had been set up on an easel. WELCOME TO HOTEL METROPOLE was printed at the top. There was more:

PLEASE KEEP CALM
TEMPORARY EMERGENCY—YOUR COOPERATION REQUESTED
ALL GUESTS MUST REMAIN INSIDE—NO EXCEPTIONS!
PLEASE DO NOT GO OUTSIDE

This last was hardly necessary, since two sentries armed with bayonets stood guard at the exit. They wore helmets and flak jackets, with black armbands on their sleeves.

The mood of the "guests" was subdued. A small tow-headed girl was curled up in an armchair with a towel for a blanket; an infant slept in his mother's lap. The mother was sleeping too, whimpering softly, her mouth open. The damp, sour smell of unclean diapers pervaded the room. An American couple was quarrelling in whispers—the woman was giving the man a hard time. His name must have been Marty—that was one of the few intelligible words between them; another word was "hostage"; none of the other guests ever uttered it.

Men sat with their shoes unlaced, or in stocking feet. Most had opened their belts for comfort. A white-haired couple slumped on a love seat; they were holding hands, their heads bobbing toward each other, then away. Only one man went through the motions of reading, but his book remained open to the same place, his finger returned to the same paragraph again and again; he never moved beyond it.

The other guests continued to stare at the curtains and the gleaming cuspidors and their own laps. They tried not to stare at the guards.

Sam fumed silently: it had been an utterly wasted day and night. He'd followed the meandering trail of the car Melus had hired from Lahore to Cyrilabad, then lost all tracks as soon as he passed the Cyrilabad town limits. There were other hotels in town, but only natives stayed in them. Sam had reason to believe that Melus was still somewhere in the city. It would be exceedingly difficult for anyone to cross the Cyrilabad–Radpur border just now.

But if Melus was in the city, why hadn't he been rounded up with the other foreigners? Unless Melus were somehow in the middle of this mess, whatever it was . . .

Sam noticed that the lobby seemed to be divided into sectors; each sector was watched over by a team of two soldiers. They changed positions on the hour, moving in simple clockwise rotation. The soldier nearest the hallway made periodic checks of the restaurant and bar; there was no way of exiting to the street from these places, and so no permanent guard stationed in them. The officer in charge had borrowed a swivel chair from one of the hotel offices and positioned it in the middle of the room near the blackboard. He spent his time slowly revolving in the chair, his eye on all sectors.

Only Sam had the temerity to question him.

"Somebody die?" he asked.

The officer hiked up his glasses on the bridge of his nose and gave Sam a particularly focused look but didn't answer.

"Your armbands, I mean," Sam persisted.

"Simple precaution," said the officer. He rose to his full height, which was considerable, and stretched himself.

None of the other guests dared to follow up on Sam's question, for the officer in charge was a fearful figure. He had great presence, but it was hard to say why; certainly his voice was remarkably small for so large a man. Perhaps it was the rows of bars and stars over each pocket, or his glasses—the thick flat lenses glinted coldly at the guests and at certain angles there seemed no eyes behind them.

The lobby looked much like a waiting room anywhere, or more exactly, a waiting room in a dream. They were travellers in a dream. They glanced at the clock repeatedly, as travellers will do, but the passage of time neither cheered nor quickened them. Unlike most travellers, they spoke little, and remained strangers to one another. Not one of them could have said what he or she was waiting for; there was no schedule of arrivals and departures; their vehicle seemed to be the waiting room itself, and they approached their unknown destination by sitting still.

Aleem and Firuz recognized one another as the only Asians in the room. Although Aleem tried to make something of this, Firuz steadily resisted the identification and did his best to keep himself apart. Their difference in station was, in any case, immediate and obvious. Firuz was clothed in his cosmopolitan best, he was more than correct in this three-piece grey suit, white shirt with double cuffs and silver links, and dark blue tie. At no time did he ever loosen his collar. He sat stiffly, a small suitcase at his feet. Aleem, in contrast, was in a state of comfortable undress, and very much the native. His hair glistened with pomade. The long trails of his shirt hung out of his trousers and dangled below his brown jacket of rough, prickly cloth, which was of local make, without lapels. His white trousers were cut like pajama bottoms, loose and flappling around his thin legs, and he wore cheap bazaar shoes with a narrow last and pointed toes that curled slightly.

Aleem's shoes were much on his mind—he longed to remove them. He pitied his feet, chafing to breathe in their cramped cells. His toes felt numb and lifeless.

But Aleem could not ease off his shoes with the Persian gentleman sitting alongside, for he'd forgotten to wear socks. He diverted himself by trying to engage Firuz's attention. Firuz pretended to understand little English, and no Urdu. Undaunted, Aleem pressed on in his best schoolbook Persian.

"I've always admired Persian poetry," he said. "Attar, Rumi, Hafez, Amir Khusrau . . ."

"I suppose Farsi is one of your required languages in school," said Firuz.

"We have a great love for the language. My grandfather wrote a *Divan* in Farsi."

"Many did," said Firuz without interest.

"Cool evening," said Aleem.

"Yes," said Firuz, closing his eyes.

"But I suppose the weather will soon be heating up," said Aleem.

"I suppose it will," said Firuz, his eyes firmly shut.

Left to his thoughts, Aleem wondered and fretted over his American friend Tom Melus. What was he doing now? Where could he be? Idle questions, for they led nowhere. And really, Aleem had worries enough of his own: his mother and sister would be out of their minds with worry if he were detained for any length of time. Then, too, he didn't know how many classes he'd be missing. A few days' absence from college would be a matter of no moment, but more than a week would take its toll.

It had been an utterly wasted day. Aleem and Melus had arrived at the outskirts of Cyrilabad late yesterday evening, and settled themselves at Hotel Pamposh, at walking distance from the town proper. The hotel, with its intricately carved balconies and ancient plumbing, had pleased Melus for it was, as Aleem had promised, not a tourist spot, and full of what Melus called "the real thing." Aleem did not know what to think of the place—he was pleased that Melus was pleased. He thought the proprietor of the hotel had seemed a little agitated, a little overly concerned for the comfort of his guests. In fact—Aleem had noticed it in passing—they'd been the only guests. They went up to their rooms immediately, for they'd already dined, and were tired. Both were unaccustomed to rising before dawn, and the day had seemed very long; they fell asleep at once. On waking, Aleem had found a note slipped under his door: *"Gone for a stroll. Back at nine."* But Melus wasn't back at nine, or at nine-thirty, and shortly before ten, Aleem had set out after him.

Aleem had not expected to find the streets so jammed. He followed the crowd, asking if anyone had seen an American or an Englishman, a tall man wearing mirrors for glasses. No one had. A tall man who walked like so? Aleem stepped like a camel. No one had seen such a man. Aleem soon learned of the stolen relic. Although he was not religious, the theft struck him as a deep insult; it touched him intimately in his manhood, a blow to his own—as well as his nation's—pride. He was concerned for Melus, too—the people on the streets were angry, it wouldn't be safe for strangers now; as soon as he found Melus, they'd have to hurry back to Lahore at once. Wherever Aleem spotted foreigners, he'd gone up and questioned them on the chance that they'd recognized one of their own. Then the police had stepped in. When he learned that all the foreign visitors in the city were being held at Hotel Metropole, Aleem had attached himself to some Swedes and gone along with them, quietly and hopefully. But there'd been no trace of Melus at Hotel Metropole and, since the Swedes had been kind enough to insist that Aleem was travelling with them, he was no longer free. And now he was afraid to mention the name of Melus, for the officer in charge had called Aleem a "foreign lackey" and said other abusive things to him.

No longer free, and unable to do anything more. Everyone seemed to be napping; even the soldiers were taking turns. As they moved on past midnight, Aleem found his head nodding on his chest. I'll take a very short pause, he thought, and was instantly asleep.

As Aleem's eyes shut, Firuz opened his. Peace at last. The boy's rattling mouth was still, he was sleeping like a baby. Firuz twisted a little to avoid grazing the oily lolling head of the native. He did not allow himself to lean back, but strained forward, hoping to minimize contact with the disreputable public sofa with its stained sleeves and discolored headcloth. Firuz wondered what the boy was doing here; all the other detainees were foreign. Most certainly, he was not a guest of the hotel. He'd probably fastened on one of the guests and made a nuisance of himself, chattering and prying until the police were obliged to take him in.

It amazed Firuz how indifferent he was to the events gripping the city. It was not his city. Nothing touched *his* shame, *his* outrage, the theft of *his* honor. At this very moment, Kate and Melus might be anywhere, committing anything, and he was powerless to stop them. And the hell of detention for Firuz was precisely this: he would never catch them in the act. They were free, drunk with sin, happy and laughing. Laughing at him . . .

Or Kate might be with another man tonight. Firuz knew nothing, really. He might be utterly mistaken about Kate. But if he was, why had she run off to a bar by herself? No respectable woman enters a bar alone, no wife of a Muslim enters a bar under any circumstances. And what did the bartender mean when he said that Kate was the sort of woman who knew where she was going? Firuz had not imagined these things. Had Kate done nothing else but go to that bar, his dishonor was complete. Complete—it needed nothing more.

Still . . . there was an old saying—"A chaste woman is chaste in an army barracks." Suppose Kate *were* chaste . . . But how could that be? A chaste woman doesn't seek out an army barracks in order to exercise her chastity.

Firuz longed for solid, tangible evidence of guilt, something he could hold in his hand, house in his pocket. If only he had a love letter, something in black and white— indisputable. He saw himself sitting down casually at breakfast one morning, and slowly opening the letter, glancing at her face as he did so, saying quite calmly: "I know, you see, I've known all along," and watching her face turn grey . . . Or, better yet, he would hold the letter and bide his time, revealing it to her long afterward, steeped in the foul vintage of her secrecy and duplicity.

But there was no letter. There were only hints, words idle and equivocal, bits and shreds of sense, whispers, whispers out of range, or silences, creases of the lips that seemed to speak, smiles—they might have been smiles —or grins or leers . . . Nothing that would count for evidence.

There was no letter, no proof. He wasn't sure.

Firuz was well aware that his upbringing had not made him the best judge of people. Wanting to be a writer, but knowing nothing of life, he'd paid his father's servants for their stories, sometimes as much as a *toumin*. As the only child of a rich landowner in a backward village, he'd grown up in a walled compound, shut off from other children. His companions were private tutors, old women, and doting servants, who gave him presents, kissed his hand, and cheated him blind because they were servants. For his eighth birthday, he'd been given a BB gun, and the gun had been his only way of leaping the wall. He loved birds, and perched at his window, gun in hand, he hoped to make contact with them by wounding them, then bringing them back into the house and taming them. He'd only succeeded once. The bird was so stunned that Firuz was able to take the sparrow in his hands. For a week, Firuz had nursed the sparrow, gently nursed it to death. With women it had often been like this, a distance, and a wounding as the only bridge.

But not with Kate. Kate had skipped free; she mocked him. And the injustice of this—Firuz's detention and suffering, Kate's exultant flight—the realization that he had come so far, to the forsaken town of Cyrilabad, that *he* was now under suspicion though guiltless and wronged, gave Firuz the look of a man who has closed his teeth on a mouthful of stones.

Aleem shifted in his sleep; Firuz shrank away, keeping

his distance. He shuddered: the boy's knees were almost touching his.

Even the UPI man was sleeping now, his lap full of phrases. Gradually, one guest after another lost the battle with sleep. Sam Curtis, alone, remained alert and watchful. He paid careful attention as the guard was reduced: there were now four soldiers standing, six sleeping. Sam studied the sleeping soldiers for some minutes to make sure they were completely out of commission.

When the officer in charge stepped outside to confer with someone, Sam knew his moment had come. He rose, staggering a little, clutching the arm of his chair.

"What's the matter?" one of the guards spoke up.

"My medicine—" said Sam, "I'm going to be sick."

"Where is it?" said the guard. Sam bit his lip, but didn't answer.

"Your medicine—where do you keep it?"

Sam raised the finger toward the ceiling.

"I don't have anyone to spare as an escort now."

Sam doubled over and made a rude sound.

"Ten minutes," said the guard, "not one more. The hotel is surrounded," he warned, "we have orders to shoot. To shoot, you understand? Eleven minutes and I'm not responsible—"

Mindful of his condition, Sam hobbled out of the lobby. Once out of sight of the soldiers, he bolted up to his room on the second floor, grabbed his walkie-talkie and ran, taking the steps in multiples, up three more flights.

The sky was cloudless, the moon full, clean and clear, a bomber's moon. Bad news for Sam. He'd hoped for a cover of darkness, but he could see for miles, and knew he could be seen as well.

Keeping a low crouch, he moved closer to the edge of the roof. He looked out: a depressing town: the flat rooftops of the city rose and fell, scattered steps, rising, descending, never arriving. He saw a line of stragglers in the street and some swarming at the crossroads. Most of the bylanes were quiet, though, and Sam could make out bundled shapes on the edges of the sidewalks.

There was a smell of burning all around, but Sam could only see two small fires, far out. The fires were dimmed by the light of the river, which burned at white heat under the brilliant arc lamps.

Less than seven minutes left—Sam had no time to spare. He adjusted the speaker of his set. He sent out three beeps and waited. The only answer was a soft sputter of static. "Anyone there?" he whispered, then pressed the receiver button and waited. Nothing. But there was the sound of something nearby, something moving—some animal about to spring. Sam made a low dash forward. Soldiers, standing a few yards apart, formed a circle around the hotel grounds. Sam heard the click of a trigger, then silence. The soldiers were quiet and preoccupied, their sights fixed outward toward the city. Bent double, Sam crept to the other side of the roof. In the kitchen courtyard, two dogs were coupling noisily in a heap of refuse; the sudden movement and noise had come from them.

No time to lose. Sam squatted down on his heels in the middle of the roof and began to broadcast:

"Hello anyone. *Salaam aleikum. Aleik-e-salaam.* Can you hear me?" He pressed the receiver button: nothing. Never mind, he had nothing to lose; he went on:

"Salaam again. This is Cyril Radcliffe speaking. My name is Cyril—do you read me? We're having a wedding party in town. Please come. The whole city's turned out for it. You should see it—everybody's dancing in the streets. Dancing the Horah in the streets—the Horah and the Kazotsky—do you read me? Soon wine will be flowing—flowing in the streets. Such a waste if you don't come. Won't you come and join us? This is Cyril Radcliffe speaking. We're dancing round the pole, going round and round the pole. Please invite all my American friends. I won't ask again—I can't. They've got us in taffy here. *Taffy*, you understand? *Wassalam*."

Then Sam went down, stopping off in his room only long enough to bury the walkie-talkie.

He was none too soon in returning to the lobby—there was little over a minute left.

One of the sleepers looked up as Sam entered. "Feeling better?" he asked.

Sam *was* feeling better and didn't deny it. He'd done what he could and now all that remained was to wait with the others. He returned to his hard chair and allowed himself to close his eyes.

While Sam slept, his message travelled; it was picked up in four places. Three of those tuned in were local police officials, and only one of them bothered to file a report, a somewhat garbled account of a rowdy drinking party. The report was typed up by a weary desk clerk at police headquarters and further garbled in the process, then the finished product was placed on the desk of the Superintendent of Police under a mound of more pressing papers. By the time Superintendent Waheed got round to it, the message was so dated and so impenetrable that he used the back of the sheet for scratch paper.

By some accident, an American picked up the broadcast. His name was Bill Cooper, and he was a Peace Corps worker, a specialist in irrigation, who spent his time going from village to village in the area. He was also a ham radio operator, and scanned the air waves with a scavenger's hunger, as a beachcomber rakes over empty sand and debris for discarded and forgotten things. The night of Sam's broadcast, Cooper was on his way back to Lahore; he'd been getting nothing but static for hours. Radcliffe's message was a find: it came through with remarkable clarity, and although Cooper could make no sense of it, he recog-

nized an accent much like his own, and thought he ought
to report the call. He jotted down as much as he could—it
sounded like nonsense, but you never knew. As soon as he
got back to Lahore, Cooper planned to drive up to the
American consulate and see the man in charge of commu-
nications.

The very first thing.

And so began—by stumbling, trickling, mazy motion—
the first erosions of the wall of secrecy surrounding Cyrilabad.

17
Entering Confusion

Nirmal had a meeting scheduled for eight that morning. Until then, he had nearly an hour to spare, sheer luxury, for he didn't know when a free hour might come his way again. He smoked his pipe with leisurely puffs and turned from his dispatches to read his matchbox; he read it carefully:

> A tiny magic wand
> That dispels gloom and engulfs the darkness
> Brings flaming warmth and happy brightness
> Amid frustration and chaos.
> HABIB MATCHES ARE NONFAILING.

He cherished the tiny matchbox with its conjuration of hope. How precious ordinary things seemed now, how tinged with strangeness. The pale morning light, falling evenly upon white cup and paper, filled the room with peace.

By seven-thirty, there came a load of fresh dispatches, full of situation reports, "sitreps," as they were called. Nirmal learned, without any particular alarm, that the town was now sealed off; there were barricades and checkpoints all around the perimeter of the city, police backed up by military contingents—nothing so tight as a wall, but the next best thing to it.

What else? A reported attack on Fathullah Din, the chief electrical engineer of the city; there'd been threats of a blackout, as well. Nirmal failed to see what earthly purpose a blackout would serve, but he was asking for logic where it no longer applied. He wrote out an order for a police escort for the engineer, and for a military guard around all electrical installations, then moved on to the next document—a letter attacking the custodians of the relic, Naseem Shah in particular, calling him a "word merchant, a money merchant . . . a poisoner of the public mind . . ." The letter was unsigned.

The rest of the heap was trifling—assorted memoranda on crowd control, crank letters, a letter of dire warning, police schedules, reports on troop movements.

By eight o'clock, the light had changed and Nirmal's mood with it. Already, he was tired. He felt old and cumbered and slow. He'd stepped into a civil servant's nightmare: as the dispatches mounted, the sense diminished—implications everywhere, hints, shreds of meaning, but no sustained sense. His desk was heaped with nothing but scraps. Among them, he sought—what? A wisp, the frailest of wisps, an eyelash could not be frailer . . .

He was deeply, inexplicably convinced that Naseem Shah and Emir Kabir were up to something, some game, the point of which he had not yet grasped. "A very deep game . . ." he said aloud, but had no idea what he meant by it. Looking back on his two days in Cyrilabad, the situation seemed hopeless, his progress negligible; Nirmal felt more mystified than when he had begun. Yet there seemed no other way to proceed than to enter the confusion.

And no choice but to proceed; it was time for the staff meeting.

"Twenty-three pieces!" Rahman exclaimed. *"Ma'shallah!* What efficiency!" Latif, Waheed, and Rahman were already in the midst of an intense discussion; they made the most perfunctory gestures of intending to rise when Nirmal entered the conference room.

"The head was missing, most of the spine, hands and feet—" Waheed was in his element.

"Anyone we know?" Nirmal asked.

But, no, they were talking about one of Scotland Yard's famous cases.

Before long, Major General Ahmed Akhtar joined them. The first order of business was to call for tea; then Nirmal gave a rundown on the latest developments, and Waheed followed, reporting on seizures, arrests, and interrogations. "Nothing much new," said Waheed, "nothing anyone could mistake for progress." All the well-known goondas had been taken into protective custody. The American prisoner was still in the overnight lockup. "How's he doing?" Rahman inquired. "Calmer, much calmer now," said Waheed. He would be kept separate from the other prisoners for the time being. As soon as the official secrecy requirements were eased, Waheed would put through a call to the American consulate in Lahore.

Tea arrived and the conversation became lax and general. Major General Akhtar took a few sips, then lit up a cigarette. Rahman, who never smoked, began coughing in reproach. The Major General ignored him; when he was done with the cigarette, he occupied himself by snapping matchsticks into little bits. After a few minutes, Waheed said: "We should discuss emergency plans," and the Major General took out his pen and cleared his throat, all attention.

At present, police patrols were supported by military contingents, each answering to their own commanders. They all agreed that firing was to be avoided as long as possible; tear gas would be used first. If the police on the spot were unable to cope with the situation, charge would be handed over to the army commander present; if the number of disorders increased, the military would be asked to take charge of the city. The Major General found these proposals unexceptionable.

Waheed was concerned with keeping police morale high. "We'll want special awards for gallantry and conscientious discharge of duty," he said. Everyone agreed that the police should have them.

"All these fine points . . ." Latif sounded the one discordant note. He brushed the table in front of him as though clearing it of crumbs. "We're wasting time."

Everyone turned to Nirmal, and Nirmal stared at his matchbox; he even picked it up and jogged it a little for courage. "What would you have us discuss, then?" he asked.

"You aren't addressing the issue," Latif explained, "no one here is. Those people in the streets are screaming with *pain*, and all we can talk about is noise abatement."

He was right, of course. Nirmal had no answer; he crossed and uncrossed his legs. He sat well forward. "What would you suggest?" He addressed Latif.

Latif spread his hands and said, very low: "You're the man in charge, remember?" The back and forth ended here. Nirmal sighed, and began to temporize. "It's a question of appropriate action, and until we know who has the relic, we don't know how to approach it, don't know what appropriate might be . . ." Nirmal's voice floated on, beside, outside, him; he only half-listened, for deep within him was a hollow echo: watery mumblings in bags. Too much tea, was all it was, but it wounded like mockery. Nirmal's eyes moved restlessly from face to face—all vacant, blank, as he knew his own must be. The rumbling continued, the sound of rumors, of emptiness. No ideas—and in their absence it was necessary to be very methodical, very busy.

"Action appropriate to causes," Nirmal repeated. Once again, they reviewed the possibilities, who might have taken the relic and why. With his civil servant's doggedness, Nirmal made a list:

1. India—border agitation
2. Radpur
3. Kidnapping for ransom
4. Factional—Muslim splinter groups—

"Municipal politics next," said Nirmal. "This business of Qureshi's sudden disappearance . . ." No one objected, so he wrote down Qureshi as a fifth possibility. While they were on municipal politics, it fell to Nirmal to mention that it was at least conceivable that the custodian of the relic might, himself, be responsible for its disappearance; Naseem Shah might have temporarily removed the relic in the hope that its loss would bring a renewal of religious fervor to the people of Cyrilabad. Or—it wasn't impossible —perhaps Naseem Shah harbored political ambitions for himself and wanted to prove that he could take charge.

The same sort of thinking would apply to Emir Kabir.

As a stranger to the city and an outsider to the faith, Nirmal felt awkward in bringing up Naseem Shah's name; it pained him that he was the only one to bring it up, but someone had to do it. Nirmal tried to broach this most distasteful possibility as delicately as possible, but he was not a tactful man; his circumlocutions made him seem heavier-footed than usual, and succeeded in underlining what he wanted to play down. Then again—it had to be mentioned—there was that troublesome question never yet answered but shunted from brother to brother, of private *deedars*, of special arrangements for private viewings which might have led to unforeseen consequences. It was not inconceivable that Naseem Shah had allowed Qureshi to borrow the relic for a private viewing, immediately turning on him and crying "theft," so that there was now no way for Qureshi to quietly put the relic back.

"Sounds a little roundabout to me," said Latif.

"All I ask is that you think about it," said Nirmal, not insisting. "There does seem to be some deep intrigue afoot to discredit Qureshi, to finish him off politically. That much you have to admit."

There was a silence which might have signified anything. Then Waheed spoke: "One detail—for whatever it's worth. I've had a man following up on Qureshi. Qureshi's mother is not at home in sickbed as we thought. Her house has been badly ransacked. We've started making inquiries at all the hospitals in the district."

"You'll keep us posted, then," said Nirmal, and returned to his list:

6. Municipal politics—Naseem Shah
7. Municipal politics—Emir Kabir

That seemed to do it. Only events could decide which of the options looked most likely. There was a general sense of incompletion, of enforced passivity, as they adjourned the meeting to wait upon events. Everyone was irritable.

As the Major General stepped through the doorway, Nirmal followed, with Latif swift upon his heels. Too swift— Nirmal and Latif bumped softly and backed away. "Sorry," said Nirmal. "So sorry," said Latif, flashing his gold teeth in what seemed to be a smile. Nirmal stepped briskly so they would not collide again.

Returning to his office, Nirmal found the anteroom full. The clerk handed him a list of names. "They all want private conferences, sir," he explained. "They all say it's important. I've listed them in the order they came."

Nirmal read off the top of the list: "Religious minorities deputation—Rustam Darrah, spokesman."

Eight men rose to their feet. They didn't look much like an official deputation. Small shopkeepers, mostly, Nirmal thought. One of the group—a stout man of middle years —stepped forward: "I'm Rustam Darrah."

"Well, come with me, and bring your delegation with you. I'll see what I can do about chairs."

"No need," said Darrah. "These are bad times and you're a busy man. We'll be brief."

"Would you?" said Nirmal, who doubted it. "I'd appreciate that."

As soon as Nirmal closed the door, Darrah began. "Our names aren't important—it would take too much time. We're Parsis and Christians. We've lived in Cyrilabad all our lives. Now we're afraid."

No one could have seemed less so. The man's build was so solid, he looked unshakable; his voice was firm and managerial.

"And who isn't?" said Nirmal.

"You have to understand," Darrah said quietly, "we're suspect now—anyone who's not a Muslim. It's unthinkable that a Muslim might have stolen the relic. So that leaves —who? Old neighbors in Radpur. Or one of us. Trouble's already started: Reddy's daughter was threatened; my shop's been looted. We don't dare stay home, we don't dare go out—what are we to do? We need protection."

"Protection . . ." Nirmal echoed absently.

"Some men have taken a pledge to kill us and signed it with their blood," a man in bifocals spoke up. He stood behind Darrah, moving when Darrah moved, a shadow. "With their blood," he repeated. "My brother-in-law heard about it. For the life of one *kafir*, they've been promised ten immortalities. Ten!—as if one were not enough!"

"Are you the spokesman?" Nirmal asked.

"No, I," the shadow faltered.

"Let Darrah speak!" the others called out. "We agreed—only one person, remember?"

"How many are you?" Nirmal turned to Darrah.

"A handful. Less than two hundred, I'd say. We might disappear tomorrow—no one would notice."

"I could arrange to have you and your families put up at the YMCA," said Nirmal, "and I could arrange for a guard . . ."

"Yes?"

"That won't solve your problem," said Nirmal.

"Our problem is security," Darrah said flatly.

Nirmal disagreed. "Your problem is trust, and the YMCA won't solve it. It might make things worse—setting you apart."

"What would you advise then?"

"You do have Muslim friends."

"*Did* have. What do you want us to do?"

"I want you to join up with your Muslim friends and act as guarantors of the peace."

"That's a beautiful conception," said Darrah in a melancholy voice.

"You don't understand a thing!" his shadow put in. "You protect foreigners, yes? We're foreigners now. Before—we were good for business. Now there's no business and no room for us."

"A very beautiful conception," Darrah said softly, touching Nirmal's desk with the tips of his fingers, "but—forgive me for saying so—a little Utopian, you know. We tried marching in sympathy with the demonstrators, some of us. I know I did. They didn't want me. Trust is a luxury, and in times like these . . ."

"There are risks," said Nirmal.

"Billet our families safely and we'll discuss this among ourselves," Darrah suggested.

"There's nothing to discuss," said his shadow.

The visitors who came after the minority delegation were even less tractable. Darrah was followed by an old man, bearing a fistful of torn pages from the Quran. "As these leaves are my witness!" he cried. He kissed the leaves, then launched into a tale of desecration. His charge was serious: he claimed that a police officer was responsible for the sacrilege. Nirmal quietly took out a sheet of paper and asked for a description of the officer; he did not question the old man's version of the story, which struck him as highly improbable; he was anxious only to move on.

"My name is Nurul Daultana," said the next visitor. He was a gardener, a convert to Islam. He came from a family of untouchables—he admitted this at once, as affidavit for his truthfulness. "I don't belong to any party," he said, "you can ask anyone."

"Come, sit down, tell me what you have to tell," said Nirmal, unable to disguise his impatience with preliminaries.

Daultana sat rigidly on the edge of his chair, a hand clamped on each knee. "I swear by Allah," he began, "I have seen a sign. I speak nothing but the truth, may God save us."

"A sign?"

"May God save us . . ." And he described a streak of light he'd seen cutting the sky in two on the night of the theft.

"Now what does that mean?"

"What *could* it mean? You—an educated man—and not know this? It means a Holy War. May God save us!"

Nirmal could think of nothing to say. There was a long pause. "I appreciate your telling me this," he said finally. Their business apparently concluded, Nirmal expected the visitor to rise and go, but Daultana sat on. "Is there anything else you want to tell me?" Nirmal ventured.

Daultana leaned forward and said in a whisper: "Leave now—you're not safe here. I'm risking something by telling you this."

"I'm grateful to you for taking that risk."

"You'll leave then?"

"How can I? I've only just come."

"No? Well . . . no help for it, then. God keep you." The visitor rose to his feet. "Wait a moment," said Nirmal. "Where did you hear this?"

"Oh, I heard, I heard," said Daultana, moving rapidly now.

Nirmal decided he would see only one more person; he could only bear one more. He consulted the list and told the clerk that Rafiq Husain would be the last; one of Waheed's men would see to the rest.

Rafiq Husain entered, carrying a briefcase in a tight grip; he continued clutching it to his chest after he was seated. He smiled: his teeth were long and yellow; there were gaps between them, like the prongs of a fork. He seemed just as intense and even more nervous than Daultana. He, too, had his preamble and his sign. They each insist upon their entrances and flourishes, thought Nirmal. Walk-on parts, yet each must make his mark.

"I have some evidence," he explained.

"Evidence?" said Nirmal. "Of what?"

"That's for you to say. I'm a simple man. Something I found near the shrine."

"Let's see."

Husain opened his briefcase and fumbled about more than was necessary. Hocus pocus, Nirmal thought, here it comes.

A tiny bundle, wrapped in a handkerchief. Husain only half unwrapped it, enough to reveal a crudely painted clay model of Ganesha, the fat elephant-headed god of worldliness, sagacity, and wealth, riding his rat. The god and his mount were so tiny that the statue fitted neatly into the cup of Husain's palm.

Nirmal had never cared for Ganesha with his bland, benign expression and hydrocephalic bulge, and this particular model was doubly repellent, a caricature of a caricature

—Ganesha clothed in a gaudy red and yellow vest with gold daubs painted round his neck. The base of the statue, below the rat, was stained with grease.

Must be a test of some kind, Nirmal thought. "What is this—this toy?" he demanded.

"You call this a toy?"

"You mean to say that the thief came and dropped a calling card—in case it wasn't clear that he was Hindu? And of all the idols he might have dropped, it had to be Ganesha, remover of obstacles, talisman for auspicious beginnings? You want me to believe this?" Nirmal made an effort not to shout, but his voice shrilled. It was too incredible.

"You're an educated man, I'm a simple man. It's not my place to say."

"If this is evidence, it's long overdue."

"I thought it might start trouble."

"You thought correctly, but evidence is evidence." The two men glared at each other. "If this is a genuine piece of evidence, I demand that you hand it over to Police Superintendent Waheed. I won't touch it."

"Very well, then," Husain said in a small, shut voice; he began wrapping the statue up.

"And please explain to him why you did not turn it over immediately."

Husain made the wrapping snug, knotting the corners. His face was calm, his motions unhurried.

Nirmal was almost certain that Husain, his bluff called, would not turn the statue over to the police. He was reasonably sure, and beyond that, he refused to think about it.

A late lunch. Hunger had not been good for Nirmal's ability to listen patiently. He dabbled curry over his shirtfront and was annoyed with himself. Letting it be known that his door was always open had been a mistake. In times like these, he reflected, all the lunatics become filled with public purpose and come forward. He had to get out, to stretch his legs and breathe a little; there was still time before the rally.

He slipped out the back way.

The sun was bright, the crowds thick as ever. The free food stalls had begun to charge a few *pice* for *chapattis* and tea; for the indigent, food was still being given out. Nirmal walked on. Wherever possible, he kept to the shade.

At the crossing up ahead, barricades had been erected, and a tense knot of people seemed to be tightening around them. Moving closer, Nirmal was able to make out placards; the men who carried them were moving in a ring. The signs were neatly lettered with a single message—NO MORE SECRECY. A young man on the sidelines was swinging a leather belt in the air in time to the chanting of the demonstrators. Two constables watched him intently; they were slapping their sticks against their palms to the same rhythm.

It was so hot. Overcome with thirst, Nirmal returned to his office before an hour was up. As soon as he entered the foyer of the building, a clerk motioned him aside, saying: "Most immediate top priority, sir," and handed Nirmal a memo to call Waheed at once.

Waheed answered on the first ring. "Bad business, sir," he began. "How bad is bad?" asked Nirmal.

Quite bad, as it turned out. A Hindu temple on the outskirts of Radpur had been robbed. Two idols were reported missing.

Nirmal pressed for more details. The temple where the thefts had occurred was small and rundown and crammed with gods. It had been neglected for years, and the doors were usually left open. Only a few devout widows came regularly to leave offerings of flowers and food. No one would say which idols were missing. Two niches were suddenly empty, that was all Waheed had been able to find out.

A temple no one cared about, Nirmal reflected. The statues might have disappeared weeks, months, before, but the timing was perfect now. It was all so hopeless. For a moment, he stared at his desk and could not speak.

Then Nirmal remembered. "Listen carefully," he said, "there's a man who can be of great help to the police. His name is Rafiq Husain—does it mean anything to you? He hasn't stopped by in the last hour? No visitors bearing gifts? No? Then let me tell you what he looks like . . ."

Paper: how nice. Ahmed, the day guard, had found a ballpoint pen and managed to retrieve a whole stack of surplus mimeographed sheets from the office upstairs. "Cyclostyle," he said, pointing proudly to the printed side, "you know this machine?" The paper was shiny—grudging to the pen, and half-used, printed as it was on one side—yet it seemed sheer luxury to Tom now, and he'd received it gratefully.

Ahmed couldn't have known, but this was the week of Tom's birthday. (Today, tomorrow, or yesterday—Tom had no calendar, but he knew it was one of those.) His birthday, and here was a gift, after all.

He was fifty-one. Fifty-one! How could that be? The years did not add up, did not accrue to anyone. Something was wrong with his memory maybe. The tips of his fingers remembered Barbara best, remembered her hair, cool and silken. If Tom had any memory at all, it was in his skin; here, all records were strictly kept, strictly assigned to him. The sags, the spots, the seams—these remembered, kept the sums.

Straining to know himself, the object of his search always eluded Tom. He'd characterized himself often enough— "all candor, tolerance . . . live and let live . . . a free spirit . . . can't be fettered . . ." All true enough, for minutes at a time. But true of whom? A flickering intermittence was all he ever grasped, nothing constant or consistent, nothing shaped.

He'd tried to get the shape into his work somehow, without ever quite carrying it off. Second-rate. At *best*. How chilling to see it so clearly and so late. "Trouble with you, Tom," Jim Thorne had warned years ago, "you're too wishy-washy. You aren't an angel, that's for sure, and you aren't enough of a heel to be interesting. You're just a poor slob, like a hundred others. Just middling-awful. To write, to really write, you've got to *burn!*" Jim had been first-rate, of course, first among the confessional poets, awesome. Top-awful. A real shithouse—even his friends could vouch for that.

Jim Thorne . . . dead by his own hand these many years. Glory. While Tom continued to muddle along, toting up the defeats. *And* the birthdays. And every now and then, in spite of himself, there'd be some small pleasure. This paper, now.

But he'd written no poems, hadn't even tried. He'd scrawled another letter to Barbara, recounting the sights, the adventures of his new life. It wasn't entirely fiction; he'd seen some sights last week. He wrote two letters of protest to the American consulate in Lahore. He doubted that any mail was moving, though, and after some thought, folded up the letters and tucked them under his blanket.

He stretched his legs, managed a short walk.

Pacing, his cell was twenty by fifteen steps (heel to toe). Twenty-five on the diagonal. Tom was immensely reassured by the fixity of these numbers; he checked and double-checked them to make sure. Even in Pakistan, the familiar geometry held. Here was stability, law.

Strangely, he was unafraid, imagining himself as safe here in custody as anyone could be in a city full of lunatics. At the time of his arrest, he'd felt only anger, then as anger subsided, even in the midst of fear, there'd been a clear presentment of relief. Whatever they did to Tom, it was no longer in his hands. For the moment, he did not have to choose.

But he listened attentively to the smallest noise.

A Stopping Place

As confusion and excitement mounted outside, Tom
found himself in a sort of tidewrack, a quiet zone, where
life was orderly, calm, desolated, and clear. He kept a running account of his thoughts, such as they were, of sights,
sounds, speculations. The visit of a fly or a glimpse of a
cloud had become an event for Tom. There were no other
events, save the constant seething in the streets outside,
the sea-sound of massing crowds and, sometimes, a shout,
a tumble, a clear voice rising above the rest, the high volute
of a wave, the rest indecipherable, broken foam, confusion,
spray . . . When Ahmed sneezed, that was a definite event,
an auditory treat, and Tom reached for his pen at once and
began recording the inflections:

> *Exterr! Echemba!*

He'd also heard sneezes like this—mostly from ladies
who were holding back:

> *Ets! Hets! Etsa! Itsa! Chmmp!*

Laughing dementedly to himself, Tom continued:

> *Contrast and compare . . .*

Such were his diversions.

18
The Rally

At the Hotel Metropole, preparations were underway for the evacuation of all detainees. By early afternoon, an American Army helicopter was waiting on the roof. Half an hour before the copter was due to arrive, the guests were told that their rescue was at hand, and ordered to their rooms to pack. They were allotted only twenty minutes, then everyone was to return to the lobby for a headcount; if anyone were missing, no one would leave. The guests cast brief, distrustful glances at one another and went about their business.

Aleem spent his time in the lavatory, rather than sitting alone in the lobby. He suffered a gnawing sense of many things left undone. Melus had left his clothes in his hotel room, and Aleem a change of underwear and a notebook in his, but there was no way for Aleem to return to Hotel Pamposh and gather their things. Leaving the clothes they'd brought behind was not important—leaving Melus behind *was*. But there was absolutely nothing Aleem could do about it. At least Aleem could take credit for one thing: in all this time, he had not once mentioned the name of

225

Melus; if the American was in trouble, Aleem, for one, had not betrayed him.

Why then did his decision to leave with the others feel so much like desertion? It wasn't Aleem's decision; he had no choice; had he made a fuss, everyone else might have been delayed in consequence. As soon as they arrived in Lahore, he'd go to the American consulate and report what had happened. The people there would know what to do.

Upstairs, on the second floor, Sam Curtis was going through similar deliberations with the same man in view. Sam felt utterly beyond his depth in this city and needed Pakistani cooperation to proceed with his search. He no longer knew if his search for one man had any importance in light of events that were now breaking. It was just as well, then, that he return to home base before going further astray.

Firuz, silent and gloomy, paced the stretch of worn blue carpet between the restaurant and the bar, his overnight case in hand. He had nothing to do at the moment, for he had never unpacked. He would never find Melus now. All Firuz could do was to steel himself for what lay ahead; as soon as they arrived in Lahore, he'd go on alone, he'd take the first flight back to Karachi. No use delaying things. It would be an ordeal returning empty-handed to an empty house, but it had to be faced.

"Everything under control," Waheed reported. And then added: "God willing."

It was well into the heavy afternoon. Nirmal stood in the middle of Jinnah Square, in the second row, close to the speakers' platform. Everyone was pushing to get closer; there was a continual surging forward and a countertow back. An old man in the front row was pushed to his knees; he was helped up, then thrown again. On Nirmal's left, a man dressed in a burlap sack was shouting joyfully: "Let the animals in! Let the animals in!" He wore a skullcap with painted wooden bobbles hanging down all around his head. Nirmal leaned away to avoid accidentally brushing the man, and soon other bodies came between them.

The crowd extended as far as his eye could see, all the way back to the railroad tracks. Since the trains were not moving, there were people sitting and standing on the rails. Even the roofs of the stalled cars were covered with spectators.

It was hot. Jinnah Square was jammed. There was a rancid smell of too many bodies too closely packed, the smell of moldering meat. The sun beat down through muffled layers of air. Every now and then, there came a brief gust of wind, a sudden swirl of yellow dust, but nothing so steady as a breeze. The speakers' platform was ringed about with green pennants; when the gust took them, they slapped themselves.

Nirmal unfolded his handkerchief, moistened it, and dabbed at his forehead and lips. The sun moved under a cloud, and still there was no relief. Something *had* to break, Nirmal felt; the air was swollen to bursting, a thick, brooding, sulfurous yeast.

Then Naseem Shah mounted the wooden platform with loud cracking strides, as though his feet were eating the boards. A man of force, his every gesture proclaimed; he took possession of the lectern, hands pounding; his eyebrows met in a fierce black knot. *"Bismillah Rahman-ir-Rahim!"* he intoned. He began to speak, but his words were drowned in cheers. He started again: "You believers, whose only wealth is the holy relic, you believers, who . . ." More cheers. And Naseem Shah paused, as politicians will, before attempting to go on. As soon as the crowd subsided, he boomed out: "Nothing must move, not a wheel must turn, until the holy hair is returned to us!"

There were shouts of assent at this, and Naseem Shah recited the *Sura of Victory:* " *'You shall enter the Sacred Mosque, if God please in safety . . . you shall not fear . . .'*

Oh, believers, the safety of our mosque has been violated
—will you stand idly by?"

The people answered in shouts: they would not stand idly
by. Then Naseem Shah's voice fell. "Our dearest treasure
is gone . . . This was all our wealth, the sign of God's great
beneficence to us. How great our wealth, how great our
loss . . ."

A mournful silence followed.

To refresh the memories of the faithful with what they
had lost, Naseem Shah began the story of the three trials.

Although everyone in Cyrilabad knew the story of the
three trials by heart, they listened raptly, as though to the
first telling—how, when held to the sun, the holy hair cast
no shadow, when coated with honey, it did not attract a
single fly. When Naseem Shah came to the part where the
doubters said it was an ordinary hair from an ordinary man,
and then to the part where the basest of slanderers claimed
it was the hair of an infidel, they pulled the lobes of their
ears and cried out *"Toba! Toba!"* as though they themselves
had doubted and blasphemed and sought forgiveness. They
strained forward, necks at a stretch, so as not to miss a
word of the second trial—the trial by honey—and when
Naseem Shah came to the story of the last trial, the trial by
fire, they murmured in unison: "yes, yes . . ."

"Oh, believers, consider this: placed in fire it did not
burn! No earthly fire could touch it, and in the fires of hell,
even there, the holy hair would not be consumed." The
crowd swayed toward him.

Nirmal dabbed at his brow again. Naseem Shah gave no
sign of heat or thirst, and went on without pausing. "Of the
Prophet—peace to his blessed memory—it is said that, on
the night of his ascent to Paradise, he was told by Allah:
With each of your sacred hairs, I will deliver thousands of
the sinful among your followers from the burning fires of
hell. And that prophecy has been fulfilled: our holy hair has
lifted thousands upon thousands.

"These are old tales. You know these tales. You know, too, that the trials of the holy hair were not to end with its third test; there was a long and perilous journey to come. The holy hair remained in Medina until the year 900—four hundred and forty-two years ago. At that time, the keeper of the relic was Sayed Nasrullah—may his memory be blessed. Sayed Nasrullah had fallen out of favor with the Caliph.

"So the poor Sayed fled from Medina, taking three precious relics with him—the saddle, the turban, and the hair of Muhammad.

"Poor, ailing, accompanied only by his faithful servant Farid, Sayed Nasrullah journeyed eastward toward Multan, where a wealthy landowner had promised him safe haven. He never reached his destination, for the way was hard, and, on the way, his sickness increased. Set upon by thieves, he lost all his treasures—save one. The holy hair remained. His servant Farid had hidden the holy relic in a place where no one thought to look. He made a gash in his arm, tucked the holy hair inside, then bound up his arm with rags, and the thieves never suspected.

"Now Sayed Nasrullah—may his memory be blessed— knew that his end was near. He knew the devotion of his good servant Farid. He knew that Farid had no other desire in the world than to cherish and protect the holy hair. Two nights before the Sayed's death, the Prophet came to the dying man in a dream and said:

" 'Don't disappoint your faithful servant. Remember, you are God's faithful servant. Give him the treasure . . .' "

There was a long sigh from the crowd, for the story was very beautiful and dear to the humble. Naseem Shah paused for breath and a tumbler of water was lifted up to him, but he declined it with the dismissive, sweeping hand of a man who has gone beyond such trifles as hunger and thirst.

"So it was that the holy hair found a home in Alminar

229

and has been here ever since. And the tomb of Sayed Nasrullah is here, too, and the tomb of his good servant, Farid
—upon them peace. Upon them peace . . ." His tone was
melting now. "Our dearest treasure is gone . . . broken in
the dust. And the dust is consecrated thereby."

Crying "Ya Rasul Allah!" a man in the front row sank to
his feet; he began stroking the dust, then slowly, dreamily,
pressed his face to the ground.

"Rise and stand!" Naseem Shah commanded. "That is
not the way. The dust will claim you soon enough!" Others
helped the man up, but he rocked on his feet and had to be
supported. Naseem Shah pursed his lips, levelled his gaze
upon the man with the streaked face, and rebuked him
sternly: "Not on your knees, not by laying your faces in dust
will wrongs be righted. This blessed ground is our own, our
spiritual home. Our home has been entered and desecrated. Will you stand idly by?"

"*Never!*" came the roar in response. "Death—death to
the infidel!"

Nirmal, infidel, was alone in this crowd. As people
pressed in closer on all sides, his distance and isolation
increased. Rank upon rank, they stood, a welded multitude
and a unity, their eyes glassy, rapt with vacancy, chins
jutted out, lips ajar, and from them came a full-throated
cry: "Death!" Nirmal felt the reverberation of many hearts
pounding in unison, a fearful fusion.

Suddenly—he was shoved from behind. Nirmal stumbled forward, unsettling the man in front. Struggling for
balance, he glanced sharply round: the entire row behind
him had advanced; the push had been impersonal, not directed at him.

Now there was even less space. Nirmal felt locked in,
although he knew he still had some small scope for the
movement of his limbs. He maneuvered his feet until he
stood with legs spread, braced, the better to stand what
ground remained to him. He was drenched with sweat, the
muscles of his shoulders clenched tight.

At once, a strong shaft of light struck his eyes. Not the sun: too sharp a ray. A mirror, he thought. No, narrower still . . . a blade? He was not imagining this: someone had spotted him, singled him out. Who? No way to tell.

More mincing gleams—coming from his left. Another: a fiery shaft, aimed and steady. This last forced Nirmal to lower his eyes, but he remained all alert, centered, his senses abnormally focused; stood rigid and immobile, as though impaled. A minute later, he raised his eyes cautiously. The reflecting object, whatever it was, was gone. Now there was nothing but the dense ranks of shoulders and heads. The crowd surged forward and back, and forward again, buoyed up by a great groundswell of emotion. Nirmal felt the currents move through him but strove to remain motionless, fighting against them.

While from the pulpit the words were hurtled down: "Fire is the answer to them!"

"Soon—soon we shall cast terror into the hearts of the unbelievers . . ." Excitement was rising, and Naseem Shah had sensed it, was skillfully orchestrating it. He had begun to recite from the holy book with a voice well trained in Quranic recitation, vowel prolongation, nasalization, supple elision, stabs, stops—those sudden detonating stops. And Naseem Shah's hands were busy weaving a spell, a conjuror's gliding hands.

The crowd pitched and tossed; people moved in one rhythm, individuals no longer, but particles, pulses in a tide. Naseem Shah was swaying, too, in the grip of the delirium he had set in motion.

"Oh, Apostle! Rouse the believers to fight. If there are twenty among you, patient and persevering, they will vanquish two hundred; if a hundred, they will vanquish a thousand . . ."

This last produced the desired effect. Cries to "Smash! Avenge! Destroy!" followed in inevitable succession. A stave was raised, an iron bar, a chain. There were calls for *"jehad,"* a holy war. Knives flashed upward from scattered points in the crowd, blades rattled. There were shouts.

"The martyr's blood will not be wasted!"

"Even the severed head proclaims—'Martyrs live forever!'"

Waheed gave the high sign and the police, some in uniform, some in plain dress, moved in without a sound. By the looks of it, one person in every seven belonged to the police. There was a scuffle, pushing and shouts. The man in the burlap sack brandished a meat knife high in the air. When the police came for him, he tossed it underfoot, hoping another would pick it up. Nirmal watched helplessly as it was kicked from foot to foot and, finally, lost in the confusion.

People seeped into the empty spaces as the men with weapons were led out.

"I have been a witness," Naseem Shah bellowed out from the rostrum. *"For shame!* For shame! The feelings of every Muslim in the world are outraged today and there is not much time left. To the government and to all who stand against us, I say: It is written in the holy book: *We have destroyed the like of you—but is there any who will mind?"*

He stepped back. A moment later, Pir Nuruddin appeared. Silence surrounded his approach, a hush like an indrawn breath, tense with expectation. Leaning on the shoulder of a young man, he shuffled slowly to the podium. Nirmal regarded the Pir with the greatest interest: a slight, unimpressive figure, stooped and sallow with age, lost in his heavy robes.

What struck Nirmal first was the remoteness of the man: the colorlessness of his hair and skin, the enlarged inexpressive eyes, brought forward by magnifying glasses, so that they seemed to swim free of his face. Only his white beard was distinctive and assertive, a small, finicky beard which grew to a point.

"Watch him carefully," Husamuddin had advised, "he's

an incalculable factor. A mystic, a solitary, the last of his line. He has power, but there's no saying how he'll use it. And there's no approaching him." Nirmal watched and waited with mounting impatience. The Pir closed his eyes for a moment, then opened them, surveying the crowd and the sky. The color of the sky had changed: it was greying over. The crowd jostled and whispered, but the Pir was in no hurry. He stood for a moment in silence, snuffling into a handkerchief. He cleared his throat. His voice was thin and wavering to start. "You are not worthy . . ." he began.

More whispers. Something was wrong with the amplification: the Pir's escort rushed forward to see to it. "YOU ARE NOT WORTHY!" Now the voice was too blasting. Still another adjustment, and another, until the voice was right.

"You have not deserved the holy hair, nor have you deserved the holy book. For you have turned your backs on them, and sinned unceasingly.

"When your treasuries were heaped and your burdens were light—when you had all good things, and a margin— what thanks did you show? Will you never remember? *Surely Allah is witness of everything, and He remembers. The Lord is all subtle, all aware. He is all hearing, ever near.* And the theft of the holy hair is a sign, a clear warning to those who understand.

"You beheld a treasure, and you said: it is safely ours. Why were you so sure? Had you earned it? Were your deeds a pledge—faithful, generous, and patient? No? What was your security then? *Sustained illusion.* How long, my children, how long will you fill your laps with dust and broken crockery and stones? What is the security of your wealth now—your harvests, your children, your homes? *Sustained illusion.* But a day will come, a day of no illusion. A day will come, and with it, a withering wind. And many a city rained to dust!"

There was no wind just then, not a breath stirring, noth-

ing but the mounting oppression of the heat, a steamy tor-
por. The crowd seemed calmed for the moment, lulled by
the suasion of the Pir, or perhaps by the stagnancy of the
air. Nirmal's thirst was appalling; he felt his tongue clump
against the roof of his mouth, a thing of rubber or clay.
Unreal, unreal! He stood in the clotted air of dreams, and
the figure of the Pir seemed to shimmer in a haze, to flicker
on the verge of insubstantiality, to founder on a sigh; his
eyes were shrouded and all was illusion save his voice, broken, fevered, rasped, the voice of fire speaking, a blistering
sibilance. "There was a shout—

"A shout—I heard it—for *jehad*. Who shouted? *Would
you teach God your religion? Jehad*—an easy martyrdom,
you think? *Sustained illusion. Jehad* means moral assault,
a fight against evil and disorder wherever they occur. You
would shout across the river, would you? Are your own lives
so pure? Backbiting, boastful, bold in hypocrisy—you call
yourselves believers? Boast on: *God will bring forth what
you forgot to fear!* For the evil lies near, very near. *Allah is
all seeing, all aware. He knows what you publish and what
your souls whisper. And the Lord is sufficient witness of all
that you are.*

"There was a call for *jehad*—I, too, sound it. I ask you to
rouse yourselves for the greatest *jehad*—within yourselves.
Let us fast, let us pray, let us rout the crafty enemy within!
And take heed: the holy hair may indeed return to us, but
if we are not deserving, it will not remain with us. Pray that
we become deserving!

"Let us fast, let us pray . . . Pray that it is not too late!
Who knows if there is still time, or if that day is near? *The
day when the Shout sounds . . . when brother flees brother
. . . scattering like moths. When the earth will be rocked
and the mountains crumbled . . .*" The Pir lifted a wasted
pale hand with fingers outspread and made a shapeless gesture—it might have signified any passing thing, the flight of
moths, the trickling of water, the sifting of sand. "*When the*

heavens are torn asunder . . . When the sun with its spacious light is folded up . . ." Here and there, eyes lifted furtively, questioningly, to the sky, for it was dull as lead, heavy with foreboding.

"The day when the firmament will be in dreadful commotion . . . when the stars fall, losing their luster. This is a fierce day . . . a day to witness. Taught by one terrible in power . . . The day when the terror descends . . . abasing, exalting . . . There is no king, no mighty legions, none, with power to ward off the approach of that day, or slow by an hour its destined course. And the Lord will judge us then."

As the Pir spoke, the sky seemed to darken by perceptible degrees, to darken and lower. A sudden wind lifted the green pennants and set them flapping. People coughed, stirred, and shook themselves. A man, not far from Nirmal, had begun striking his breast and wailing softly. Another took up the lamentation. The Pir's voice was all effort now, a terrible scorched whisper.

"And the Lord will judge us then . . . A mighty wage is coming to you—generous recompense to the generous, to all a payment in full. And anyone who has done an atom's weight of good shall see it then! And anyone who has done an atom's weight of evil shall see it then!"

The sun went under a cloud. Stretching both arms upward, the Pir went on: *"In the name of the merciful and compassionate God . . . Say: I seek refuge in the Lord of the daybreak . . ."* It was the *Sura of the Daybreak* and, to be sure, something was breaking.

"Not to fast, not to wait, but to fight!" came a strong voice from the crowd. Again, there were calls for a war against the infidel—if not a holy war, then an unholy one. Who spoke? Heads turned. But, now, all voices were dwarfed by sounds overhead, a mutinous rumbling, the sound of muffled drums, of distant runners in the sky. "Only listen!" someone called out, and the Pir raised an admonitory finger. *"Say: I seek refuge from the Lord of the daybreak, from the evil . . ."* The Pir never finished: a white fork appeared in the blackened sky, thunder with it, and the rain swept over them all, a low, swift slant, as though a tide were coming in.

Utter confusion. The speakers on the platform disappeared with the second stroke of lightning, taking the Pir to shelter. In the commotion of the sudden downpour and their concern for the frailty of the Pir, the leaders of the Holy Relic Action Committee had issued no instructions, so for the first time in three days, people were left on their own to decide what to do. There was no shelter in the square, and the crowd rapidly dispersed.

Nirmal continued staring at the deserted speakers' platform with its limp pennants; he dabbed his sopping brow with a sopping handkerchief and remained standing in place as the square emptied out. His feet were cold; the ground was full of puddles; they spattered upward and seemed to smoke in the air.

He remained standing. The rain was everything he could have wished. The ground had become a shallow lake, his shoes were soaked, his shirt pasted to his skin. Still, he had no complaints; he was more than grateful. Where armies might have failed, the rain advanced and continued to advance, invincible.

Finally, Nirmal turned and left. It was a long walk back to headquarters, but easier going now than in sunnier times; the streets were open passageways for the first time in days. A ditch ran filth—the broken rinds of fruit, clay shards, paper scraps, raw sewage, straw . . . A few blurred figures scurried past, soundless in the noise of the weather.

So tired. Nirmal was rinsed with a weariness like an exaltation. Ever since Husamuddin's summons, he had been running, running in place. When he returned to his office he would sit still for an hour, even lie down, perhaps; he would cover no less distance.

Soaked through, Nirmal returned to headquarters to find the building half empty, only the front desk clerk, a switchboard operator, the bearer and his family rattling around officiously with nothing to do; everyone else had been detailed to the rally and now had fled to shelter. Drying off and changing his clothes, Nirmal glanced in the mirror. He got back no reflection. Dizzy, he gripped the frame of the mirror and waited. He stared intently into the blankness. It will come back, he told himself, you've only to wait. To believe and to wait . . .

And there it was; the familiar face. Slashed with fatigue now, eyes bruised with shadow. When did he grow old? He felt feverish, cold and hot at the same time, restless; the slightest breeze made him shiver. But he wasn't ready to lie down.

The room was damp and inhospitable: mice pills in the corner, dust, ants, and crumbs—Nirmal had been taking his meals at his desk.

He settled himself at his desk now. He confronted the array: three heaping files took up most of the available space. Each clamored for attention. Moving from right to left, the labels read: URGENT, VERY URGENT, MOST URGENT —he could take his pick. Memos, bulletins, agendas, crank letters, prophecies, warning letters—"your house is burning," "your life is done"—lists, nothing out of the usual. Nirmal sighed and stretched. Inside, the office was quiet, echoing only the rain. The window panes bumped and creaked softly with the wind; then there'd come a noisy spatter of drops.

Late afternoon: the rain continued, a measured, myriad, ticking, for the wind held steady now. Nirmal sat on without moving, his hands locked together, nodding over papers that had become indecipherable, as though rained on, obliterated by water. His neck and shoulders were cramped. He wanted desperately to talk to Husamuddin, and then to Meena. His personal line seemed dead, so he tried a party line, hoping to get through to the operator and have service restored to his private connection. He stumbled into a conversation he wished he hadn't. One voice was unfamiliar; the other sounded like one of the clerks. The familiar voice said: "I'm telling you, he's a Christian. His name is *James*. I have the bulletin here on my desk— 'James Nirmal Roy.' I'm reading it now. Do you want to see it?"

"What sort of proof is that?" the other cried. "You talk like a child. Anyone can call himself a Christian. His friends call him 'Nirmal'—is that a Christian name? You know very well . . . Just think a moment, won't you? The name is Sanskrit—it means 'purity.' "

Nirmal held on in silence. "*Hindu—*" the unknown voice thickened with contempt. "All wrapped up in his karma, too busy to care, too busy breathing through one nostril at a time. Hoarding his semen, hoping it will turn as white as cream! Purity! And that's the least of it—the question is: why did he come? *Whose* side is he on?"

In the corners of the room, beyond the circle of his lamp, shadows were gathering. Nirmal sat on, glancing every now and then at the phone, which he did not pick up again. Well, and what did he expect? Now was not the time for the luxury of personal feeling. He sat on at his desk, shifting papers from right to left.

First dark, and still the rain continued. Nirmal turned off the desk lamp and walked over to the window: there was nothing to see. He stood there, waiting without expectation, staring out at nothing, his fingers resting lightly on the sill. He touched the windowpane: it was cool. Rain rattled the glass.

The wind seemed to be rising.

19
Sad

Spreading the fingers of her left hand, Kate studied her
wedding ring. A plain gold band, familiar, homely as a
kitchen spoon, it gave no reassurance now, where once it
had filled her with a vast complacency.

It was all true—Snow White, Rose Red, the years in the
tower, abeyance, the numb sleep of waiting—only in re-
verse. The arrest began after marriage, not before, the long
leaning after the light, after the light has moved on.

I live here, Kate said to herself, but could not believe it.
The house was silent, with so large a silence it dizzied and
sickened her. When she spoke, did the sound come out?
She was no longer sure. If the sound came out, did anyone
hear? If they heard, did they understand? No word came
back, so how was she to know?

The exhilaration of her night at the cabaret had quickly
faded. She'd done nothing but move counter to her husband's wishes, within the ambit he had set for her—what
kind of freedom was that?

She made two calls on Monday morning after a fearful
night waiting for Firuz to return home, dreading an out-

burst that never came. Her first call was to his office; she identified herself as a "Mrs. Roper," the first name that came to mind, and asked to speak to Mr. Nazar. The clerk informed her that Agha Nazar had been called away to Teheran; if she wished to have her call transferred, Agha Emiri would be delighted to assist her in any way he could.

Emiri was the last person Kate wanted to talk to; she declined with abrupt thanks. So that was the official story —Teheran. Kate doubted it. But she could think of no other plausible place, nor could she hope for a more truthful answer without giving her real name.

That, she was not willing to do. She wanted no visitors; she'd given Firuz's circle enough food for gossip, long before anything ever happened; she would not offer them more. So she taught Abdul Ghani a simple message for all callers, the same as Sylvia's: the sahib and the memsahib were away; they had not said when they planned to return.

It was not a lie. The sahib was away. And so was the memsahib. Every gesture Kate made was with the motion of a person throwing something away.

Kate's second call on Monday had been to the American embassy. The last contact she'd had with the embassy had been in November when President Kennedy was killed: Kate had written a long, careful letter of condolence, which was answered with a form letter. Not even the signature was real. She hadn't been considered close enough to the American community in Karachi to be invited to any of the memorial services.

It was not an easy call to make. She spoke to a man named Bellman about passport procedures. He asked her a few questions in return. He seemed especially interested to know what passport she'd used to enter the country. "Iranian," Kate had to admit, "diplomatic."

"I'd call that taking advantage," Bellman said, "cashing in on both worlds, taking advantage of another citizenship. What was the idea?"

Kate tried to explain to Bellman, as Firuz had once explained to her, the purely practical advantages of traveling on a single family passport of whatever nationality. "If it's so practical, why do you want to change it now?" Bellman asked. Kate hadn't thought it through and, improvising, said she planned to do some travelling on her own.

"Call back in a couple of weeks," said Bellman. "I'll look into it, but I can't promise anything. The Vice-Consul will have something to say about this." His tone was disapproving. "Being an American citizen is a privilege, you know, it's not a right. Are you planning to leave the country soon?" The question surprised Kate. By indirection, then, like someone learning of her own wounds through a mirror, Kate learned that she was thinking of leaving. Numb Kate—she had not known she was thinking at all.

In a last effort at connection, she tried writing a letter to her father, got well into the fourth paragraph, then gave it up. There was too much to explain, so much of it new, and she'd never been able to make anything clear before.

It had been a civil wedding, and she'd only told her father after it was over, calling long distance from New York and talking longer at one stretch than they'd ever done at home. "Is he as rich as that man from Monaco?" her father had asked, and when Kate said he wasn't, her father had laughed a little and confessed: "That's all right, honey—it's a load off my mind just to know you won't be running around, that someone will be looking after you." He meant it—it was a relief. As a widower, getting Kate "set" had been on his mind for a long time. He'd remarried a few weeks before Kate left for New York, and had taken on new worries—there were stepchildren.

How could she even begin to explain to him? Kate was convinced that her father didn't really know what country she'd married into; he'd only met Firuz once and his geography was hazy; she was certain he confused Iran with Iraq. Once, she caught him at it, but he shrugged the distinction off, saying: "Same difference." When Kate insisted that Iran and Iraq didn't even like each other, he returned: "Don't you believe it! They're like Goodrich and Goodyear. Thick as thieves, I bet." It was hopeless trying to explain now.

Besides—Kate herself didn't know what she wanted to say. So she moved around the house instead of writing, plumped the cushions, tried to remember her mother—a plumper of cushions, sat in this chair, in that, did not settle anywhere.

At moments, mulling over the past few weeks, trying to sort out the havoc reaped by Alavi's remark and Firuz's anger, Kate felt herself a victim of chance, of events that were randomly malicious, but then, the next moment, she wasn't sure: there was something deserved, causal, entirely fitting in what had happened to her. An apt punishment, in fact. By marrying as she had she'd broken with her tribe and could expect no comfort, no quarter, anywhere. She belonged nowhere.

How quickly she'd lost touch with everything familiar! In only a year away . . . Marge, the one friend who still held on, had moved from New York to San Francisco. They continued to send picture postcards back and forth, the tiny writing spaces crammed with exclamations. Marge thought Kate's life "an adventure—so exotic!" Her enthusiasm had a fine irony now.

Still, it had been an adventure to start: meeting Firuz, their whirlwind courtship, all of it so unlikely, so different from what Kate had ever expected. The honeymoon in Naples, then off to Iran—Shiraz, Takhte Jamshid, Isfahan with those turquoise domes and skies, the sun smiling, a blue-gold glaze over everything, her eyes dazed, dazzled with splendor. Even the beggars in their picturesque rags, seemed part of a pageantry. The melon vendor passed by, crying his wares, "red as gold, all good, no evil in them." Even in commerce, there was joy. Whatever Firuz translated was charming. Here was an older, simpler, more innocent world. Kate drank *sharbat* flavored with rosewater, basked in animal contentment, filled with languor. Firuz was radiant, tender.

Then, all too soon, there'd come that long week in Teheran, the visits and countervisits, the relatives looking Kate over with shrewd, appraising eyes. What do they *think?* she'd wondered for the first time. And: Will I pass?

She did pass. Firuz reported that his aunts had found Kate not at all frivolous, as they'd imagined her to be, but "grave" and "noble"; they'd been favorably impressed. Kate's mute condition had helped, of course, she realized that now. They'd left for Karachi soon after that. Firuz was no longer translating, and Kate had begun to listen and learn for herself; she was no longer touring. Her adventure had ended here, within four walls.

Such a nothing feeling, watching the nothing clock. Kate read her skin; she pressed her head to the wall: she seemed to hear the sea. But it wasn't the sea, only the soft surge and thunder of her own blood. She tabulated her heartbeats—it was that quiet all around her. Once, she struck her head against the door so as to feel something, just to feel. She tried to read, but even the simplest novel seemed incomprehensible to her: words dissolved into letters, letters into blots. Unable to read or write, or to meet and talk to people, Kate went for hours without anything so shapely as a thought. She touched her face in the looking glass: it was smooth and cold, composed and passionless. To an outsider, nothing was visible, there was no sadness showing, no tear stains, no swollen lids, no downcurving lines. Her face was perfectly composed, her lips closed, her hands folded lightly and evenly, one over the other. She'd learned finally, belatedly, as everyone learns, to weep behind her face, deep in the pit of her throat, too low for sound.

She stood up suddenly; her keys fell from her lap in a jangling heap. She stooped to retrieve them. The keys had always been an issue between Kate and Firuz. There were seventeen keys on a heavy ring; they might have been keys to a public institution, a janitor's bundle, keys to every cupboard and closet. Firuz insisted on keeping every cupboard locked. "Trust is a luxury," he'd explained. "You come from a rich country. Here, it's different." So Kate made an effort to always lock up. And always managed to lose the keys. And Abdul Ghani always found the keys; he brought them back to Kate, coughing as he did so, trying hard not to laugh—it was a game. Servants sized Kate up at first glance as "an easy mistress," a soft touch; the household accounts were adjusted accordingly: sugar and tea were slowly siphoned off, the rice dwindled pinch by pinch. She wasn't fooling anyone.

Mealtimes were very hard now, suppers most of all. In other houses, families gathered together and ate together. Kate sat alone at the head of the long oval banquet table. She lifted her fork, but had difficulty raising it to her mouth. Abdul Ghani stood over her, hovering and concerned. He would have stirred her tea for her and buttered her bread, had she allowed it. Kate ate four bites, then rested. Abdul Ghani tried to soothe her; when that brought no result, he began to plead: "American dish—cutlet— tasty, yes?" She tasted. "Yes," she said, "very tasty." She made an effort, but the heap of rice and curds in front of her did not diminish; she dawdled so much that the rich sauce over the cutlets grew cold and congealed with fat. It was no use—she simply wasn't hungry. "I work—you eat!" said Adbul Ghani, raising his voice. Kate did no work, so why should she be hungry? Ladies here often referred to themselves as "we useless women" and, really, Kate thought, that's what we are, we have no right to be hungry.

Sometimes, though, she thought it was really anger that would not let her eat, anger, heavy and indigestible, something she could not swallow or cough up.

Abdul Ghani, much troubled, puzzled over Firuz's disappearance and feared for the worst. With only the Mem to cook for, his own job was on the line. So he cooked with a vengeance, and Monday evening, produced an elaborate dessert of heavy meringue and biscuits; it was shaped like a Swiss cottage with a peaked roof, and covered with snow, a thing more sculpted than cooked. To Kate, it looked inedible: the happy cottage under its snow of sweetness seemed to mock her. She knew that Abdul Ghani's intentions were innocent enough; he was practicing up for company, was all it meant. She ate a corner of the roof and the front door with its surrounding masonry, and the thing crumbled.

She must have lost control when the house tumbled down, for when next Kate looked up, Abdul Ghani was clearing the plates, rattling things, as if calling an unruly meeting to order. He said gruffly: *"Burra Memsahib*—no cry."

His conviction that great ladies didn't cry, and that she was a great lady, touched Kate, reminded her of the presence and dignity expected of her. She was, after all, a woman of position, but of what position? Alone, she veered from tears to laughter, and back again, but she made an effort to control herself in Abdul Ghani's presence.

Two people alone together, and each might have alleviated the loneliness of the other, but for the proprieties. They were under a tyranny of forms so rigid that Kate could never meet Abdul Ghani's eyes on a level with her own. She was forced to look always a little to the side, a little above, a little beyond. It was almost as if she could not withstand a direct gaze—she might be found out.

Their conversation was also severely restricted, Kate rarely moving beyond "do this—do that," her servant confined to the compliant responsive. There were only momentary lapses, words which might have seemed banal and indifferent to an outsider. A simple comment like: "This is fine weather," or a seemingly casual question: "Are you tired?" seemed, in so parched a silence, full of solicitude, moist with tenderness. Often Kate asked him: "*Is ka nam kya hai?*"—What is the name of this?—for she knew only the scantiest Urdu. Abdul Ghani was delighted; he loved taking on the role of teacher. For the moment, for as long as the question lasted, he was the master.

Once Kate asked him if he had any relatives, a daring question under their circumstances, a lapse from the prescribed code. He answered that his wife, children, and grandchildren were in Kashmir; he hadn't seen them in more than six years. More than this, Kate could not inquire.

Now that Firuz was gone, Abdul Ghani slept in front of her door. He had done this before when Firuz went on a trip. There, like a doorstep, the old man spread his thin pallet and himself upon it, his body interposed between Kate and whatever dark forces of the night might violate her honor—which was, of course, her husband's honor as well.

How close and how distant they were, Kate and her servant . . . With speech so constrained, they had a rich life of gestures and hesitations, silences and inflections. They were totally at each other's mercy and the slightest hint of irritation made life miserable for both of them; he'd sulk, she'd sulk, they'd spend the next few hours cutting down on their bare minimum of speech, or else bullying and bribing one another. What was needed was a reassuring pat of the hand and such a liberty was out of the question. So the misunderstandings multiplied: Abdul Ghani, feeling

abused, his job threatened, abused the sweeper, who
abused the pariah dog, who snarled at his mate. How sadly
alike we are, Abdul Ghani and I, Kate thought; we have no
arts but those of pleasing, and when we do not please, we
have no arts at all.

Mornings, the sweeper woman came. Bent double, she
moved through the house with her filthy cloth or bundle of
straws that passed for a broom, eyes on the ground. In her
dark skin and coarse, dun-colored sari with muddy hems,
the old woman seemed part of the ground, and passed from
room to room as a shadow passes.

There was no relief—they were in a spell of drought with
rain long overdue. The palm trees in the garden had a fluid
motion in the wind, like seaweed, but gave out a dry papery
sound. The wind was dry and scouring, abrading where it
touched. It brought into the house a harsh yellow dust.
Lacking a bearer, Kate was allowed to dust. She moved her
cloth over the surfaces of tables, shelves, and chairs, she
redistributed the dust; she took down the living-room curtains and shook them out in the yard; the wind threw the
dust back into the house. She changed the places of the
lighter chairs, then moved them back. She dusted the guest
room; stashed away in a drawer, she found some things that
puzzled her. There was a framed portrait in green and
white of Muhammad and the twelve Imams. All the Imams
looked alike, except for the inscriptions under their feet;
each had a little curtain over his face. She touched the tiny
earthen prayer plaque. Firuz's mother had given him that,
and the rosary beside it, made of the same clay. Kate had
never seen Firuz use these things, she'd forgotten all about
them. She shut the drawer quickly.

In the dining room, she lifted up the knicknacks, arranged the spaces between them. Most of the knicknacks
were wedding gifts—the porcelain ballerina on her stiff toe,
the tile trivet, the blue teapot with raised gilt roses, which
played "Tea for Two" when tipped. She left her keys in the

cupboard door; Abdul Ghani found them and brought them to her. There was nothing she wanted to do.

Her hands, idle, scattered and flew. She brushed her hair, a hundred strokes, morning and evening; she made up a chant to go with it: "to behave properly/to bathe fully/to dress nicely/to brush the hair well/to behave—" The last stroke was so savage, she cried out. Her hair sizzled and billowed, a nest of flames. She laughed, and the laughter caught in her throat, she coughed, and the brush fell, clattering.

The night was endless; there were no landmarks. The empty day stretched like a month.

Kate envied Abdul Ghani's little routines that carried him through the day. They never varied. First thing on rising, he coughed and spat until his chest was clear, then blew his nose between thumb and forefinger and wiped his hand on the grass. Next, the lavatory, where he occupied himself for some minutes. Ablutions, after that, and then his morning prayers. After starting up the kitchen fire, he prepared a pellet of opium, grinding it down from a stick that looked like a brown crayon. He mixed the grindings with oil and saffron, rolling the mixture to a tiny ball between his fingers. Only when that was finished did he begin his chores. Evenings, when the supper dishes were done, he'd spread a mat and stretch out on the back verandah where he'd slowly consume the pellet, his hands folded under his head, his eyes wandering over the garden with an expression languid and indifferent. Once recumbent, it was all but impossible to rouse him.

Abdul Ghani had one other recreation—a woman in town. Kate assumed it was a woman, she had no way of knowing. He visited her on Mondays. From Monday noon until five was one of his half-days off, but long before midday he'd be ready to set off. The transformation was dazzling: his clothes were span white and so starched that they crackled when he moved; the ruff of his turban was elaborately pleated and stood high; his sparse beard was fluffed out and reddened with henna, and the whites of his eyes gleamed with antimony. His scent was pronounced, floral and festive: he'd soaked two dabs of cotton wool in rosewater, tucking a tiny wad behind each ear. Only his gap-toothed smile kept the air of sad dishevelment of ordinary days.

Another Monday noon came round. Kate watched Abdul Ghani leave the house, and remained standing at the window long after his form diminished, feeling as if her sole link to the world outside were cut.

Locked up here all alone, she said to herself.

But that was absurd—she held the keys in her own hand. I can leave, too, she thought. I'll go out shopping, that's the cure.

It was the cure, clearly, for her blood quickened with the thought, her limbs moved efficiently. She dressed and locked up the house.

Leaving the house, her dark *anderun*, Kate was shocked and bewildered by the brilliance of sun in the street, at the people, so many people, living, moving unconcerned past her. It was as if she had suddenly emerged, from hours in a blackened cinema, into the fullness of day—she was stunned and amazed at the persistence of the world.

She had no idea where to go.

She took a taxi to the center of town. Traffic was slow; the streets were clogged with pedestrians; there was some shouting. The driver took her on a detour, nearly a half mile out of her way, but there were crowds of pedestrians everywhere, an aimless, noisy milling about.

In the shopping district, business was brisk. Chickens stood on the curb in bunches and squawked, their legs tied together. Servants with market baskets went from stall to stall, pricing and comparing; some of them, the servants of the very rich, swaggered with importance as they walked. A prostitute passed, heavily veiled, disguised as a student, complete with book under arm; her exposed fingers were covered with rings, the nails painted, a string of scarlet flags fluttering out from under a black tent. Three young girls, trying to keep fair, tilted their multi-colored umbrellas against the sun. Kate simply followed them, content to be swept along in that stream of umbrellas and wheels.

She moved mindlessly, indifferently, carried by the motion of others. There was nowhere she wanted to go. It would rain soon, by afternoon or early evening; dark clouds scudded over the sun, racing by furtively, like scene-changers on a curtainless stage.

Kate walked on until she came to the street of the plastic vendors. Here, the stalls were heaped with brightly colored sandals, pitchers, flowers, baskets. She lingered over the baskets for a moment, but there was nothing she wanted to buy.

She moved down the street: a white woman in a thin frock, her red hair blazing. Someone brushed against her lightly. A hand touched hers, softly and tentatively—or did she imagine this? She was aware suddenly of the density of her flesh, the whiteness of her arms, the thickness of the crowd, the fullness of her thighs. An elbow bruised her breast. These things happen. Then she felt the palm of a hand on her left hip, lingering. Not quite accidental, it clung to her as she moved forward. She slapped it off. It returned, this time cupping a buttock. Kate abruptly about-faced and the hand disappeared; she tried to locate the face to which it belonged, but the faces she scanned were expressionless, gave no clue.

Keep going, she said to herself, you'll throw him off. She pushed forward and a hand crept down her palm and damp alien fingers twined among her own. This time she swung out with her purse, striking the boy closest to her on the left side; he backed up sharply, but the fingers remained: a bad mistake.

Now someone pressed his whole torso against her; she

felt a particular stiffness, like the beak of a bird, touching the small of her back. She swung out with her purse again; heads turned; someone cried out; she cut across the stream of traffic, twisting and swinging to create boundaries, to free herself from the smutch of hands.

Part III

Tashkent will fail, but its value is a stopping place; if you stop you think and feel, and if you think and feel your humanity may lead you to reason, good sense, civilization. It's a chance, and yet an accumulation of chances may build a chain of reality . . .

E. N. MANGAT RAI
Commitment my style:
Career in the Indian Civil Service

20
Rain

Cyrilabad, Monday—Tuesday

The stridence of voices had subsided before the wind and
the rain. Tom glanced up from his Urdu conversation
book. The rain made a sizzling sound. Tom paused to listen. Then he returned to the page before him.

A murder was committed this morning. *Aj fajr ek khun
hu'a hai.* The murderer was imprisoned. *Khuni kaid hu'a
hai.* The murderer is to be hung. *Khuni phansa jawega.* He
was born before you. *Wuh tumhare age paida hu'a tha.* He
died yesterday. *Wuh kai margaya.* They will be married
tomorrow. *Un ki shadi kal hogi.* This is wonderful news.
Yih 'ajib khabar hai. I am learning Urdu quickly . . .

Tom was, in fact, learning Urdu quickly. Unprecedented
progress for just a few hours. Of course, it was only a phrase
book—no grammar to slow him down. Then, too, there
were no distractions, there was nothing else for him to do.
As far as he could see, the country was in a state of war,
and under the circumstances, learning Urdu was a fine occupation, prison as cozy and safe a place as any. Safer,
probably: the walls were fortified. As a forgotten man, Tom

offered no target to anyone. No point, then, in reminding anyone of his existence.

Early that afternoon, Ahmed had produced the phrase-book—another gift from the clerk upstairs. Tom opened it and at once found the question that seemed to unlock everything else: *"Is ka nam kiya hai?"*—What is the name of this? He pointed to his bed, basin, pitcher, and Ahmed, beaming with pleasure, recited each name slowly, twice. Ten minutes later, he gave Tom a little quiz, and Tom didn't do too badly. Ahmed was quite a good teacher; his English was a little erratic, though, courtly at best, but he could not read or write it.

"You are my guest for now," he told Tom.

That was a gracious way of putting it. At suppertime, when no one was looking, Ahmed opened the door of Tom's cell and the two men dined together, each on opposite sides of the threshold.

A small thing, yet Tom was grateful for it. He had no feeling at all for Hassan, the other guard, who worked the late night shift and preserved all the barriers between them —silence the strongest of these. But Tom was growing fond of Ahmed.

Ahmed was uncommunicative on only one particular, and that was the subject which most concerned Tom— what exactly was going on outside. "Trouble," he'd say, and refuse to elaborate further. "We begin the lesson now?" Tom agreed to learn Urdu mostly as a way of killing time, but also to assure Ahmed of his friendly intentions.

No problem now deciding what to do with his time: there were his jottings, the Urdu phrase book, conversation with Ahmed, silent reflection, eating, voiding, pacing, sleeping. And that was all, the sum total of possible options. Any more letter writing seemed futile with the city under siege as it seemed to be. Poor "little fox" . . . But it couldn't be helped.

He was often thirsty. How he would cherish a glass of something golden, warming . . . Never mind. *Kuch parva nahin*. The light was dim in the yellow room. It was true about real trouble chasing away small troubles. All the clichés were true: hence their persistence.

A late learner, ancient Tom. But a learner, nonetheless. Come what may. *Jo chahe ho.* As soon as possible. *Jitni jeldi ho sake.*

A flood seemed to be in the offing. The rain beat down, shimmering, a marimba of sound. There were no voices. Tom returned to his book: I clasp your feet . . . No, skip that one.

It may happen. *Yeh ho sakta hai.* Learn it by heart. *Ise zubani yad kar dalo.* At the point of the sword. *Talwar ke zor se.* These phrases are useful. *Yeh fikre kam ke honge.*

Curious, the phrases deemed useful.

The wind was rising, and the river would soon be rising, too.

All through the night, as the wind rose and fell, the rain continued. Unwilling to take to his bed, Nirmal slumped at his desk, and sleep overtook him there, as a patient creditor who waits and seizes.

He slept for nearly an hour at his desk, head on folded elbows, mumbling into his dispatches, then shook himself awake. His head and neck throbbed; his arms were numb. It was still raining, though quietly now, an unwearying tick tick tick . . . There would be hours yet. Unable to think, and thoroughly chilled, Nirmal relinquished his desk and staggered to his cot.

A long sleep followed, but there was little refreshment in it. Dream followed dream, but he could only remember the last one before waking. He stood on a beach, a stony crescent full of gleaming mica, like the beach at Clifton. He was pouring milk into the sea to appease some god or other. Tumbling through blue waters, he woke. His cot flowed past him, then lurched still.

He turned on the standing lamp and saw the familiar

room, everything in its place—files, desks, papers, chairs —all in place and holding firm. On the wall beside him were the twin maps of the cities of Cyrilabad and Radpur, whose details were already as familiar to Nirmal as the markings of his right and left palms: the intricate branchings of streets and avenues, webbed junctions, knotty roundabouts, the fine traceries of alleyways and lanes. The lamp beside him was familiar, the light steady and warm; these things should have soothed him, yet did not.

He listened, seemed to hear a faint knocking. His door? He waited. There was a long pause.

"Who is it?" he called.

Only a rustle of cloth for answer.

Nirmal stepped forward.

A young girl stood in the doorway. She was in Punjabi dress—all white with a blue *dupatta*. She lowered her eyes modestly when Nirmal stared at her. Her *dupatta* fell back, exposing her hair, which gleamed blue and violet; she had round, shell-like ears, with a tiny rose tucked behind one of them. Her skin was fair, the color of wheat.

"What do you want?" the words came out more gruffly than Nirmal intended. The girl looked down at her shoes. Nirmal wondered whether she'd just come in out of the rain—her hair shone so. But her clothes were dry.

Her clothes were dry . . . Someone from inside the building? One of the servants? Nirmal couldn't remember —there'd been so many new faces.

"Why have you come?" he asked.

She raised her face a little, and stared at him as though the answer were obvious. "*Huzoor*," she said softly.

A trap, he thought. "Who sent you? Who paid you?" he demanded.

The question was insulting to both of them, and the girl glanced away. He was about to say: "I am sixty-two years old. You see how I am—my hair is white." Instead, he said angrily: "How much were you paid?"

"*How much?*" he persisted.

By way of answer or distraction, she plucked the tiny rose from her ear and pressed it into Nirmal's hand. Her fingers were soft, insistent.

"You go now," he said.

"Go home, you hear?" He was beginning to raise his voice again. "Who do you belong to?" She didn't move. "Are you deaf?" he shouted. She didn't answer, only stared at her shoes. A most unlikely temptress, Nirmal thought, as starched and scrubbed as a schoolgirl in her narrow chemise. She couldn't have been more than fifteen. Small, lemon-shaped breasts, smaller than the hollows of his hands. "Please go home," he said again, "or wait downstairs until the rain stops. This is an office."

She salaamed, touching two fingers to her forehead, and turned away. Nirmal stood, following her with his eyes, listening to the light pattering sound of her feet. Her footsteps faded. He thought he might have dreamed her, were it not for the tiny rose he held in his hand. The flower was fully open, but minute, smaller than his thumbnail, the kind of rose that does not drop its petals one by one, but saves itself and withers on the stem.

He turned back into the room. Noticed damp stains on the far wall.

Without thinking, he crushed the rose between his fingers. He hadn't wanted to—it was the tension, his will clenched like a fist. He dropped the pulp into the wastebasket. A petal clung to his thumb, the light flicking of a finger. He tore it off with a rage that stunned him. His fingers were stained. He walked over to the iron basin and turned on the faucets; the water from both taps was cold and left a sandy brown sediment. He scrubbed until no trace of the crimson remained, then dried his hands—they looked immaculate. But, bringing them close to his face, he was irked to find that the scent had not washed off; he'd have to start all over again. He stoppered the basin this time, soaped his right hand, and then soaked it, taking his time. The scent was much fainter now.

After that, he sat on the edge of his cot in darkness for a while, reluctant to resume his dreams, yet craving sleep. Perhaps his dreams would be better this time. Doubtfully, he stretched out once again, drawing the cover up to his chin. It felt luxurious. How peaceful it was: no glare, no voices, nothing he had to do, nothing he *could* do. The rain dinned softly . . .

Sometime before dawn, the rain stopped; there was only a slow, erratic trickling from the eaves. Slowly, the darkness thinned out. Nirmal greeted the morning with unreasonable disappointment. He'd known of course that the rain was temporary, a reprieve only. With the return of the sun, he would have to act and act decisively.

Husamuddin phoned before Nirmal had quite finished his first cup of tea. "How's your weather?" he began. "You haven't called to talk about the weather," said Nirmal. "What's that?" said Husamuddin. The line was bad; their voices fizzed and crackled. "Can you speak louder?" Husamuddin asked. Nirmal made an effort, which brought on a cough. An ant fell out of the earpiece—the office was overrun with ants. "Can't have you getting sick," said Husamuddin, "are you taking care of yourself?" Nirmal mumbled something reassuring. Then Husamuddin moved on to business, the nasty part: "You'll have to move. You'll have to take some action immediately. The news is out—the whole business leaked out yesterday morning. The Americans started it, don't ask me how. And now we have word from Delhi—there's been rioting in Batala—the Indians hold us responsible—"

"Responsible for what?" said Nirmal.

"But surely you've heard . . ." said Husamuddin, "about that plundering of a Hindu temple in Radpur."

"Let me clarify that," Nirmal interrupted, "I'm not sure it was a plundering at all—"

"No need." Husamuddin would not let him finish. "If it hadn't been that temple, it would have been another—or something else calculated to provoke. Passions create their occasions, haven't you noticed? You'll have to move, Nirmal."

"I can't. Not yet."

"Don't you have any sense of the situation?"

"Less and less. I don't even know that the relic has been stolen."

"What do you mean?"

"I don't really know. It's possible that the relic is here, safe and sound, in Cyrilabad. It's one possibility—out of six, seven, I don't know how many. And even if the relic has been stolen, the whole affair might be much smaller than we thought. It may be nothing but a municipal squabble."

"It can't be small, Nirmal. You're very mistaken if you think that. This may have started as a *household* squabble, for all I care. The repercussions are going to be large— large and awful—if we don't take action soon."

"Well, I sometimes wonder whether I'm the right man for this," Nirmal confessed. "I'll tell you one thing, and I'm all alone in this . . . I have no evidence, nothing to back me up, but I don't think it's an Indian plot. People think I'm partial—my Hindu blood is telling."

"You're the right man for the job, Nirmal. I chose you, and I'm not backing down. You'll have to make some sort of move, though. The Governor is on my neck, and the Minister of the Interior on his, and the P.M. on his. You know . . ."

Nirmal made a murmuring sound. I'll be moving blind, he thought.

"And Nirmal—" an afterthought: "be careful!"

Breakfast: a bowl of curd and a second cup of tea. The newspapers were brought in. Husamuddin was right: the news was certainly out, and everywhere in headlines. He

261

picked up *The Morning Messenger*, a Karachi daily; he scanned the front page. WE HAVE BEEN EMASCULATED! the single headline read; the bold black letters were an inch high. Yesterday, suddenly, due to circumstances nowhere explained, the news blackout surrounding Cyrilabad had been lifted. "In these troublous and malicious times . . ." a commentary began. In cities across the nation, flags were reported flying at half-mast, rallies and strikes were being planned, and editorial phrases were rife.

Nirmal threw down the paper—he had to get out.

But outside, little was happening. The streets were still wet, although the rain had stopped. There were army checkpoints at every other corner now: the soldiers stood huddled and shivering in the damp, their gunshafts dripping. Walls and branches, overhangs and lamp posts—everything glistened and ran.

It was after nine and Nirmal noticed that many of the free food stalls remained closed. When he asked about it, Nirmal learned that the period of fasting proposed by Pir Nuruddin had officially begun. Nirmal wasn't in the least cheered by this development: fasting would only postpone things; like the rain, it would make a redoubled reckoning inevitable.

Near Khem Karan Street, a flagellant's procession lumbered past. A crowd had formed to watch it go by. Nirmal also stopped to watch. To the refrain of a melancholy dirge —"the faithful come Allah to Thee!"—the breast-beaters, naked to their waists, raised striking hands and chains and let them fall upon their chests in a single crash. A straggler at the end pitched drunkenly into the crowd; he moved forward, scraping his chain after him, dazed but upright, his face veiled under a thin film of blood. Nirmal saw him coming, but was too horrified to move. As their shoulders brushed, Nirmal shuddered violently. The man stumbled forward, stiff with lacerations over face and chest, blood streaming from his side, his head thrown back, eyes wide and vacant with ecstasy. He was muttering "Al-lah! Al-lah! Al-lah!"—six heartbeats. Nirmal turned away, pale, shaken.

Back to the office to find his desk heaped with dispatches. Nirmal ordered tea and settled himself in. On top, was a memo from Waheed: all the kidnapping leads were blind. Nothing surprising in that.

Here was some news. One of Waheed's men had found a suitcase in a storage shed on Khem Karan Street, not far from the Holy Relic Action Committee's godown. The valise was full of what Waheed delicately called "supplies:" 260 sticks of dynamite, 350 detonaters, 344 fusewires . . .

The phone rang. It was a call from the American consulate in Lahore. Something about an evacuation and an American who'd been left out.

"I don't understand," said Nirmal.

"One of our own left behind. We only learned about it after the group got back here. I've spoken to a Mr. Waheed in charge of police, and he referred us to you—apparently, you've taken the man in custody. Name of Melus . . ."

Nirmal didn't remember the name, but he did recall an American with a very red face who'd been taken in some days back. "What would you have us do with him?" he asked.

"We'd like you to keep him on ice for us."

"Ice?" said Nirmal.

"Right. Safe and sound and out of trouble until the commotion dies down."

"What if the commotion doesn't die down?"

"We'll be in touch," said the American.

There was a knock at the door. "Come in!" Nirmal called eagerly, hoping it would be the bearer with tea. It wasn't. Instead, Munim entered; he had a memo pad in hand.

"Important news," he said without preamble. "So I came right up."

"Yes?"

"I've been asking questions as you suggested . . . Something interesting. I met a travel agent. Qureshi's mother isn't sick at all—she left for Mecca two days before the theft."

Nirmal straightened in his chair, all alertness. "You're right," he said, "that *is* interesting." Then demurred, "But I doubt if it's anything more than that. You're not to speak a word of this to anyone, Munim, understand? You've done a good job—leave the name of the travel agent with me so I can keep it on file. There's some intrigue afoot to discredit Qureshi. I'm not at all sure that this information is true— or what it means if it is true."

Nirmal had said more than he should. It was painfully clear to both men what the information meant if it was true, and Munim smiled a little at the transparency of Nirmal's bluff. "Will that be all?" he said.

"If that's all you have to tell me—yes. I want you to stay with the Action Committee. Those people want watching."

The bearer entered with a steaming tray.

"Will you have a cup before you go, Munim?"

Munim declined the propitiatory cup.

Matters had now taken a turn. Nirmal rang up Latif as soon as Munim had left. "I'll be over directly," said Latif, after hearing the news. Nirmal had never heard him sound so cheerful.

21
Chahar Shambeh Soori

Karachi, Monday–Tuesday

Lurching home in a three-wheel scooter cab with a gaudy striped awning, its gilt tassels spinning, Kate clung to the side panel of the seat. The driver went too fast. When he put on his brakes, Kate fell forward, hitting her shoulder. She didn't bother to say anything then; only when they turned down her driveway did she begin to weep, openly, uncontrollably, past the point of caring.

Someone was waiting, standing on the verandah. Not Firuz: a woman. Kate pretended not to notice; she wanted no visitors. She stepped out of the taxi and turned her back on the house. Now what? Money? Fumbling in her purse, she discovered there wasn't enough. She continued rummaging, certain that the right amount and more would be found tucked away in one of the seams. It was not. She put forth all she had. The driver refused to accept it. In a fury, she turned her purse inside out—matchbox, comb, compact, lipstick, postcard, dusty soda mints, stamps, a stick of tampax, a packet of hairpins, all tumbled out onto the driveway. The driver shook his head and stubbornly pointed to the house: "*Burra* bungalow," he insisted, *"burra* sahib—many moneys." Kate began to weep afresh.

"Jao!" Another voice broke in. It was Sylvia, all two hundred pounds of her. She lumbered toward them, rattling coins. *"Jeldi jao!"* she said angrily, pointing the way out. The driver pocketed the coins and returned to his scooter. The women stooped to gather the spillage from Kate's purse.

"I don't know what came over me," said Kate, her hands trembling.

"Don't you?" said Sylvia.

There was a rumbling in the air. The sun was completely covered up. They went in quickly.

Sylvia put her arm around Kate's shoulder as they stepped into the vestibule. "Think of me," she said, "as a shoulder, a well-padded one." Rounding the passage, their bodies swayed together, and Kate felt she might simply flow into Sylvia's arms, simply grateful. Instead, she pulled away sharply; if it seemed rude, it couldn't be helped. Kate had learned long ago that women were not to be relied upon; they belonged to others, not to themselves.

Sylvia dropped her arm and the two women seated themselves facing each other, a clarifying distance between them.

"You must tell me all about your trip. I'll make some coffee," said Kate, making no effort to rise.

"You'll do nothing of the kind," said Sylvia. "There's nothing to tell—we went to Abbottabad. It was dull there. I just got home, saw your note, and ran right over. Now you're going to sit here and tell me what's been going on. *Something* is going on—I'm no fool. You've got to tell me, Kate. Where in hell is Firuz?"

Kate repeated what Firuz's embassy had told her. She dressed it up a little, saying: "He's been called back to Teheran."

"I wish you'd just trust me," Sylvia said.

"But I don't know anything more," Kate insisted. "And I want you to know I'm fine now." She bent all her efforts to recomposing her face. Her hands still shook, betraying her face and, really, it was useless—Sylvia had witnessed all she needed to know.

"I feel . . ." Kate said.

"How? Tell me how you feel."

"Not enough air."

"I'll call a doctor."

"No—no doctor. I'm tired, that's all. All I need is some sleep. I haven't been sleeping much lately."

Sylvia advised seconal and bed. "What—in the middle of the afternoon?" Kate protested, then agreed with such alacrity that Sylvia was alarmed. And when Kate asked: "You'll get home all right, won't you?" Sylvia could not fail to notice that it wasn't a real question.

"Don't worry about me," said Sylvia, doling out two capsules. "I won't be able to beat the first downpour, so I'll sit on for a bit. You take these now."

"You sure you'll be comfortable?" Again, it wasn't really a question.

After Kate went to her room, Sylvia sat on in the empty living room, shredding an unlit cigarette, and wondering what to do next. If Firuz were in Teheran, as Kate had been told, there ought to be a way of reaching him. Someone ought to let him know how things stood with his wife.

Sylvia waited until she was certain that Kate was asleep.

Fortunately, the time for international calls was right, and the Pakistani operator sounded bright and efficient. "Teheran, Iran? No problem," she assured Sylvia, and she was as good as her word. They were through in minutes. The only difficulty now was in getting past the Teheran operator, who fell into a deep silence after hearing the name "Nazar." She seemed to be sighing, but perhaps that was only the connection.

"Have you got the number?" said Sylvia.

"Hallo?" said the Teheran operator.

"Hello."

"Hallo."

"What is the telephone number of Firuz Nazar?"

"I don't know, my dear," said the Teheran operator.

"Well, please look it up."

"My dear, I don't know. He is gone travel."

"How do you know this?" Sylvia demanded. "Do you have a list of people travelling?"

"Germany," said the Teheran operator. "He is gone to Germany. He is gone."

"Listen," said Sylvia, speaking very slowly and enunciating each syllable. "Listen carefully now." There was no sound. "Are you listening?"

"My dear?"

"I'm calling for his wife—she is sick with worry about him—about Firuz Nazar, her husband. He's in Teheran—his embassy says so—his wife says so. His wife ought to know." Sylvia tried to project conviction, but the phrase "he's in Teheran" emerged without force; she didn't know. That was the embassy's official word, and Sylvia deeply doubted anything official.

There was no response from the Teheran operator.

"Hello, Teheran?" the Pakistani operator prodded.

"Have we lost the connection?" Sylvia asked.

A voice came through faintly: "Hallo."

"Are you looking up the number of Firuz Nazar?" Sylvia persisted.

"I don't know, my dear," said the Teheran operator.

"*Of course* you don't know," Sylvia said. "Please look up his number. In the phone book. Do you have the phone book? The directory? The list of telephone numbers? Are you trying?"

"My dear, I don't know."

"You don't know if you're *trying?*" Sylvia's voice rose

steeply. "*Vous parlez* . . . What's the use? Are you the *international* operator?"

The Pakistani operator intervened here, saying crisply: "Hello, Teheran—I want to speak to your supervisor. Your boss, understand? Bring your boss to the phone. Hello. Hello? Hello, Teheran?"

There was no answer. The Pakistani operator said to Sylvia: "I don't think she understands English. There's no answer. Hello? I don't think she disconnected us. I think she fell off the chair. Hello!"

A voice came through faintly: "Hallo?"

"Should I keep on?" asked the Pakistani operator.

"My dear?" said Teheran.

"Some other time," said Sylvia, who had a liking for decided matters and couldn't bear a moment more of this. "I'm sorry," said the Pakistani operator.

"You tried," said Sylvia, winding the telephone cord round and round her thumb, "you did all you could. You've been very helpful, very kind . . ."

"Only my job," said the Pakistani operator; she began to say something else, but already even the local connection was bad. The sky had opened up. A clap of thunder and the bursting of the rain effaced the rest of Sylvia's good-bye.

Firuz returned only a few hours later. It was barely twilight, but the lights in the living room were on. There was a fat woman he recognized, but wished he hadn't, asleep on the couch, head slouching on her ample chest, legs sprawled out. Slattern! She wore a short skirt and no stockings and he could see right up her legs to where the thighs spread and the swamp began. Firuz went on past, straight to the bedroom. He found Abdul Ghani stretched out in front of Kate's door, insensate. When Firuz prodded the sleeper with his foot, the old man whimpered and shifted sides. Firuz simply stepped over the body. Kate's door was

closed, he threw his whole weight upon it. Abdul Ghani
shot up to a sitting position and clapped his hands to his
ears; he gave a little shriek. Kate heard a muffled small
outcry.

"Firuz?" She stirred, shading her eyes.

Firuz stared at her in a silence of bitter recrimination.
Finally, he said, "I congratulate you, Khanum!"

Kate had nothing to answer; her mouth was dry as alum.
Muggy from the heavy sedation which had not yet run
its course, she struggled to get Firuz into focus. Unshaven,
his shoulders stooped, he seemed very changed. There
were grey smudges around his eyes; his clothes were rum-
pled and creased, as if he'd been living in them for
weeks.

"So . . . you tire of your lover and come creeping back.
You are a hundred cats!"

"You need a shower," said Kate.

"Get rid of that woman," he ordered. Kate looked puzzled. "Oh, don't tell me you don't know!"

Slamming doors, he went off to bathe.

Firuz's banging and shouting had wakened Sylvia. She
prepared to leave at once. None too soon, either. She felt
as if she had a touch of flu, she was so stiff and chilled.
Kate came in and sat down beside her: "Firuz is in one of
his moods," she explained. "That's all right," said Sylvia,
"I know when I'm not wanted."

"Nothing to do with you," said Kate, "I'll walk you to the
road." She was wearing only a thin housecoat, and shuddered a little from the chill. "You shouldn't go out in that,"
said Sylvia. "I'm going anyhow," said Kate. They crossed
the garden together. It was dusk. The rain had stopped, but
it was still wild and windy; Kate thought there might be
more rain to come. They stood together at the edge of the
road waiting for a taxi.

"I want you to promise, Kate. If you need anything,
please call, let me know—"

"We'll be in touch. Mike will be worried."

"Fat chance. He's on a flight to Bangkok. I knew what I was getting into when I married an airline pilot, so I can't complain. Feel just like a sailor's wife. Did you know what you were getting in for, Kate?"

"Who could?"

"You promise now? I'll keep on calling if I don't hear," said Sylvia. "What friends are for—" A taxi had come up. She blew a kiss.

"Promise." Kate waved her away with a sensation of water rushing through her fingers.

She turned back. Her hair was wetted dark and streaming, it fell over her shoulders in long clumps, like ropes. Crossing the garden, she watched her feet. The grass was shimmering, strung with tiny flowers whose names she did not know, frail hectic lamps. The grass shone darkly. Her slippers were heavy, soaked.

The longer she lingered in the garden, the less the dampness touched her. She was amazed at how quickly the spring came on in this country. The jacaranda looked blue and spiky in the fading light. Already the green mulberries were whitening on the trees, shaped like tiny hearts, the color of smoke or cobwebs, faint, faint-hearted . . . Kate no longer knew whether she was hot or cold. As she mounted the verandah steps, a sharp gust shook the overhanging trees. A leaf in the shape of an open fan swooped down and blotted out her mouth. She snatched it away with a violent motion.

Abdul Ghani was up and fussing in the dining room. "Sahib wanting dinner?" he asked. Kate didn't know, and neither she nor Abdul Ghani had the courage to ask Firuz. They waited in silence.

Firuz went directly from his bath to his bed in the guest room. He shut the door and locked it. "That seems to be the answer," said Kate, "no dinner." This time, Abdul Ghani did not protest. Kate turned off the lights and returned to her own bed, relieved at the postponement; but her sleep had been badly interrupted and it was a long time before she fell off again.

Early the next morning, she rose and went directly to the dining room. Firuz had been up and stirring for a long while, but he'd not yet emerged from the guest room.

The table had been set, but not in the usual way. Normally, Firuz and Kate sat side by side or just across the breadth of the table, but today it was set at head and foot, at the farthermost ends, as though for visiting dignitaries. A great array of silverware, too, and cloth napkins. In Abdul Ghani's mind, at least, this was an occasion of great solemnity.

There was still time to rearrange the setting; Kate could have done it, or a word to Abdul Ghani would have been sufficient, but she could not utter that word. What would be, would be. She could alter nothing.

Firuz entered. Husband and wife faced one another across the gleaming expanse of the great banquet table. They sat stiffly, staring at their plates. Only the clashing of silver and the sounds of eating could be heard.

Since Firuz and Kate did not speak, Abdul Ghani spent his time shuttling from one end of the table to the other, passing the salt, cream, and sugar, shaking his head and clucking to himself all the while. Finally, Firuz said: "You can go now. Memsahib will call you when it's time to clear."

As soon as the old man left, Firuz said to Kate: "I think you better get out of the country as soon as you can—while you still can. There's something like a war on."

Kate did not know what war he was referring to. All she knew was that she felt laid waste by his words, and more than the words, by the tone of them. It might have been a machine talking: nothing was resonant, nothing was warm.

Waiting for a response, Firuz set down his teacup, then

lifted it a finger's breadth to study the ring of wetness beneath. "You have nothing to say? You're smiling."

She did seem to be smiling faintly. She touched her lips to feel the thing spread, like a wound.

"Why don't you answer?"

She did not know what answer to give. She touched her lips again with her forefinger: a thin even line. The smile had retreated. It surprised her, the smile before, the evenness now.

"As you came with no dowry, you can hardly expect anything back." He dabbed his lips delicately with his napkin. He folded the cloth into fourths and placed it on the spoon side of his plate.

Kate felt a rush of heat. Everything she looked upon, cup and spoon, her own clenched hand, all throbbed with life. "I am," she said, and couldn't finish. Blood clamored in her ears. "I'm tough!" she managed to blurt out.

"Really?" he said with quiet scorn. "You don't say."

"I will be," she amended. And then, when she saw he didn't believe her, she announced: "I've already called the embassy. It will take a couple of weeks to fix up my American passport."

Now the balance had shifted, and Firuz—his bluff called—reached unsteadily for his napkin to cover his mouth. His lips quivered, he covered them hastily. He made some low sounds into the cloth as though he were clearing his throat. His eyes were red.

Let him weep, she said to herself, he has enough reasons.

She would not go to him. He wept in another language, it was nothing to her. No sympathy now, none, or she'd be swept away. She made an effort to continue eating.

Firuz was certain now: he'd been wronged and wronged again. She had no remorse, no shame; she was not worth his sorrow. The realization made him bitter, cold, efficient. "I'm glad," he said at last, "you really must go."

They exchanged no further word that morning. After

breakfast, Firuz left for the office. He stayed away until evening, when they attended a reception together.

It was an all-Iranian affair, celebrating Chahar Shambeh Soori, and, despite the unusual agitation in the city, the festivities were proceeding as planned. Only one alteration: the ambassador would not be present. Alavi was tied up with the local officials, and Agha Sorabi, the chargé d'affaires, presided.

Together in that public room, Firuz and Kate were more cordial to each other than they had been in weeks. They were able to smile at one another and say pleasant things —a truce of sorts, and very restful for both of them.

The usual people were present. "Sit here! Sit here!" they cried, making ritualistic motions of attempting to rise—a slight falling-forward, accompanied by murmurs of "Ya Ali!" A flutter of many hands indicated the place where they should sit: the place of honor, farthest from the door. This was another ritual. Firuz and Kate then refused pride of place, as they were expected to do, seating themselves at a modest distance from the door. Kate found herself sitting next to Khanum Emiri; they greeted one another with elaborate ceremony. "How are your children?" Kate asked. "Fine, thank God," Khanum Emiri replied, "they kiss your hands." Kate had to keep the conversation going, so she said: "What a lovely dress!" Khanum Emiri replied: "Your eyes are lovely." Khanum Emiri lifted a silver dish: "You will have some sweets?" Kate replied: "No, thank you, may your hand not ache." The two women went on like this for some minutes.

Mercifully, Khanum Emiri asked no questions about Firuz's trip. Kate, herself, had asked Firuz nothing and, of course, he'd answered not at all to the questions she failed to ask. From time to time, Kate noticed people glancing in her direction. What did they know about her? Agha Emiri knew *something*. Was he the man she'd seen at the cabaret? He stared at Kate openly, rudely, smiled at her repeatedly with an insinuating expression. His gaze traveled the length of her body, slow and clinging, and left her feeling soiled.

Then Shirin, one of the Emiri daughters, came up to Kate, whispered something in her ear. Kate stood up and excused herself. As they walked out of the room, they could hear Khanum Emiri speaking quite loudly, as though for Kate's benefit: "People don't say a thing like that unless there *is* something!"

Shirin wanted to show Kate how Iranian children celebrated the end of winter. In the middle of the courtyard was a small fire, built of twigs. Children were jumping over the fire, chanting to it: "My paleness to you! Your redness to me!"

Kate lingered by the fire, watching the sprinters, smiling —her face shattered with smiles. A young woman had gathered over in the corner all the toddlers too small to jump over the fire. About to tell a story, she raised a finger to her lips. Kate was able to recognize the traditional invocation when it came: "There was one, there was none, there was none but the One . . ."

The eve of Chahar Shambeh Soori was a harbinger holiday, preceding the Persian New Year. The new year fell on the first day of spring. Kate wondered what the year ahead had in store for her. A journey, she was almost sure of it.

Yes, most certainly, there would be a long journey . . . The garden was full of shaken lights. Kate wiped her eyes. "The fire," she explained to Shirin, "it makes my eyes sting." They went back inside.

Supper was buffet. Kate mixed and mingled skillfully. She was doing better all the time. The less she cared, the better she performed. Her command of the language was growing, just when she no longer needed it.

Firuz, too, marveled at Kate's performance: the false glittering smile, the facile courtesies. How socially adept she

had become, how consummate in deception! An actress
. . . He turned away, it made him sick to watch her.

While the women chattered, the men discussed politics,
always returning to Iranian developments. Land reform in
the provinces was the great issue: it touched most of the
men directly, for nearly all were from landowning families
and now felt themselves disinherited. One by one, the
Shah was cutting up the great estates and distributing them
to the peasants. Selling it to the peasants on installments,
actually. Everyone knew that the peasants would be unable
to afford it, that they didn't know how to repair wells, or
look after improvements, or plan for the future. Sorabi had
questioned one of his father's oldest tenants on the
changes. He'd asked about the parliamentary elections that
were coming up: "Now that the landlord won't tell you how
to vote, who will?"

"Oh, the government," said the peasant cheerfully.

They laughed a little at that, then faltered, wondering
whether they should have. Sorabi's loyalty to the government was, of course, above suspicion, but others of the
group . . .

No one spoke of the mounting agitation in Lahore, although Kate had noticed one of the bearers going round
earlier, passing out mimeographed sheets to each of the
men. Kate had caught some mention of curfews in connection with the paper, but more than that, she couldn't follow; Firuz had folded up the memo without seeming to look
at it, placing it in his breast pocket. Kate would have to wait
to be told.

Not long after dinner, Firuz signaled to Kate, and they
rose to go. Everyone protested their leaving so soon. The
Sorabis saw Kate and Firuz to the door; they said what was
always said on leaving:

"May your shadow never grow less."

"May your favor never grow less."

"May I be your sacrifice."

By accident or habit, Firuz put his hand on Kate's shoulder as they stood at the door. He withdrew it quickly when the rituals of parting were over.

The minute they were alone in the taxi together, their faces hardened and the long silence resumed.

22
Power

That night, once again, Firuz and Kate slept in separate bedrooms: Firuz in the guest room, Kate in the master bedroom next door. Kate took the precaution of locking the adjoining door from her side before getting into bed, but it was only a half-hearted measure. Firuz had his own key, and Kate had never drawn the upper sliding bolt—she was afraid that it would make too much noise and further anger him.

Shortly before midnight, Kate was awakened by the glare of the overhead light. She struggled to sit up, alarmed, but not really surprised: she knew who it would be. Firuz hesitated in the doorway, regarding her without speaking.

"What's up?"

"You needn't make your feelings that clear," he said, coming forward and settling on the edge of her bed. She shifted her legs so there'd be no contact.

"What do you want of me?"

"What any man wants of his wife—'*ezzat*,' we call it. What you call 'honor.' A wife is her husband's honor . . ."

He stared at her, hoping for signs of remorse. There were none.

"It's possible—barely possible—that I've made a mistake," he said. He offered this. But Kate remained impassive.

"Big of you," she said.

"What? Speak up!"

"An expression," she said, too weary to explain.

"One chance in a thousand," he said. "After all, I have proof."

"Proof!" she spat the word out. "You'll never know."

Firuz stared and Kate followed his gaze, resting on a patch of darkened skin. "A bruise . . ." she said absently, "I bruise easily." She adjusted her nightgown, covering her shoulder.

At last Firuz was on the trail of something, something which had eluded him before. Assured of his purpose now, he took hold of the nightgown and uncovered the bruise again. It was shaped like a crescent.

"What are you doing?" Kate cried. Her eyes were a blue blaze. The devil also had eyes of that color.

"What do you think you're doing?" she cried. The light hurt her eyes. She raised her pillow to cover the exposed shoulder. Firuz tore the pillow from her hands and applied himself to the bruise. He traced its shape with the greatest care, as a painter might copy the fold of a drape or the curvature of a lip. This, then, was the mark of her lover's mouth: a narrow, pinched ellipse, the mouth of a viper. Touching the bruise, Firuz touched the mouth of the strange man who had so wounded him; the man's head pressed against his neck. Firuz shuddered; he felt a stranger's sweat, cool upon his own skin, the man's breath hot in his ear . . .

Here it was at last: a tangible mark, indisputable evidence, a signature. Firuz's hand strayed and brushed Kate's neck, lifting her hair, he moved softly, trailing his fingertips. Lightly . . . Kate stared at him without moving, she seemed to be paralyzed. For an instant, Firuz did not know what he was going to do next. His fingers were almost caressing her skin.

The sight of his hand with its black hairs, creeping, crawling, the servile, spiderlike, crouching motion of that hand, brought Firuz up short. She was lying to him now, she had lied to him before. She brought mud into his house, she blackened his face with shame, she whored through the night and came creeping home when she was done! He drew his hand away suddenly and as suddenly returned, this time, the rigid flat of his palm—hard—

As Kate fended for her face, Firuz struck blindly at her hands, the offending shoulder, her ear. She buried her face in her hands; he pulled them away and struck again.

For once, she did not weep; she made no sound at all.

His wrist ached, and now Firuz paused and wept without shame, brokenly. What had he done? Kate's body was his own, flesh of his flesh. But opaque to him, opposed to him. He hated the broad muscles of her neck as she tensed herself against him, hated the solidity of her bones, the impenetrability of her skull, the wildness of her hair, the chill blueness of her eyes.

Her eyes were so blue they seemed to him unreal. He saw himself, minute, diminished in her eyes. His hand ached and his head, too, as if he'd been slapping his own face.

She turned away from him: when she spoke it was with eyes averted. Her left ear was ringing. She spoke quietly, without emphasis. Without interest, as though she were speaking of someone she knew only second or thirdhand. "I was riding in the rickshaw, one of those scooter cabs. The driver was going too fast and tipped over."

But Firuz didn't seem to be listening. He stretched out his hands and stared at them, and then at Kate's shoulder.

He raised one hand to his mouth. Carefully, almost experimentally, he bit into the palm of his right hand. The curvature was wide, unexpectedly wide. No grown man could have made the mark on Kate's shoulder, only an infant's mouth was that narrow.

Firuz sat perfectly motionless, so arrested by his new perception that he did not seem to breathe. He'd made a mistake: his one certainty had been dead wrong. He might have made other mistakes . . . But no, there was still the question of Kate's night at the cabaret; he had a witness to that. *That* was something she'd have to explain. Let her try. No—it would be full of lies, he couldn't bear to hear it.

Still . . . the bartender had told him she'd gone with no one. "That night," he said, "the night we came back from Lahore."

She shrugged but didn't answer. One of her cheeks was red, the other dead white.

He reached over, took Kate's downcast head in both hands, and raised it until their eyes met.

"I wouldn't care if I didn't love you," he said softly.

"What?"

"I forgive you," he said with some congestion, and the words were performatory; he was at once full to the brim with forgiveness. "I forgive you," he repeated.

"Forgive?" she echoed stupidly. Who was doing what to whom? He was out to confuse her, to destroy her mind. She gazed at him, eyes wide. His words reaped confusion, but his hand had clarified.

"You have nothing to say?" Firuz regarded her fixedly, certain that she would give in and speak, or else crumple in tears.

But he'd miscalculated. Silence gathered between them, and the phone ringing just at that moment interrupted nothing. Kate locked the door when Firuz stepped out to answer it. This time she drew the upper bolt.

The phone continued to ring. Firuz hesitated before answering; he'd been listening to Kate struggle with the bolt and ram it home; this sound, more than anything she had said or not said, gave him pause. "Yes?" he spoke absently into the receiver.

It was Ambassador Alavi calling. He made the faintest of apologies for the lateness of the hour: the situation was urgent. There were three emergency meetings scheduled for tomorrow: one at the embassy, one at a mosque, and a third, scheduled for late in the afternoon, with the Governor of West Pakistan at a location yet to be disclosed. The Governor had most particularly requested Firuz's presence as an eyewitness to events in Cyrilabad. Firuz was at pains to explain, as he had explained before, that he had spent his time in detention at the town hotel and had seen nothing. No one believed him.

Firuz returned to bed, and troubled as he was, sheer exhaustion overtook him at last. He slept deeply and dreamlessly for several hours. When he woke, the house was already bustling; Kate must have been quarreling with Abdul Ghani, for Abdul Ghani was hurling abuse at the sweeper, quite as other mornings. Yes, everything sounded rather normal.

Firuz stepped out onto the verandah in his pajamas and ordered the gardener to hop on his bicycle and pick up a newspaper. At breakfast, he surveyed the morning's headlines. The news was not good. International news was crowded into insignificance by conflicting local reports. The lead story, phrased to produce reassurance and calm, did not reassure. Its banner read:

SITUATION NORMAL ALL OVER COUNTRY

Underneath that:

Incidents In Some Cities

In a single article, statement and contradiction followed so quickly upon one another that they succeeded only in cancelling each other out. The situation might not have been so confusing if two voices were apparent, but there was only one voice blandly narrating, uttering contradiction after contradiction with robotlike composure and persistence.

The other headlines were similarly dizzying:

RIOTING IN AMRITSAR AND FEROZEPORE: PROTEST TEMPLE THEFTS . . .

RALLIES IN RADPUR—CURFEW IMPOSED . . .

MILD LATHI-CHARGE IN LAHORE. CITY CALM . . .

DAYLONG FAST IN CYRILABAD . . .

ARSON IN CALCUTTA. CURFEW CALLED . . . COMMUNAL VIOLENCE SPREADS . . .

12 HURT IN MULTAN TEARGASSING . . . NEW CASES OF SMALLPOX . . .

FIRING IN HYDERABAD CONDEMNED—CITY NORMAL . . .

COMMENTARY: HAMLET-LIKE MOOD OF THE NATION . . .

STRIKE IN KARACHI: PRIVATE TRANSPORT TO PLY NORMALLY . . .

ISLAM GROWING AT TREMENDOUS RATE IN U.S. . . .

Oddly enough, the most reassuring piece of news was the most grotesque; it gave an air of normalcy, of normal insanity, to the day. A cannibal had been apprehended on the footpath near Government College for Women—he'd been caught in the act of removing the liver and heart of his victim.

Firuz's long reading went on. He held the paper close to his eyes, and Kate couldn't see his face behind the little barrier. She listened to the crepitation of newsprint, heard a cough, two coughs, a dry scissoring sound. She had no intention of being the first to speak.

Then, after what seemed an inordinate time, Firuz

folded the paper neatly and set it down. "I have to go soon," he announced. Kate did not reply. He'd begun sucking his tea through a sugar cube held between his teeth, and the sound was abnormally grating to her. "I might be held up. Meetings all day. They might go on all night, I don't know when I'll be back. Don't bother to wait up for me—not that you would." He glanced at Kate to see how she was taking this. No response. "You're not to go out today, do you understand? Can you do this one simple thing for your own safety?"

Kate seemed to have heard; she nodded slightly.

"I suppose you have no idea what's going on here—all around you."

That was too much, and Kate was forced to speak at last. "I have no idea. You never wanted me to know anything before. Since I'm leaving, it hardly seems worthwhile finding out."

Firuz said nothing to dispute this. He rapped loudly, with his ring, on the table. Abdul Ghani approached at a leisurely pace, stood in a sloppy parade-rest position and said:

"Yes, sahib—you called?"

"When I call you're to come quickly—*jeldi*. Understand?"

Abdul Ghani hitched up his billowing trousers. "Very good, sahib. What you say."

"And stand up straight. Look sharp."

"This is old man, sahib. Much work—many *burra sahibs* I working. All say Abdul Ghani *accha*, first class. Abdul Ghani good service. All say—English mem—all."

"Did you hear that?" Firuz seemed to be addressing Kate. "He loves telling me he was trained by a British mem—can you believe it? A pimp from Kabul, more likely!"

Firuz fished in his pocket for some bills, counted them. "There you are." He placed them on the table. Abdul Ghani took up the packet, wetted his thumb, and proceeded to count the bills for himself. "No, sahib," he said, returning the packet, "this not right."

"Oohoo—not right? This magistrate says his pay is not right!" Firuz began to shout. "I suppose you want a raise?"

"Yes, sahib."

"And you deserve a raise?"

"Yes, sahib!" with conviction. "Much owing, sahib," and Abdul Ghani went on to explain rapidly in Urdu and English. Due to strict fasting during the entire month of Ramadan, he had managed to save the Nazars quite a few rupees. It had given him a flux and he'd been sick for two weeks afterward. He'd eaten nothing but rice and tea when he was sick, so that also was a saving.

"What did you say you were sick with?" Firuz asked.

"Flux, sahib."

"Flux comes from overeating, Abdul Ghani."

"No—no eating—" Abdul Ghani was prepared to give an account of all the food he hadn't eaten.

Firuz grew quite pale listening. "How many months ago was last Ramadan? You think I'm a fool? You have such faith that you want to be paid back? What kind of faith is that?"

"This pay not right, sahib."

"Why should I pay for your fasts? That's between you and God . . ."

"No good, this. Sahib, sir."

"Why are you shaking so?"

"Flux and thunder, sahib!"

"You're upset—why are you upset? Have you done something wrong?"

Abdul Ghani was trembling from head to foot. "I working good service. I go now—first-class house."

"Go, then. What? Aren't you gone? Go! By all means, leave. Do you think you are such a treasure that I can't do without you? I'll get a new servant. A new servant runs like a gazelle. Not like you, Abdul Ghani—"

Abdul Ghani gave a little snort and stamped out of the room. Firuz scraped back his chair and scooped up the newspaper. The money fluttered from table to floor. Kate watched the bills scatter.

"My palace . . ." Firuz said bitterly. The rest of his sentence was lost in the hallway.

Kate remained sitting at the breakfast table until she heard doors slam at opposite ends of the house. "Money seems to mean nothing to them," she said to the air. She stooped to gather the bills and stacked them under the salt shaker. She knew that Abdul Ghani would creep back to them. Pride was, after all, a luxury here.

23
Nightwatch

After his conversation with Latif, Nirmal had acted swiftly and without hesitation; he had moved like a man under orders who knows clearly what he must do, because it is the only thing he can do. Both Latif and Rahman were supportive, although Latif pronounced it a stratagem of last resource, and Nirmal did not correct him.

The plan was called "honorable retreat." It was something more radical than amnesty that Nirmal proposed to announce, it was oblivion, indifference; if the relic were returned before a certain deadline, there would be no penalty, no attempt at investigation, the record would be closed. But once the prescribed period had lapsed—Nirmal was as adamant as the others on this—the authorities would prosecute in full measure.

Only Waheed had balked, disagreeing, as he made clear, "in principle." "Thieves must be punished," he said flatly, with the air of a man reciting an axiom. "As Superintendent of Police, that's what I'm here for."

Nirmal put the question bluntly to Waheed: "Which would you prefer—the holy relic safe in the place where it belongs, or the thieves without the relic—the relic destroyed in an effort to avoid incrimination?" A loaded question, and Waheed muttered a little about the unfairness of the choice, then admitted he would prefer having the relic safe and sound. "Then," said Nirmal, "the only item up for discussion is implementation." Nirmal had gotten out of the habit of authority, but it was coming back to him now.

Implementation was another matter, and Waheed, having vented his reservations, raised no further objections. He turned out to be most helpful. Whatever his unhappiness with Nirmal's plan, Waheed believed in an orderly chain of command, in stability and structure, and he would work to preserve it.

Together the group drafted a public announcement giving instructions for return of the holy hair. The reticule should be wrapped to withstand shock—several layers of cloth were recommended—then dropped into any post box in the city. By midday tomorrow, the police and postal authorities would be out emptying them all. The night of honorable retreat would begin at sundown. People were advised to return to their homes and pray for the recovery of the relic.

No effort was made to consult with the members of the Holy Relic Action Committee or to solicit their approval. Nirmal felt strongly about this: his crisis management team was the legitimate authority in the city, and the Action Committee was spurious, self-appointed.

Husamuddin thought the same: "It's about time you took the initiative from them." The two men were in constant touch, the Chief Secretary still steadfast in his support. "You're the man on the spot. It's up to you to make the decisions." Husamuddin then proceeded to regale Nirmal with the latest bad news. Communal violence had spread as far east as Calcutta. "Calcutta?" said Nirmal, his voice sinking, "I don't see—"

"You know the story as well as I. Any excuse. Some

Hindus deface a mosque in sympathy for the theft of that temple in Radpur. Naturally, an insult like that can't go unanswered, it's the old story . . ."

Back to the strategy of honorable retreat: Indian representatives and the Radpur town officials would have to be informed of the deadline and the general features of the plan. It was extremely short notice, although Husamuddin was in full agreement that they had no time to lose.

Word from the High Commissioner for India in Karachi came to Nirmal promptly; the message was sharp and clear; the trouble in Cyrilabad was Pakistan's problem; India had no interest in Pakistan's internal affairs.

In any event, there had been no opening up of the border, although, for this one night only, the boundary force had been reduced on the Pakistani side. If the thieves came from India, Nirmal assumed that having successfully come across once, they'd manage to do it again. But the plan of honorable retreat was based on the premise, never stated, yet clear to all who thought it through, that the theft was a wholly internal matter, that there'd been no Indian involvement.

Gradually, the building emptied out for the evening; tonight only a skeleton staff was to remain. Footsteps sounded and resounded in the half-deserted building. Nirmal heard a solitary typewriter tapping.

Dusk.

Silence, the stammering of his heart, a dread incertitude. How hard it was to wait and do nothing!

Nirmal settled himself in the familiar posture at the familiar place. He cleared a space for his elbows; the heaps of dispatches were nothing but clutter now, all out-of-date. He loosened his belt and his shoelaces, but remained in place—he felt he had to hold himself in readiness. For what, he could not say.

He would take the hours one by one.

The dark came on rapidly. By nine o'clock, nearly everyone had gone home. The dial of Nirmal's watch was luminous, with feeble white pulsings; the numerals seemed to be faintly humming. It was so quiet . . . not even the rain for company. Nirmal could hear the bearer with his wife on the floor above. He heard panting and grappling, a dark stifled moan. Animal sounds, he thought. But he knew they were human sounds, human, and lost to him now. He tried to remember, but couldn't recall, the fever and the ache, he couldn't remember, it was already so far away.

Nine o'clock. What was Meena doing at this hour? Locking up, probably. Or waiting on the verandah until the darkness was complete.

Meena was much on his mind. He fetched a sheet of paper and uncapped his pen. He wrote the date and then: *"My dear sister—I am working nine days out of seven."* Then paused, pen tipped to his ear.

He wrote: *"If only . . ."* He cast a lingering glance over his cot. If only . . . what?

No, no use sleeping, in case he were able to sleep. He would only open himself up to what he could not control; he did not trust his dreams. Besides, he told himself, a man responsible for public welfare does not sleep. He thought irreverently of that Tartar, Mongol or Hun, who was buried upright mounted on his horse. And if the weight of the earth hadn't unhorsed him, he was mounted still.

"If only . . ." The words stuck; he crossed them out and started a new line. There was not much Nirmal could safely say to his sister; each sentence would give new grounds for worry.

If you asked Nirmal why he had never married, he would have said "for Meena." Meena, if asked why she had never married, would have said, "because of Nirmal—he's alone." The truth was—Nirmal did not know what the truth was. Meena had no real choice, that much was clear. And Nirmal? Nirmal had his reserve, which he had not chosen, a need for privacy so ingrained and deep he could not explain it. His diffidence had only increased with the years; at first, he'd held himself back so as not to be misunderstood—for protection, he supposed—but, little by little, laying reticence upon reticence, it was as if he'd raised a wall around himself, which precluded understanding, too, and now the wall encroached as much as it protected. It was more than simple castelessness, devastating as that was, that had worked against his one sally at courtship. The girl he'd wanted had come from a strict Hindu family, but there had been no dearth of fine and willing Christian daughters to choose from. The impediment was in himself, a need for distance, a certain habit of refusal. Passions obscured, proprieties compromised, narrowed. Unattached, Nirmal retained his clarity. His immaculate clarity. Yet there were times when he was overcome by a sense of impersonality, remoteness, the attenuation of things, a fading within hours when he wandered among abstractions, bodiless among the bodiless, an estrangement so great he was forced to touch everything in sight. Strange, that only touch could center him.

He hadn't married, but at least he'd had his chances. Life had not been so kind to Meena; bright and loving and beautiful, she'd grown up expecting nothing. Although she had fine features, and gold and silver were brilliant against her skin, she was far too dark for beauty. As an infant, she'd been massaged with saffron, whitened with flour, bathed in goat's milk, stroked with unguents, oils, bleaching agents, salves—anything to achieve a decent sallowness. Nothing worked. One special lotion, tried in adolescence, had burned off patches of skin on her hands and cheeks, leaving her mottled for months. And that was the final indignity; after that, everyone left Meena alone.

It was odd . . . Islam and Christianity were color-blind, caste-blind; that was why so many untouchables converted. And yet, when it came to marriage, the same rigid preferences remained—"fair" or "wheat-colored."

So, for one reason or another, neither had married. And what difference did it make, really? Nirmal and Meena had their domestic rituals, their shared memories, much as any couple. For other needs, Nirmal had gone elsewhere—as did many married men. Except for children, there was nothing lacking.

Except for children . . . No use raking that particular ground.

"Crisis is tiring," he wrote, "I'm counting on that." The letter came quite easily now. Nirmal wrote on without stopping, hesitating only at the end. He did not sign or seal the letter. If all went well, he might be home before the next post. It was possible, barely possible. He wasn't counting on it, though.

Nirmal leaned back and lit his pipe—four matches until the pipe took hold. The smoke rose in lazy clumps and coils. His eyes kept making horizontal tracks, as though he were still reading dispatches. What if the relic were returned and stolen again, all in the same night? It *could* happen, there was no comforting answer.

Allah's reign, and I—the instrument of Allah, he thought wryly. Instrument or plaything? he wondered. Time would tell.

Nothing for Nirmal to do now but to wait for the end of the retreat, still many hours off. The city would manage itself in the interim, the new day would come punctually, the morning, the fateful morning would come.

The long night dragged on. Nirmal was reluctant to extinguish the lamp, although darkness might have refreshed his eyes. His pipe went cold; he set it down; his hand fell of its own weight; his lips closed indifferently. It was the time of night when the tides of life ran low.

Three in the morning. Nirmal remained at his desk. He clicked his tongue against the stones of his teeth, then paused to listen. He thought he heard someone barefoot, running in circles. He waited. Silence. The sound—faded, gone if it ever was. Not a mouse stirring.

How far away everything was . . . His own hands seemed to live at the other end of the table. He raised his right hand to the lamp and cupped the bare bulb; his fingers shrilled at the touch. The pain restored him to himself for as long as it lasted.

Half past three. Nirmal's wakefulness was bringing in steadily diminishing returns. Still, he would not sleep. To make the time pass, he began to calculate: minutes in an hour, seconds in a minute, seconds in a day, in a decade, head hairs per square centimeter—two hundred to three hundred, he imagined. The minutes went by, but the hours lingered.

Tom was cold, chilled through and through. He didn't know why. Inadequate food, maybe. He'd been given a blanket, but it wasn't much use—a threadbare brown blanket, long since denuded of its warming hairs.

He dreamed of escape, but even in dreams, his plans went bust. He was in parts and scattered. Quickly, he tried to gather up his arms and legs, fingers and toes, to scrape the little bits together and try and dash out the door while it was open. But there were too many scattered bits. He lunged forward, dropping a finger, stooped, dropped another— The door slammed. He woke with a start.

Too many details, his hands useless . . .

He missed his pipe and reamer, the little pick, spoon, and press that had given him so much innocent pleasure. Tom stared at his hands often these days, at the speckles like foxed paper, where the fats had begun to fry.

His vision was, by turns, flyspecked or spotted with tears, encapsulated tears. There was one consolation in this: he was never alone. His floaters enlivened the walls before him as graffiti might have done, they brought a touch of home into his cell.

Barbara came often to mind—an endearment, an image, sometimes a little rash of remembrance in the crook of his arm, where she liked to rest her head. He thought, for moments at a time, of marriage. What if he'd married Barbara, what then?

But he knew the answer all too well. Then the very predictable would have started again; there'd have been some other "dear little fox," and Barbara would have begun to chafe and whine in the manner of all wives. Tom's mistresses had always been "little foxes" and "minxes," animals wily and mischievous, corresponding to the sly things in himself.

Tom brooded monotonously over his predicament, but there was little progression in his thoughts. His imprisonment had come as a rather severe surprise, a definite fall. A fortunate fall, perhaps? Perhaps. Fortunate—how? As a poke in the scrotum is fortunate: an awakening at least.

Tom had been spoiled since his earliest days; he'd been aware of it before this, but had cause to give it more thought now. As a doting mother's only child, it had been unreal expectations from the start: boundless exclusive love and unfaltering reward; she'd even filled his sandbox with trinkets and seashells, marbles, wrapped sweets and toys, so that every turn of his shovel was blessed. Clearly, this set no realistic precedent for actual life to come. The impact of reality, impersonal, profoundly indifferent, utterly random in the bestowal of favors and gifts, had always been unexpected, shattering.

Outside, a sudden hammering began. It had been unusually quiet for some time. An eerie silence, after so much seething. The hammering ended, and the silence resumed. Peaceful, yet Tom didn't trust it. He could hear someone coughing on the floor above him, it was that still.

Tom moved to the window. Still quiet. A single star, incomparably high, far, and cold. Nothing that matters to us matters. He pressed his face against the bars. The hammering began again. Louder this time, sharper. He heard wood snapping and splintering—a single musket shot—a cry: "hai!"—

"Hassan!" Tom called.

There was no reply.

Tom went over to the door, peeked through the viewing slot: no sign of the guard on night duty. He rattled the door.

To his amazement, it gave: simply swung open. The noise was considerable—the creak of oars in tholepins. Tom stood for a minute, too stunned to move. This was no dream, yet all the barriers seemed to have dissolved. He stood on the threshold of an open door, on the brink of freedom, unopposed. Was it a trick? Tom considered simply shutting the door, but to do so would cause it to creak again—he'd be guilty in any case.

He leaned out. The hallway seemed to be deserted, but it was so dark, Tom couldn't tell for sure. He crept out, two, three steps. Dark and dank. No one about. His flipflops made a slapping sound on the tiles, so he took them off and tucked them under his arm.

The corridor was long and straight and dim. Where would he go when he got to the end of it? Tom had no idea. He hadn't a brown Abe in his pocket. No pockets. Suppose he managed to make his way into the streets, what would he do then? There was nowhere he wanted to go. He thought the sounds he'd been hearing might have been a gun. Dark streets, strange ones, strangers, a loose gun, were waiting for him out there. The police were holding his passport, so he'd have no way of explaining himself.

Tom halted in midpassage, debating his next steps. He heard a soft scraping, a phrase "tat!" repeated twice, a dot of thunder. Then a voice whispering: *"Deko!"* It came from somewhere in front of him—the stairs? The landing? He froze in place. But the voices dwindled away. Now! The coast was clear.

Clear to where?

He turned and crept back to his cell. The familiar scene, bed, basin, pitcher, welcomed him back. Tom was overcome with relief. How strange to be closing the door on himself! He eased it shut gently, but the door sounded, seemed to speak: "ah, oh . . ." The noise was shocking.

Nothing happened.

Some minutes later, he heard footsteps. Tom knew the spacing of that tread—it was Hassan, the negligent, returning to his post. It was more reassuring than not, actually, having Hassan close by. Tom stretched out on the bed. He decided to keep his ears open for a while.

Soon the new day would be breaking. Everything was possible still, or so Nirmal liked to think for the day had not yet happened, a white thread could not yet be distinguished from a black, it was not technically dawn.

The *azan* for the setting of the stars broke the predawn hush. "Prayer is better than sleep," the voice of the muezzin rippled over the housetops. Perhaps . . . Nirmal thought, but sleep can be very sweet. Nirmal was ravenous, with the hunger of a man who has labored all through the night, although he had only sat on patiently, waiting for the night to end. He rambled down the hall to see if anyone was stirring. Not a soul. He had no idea where the tea things were kept; in fact, Nirmal had no idea where he was heading.

At the end of the hallway, he ventured down a short flight of steps. There was another corridor, and at the end of it, an overnight lockup; the night guard was sitting on a stool alongside the door, sound asleep, his head nodding. I ought to wake him, Nirmal told himself. He coughed; when that brought no response, he stepped forward loudly. The jailor failed to stir. Nirmal peered though the viewing grate; the light was bad.

A man with greying hair was stretched out on the *charpoi*. His legs extended over the edge; he was tall. Was this the American? The one he'd been asked to refrigerate? It must be. The man slept in a wide sprawl, with an abandon Nirmal thought typically American. All energy, no discipline.

The sleeping figure drew his limbs closer together, as

though aware of being observed. What's he doing here? Nirmal wondered. As soon as he straightened out other, more pressing matters, he'd have to look into it.

It wasn't until Nirmal reached the top of the steps that he realized he'd forgotten about waking the jailor. He ought to go back, he told himself, but then he'd have to come up again and he was too tired for that. He wasn't thinking at all clearly.

Tom listened as Nirmal's footsteps faded. He had not been sleeping. He'd heard the new man approach, and held his breath as the stranger looked in. Tom could tell the man was a stranger, because his footfall was unfamiliar, slow and uneven, with wide intervals between the steps. A tall and exhausted man, Tom judged. Neither of his jailors were tall. This was the hour when. Before dawn, wasn't it, when . . . ? Tom couldn't finish the question, even to himself. One eyelid jumped: Tom ordered it shut—without result, then lifted it ever so slightly in appeasement. He'd seen the flaring wedge of a nose, a dark eye. The eye seemed huge in its hollow; it blinked and stared. Tom had tried his best not to breathe or shift his limbs.

Nothing but silence after that, and an empty grill where the eye had been, and, finally, Tom slept.

No sleep for Nirmal; he returned to his office. He would have to wait for his tea.

The room was cold, with that peculiar chill that comes just before dawn. It was the odd hour, grey out and bone cold, with the sun coming up and the street lamps still shining—a thin, shivery light. He'd left his desk lamp burning. How pale it seemed now, such a dim solace, as the light gained all around him.

There was something on his desk that had not been there before.

24
Daybreak

So—

A small parcel wrapped in a shawl of white wool. It glowed in the chill greyness of the room, and Nirmal stretched out his hands to it as though to a warming fire. He folded his stiff limbs into a chair, lifted the bundle onto his lap, and began to unwind the cloth. Fold after fold, his hand went round in narrowing spiral motion.

Lulled by the motion of his hand, by the light grazing of the wool against his skin, Nirmal did not pause to ask what he would find: he knew. The reticule when he came to it, was small and unimposing. It looked quite ordinary—like a stout thermometer, with silver caps at both ends.

Neither cold nor warm.

It radiated nothing. Holding it carefully by the tips, Nirmal lifted the capsule to the light. It certainly looked ancient enough; the glass tube was encrusted and murky— from reverential rubbings, he assumed. All but impossible to make out what it contained. The tube wasn't empty; more than that, Nirmal couldn't say.

Lamp, cup, paper, relic, pen: Nirmal stared at the objects

in front of him. He felt—numb. He thought: I'm glad, I've been granted my wildest wish, who would have dreamed . . . He thought: I've been set up as a target—why?—why me? It was signal of his exhaustion that he held these disparate thoughts side by side for a long moment without one modifying the other.

Then unease filled him. I must do something, he said to himself, and picked up the telephone and dialed Latif's number. "Good news," he began. His voice floated. "At least, I hope it's good news."

Nirmal explained; Latif heard him out in silence.

"So it came back to your desk," Latif said finally.

"Yes," said Nirmal, "it's in front of me now."

"On your desk?" said Latif.

"Yes," said Nirmal, "I told you that already."

Finally, the news seemed to register. Latif suggested they convene a staff meeting in the next hour and Nirmal said, yes, that's what he had in mind, no, he'd tell the truth—just what had happened, no, he was not afraid, yes, it had been a long night, tired, yes, tired.

Rising from his desk, Nirmal fell forward to walk; his knees were forceless. He washed, shaved—badly, but managing not to cut himself; his face in the mirror looked grim, ghostly, bleached out, as if after a night of fearful debauch. He toweled harshly, restoring some sort of sensation to his skin; he changed his clothes. Neither happy nor sad, he did not know what he felt.

After his tea, Nirmal ordered chairs brought in. Then sat back and waited, his gaze nailed to the door as though to the opening curtain on a stage. The wait seemed interminable. He rubbed his eyes: the lids were swollen, granular. He made a visor of his hands and narrowed his eyes to cut off the glare. Actually, there was no glare; the morning was mild, the light pale, cool and tentative, but to eyes that had been open all night long, even the mildest sunlight was painful.

Less than an hour later, Latif, Waheed, Rahman, and Munim gathered in Nirmal's office. The Shah brothers were late and Nirmal began the meeting without them.

Nirmal told how, just after dawn, he had stepped out of his office to look in on one of the prisoners in lockup and returned to find a bundle on his desk.

There was a burst of questions, all at the same moment. Nirmal offered to answer them one at a time. He did his best: where he was ignorant, he frankly avowed it. He was largely ignorant, so his answers satisfied no one; the others thought he was being willfully mysterious, suspected Nirmal was protecting someone, and hinted as much, though no one dared say so outright.

Nirmal did have an air of visible distraction about him, as though his true interest were elsewhere—but there was no mystery where that was. Everyone waited for the Shah brothers whose verdict was so crucial, and each time a footfall was heard in the corridor, heads turned to the door expectantly. Nirmal was on the verge of sending another messenger when the brothers arrived. They greeted the members of Nirmal's team with offhand courtesy and seated themselves close to the door.

Naseem Shah wasted no time in coming to the point. "You say you have found the holy relic," he began. "Perhaps . . . God willing . . . how miraculous that would be. But, please, permit me to intrude . . . I don't understand the circumstances."

Nor did Nirmal. Why had the relic been returned to his desk when it would have been so much safer to drop it in a post-box? Why *his* desk with so many other desks to choose from? He didn't know, and might have spared himself by telling another story; instead, he said evenly: "The holy relic has come back to us the same way it left us—in mysterious circumstances." And he repeated the story of how he'd come to find the bundle for the benefit of the Shah brothers. It came out more smoothly on the retelling. Too smoothly, perhaps. Aslam Shah examined his fingernails with a studied indifference. Naseem Shah's lip curled. "Why are you smiling?" Nirmal asked.

"Was I smiling?" Naseem Shah fingered his beard slowly. "Well, it must be happiness. I find it perfectly magical—the way the holy relic found its way to your desk."

"I was as surprised as you are," Nirmal confessed. "I might easily have waited until midday, after the postboxes were cleared, and told you a different story, a story that didn't involve me in the least. But I've nothing to hide."

"Perhaps it is as you say," Naseem Shah pursed his lips. "Might we see *what* has been recovered?"

"By all means." Once again, Nirmal unwrapped the tiny vial. Naseem Shah strained forward, stared, and said nothing.

"Has everyone here seen the holy relic before this?" Nirmal asked. There was a low hum of assent.

"Will each of you go on record that this is indeed the *mu-e-muqaddas?*"

Going on record was a different proposition, and the men crossed and uncrossed their legs restively before answering. Latif continued poring over the reticule; Waheed stepped forward and prodded it with the end of a ruler, as though it were alive, but no one, not even Naseem Shah, touched it directly. One by one, Nirmal asked each man for his verdict. No one wanted to be first. Nirmal decided to start with Naseem Shah. "Please give us your judgment."

"It seems very like," Naseem Shah conceded.

"Seems!" said Nirmal. "What do you mean by that?"

"As Allah is my witness, I cannot speak—not here."

"Why not?"

"This is not the place."

"One word—yes or no," Nirmal persisted.

"I can only speak in the presence of my people."

His people! Yes, that's been perfectly clear all along, Nirmal thought. He raised his voice: "Then we'll make the announcement without you."

"As you please," said Naseem Shah.

"Next!" said Nirmal quickly, turning to Aslam Shah.

"The resemblance is striking," said Aslam Shah.

"And you?" Nirmal turned to Munim.

"It's pointless for me to say anything," Munim explained, "unless . . ."

"Unless what?" Nirmal wanted to know.

"Unless the custodians speak."

"We'll manage without you, then," said Nirmal, turning to Waheed.

"Well, I would call it the same," said Waheed, "unless my eyes deceive me." And the others followed suit, affirming and qualifying at the same time.

There was a silence after everyone had spoken. A joyful occasion, yet no one looks joyful, Nirmal observed, myself least of all. Nirmal was at a loss as to how to proceed further. Better brazen it out, he thought. "First I'll telephone the Chief Secretary, then, with his blessing, we'll all proceed to Jinnah Square and make a public announcement."

"So that's settled, then," said Naseem Shah with heavy sarcasm. He continued to stare at Nirmal.

Nirmal stood up to the man's gaze, trying hard to look equable and assured. His left eye, absurdly, began to tear.

The Shah brothers were the first to leave the room; the others followed: they would wait in Waheed's office while Nirmal made his call.

As luck would have it, the telephone line was dead. Nirmal sped down the hall, fairly strangled with frustration. A young army officer was sitting at the switchboard, playing with the wires. "You'll have to revive that line at once," Nirmal demanded. "God willing," said the officer. "You must!" said Nirmal. "You are at liberty to hear everything I say to the Chief Secretary."

That ought to give him an incentive, Nirmal thought. He'd eavesdrop anyway; this way, he has my blessing. He returned to his office: he'd left the door open with the relic in plain sight—unbelievable carelessness! There it sat, in

its fat wrapping, between the URGENT and VERY UR-
GENT files. He took the bundle and stuffed it into his lap
drawer, the only drawer with a key. It was difficult squash-
ing the wrapping flat into that shallow space, but after a
few tries, he succeeded in forcing the drawer shut and locking it.

For a moment, he put his head down on his arms and
closed his eyes. Too much had happened too fast; he
couldn't sort it out. So tired he could weep.

He sat up abruptly and tried the phone again.

The line was clear. As soon as he had satisfied himself
that it was Husamuddin on the other end, Nirmal announced the news.

"What?" said Husamuddin.

"We're recovered it."

"You recovered it?" said Husamuddin.

"Yes, yes, we've recovered it." And Nirmal went on to
tell how he'd stepped out of his office and returned to find
a strange object on his desk.

"And where is it now?"

Nirmal told him.

Husamuddin was horrified: "I know you're tired, but
really . . ."

"You're right. I'm so tired."

"Get it into the District Magistrate's safe and have it
sealed with his seal. And have a special guard posted
around it night and day."

"You're absolutely right."

"You've every reason to be tired," said Husamuddin.

More reason than you know, thought Nirmal. "There's
only one little problem," he said. "The others are willing to
stand with me when I announce the recovery publicly—
but the Shah brothers won't come along."

"The others all verified it?"

"Yes. Well, in a way . . . Each had a saving reservation."

"But they're willing to stand with you?"

"All but one of the police constables—a man named Munim. He's been spending most of his time with the Action Committee, so it's understandable. I don't know whether he refused from conviction or whether it was a calculated gesture, so as not to poison his relationship with the committee."

"Forget him. Naseem Shah wants a *deedar*, I suppose, with all the maulanas in on it."

"I imagine."

"But we can't risk that now."

"Exactly."

"Announce the recovery, Nirmal. Or, better—have the District Magistrate or the Deputy Commissioner do it. Move over the heads of the Shah brothers if you have to. If they're not going to cooperate . . . I've learned a few things about Naseem Shah. Let me tell you he's in politics up to his neck. Be forceful. Make the announcement and ring me back at once. I'm anxious to know how it goes."

There was a tiny catch in Nirmal's voice as he said good-bye. Husamuddin tried to detain him a moment longer. "Well, my friend . . . you're not going back to retirement after this. What are your future plans?"

"Plans?" said Nirmal. "The future? I can't think five minutes from now." You tell me the future, and I'll tell you my plans, he thought. For the moment, he could think of nothing better than retirement, nothing happier than his quiet mornings on the verandah, a life with the taste and texture of bread, as solid, sustenant, and mild.

Before going out, Nirmal composed a short press release so as to have it in readiness. He left it on top of his other papers, so he could find it easily when it came time to add a note concerning the celebration of the crowd. Wishful thinking, he suspected.

Soon afterward, the tiny crisis management team, Nirmal and Latif at its head, made its way to Jinnah Square. Small crowds were massing at the crossroads, for the news was already out; it must have traveled by word of mouth. Latif overheard someone saying: "The police sahibs made life hot for the thieves, so they made a deal."

A bent old man touched Nirmal's sleeve. *"Mubarak!"* he said gratefully.

Other bystanders were less expressive. It was hard to read their faces; they were so full of conflicting indications: doubt, joy, surliness, doubt, hope, bewilderment.

The crowd was straggly at the square. Nirmal and his entourage mounted the platform. The boards were sodden even now. The microphones, still in place from the rally and the rain which followed, were not functioning. Latif would have to shout.

From where Nirmal stood, he could not see any readily recognizable members of the Holy Relic Action Committee. Good, he thought, if they are not assisting us, at least they are not interfering. Unless they're hatching plans at a distance . . .

Latif began to bellow out the news. When he said: "It is time to give thanks and go back to work," there were mixed cries. Someone began reciting the *Kalima*: *"La ilaha illal'lah . . ."* the soft palatals hard with hate.

"Not so fast!" someone shouted.

"Where is Qureshi?" another voice.

"Can't hear!" from the back.

"Let's see it!" a chorus now.

When Latif explained that there were legal difficulties in the way of displaying the holy relic at this time, and Nirmal interrupted to promise that the holy hair would be installed in the shrine in due course, the response was swift: "We want it now—a *deedar* for the people!"

Nirmal tried to speak, but it was impossible for him to be heard above the shouting. Jinnah Square was in turmoil, a sea of lifted arms.

"Now! We want it now!"

"Expose the plot!"

Cries of "fraud" and "Hindu trickery" were flying thick and fast. Waheed's men appeared from nowhere and began pushing the crowd back with their lathis held across their chests. Nirmal was taken firmly by both elbows and rushed off the platform. For a moment, he did not realize that he was in the grip of the police, that he was being forced to safety. Latif was close behind him, also under escort. They were propelled into an alleyway, down side streets, until they came to a corner where the way was clear. Waheed joined them there: his nose was bleeding, his sleeve torn. "My men are holding," he said, "there's nothing we can do here."

"I suggest—if you'll pardon the expression," said Latif, "that we beat an honorable retreat."

Back at headquarters, Nirmal found his group shaken but intact. "Those are—I am sorry to say—Muslims," Rahman kept repeating to all who would listen.

Munim was waiting with a message from the Holy Relic Action Committee. "They've been meeting ever since your meeting. They demand a *deedar* for the people, a public verification."

The message came as no surprise to anyone. The Holy Relic Action Committee had again seized the initiative. Once again, for all practical purposes, the city was in their hands.

"What are their terms?" Nirmal asked wearily.

"No political figures participate—no city officials, no district officials."

"How about *candidates* for political office?"

"You mean Emir Kabir? But he wouldn't be included in any case. The committee wants a religious panel."

"We'll let Naseem Shah know in due course," said Nirmal. "You may go back now, or wait, as you please . . ."

Munim, quite sensibly, decided to wait.

Rahman stared at Nirmal, Nirmal stared at Latif, Latif stared at the wall. No one spoke. What choice did they have? They closed the door on Munim, so that their deliberations could be private, and in five minutes had decided what no one of them had ever doubted: they had no choice, there was no time to lose. The sense of the meeting was unanimous: they had no alternative but to take the risk. Nothing remained but to agree to a public verification, and to call Naseem Shah in to discuss it. Munim was sent off with a note of accommodation.

Nirmal paced the hall as he waited for a response. He peeked into Latif's office. The safe, sealed with the District Magistrate's seal, stood fast. A police constable, heavily armed, stood alongside it in a posture of rigid attention.

A call from Husamuddin brought Nirmal back to his desk. The connection was bad, buzzing with static, and Husamuddin was frantic. In Karachi, the news of the miraculous recovery had been received with an outcry of rage and disbelief. He'd caught the early wireless reports from Quetta, Hyderabad, and Multan; they all said the same thing: rallies, riots, arson—can you verify?

This time, Naseem Shah came without delay. His step was brisk in the hallway—Nirmal heard it—but he entered the room slowly, with great solemnity, an air, Nirmal thought, of injured righteousness, of a man who has finally been accorded his due, but ungraciously and too late. He nodded to the company and cast an especially heavy glance in Nirmal's direction, an insinuating look from under hooded lids. God alone knows what he's up to, Nirmal thought. Naseem Shah's voice, too, was calm and slow to the point of insolence, as if to say—you made me wait, now you'll wait. Yet there was little to discuss. All that Nirmal could do was to demand that his group have some voice in choosing those who would perform the public verification.

"There's no problem. We'll select the most respected religious leaders in our community," Naseem Shah assured the group.

"Please give us their names," said Latif.

"As one of the faithful, I'm sure you are familiar with all of them," said Naseem Shah.

"Just the same, I'd like their names," Latif insisted.

"My committee is discussing that list now. It's not quite complete. I give you my word—they're all honorable men."

"You doubt our word—we're free to doubt yours," Latif answered.

"Excellencies . . . excellencies, be reasonable," said Naseem Shah, in a tone of perfect reasonableness. "There are certain rules of order. You observe them. My committee also observes them. The list is under discussion now. I must return to that discussion."

"How many names?" Waheed asked.

"When I left—between five and fifteen. And now, with your permission, I'll take my leave."

"Wait!" It was Nirmal who called out. They were in a bind. All they could do was to demand a copy of the list of names as soon as it was decided upon. At the very least, they could check out antecedents and credentials, so as to be ready with challenge if needed.

Nirmal demanded a copy of the list by three in the afternoon. Naseem Shah departed, and the members of Nirmal's team put their heads together on the question of security arrangements, which would be massive. For they were all public men and realists. Major General Akhtar was called in.

Having granted permission for public verification of the relic, they now had to prepare themselves for the aftermath of a negative verdict. The details were endless: precautions for keeping reporters and photographers away from the scene, plans for a massive infiltration of army reservists at the shrine, reinforcements at the Hafsa embankment and at all points where the boundary force was stationed.

Nirmal tried calling Husamuddin but the lines were down

again. Wireless would have been too risky, so he dispatched
a note by courier:

STRICTLY CONFIDENTIAL
From N.R. for C.S.H.H.
    No lines. All troops present engaged. Want unobtru-
sive but firm arrangements for riot control and border
reinforcements. Matter grave. Advise at once if unable.

As soon as Nirmal stepped out of the office, he was besieged with reports on the local situation. At the junction
of Khem Karan and Allan Octavian Hume streets, someone
had thrown a pot of burning coals into the face of an army
lieutenant. The soldiers with him were frightened and had
begun shooting into the crowd, wounding and killing. The
number of casualties was still uncertain.

An army contingent stood shoulder to shoulder around
the police headquarters building. There'd been a bomb
threat earlier, but Nirmal only learned of it when it was all
over.

At three-thirty, no list had come.

Nirmal sent a messenger to be sure.

At five, the phones were working again and Nirmal spoke
to Husamuddin directly. The courier had arrived, and Husamuddin promised his full cooperation.

More local reports. Except for a small crowd that could
not be dispersed at the scene of the shootings, the city was
gradually quieting. News of the impending public verification had gone round, and people were going home to prepare for it.

At five, six, seven, on the hour, a messenger was sent.
The answer was always the same: the Action Committee
was still meeting; the list was not yet ready.

At midnight, Nirmal gave up. There was nothing they
could do; there would be no time to check the names.

After midnight, no messenger was sent.

Nirmal went to his cot and stretched out. It was a relief to lie down but, again, sleep would not come. The night before had been the "last night before," and here it was all over again. This would certainly be the last time.

At some point in the small hours, Waheed called. A body had been found in the river. First identification was only: circumsized male, well-built, tall, in his middle forties.

"Can't you tell me more?" Nirmal urged.

"Recently drowned, I'd say . . . only an hour or two before. The border patrol thought it was timber floating downriver."

"How about fingerprints?"

"No fingers," said Waheed, "so no prints. Hands cut off at the wrists."

"No distinguishing features?" Nirmal asked. "A moustache? A birthmark?"

"He might have. Right now, he has no face. He made someone rather angry, I'd say."

"Nothing else? No cards in his pockets? Labels? Anything at all to remind you of Qureshi?"

"Not a thing. We'll let you know—but not today—everyone will be busy today."

Nirmal put down the receiver slowly. He returned to his cot and closed his eyes, but remained wakeful.

Before dawn, Nirmal could hear troop movements along the perimeter of the city. Waheed did not ring back and Nirmal did not expect him to, although he half-hoped for the impossible. He knew that the entire police force had been mobilized for special duties during the day of public verification. The day which was now breaking.

25
Unfolding

Cyrilabad, Thursday

From sunrise on, Nirmal could hear the rattle of helicopters overhead; they darkened the sky like an incursion of locusts, their blades eating light and air. If this was Husamuddin's idea of *unobtrusive* troop arrangements, what would obtrusive be like?

The list of names arrived by courier while Nirmal was eating breakfast. He read it through, twice. There were six names and Pir Nuruddin headed the list; the Shah brothers were also part of the six, and the three other names meant nothing to Nirmal. He sent the list on to Latif by the same messenger. Latif phoned back at once. His only comment was that events were now in the hands of Allah. The Pir, at any rate, was his own man—no one could buy his loyalty. No one could second-guess his thoughts, either, he had never been predictable.

Nirmal waited on the front steps for the rest of his team. An old woman, leaning against the facing wall, regarded him steadily from under her many folds of cloth. She was a sweeper, to judge from her sari, which was coarsely woven and mud-colored; but Nirmal had never glimpsed

311

her at work, he'd never actually seen her with cloth or broom in hand. She seemed to do nothing but watch comings and goings in the building.

He glanced up. There were clouds gathering in the east. Nirmal didn't know how seriously to take them. It didn't matter what the weather, he reminded himself, the rain could bring no reprieve now. The time for a verdict had come.

Nirmal's group assembled. They went forward on foot. Hamid, the strongest of the peons attached to police headquarters, carried the safe on his head. Nirmal and Latif followed behind him. It looked, for all the world, like a victory procession, but Nirmal felt far from victorious. The three men formed a moving triangle, Hamid with the safe at its apex, Nirmal and Latif at its base. Armed police flanked them on all sides. As they moved, the safe was bombarded with flowers. One entire contingent of police trainees in plain dress had been scattered along the route to do nothing but throw petals in welcome. Each of them was armed with a basketful of jasmine and marigold. Many women and children were also sweetening Nirmal's path, and some were hurling roses. There was a sickly, cloying odor of crushed blossoms underfoot.

To a practiced eye, it was a very mixed crowd. Some of the children were carrying colored paper streamers in anticipation of a joyful outcome, but the older boys carried sticks and daggers in their waistbands; Nirmal could tell from the awkward way they walked, as though they had splinted legs or third testicles.

In the courtyard of the shrine, the formations were strained but orderly; women and small children were gathered against the left wall. Two chalk lines had been drawn along the crowd at ten-foot intervals. Between them, stood police with *lathis*, dividing the crowd into manageable sectors. A line of soldiers with bayonets stood back against the wall. There was an empty space, like a moat, around the speakers' platform, and barricades between the first row of onlookers and the moat.

The platform itself was fringed with green boughs, and the table on which the safe was to be placed was already covered with jasmine. Here, too, the smell of flowers was overpowering. They mounted the platform slowly, unsure of their footing; Hamid stooped to lower the safe. Under the table, baskets of garlands were waiting; Latif and Nirmal unloaded the baskets onto the safe, string by string. As Nirmal placed the last garland, he moved quickly so the trembling of his hands would not show.

Then the men separated to find places in the crowd. From where Nirmal stood, the safe seemed drowned in petals—all he could see was a door with a heavy lock and an important-looking seal peeping out of a floral mound.

A lectern, bristling with microphones, stood to one side of the table. Next to it: a solitary wooden armchair; it had a microphone on one of its arms—for the use of the fasting Pir, Nirmal assumed. A blackboard on an easel had been set up beside it.

Minutes later, the judges entered. They emerged from an inner chamber of the shrine, the aged Pir leading the way, the others following at the same broken pace, an old man's gait: step, hesitation, step. A hush went up. Nirmal could feel the silence on his skin, a sudden chill, a river's rising.

Just then, Nirmal was summoned inside to discuss disaster plans with a military officer who'd been having some second thoughts. He was unable to witness the start of the ceremony.

The safe was open when Nirmal returned. Naseem Shah was carefully removing the bundle, still in its heavy wraps.

The bundle was passed from hand to hand and, finally, to the Pir, who uttered a barely audible *"Bismillah!"* and rose unsteadily from the armchair to receive it. Chanting softly, mysteriously, to himself, he began to unwrap the covering of white wool. The reticule was tiny, the shawl longer and broader than a man, so there were many windings to unravel, and the Pir seemed to move more and more slowly as they came to the end.

Finally, the tiny capsule came into view. The Pir held it by the endpieces, lifting it above his head. The crowd pressed forward. It was hard to tell what anyone else was able to see. Close as he was, Nirmal could only make out a stem of murky glass, stoppered with metal at both ends.

The Pir then returned the reticule to its resting place on the shawl, and took up a copy of the Quran, saying: "All of you are Muslims and the Holy Quran is before you. Whatever you say must be the truth." He administered an oath to the man closest to him, who took up the Quran in turn and gave the oath to the man standing on his right. When each member of the group had been sworn in, the Maulanas and the Pir formed a circle round the table, and went into a huddle. The crowd was silent, but from the circle of judges came a low droning, the sound of bees in clover. Now and then, one of the group took up the reticule and lifted it. A careful man, Pir Nuruddin did this several times, turning the cylinder this way and that to the light, holding it always very close to his eyes. Nirmal made a concentrated effort to look on calmly, to appear casual and unconcerned, but he was aware of troops and tanks in the wings, of helicopters waiting at a little distance, and the effort nearly suffocated him. His head ached; he felt as if a thumb were pressing against each eyeball. The silence was overpowering, hypnotic, the tension—after so many days of it —close to unbearable. A little more of this, and Nirmal would begin not to care. He looked away to the far wall, to the branches of the trees above it, the indifferent sky.

Pir Nuruddin was hobbling to the blackboard. He picked up a piece of chalk and began to write slowly, forming large angular letters, like a schoolboy just learning. The chalk was new and squeaked.

Haq hai, the first line emerged.

And the second line: *Haq hai*.

And the third: *Haq hai*.

The other verdicts followed swiftly. "God be praised," from Mir Ali. "Yes," from Mahmud Maqbool. "Thank God," from Fathullah Rehnuma.

A whisper, inaudible, from Naseem Shah, a twist of the hand from Aslam Shah. The first verdict had clearly been the deciding one.

It was done. Pir Nuruddin moved to the lectern, where he took hold of the microphone with both hands, swayed, and tried to speak. The microphone tilted precipitously. Assisted to the armchair, the Pir tumbled into it. The crowd waited quietly as the Pir gathered breath. Then, in a voice thin and whistling, he began to speak.

"It is the holy hair, the same, the very same."

Once again, the reticule was brought to him, and the Pir raised it, kissed it, touched it to his forehead, waved it over the crowd. "Our shrine is bright with the light of Muhammad. The light of the Prophet is reflected in every face, in every leaf, in every flower . . ."

Nirmal glanced about him. Joy—could he trust it?—welled up in his throat. Men had begun to weep—even Latif was wiping his eyes. Rahman was sobbing unashamedly.

The Pir went on: "The *mu-e-muqaddas* traveled all the way from Medina to Multan and Lahore, to rest finally in our own city. The mighty of the earth failed to interrupt its passage to our shrine, and all attempts to delay it or to take it from us have failed. The holy relic has come home to us. Truly, Allah is *rahman* and *rahim!*"

Knives were flashed in the air, but only to celebrate the sun. A bearer rushed to the Pir's side with a glass of water on a silver tray. The Pir reached for the glass, but missed it in his excitement; he pinched the air, then waved the tray away, frowning. He took off his spectacles, breathed on

them, wiped the heavy lenses on his sleeve. It was warming
up.

Rehnuma took command of the microphone: "Is this
your welcome to the holy hair? What little thanks you
show!"

On all sides: blessings, smiles, cheers.

A single heart could not bear it. Nirmal could not contain
it—there was a surge of happiness so large in him, it could
not be contained in one body. His lips broke open and—

He paused, heard shouts—two, three voices only,
though strong and discordant:

"Expose the plot!"

From the platform: "Is this your thanks? Truly, we are
weak, ungrateful!"

A roar.

"Louder!"

All right, then. Time for Nirmal to be on his way. There
was dissension, that was only natural, but the mass of the
crowd stood with the Pir and his verdict. Latif, with all his
reinforcements, should have no difficulty keeping control.
There was work yet to be done.

As Nirmal walked off, an old man followed him, tugged
at his sleeve and mumbled something. "Not now, father,"
said Nirmal. "I can't hear a thing." The old man gibbered
and made a shadow picture with his hand—a swift bird,
flying across his throat—his corded neck thrust out. "I
don't understand," said Nirmal.

The old man touched his forehead and his heart, then
quickly vanished.

No time, no time! Too much to do. First, to speak to
Latif and Waheed. They would stay here until the relic was
safely escorted into the shrine. Soldiers would remain
posted around the shrine and in the special chamber itself,
until the Department of Public Works put in new doors and
special locks. Next, to call Husamuddin, who was waiting.
And then the slow, cumbersome business of returning the

city to normal. Soon schools and shops would open, factory whistles would blow. Before that—a real holiday, a day of celebration. By Monday—no later—everything must be back to normal. The troops that had come in by helicopter would go first; the others had best stand by for the next few days at least.

These were his plans. Suddenly, Nirmal was filled with plans.

26
One Day after Another

"Everything *accha*, sahib?" Abdul Ghani whisked away a fly that was in danger of falling into the gravy.

Firuz ate his supper slowly and punctiliously, as a duty to himself, although he had no appetite. The windows were open and the soft air of the garden filled the dining room. Spring . . . the season made him melancholy. The grass, everywhere he looked, was full of flutterings, faint cries; buds strained at their taut coverings and burst. Everything stirred and stretched, boiled over and breathed out, but Firuz did not. He might have been dressed in lead, he felt so heavy, so narrowed, tunneled in.

From time to time, he glanced up and caught sight of his reflection in the glass breakfront. The experience was not a pleasant one: his face was grey, his moustache—his strongest feature—a smudge of disappointment over a mouth he had always considered weak and small.

He made no attempt to call Kate in to eat with him. What was the use? He continued to lift his fork, though, eating on in silence, itching to shout something. The itch took the form of a cough. He coughed self-consciously a few times, then stopped.

He had forgiven her. Why then did Kate remain sullen and incommunicative? It was donkeyness—donkeyness! Last night he had explained to her, explained slowly and gently, as a mother might, why she must not persist in her stubbornness. "Marriage is sacrifice," he'd said at the end. "Quite," she agreed. And he thought that had signified the beginning of an understanding.

But he'd been sadly mistaken. Early this morning, before breakfast, Kate had slipped a note under his door, informing him that she'd be leaving in a month. He stormed into her bedroom to answer it in person. "You leave me and your suffering has only begun!" he warned. "I suppose you're right," she said without heat. She was emptying one of her drawers, sorting stockings, bundling them into balls. "Get off Satan's ass!" he shouted. But she didn't pause in her motions. "*Look at me!*" he demanded. She turned her back to him and busied herself in the closet. He dragged her out of it, using her hair as a handle. She had the insolence to smile. The provocation was very great.

This was the second time he had raised his hand against her, and this time he knew what he was doing. It was easier now. He struck her across the mouth and then, when she persisted in smiling, threw her to the ground. "Now may you eat dung!" he cried. She didn't resist, only lay there, limp as a pile of rags. Women! Why did they never strike back? Her docility filled him with contempt, and he put his foot on her ear and ground her face into the carpet for good measure. Not hard—lightly—only enough to give her a taste of how she made him feel. But for a moment, he'd wanted to grind her into the floor.

She rose to her feet and stared at him in silence after he was done. There was no expression he could name on her face. Her blue eyes were so cold, like bits of glass, not really alive.

She spat into her hand, wiped her mouth and walked away.

Now she was playing at *what?*

He had fed her, clothed her, loved her—loved her as wives were rarely loved in his country. He had made himself vulnerable for her. In return she had wronged him deeply.

"Out of the cage into the well!" he shouted after her. But she had locked herself in the bathroom and the faucets were on full.

And now, sitting over the remains of his supper, even his rage was cold. He could not call Kate back. He was a man and had his pride, and he thought of the old saying, "The heart is not like a table to spread before anyone." How true that was . . .

He thought of another proverb: "The world is like two days, the rest—one day after another." How true! All the old sayings were true.

The sorting of her clothes brought a great sense of order and peace to Kate, a sense of definition. It was rushing things, of course, the passport wouldn't be ready for a while yet, but she'd been packing in her mind so furiously the last few days, it was a relief to stop imagining and actually begin.

She was no longer waiting.

She had decided to leave behind the dresses Firuz had chosen for her: the brown semiformal with its dull sheen, the indigo formal, peppered with tiny white dots, which always made her want to sneeze, the grey floral—all the refined, serious, suitable frocks, that made her look twice her age.

Colors! She embraced them all, taking them all back. She would take her joyous flowered prints, the lime and yellow, the rose and umber, the shamrock green from the flamboyant days of her freedom. And this one as a re-

minder, she would take this, too—the sky-blue dress she'd
worn when she first met Firuz.

How lost and strange he'd seemed that day . . . It was his
first time abroad, and he couldn't understand the money,
or the gestures, or the pace. His English, though grammat-
ical and fluent, was a touch Victorian. They'd met at a
Nedicks counter—Firuz was spilling change in an effort to
compose the required sum—he had no idea of what the
denominations were worth and was relying on the waitress
to stop him when he'd given enough. His incompetence
made Kate feel competent and protective. And then those
large, soulful, grateful eyes he'd turned upon her—eyes so
black they seemed all pupil, all openness, of a bottomless
profundity . . . Before she knew it, she was showing him
the city, guiding and explaining, and after a little interval,
he was guiding and explaining . . . before she knew it, he
was dragging her by the hair.

Kate glanced at her face in the mirror: a little blanched,
but that was all. She could see no sorrow written there, but
that precisely was her sorrow and her devastation, the deep
anonymity she felt within her. Gradually, so gradually, she
never noticed when, all her force, her very sense of herself,
had ebbed away. How had this seepage begun? One tiny
adjustment, a substitution of no great account, a slight accommodation here, a concession there. Little things.

Actually, it's an old story, Kate thought, and began once
again to tell her story to herself. This time, there would be
no softening embellishments. She was angry, but more
angry at herself than Firuz, angry at her own self-betrayal.
She had been a more-than-willing accomplice in her own
undoing. She had sold herself.

But no, that wasn't quite it. She had turned to Firuz in a
funk, at a loss what to do with her life, and he'd told her
what she'd always been told: a woman's destiny was to be
rescued. He would rescue her. He would take her away, far
away, and she would begin a new life.

A *Stopping Place*

Such an old tale, a fairy tale, really, a tale for the very young . . .

When would she ever grow up? In less than a week, she would be twenty-four, a fully adult age. Her face did not reflect it. Such a drab nothing face, no character. She would assume character; she would begin by acting a part. She would choose her mask and grow into it; choosing a mask of strength, she would become strong. She didn't feel so very strong just at the moment, but that didn't matter.

Even to Abdul Ghani it was clear that Kate was leaving. By afternoon yesterday, he'd returned to pick up his inadequate salary, and by suppertime had settled quietly into his old routine. Today, Kate had trouble remembering how he'd stormed out of the house yesterday morning, vowing he'd never return.

All day long he'd been busy buttering up the master. Kate smiled as she caught him hovering over Firuz, but it hurt a little to watch him.

No one to count on.

I don't in the least know what I'm doing, she thought, but I'm managing all the same. She consolidated the two bottom drawers and emptied the top one. Into the middle drawer, she folded the dresses she would never wear again. How had they ever constricted her so? They would not again. Deflated, banished, in the shut drawer they were vanquished forever.

When the bureau was settled, Kate sat on the bed and made a list of all she had yet to do. She wrote: *Passport, Sylvia, letters, bank, American Express.* Then added: *newspapers—what's happening?* She hadn't a notion what had been going on in the world while she'd been away.

27
A Stopping Place

Cyrilabad, Saturday

TELEGRAM—ORDINARY
JAMES NIRMAL ROY
POLICE HEADQUARTERS
CYRILABAD
   MIRACULOUS RECOVERY ANOTHER FEATHER IN YOUR
CAP

HUSAMUDDIN

Nirmal had not slept at all that night, although he'd tried. He kept getting up to jot down some detail of normalization he'd forgotten. Between jottings, he stretched out on his cot and closed his eyes. But he didn't feel rested: his eyelids were dry and chafed, his neck stiff, knees unreliable. He'd lost the rhythm of sleep in the nights when time was too precious to be wasted. And last night, there was something more—an awful sense of how close they had been to collision, how narrowly they'd come through.

He'd gone up on the roof to catch the dawn. From there, Nirmal could see the broad gleam of the river, the dark banks heaped with sandbags. There was a brown mist rising

323

up over the water; it looked like brushfire, smoldering grass. Nirmal's head ached with the early morning chill. He waited until the sun touched the river, the sky burst into color. The gala day had begun.

Back in his office, Nirmal found his tray of morning mail as cluttered as ever, but only the top crust was up-to-date, post-recovery. There were several notes of congratulation in this layer, but even here, a few were still threatening. Nirmal ruffled through them mechanically, absently, for the sake of completeness.

He continued digging down through the layers of correspondence. Here was another letter of warning. He'd received so many now that he'd lost count. The format looked familiar—a collage made up of words cut from a newspaper; the message was familiar, too—that Nirmal should leave town at once. But the letter was undated, he'd found it deep down in the pile, close to the bottom of the heap, so Nirmal supposed it was something left over from the last hours of uncertainty before the relic had been confirmed.

No time—too much to be done. First, a memo to the Department of Public Works concerning the locks and doors in the shrine. Then a note to Waheed. Ample work ahead for the police—the drowned man was still to be identified, and the search for the whereabouts of Qureshi would have to be taken up again, the two cases to be pursued independently and no linkages assumed beforehand. For the town officials, there would be work and more work ahead, since normal services could not possibly be restored all at once, but Nirmal, for his part, felt that his job was substantially done. There was only the business of tidying up—another day at most.

Munim was brisk this morning.

"Sit down, sit down—you've earned it," Nirmal greeted him warmly.

Munim sat, on the edge of the chair. He pressed his

thumbs together—hard, so that they seemed to curve backward. "About Pir Nuruddin—" he began.

"What about him?"

"His eyes are failing."

"I'm sorry to hear that."

"You see what I'm saying," Munim directed a long and level gaze at Nirmal. "It isn't at all hard to understand. With his glasses off, the Pir can barely make out the face in front of him. Even with his glasses on, he has difficulty reading."

"How do you happen to know?"

"My uncle is his oculist."

"Oculist . . ." Nirmal repeated, as though the word were foreign to him. "So your uncle told you this . . . Anyone else mention it?"

"No."

"A man's health—that's a private matter," said Nirmal, tapping the desk combatively. "I don't want to know anything more about it."

Munim blinked slowly, said nothing.

Nirmal stared at his desk, unable to look up. He did not know what he thought. He made an effort to say something. "It *should* be a private matter. You see that, Munim, don't you?"

There was a measured silence. "No," Munim said finally, "I don't see. Your job is—"

"My job," Nirmal cut in, "was to recover the relic and restore peace to the city. To end the madness." He tried to speak slowly, evenly, without stresses. He was amazed at the sound of his voice, a recorded voice, it did not seem to be coming from his own throat.

Another long pause. Nirmal struggled for composure; he had used up his strength, his patience, all his sanity, and the muddle had only grown deeper. The ordeal was telling now. He sat heavily in his chair, as though his legs were grasped; he studied his hands: they were blurred, with wav-

ering separations between the fingers. What was he to believe? Had the Pir merely been careless, then? Or careful,
more careful than anyone had ever dreamed?

Again Munim objected: "It's most unsatisfactory."

"What is?" Nirmal asked. "Is today's celebration unsatisfactory? You like a bloodbath better?"

"It isn't natural . . . not to see this through. It's not over,
you know."

"No, it's not over," Nirmal agreed. "We haven't put an
end to speculation, rumor, resentment. No one ever does."

"The case is not solved," said Munim.

"When did I say it was?"

"It's my duty to be curious—professional curiosity."

"Tell me, Masud, how many cases of theft are ever
solved?" Munim frowned. Nirmal didn't wait for him to
answer: "You know and I know it's less than half."

"That's no excuse for not trying," said Munim stubbornly.

Nirmal realized that his patience was exhausted, and that
his voice showed it. "I promised there'd be no penalty, no
prosecution, if the relic were returned safely; those were
my terms, and I mean to keep my promise. But there's
plenty of work to be done. Find Qureshi if you can. That
should keep you busy. And . . . who knows?"

"I don't like loose ends," said Munim.

One last attempt: "Masud . . . listen. You're a religious
man, aren't you? When a man as saintly and as wise as the
Pir comes to a decision, his reasons are not for us to judge.
Trust him."

"As you wish," said Munim, lengthening the phrase con-
siderably. "We'll see what the Qureshi business turns up,
God willing. And the case of Rafiq Husain—you remember
him?"

"Husain?" Nirmal echoed, trying to remember.

"You had him taken into custody. For picking up an idol,
I believe."

"Oh, yes, I remember. A little statue of Ganesha—his 'picking it up,' as you put it, happened to coincide with the ransacking of a Hindu temple. Tell me something, Munim —why do you resent me so?"

"I don't resent you, sir."

"Tomorrow or the next day, I'll be gone. I don't want anyone's job."

"Nothing personal, sir. I'll be going back to the Superintendent's office now."

"Yes, your work for me is done. I thank you." Nirmal rose from his chair.

Munim bowed slightly from the waist and touched his fingers to his forehead.

"And—Munim?"

"Yes?"

"This matter you've mentioned—it's between ourselves. I'll take the responsibility. You understand?"

"As you say."

After Munim had left, Nirmal turned over a paper or two more, then abandoned the rest of the heap—he had almost scraped bottom, not quite, but very near. He found himself unable to concentrate, and after the final report on the verification ceremony was brought in for his signature, he could not face his desk again. Nothing coheres, he thought, or rests, ever. He glanced at his watch: it was getting late. Almost time for the official procession to begin. The Prime Minister must have arrived by now; Nirmal would have all he could do to catch up with him.

It was good to step out in the open. Cool. Not a cloud, the sky a clear lens. Nirmal felt revived almost at once. More resurrected than revived, a miraculous second wind.

The streets were swept and watered, and lined with white chalk; green boughs fringed the balconies of the houses. Faces were smiling for a change, voices cascading laughter, shouting gaily. Here and there, shops were open, catering to the holiday crowd. Pushcarts stood at the corners, selling tiny *shami kababs* for two *annas* each. Up ahead, a small boy was leading a ram to slaughter. The animal, adorned with garlands and tinkling bells, was undeceived by so much festivity; his nostrils bursting, he seemed to smell foulness in the fine air, and stared, bleating at the place, only a little distant, where a man with two sunny knives was waiting; he dug in his hooves and refused to budge. The boy seized the ram by the horns and tried to drag him forward, but the animal stood his ground, legs splayed out, dropping his tiny pellets, bleating mournfully. Finally, he was carried.

Nirmal went on past. A glittering blue fly came with him, circling slowly round and round Nirmal's ears, settling on his lip. He blew the fly off but it returned.

The sun was high overhead. The air seemed freshly rain-washed, although there had been no rain since the day of the rally. This morning, even the beggars were smiling. A fine day! As if trouble had never been. Only now and then, glancing down a side street, stung by something acrid drifting up from the alley, did Nirmal spot the charred places and remember how it was.

In Kohlu Park, a handful of boys were playing cricket and, along its border, under the trees in their new lustrous leafage, itinerant barbers shaved their customers. Nirmal touched his chin and decided a professional shave was in order. A decent shave. And a haircut? He fingered the fringe at the base of his neck—not too bad. Give it another week. But a shave was a must—he would treat himself to some luxury, a proper place with fans and unguents. Padded chairs. The padding seemed very important.

The crowd grew denser as he neared the center of town. Three black cars nosed into view, and when the middle car passed with its green flag rippling on the hood, the cry went up from all sides: "Azam *zendabad!*" Petals flew, raining down from windows and roofs, until the hood of the car and the heads of the bystanders were white and fragrant.

Unable to touch the Minister himself, people stretched out their hands to touch the fenders of the car, and the people standing behind them stretched to touch the touchers, and the ecstasy was transferred.

The Prime Minister's limousine, with a security car fore and aft, inched down the street. Dust rose, petals continued to fall, and the cars drifted forward with motors disengaged, a grinding slowness. The sun mounted to its meridian: tall trees cast ever smaller shadows.

Nirmal followed the third car on foot. By his own choice —his own insistence, to be exact. He needed the exercise and—it was his habit—he wanted to see the crowd for himself. Latif and Waheed signaled to Nirmal to join them in the Prime Minister's car, Rahman smiled and beckoned, but Nirmal waved them on.

To those passing in a car, the crowd might have seemed wholly jubilant, but walking by slowly as he did, Nirmal was able to detect shades of difference—there were smiles and smiles. Here and there, a face blank of emotion, or crimped with sorrow. "Alive only three days ago!" someone cried. A man he did not know greeted Nirmal, saying: "The story is not finished yet." Nirmal went on without answering. He came to a humped old man, leaning against a shed, who must have been weeping for hours—his sobs were so dry and rasping. "What is it, father?" Nirmal asked. But the old man did not pause in his weeping to answer.

It was growing late. Nirmal had to quicken his step to catch up with the cars. Eleven thirty-seven. It was lucky his watch was still working, for on this street Nirmal saw three clocks in a row on neighboring buildings, and each told a different hour.

A wooden welcome arch, strung with flowers and colored cloth, had been raised in front of the courtyard of the shrine. Everyone entering the courtyard had to pass under it. The Prime Minister led the procession and, approaching the archway, was loaded with strings of garlands; seventeen times he dipped his head and the garlands were loaded up to his ears. Nirmal and the others received lighter loads— three to four strands apiece. Reporters jostled in on all sides with microphones on long booms.

From the moment the Prime Minister stepped out of the car, the tiny group of dignitaries found itself surrounded; the photographers were everywhere. Shutters clicked: Prime Minister Azam receiving a tribute of garlands in front of the entrance to the shrine; Azam, flanked by Latif and Nirmal, making a short speech of congratulation; Nirmal clarifying some point or other, expostulating with his hands; Azam entering, leaving, the shrine; Azam rumpling the hair of a small child, giving money to a beggar without arms; Azam and Latif embracing; Azam and Nirmal embracing; Azam issuing a final statement to the press, front view, side view, view from squatting position; Azam saluting the crowd in the street outside; Azam and Naseem Shah standing stiffly side by side; Azam waving goodbye to Cyrilabad.

Only Pir Nuruddin was absent. He'd sent a note to Rahman, pleading a temporary indisposition, assuring his followers that his spirit was with them in their shared rejoicing.

When the Prime Minister's limousine drove off, its green flag streaming, Naseem Shah made a low bow to the company and withdrew. It was over. The men unloaded their garlands on the first beggar to approach them.

Nirmal walked on with Rahman and Latif. Rahman was brooding and silent; Latif carried the burden of the conversation. "Where are you off to after this?" he asked Nirmal.

"I thought I'd find a barber," said Nirmal. "Must be a shop nearby."

"The closest is Shamsul Khordad's—a few minutes from here. Better . . . Better not. There's another place, not much farther, if you keep walking this way. Forget Shamsul's."

"Why do that?"

"It may not be open."

"The next may be closed as well."

"You really shouldn't be wandering about this neighborhood alone."

"I managed on my own when people were at their angriest," Nirmal reminded him.

"Anger needs time to cool," said Latif. "Shamsul is an unforgiving man. Any imagined insult and he flies."

"Insulted? How could that be? I never met the man."

"Why subject yourself to any unpleasantness? Shamsul is a friend of Rafiq Husain—you remember him—"

"No one lets me forget."

"Husain has friends everywhere. Forget Shamsul. Mansur's shop isn't that much farther. It's very decent."

"All I want is something very simple," said Nirmal wearily. He thought he'd like to pay his respects to the Pir, but decided not to mention it. The Pir's house wasn't far.

Latif took his leave at the next corner. Rahman and Nirmal walked on together. At the edge of Jinnah Square, Rahman asked: "Won't you stop by? My house is round the corner. My wife made some sweets for the holiday. It would be an honor for us." But Nirmal thanked him and said no, not today. He thought, momentarily, of all the sweets he'd refused in his life, all the chances to "stop by" never taken; he didn't know why, but it was necessary to be always on his way, never beholden to anyone.

"Another time, then. *Enshallah*."

"This won't be good-bye," said Nirmal.

He continued on straight after leaving Rahman. His thoughts were very simple: first, he wanted a shave, then maybe just a word with the Pir, if that were possible. Then on to Rest House and a bath. After that, as many hours of sleep as he could—he had some catching up to do. Creature comforts . . .

And now what?

He stepped softly, listening.

Someone seemed to be shadowing him.

How could that be? Imagination becomes part of the air, he thought. The smallest suggestion from Latif and now—

Still, the impression persisted. Someone in sandshoes, or sweeping in short swipes, the sound gaining, fading, gaining again.

But that was absurd. No one was following, although there were pedestrians going his way. Only natural.

He badly needed sleep, that was all.

Shamsul's shop was open: Nirmal peered through the window. There were no customers inside. The place looked comfortable, if not luxurious. Three thickly upholstered chairs awaited him. The chairs had tilting backs and foot-rests. There were fans and wall mirrors. It was very tempting.

Then the assistant, a boy of twelve or thirteen, rushed forward to greet Nirmal, his hands pressed together in an awkward *namaskar*. The barber also turned and gestured to Nirmal, bringing his hands together in the Hindu greeting.

Nirmal felt there was mockery in it, and decided not to enter after all. He gave the traditional Muslim *adab*, touching his fingers to his forehead, and moved on. Once past the shop, he ran his fingers over his chin and neck again and thought: it can wait. A bath and bed are the important things. Might as well pay my respects to the Pir . . .

The Pir's house wasn't much farther. Nirmal decided he would simply leave his name at the door and go on. He turned down Russell Road. The street was almost empty, the sky above it—crystalline, without a cloud. Nirmal had never seen such light at midday, only before sunset, just before the light fails, when the edges of things stand sharp, and the separation between leaf and leaf is absolute, nothing blurs or clings or leans.

He heard steps approach. A young man walked up on

Nirmal's left and greeted him. *"Salaam aleikum,"* he smiled.

"And on you peace," Nirmal replied.

"Nice weather," said the young man, keeping abreast.

"Yes, lovely," said Nirmal.

The young man continued walking alongside, although Nirmal was not aware of having invited him to do so. They walked in silence. When Nirmal slackened his pace, the young man also slowed down. Nirmal lurched forward with quick, long strides, but the other kept in step. "See here!" said Nirmal irritably, but the young man's face was turned away, he couldn't have heard. Willful as a child, Nirmal thought, and, really, he wasn't much more than a child; he wasn't a man at all. Only a boy, tall, gangly, with a faint moustache, a weak chin, and a long throat. His lips had the sticky redness of the young and fair.

Boy or man—it made no difference to Nirmal. Had he wanted company, he would have much preferred Rahman. "Now, listen . . ." he said, but the words emerged without force.

Too tired to make a fuss, Nirmal reflected. Doesn't seem worth the effort. And I'm not thinking clearly. Visiting the Pir—is that wise? Is it even sensible?

Better turn back.

But his feet continued to move forward, carried by an earlier momentum, and his companion moved alongside at the same tempo.

"A festival," said the boy, "even the flies are festive today."

"I noticed that," said Nirmal.

The narrow street stretched ahead, still and empty now, a diminishing perspective. The boy said: "They say that the holy hair was delivered to your desk—a blessing to you personally." There was muffled anger in his voice.

Nirmal made no reply. He felt more than a little uncomfortable; the walk had gone on too long, and he'd found no way to shake his companion off. There were no shops to dip into; this was a residential district. Nirmal took another quick glance at the boy, and told himself to be calm, there was no reason to worry. Only a schoolboy, young and impatient with an imperfect world.

"So you'll soon be leaving us," he said.

"Soon as I tidy things up," said Nirmal.

"Tidy things up? You should—yes," said the boy.

Wasn't this the Pir's house on his left? Nirmal wondered. He hesitated now: there was a high wall all around it; the shutters were closed. Nothing invited him to enter, and he thought: I'll go on past . . .

But now the boy had turned to face him. He said—or seemed to say—it was hard to tell, he spoke so quickly: "Someone's got to pay. We don't like government stooges. We don't like people who make deals."

Let the boy have his say, Nirmal thought, I'm too tired to argue. Besides, anger seemed such a waste. The sky was so blue, the sun so mild.

The boy repeated, as if he were arguing the point: "Someone's got to pay."

"I have to go now," said Nirmal wearily, "I want—"

"One of these?" said the boy, reaching for something in his pocket. "*Bismillah!*" he invoked God's blessing. He put out his hand. In it: something shining—

"*Who's this?*" Nirmal cried out. Recoiled sharply—the pain was very great. *The shock.* And yet he'd known . . . Only the cold, the knife cold, knife-touched bone cold. "Run!" he said to his feet, his feet pumped, running against a great headwind—he did not move.

Then he saw the red runner beneath his feet, the carpet red for him. He'd never asked for never wanted things like that but if it was expected why then—

28
Free

Lahore, Monday–Saturday

He was free again.

Stepping outside for the first time on Monday, Tom was overcome by the amplitude of the sky, then by the violent bustle in the streets, the speed, the dazzle, the din. There was sex in the air—people, foliage, flowers—everything going berserk.

Tom left Cyrilabad under police escort late Monday afternoon and arrived in Lahore early that evening. The evening was cool and mild. Nearing Lahore, the river looked splendid as the guidebook said it would be; the Badshahi mosque loomed ahead, three-breasted: the milk-white domes beckoned and shone against a sky of azure. A sky like silk, like glass. Only his floaters marred it.

There were several letters waiting for him at the hotel. Two were from Barbara, mildly frantic for news.

And Aleem was waiting, unsmiling, his eyes plaintively round and moist. He seemed to have great difficulty finding words—when he did it was to beg for forgiveness. But Tom would have none of it: "My own damn fault," he said. "I was asking for something to happen." He sent Aleem home with promises to meet again soon.

A shower was the first thing: Tom hadn't washed properly in days. In a very few minutes, he'd shed a week's grime. Should he shave? he wondered. He had the beginnings of a beard and was curious to see how it might turn out, so he decided to wait.

He hadn't brushed his teeth in days, and that was what he did next. As he reached for the toothpaste, he noticed the big amber bottle on the shelf. Couldn't be much left, he thought. He lifted the bottle to the light, assessing the contents, holding it out at arm's length to demonstrate how completely he had vanquished it. For an instant, he thought the label read *Not To Be Used For Navigation*— but how could that be? He brought the bottle closer to read the label correctly. Was he feeling tempted? Yes, he had to admit, a little. No virtue without temptation, he thought. Angels have neither, and therefore . . . Therefore? Therefore, I am not an angel, since virtuous, since tempted. Some flaw in the argument somewhere, although his first premises were surely sound, and Tom was surely, sorely, *tempted*. He'd take one tiny sip as a concession to temptation, then cap it up at once to show the measure of his control. The taste was unpleasant, musty and sharp—brrr! He was cured. He took one more to make certain: the taste was certainly not addictive. Definitely cured! One last sip to mark the success of his cure—that did it! Tom smiled to himself in the mirror. His face had a boiled look. Quite enough now. Capping the bottle and setting it back on the shelf, Tom noticed there weren't more than a few drops left. Not worth leaving, really. This would be it, the final final, a toast to his freedom, his new beginning.

He slept through noon Tuesday and had his brunch sent up, a glass of gin and lime with it. The ice in his glass made a glad sound. And Tom would have been glad, if only—

He tried to write for two aching hours, relinquishing page

after page—a clean sheet for each fresh, false, start. "The well is dry," he pronounced in a sepulchral voice.

No use forcing himself. It was the heat, utterly debilitating. His thirst raged. Water did not assuage it.

The heat was grilling. When Tom called the manager about it, he was told it was too early for air conditioning—call again in April. Throughout the afternoon, Tom was obliged to return to the basin, where he sought relief by splashing water over his face and neck, and stood, for long intervals, soaking his wrists. The beard, he decided, had to go; it only made him hotter.

Wednesday morning, Tom stopped off at the consulate and asked to cut short his tour. Iran, the next stop on his itinerary, had no appeal for him; he wanted to return directly to the States. "After what you've been through," said Kenny, "don't blame you a bit. Shall we say 'for reasons of health'?"

"Say anything," Tom agreed, "but get me out of here."

On Wednesday night, there was a small dinner party at the Wicks. Tom was very much at the center of it. "You were . . . tortured?" one of the guests ventured to ask. Tom ignored the question as preposterous, and when Nan pressed: "Tell us all about it!" he said: "There's nothing to tell."

The eager faces surrounding him fell slack. "Nothing," he repeated, taking a mouthful of cake. "Really." Stashed for reasons of convenience, as he'd come to understand it, he'd been safe all along. He was safe now. Nothing would happen to him, ever—except the last thing . . .

"Oh, come," Nan insisted, "it couldn't of been pleasant."

"Well, the accommodations weren't quite first class," Tom said thickly; heavy with a sense of anticlimax, his mouth seemed full of paste. To have travelled so far, only to discover the walls of a slammer and his own visual debris! He'd have done better at home.

Home . . . a word he never used.

By Thursday, there was nothing to detain Tom. It was hard to think of anything but ways of keeping cool. Tom's thirst was nagging, fierce; nothing quenched it. From here on out, the sun would be gaining steadily. Summers in Lahore, people actually wept from the heat, so they'd told Tom at the consulate. He'd no intention of staying on, whatever the weather, no desire to take to the hills.

Luckily, he was able to book a reservation for the flight on Saturday. He turned in his keys at two that afternoon. Aleem was already pacing in the lobby and Howard Wick was waiting outside in his air-conditioned car. They formed an awkward threesome; Howard seemed especially irked by Aleem's presence, and the conversation between them was halting and stiff.

The car made good time. Heat had emptied the streets for them. Entering the wire enclosure around the airport, Tom felt he had already left the country. The airport waiting room, stocked with the usual magazines, watches, Swiss chocolate, Pepsi, lemonade, and flyblown fruit, was a placeless zone. The air in the hangar did not stir; a ceiling fan, and a wall fan with faded paper streamers, churned heavily, without effect.

"What's that?" Tom asked again and again. There were so many announcements and the fans were so noisy, he kept skipping words. Yet they talked on, each of them strained to keep the conversation going.

Tom had no knack for bringing people together. Parties in his honor were always discordant or silent, his friends were rarely friends of one another; this signified something about himself—just what, he preferred not to think.

Suddenly they heard a voice over the loudspeaker calling Howard Wick to the phone. "Who do you suppose?" Howard asked; he sounded annoyed, but walked off with a springing step.

"Wife, I bet," Tom confided to Aleem as soon as they

were alone together. He could see Howard in a corner stall, gesturing uselessly with his free hand.

"I shall never marry," said Aleem fervently, "never!"

"We all say that," said Tom, "and we all marry. I bet your family has a girl set up for you right now . . ."

"I won't marry her," said Aleem.

Howard returned, huffing a little. "Sorry," he said, "have to be off. Business, I'm afraid." He spoke with more breathlessness than was possible for such a short jog. "Embassy business, I suppose," Tom probed. Howard nodded, failed to supply details. Nan must have chewed him out—why else would he look so sheepish?

"*C'est la vie*," said Tom.

"Till next time, Tom— Soon!"

Howard and Tom both doubted there would be a next time. Aleem regarded them with astonishment as they shook hands stiffly and vigorously. How cold, he thought, how cold Americans are, touching only at the antipodes, like blind men crossing canes.

After Wick left, Tom and Aleem sat down on a bench together and talked more freely. It was easier now. Once again, Aleem asked Tom what the New York underground was like, how much it cost to travel from one end of Manhattan to the other. Tom promised to write as soon as he arrived. Aleem said no, he would write first. "Don't know where I'll be exactly," said Tom, "so you better wait." Aleem turned his head away. Tom would forget to write; Aleem's letter would never connect. We are saying goodbye for the rest of our lives, Aleem thought; he wanted to shout the truth, but only stared silently at the clock cutting the minutes, his face screwed up.

Tom's floaters were with him now, two trembling wisps in the right eye. He swerved and twisted his head to peer through his left eye, which was clearer. As Aleem noticed Tom blink and twist, he decided he'd misjudged the man; the American seemed to be struggling to hide his tears.

Then came the boarding announcement for the flight to London.

"It won't be long," Tom stood up. "We'll meet again."

"*Enshallah*," said Aleem. "Maybe." And, despite his bleak certainty of the moment before, he was beginning to hope again.

"I'll show you round," said Tom. "My turn."

"Would you?" said Aleem. "I'm such a greenhurt."

"Greenhorn," Tom corrected.

"Horn? Why this horn?"

The loudspeaker cracked and coughed. Bearishly, with some embarrassment, Tom returned Aleem's embrace. Custom of the country, he thought. And, hell, why ever not?

"See you in New York!"

"*Enshallah* . . ." Aleem waved after Tom's departing back. New York . . . the name conjured up images of white towers shutting out the sun, of streets black and glittering with sin. "*Enshallah!*" he repeated when Tom turned and waved, halfway to the plane. Mica—or metal—in the tarmac glinted painfully in Aleem's eyes, the wires of the fence scorched his fingers, but Tom did not look back again.

29
Sorting

Karachi–Athens, end of April

Faced with Kate's determination to leave, Firuz waxed hot
and cold. For days at a time, he was accommodating, reasonable, full of humor and charm—he would tease her out
of her stubbornness. It was childish. He had forgiven her;
they would start afresh. All marriages, even the best of
them, had their ups and downs. Children would make a
difference, give Kate something to do with her time. They
would start having children now. Whose idea had it been
to wait until they had two years of marriage behind them?
"Mine," Kate said with some pride, for it had been her one
sanity.

When Kate did not relent, Firuz accused her of ruining
both their lives. He wept openly.

Too many tears. Kate tuned him out. She was becoming
deaf, stone, cold. She had to be—or else he would confuse
her utterly. If he told her that her hair was black often and
vehemently enough, she might, against all the evidence of
her senses, come to believe him; for his forgiveness, she
might in time become grateful. In front of Firuz, Kate
never wavered, but there were moments when, left to her-

self, she was filled with misgivings. She had simplified, falsified. She'd never known Firuz. Here was love, as turbulent—but as true—as it ever was. She was turning her back on it. For what? She'd come to a dead stop in the hallway, wondering where she was going. I don't in the least know what I'm doing, she'd say to herself, I haven't the faintest idea what I shall become. Why leave, then? The answer was always the same: because I must, because I cannot breathe, because I know for a certainty what I cannot be.

It was only a month into spring, but broiling. A bowl of milk with a drop of yogurt in it became a bowl of solid yogurt after standing for half an hour on the shelf. Even the nights were hot: Kate sprinkled her pillow with water before going to sleep.

They left Karachi in the bleached hours of early afternoon. The city seemed deserted, the sun so white, it seemed to have annihilated colors, gradations, the street itself. It was the time of day when shops and offices draw their shutters, the hour when everyone lies down in the shade or under an electric fan, all lie down heavily, the flesh a burden. Only lovers and messengers of the dying venture out, mindless of comfort, sick with urgency.

Kate was desperate to leave, and the taxi could not move quickly enough away from the house she had never loved or tended, down the metalled Airport Road with its borders of dust and sand on either side. The new golf course redeemed nothing, and the Imperial War Graves Cemetery seemed an oasis of complacency in that barren, mocking waste.

Firuz had an assignment in Lebanon, so they went on to Athens together. From Athens, they would each turn: Firuz to Beirut, then back to Lahore and the house they had chosen together, Kate to New York, and then to California maybe—she wasn't sure. She had chosen to return by boat, slowly, hoping to begin to sort her life out on the way.

They stood at the dock in Piraeus at a distance from the ship, looking out on a sweep of sunstruck water and a far shore of scoured stone. They'd left the murk and the heat behind; here everything shone with the purity of Mediterranean light: clear and mild: this was temperate ground. For Kate, the very air was cleansing.

They stood facing one another, glancing at the water, and glancing away. They did not look at the ship itself. Firuz's eyes were red—from the sun, he explained. Kate was wearing dark glasses, her eyes protected.

Kate's luggage had already been carried on board. She had an overnight case in her hand, but that was all. She could have rested the case at her feet, but didn't, she didn't want to put it down.

There was a call to go on board. "Plenty of time, plenty of time," Firuz said. "Why be first?" So they waited, facing each other but not touching, while the other passengers lined up.

There was nothing to say. Soon Kate would have to move, and it seemed to her that she stood on the edge of a clearing; she was afraid of the openness, afraid of the light. The crowd on the gangplank was thinning out.

When they heard the final call to board, Kate lifted her sunglasses. It was too rapid a gesture for Firuz to catch the expression of her eyes. They rushed to kiss—an old habit, even now not easily broken. Then fell apart clumsily, both embarrassed that they had not been able to keep up a consistent attitude to the end. But what did it matter now?

Then Kate turned and stepped out into the clearing, mounting the ramp without hurry, yet without lingering or backward glances; she moved with wide, deliberate steps, as though across a stage.

Firuz's hand, lifted as Kate stepped away, fell to his side as she went forward without once looking back. He followed her with his eyes. There was not much distance between them, only a little lapsed time.

Only a little lapsed time and, had he wanted, Firuz still might have called her back. But he didn't want to—not yet. I'll call her back when she has learned what separation means, he said to himself, when she has begun to fathom what she has lost.

Firuz seemed to have already lost her: he squinted to make out where Kate might have gone, but it was hopeless, there was a dense weave of bodies, a tangle of arms.

Kate stood at the outer rail of the middle deck, levering with her elbows to make space for herself. Everyone was waving, handkerchiefs streaming, women were crossing themselves, weeping, shouting endearments. Kate scanned the pier, waved, paused with hand in midair, waved again. It was easy enough to spot Firuz: he was standing apart from everyone, a disconsolate dark shape, his shoes seemed burnished with gold, so immaculately shined.

He did not wave back, and Kate tried to shout, but it was no use—everyone was shouting. And then, suddenly, she knew he had spotted her. He'd begun to wave with both hands, holding them high above his head.

The sun had touched Kate's hair—a blaze—and now there was no missing her. Firuz waved until he was dizzy with it.

There was no way to tell when the separation began except for the churning of the motors; no power yet, but the promise of power. Kate felt the great heartroar of the engines travelling upward, outward—

Outward bound!

Kate peered down: she saw nothing at first, the ship was still flush with the dock, but fixing her gaze steadily, she noticed something move. The crowd on the pier seemed to recoil, shrink ever so slightly away.

Now the ship was starting to move. The waving hands strained not upward, but outward, as though to touch.

Kate, too, leaned far over the rail, her hand motionless, stretched out. Firuz was shading his eyes with one hand, waving with the other, and the ship was moving out to sea, keeping parallel with the pier, the water coming between them, imperceptibly at first, the merest thread, an edge of brightness that severed and defined—a hair, and then a blade.

30
Alone

My dear sister—
  The neem tree was in its yellow leaf, Nirmal's letter was in her hand. Meena stood on the verandah where they had so often taken breakfast together in the past. It was evening now, with the first cool breezes coming in. The garden was quieter, more subdued than a month ago; the delirium, the season of blossoms, was over. The season of fruits had come.
  With her empty hand, Meena pulled absently at the fringe of leaves which beat against the railing, then repented and peered down nearsightedly to study what she'd plucked: a leaf, fish-shaped, riddled with tiny holes.
  Blight . . . Everything she touched was touched with it. Everywhere she looked something of Nirmal remained. She'd given away all his clothes, but there was always something turning up—a pipe, a pen, a broken compass, a long lost slipper, a letter he'd forgotten to mail, his last letter. Here his hand had moved . . .
  I am working nine days out of seven.
  For what? What had changed? Nothing ever changes.

There was more trouble on the border only this week, another border to the south, and to the north in Kashmir—more riots. Cyrilabad was all but forgotten in the new clashes; the cause of the theft of the holy hair remained unknown, but the case was considered closed, and the relic which had cost so much, which had cost Meena the earth, was resting comfortably; there was no news at all from the town. Not since the Pir's death, which had followed swift upon Nirmal's own. Unlike Nirmal, the Pir had died a peaceful, natural death in bed, and in the great access of emotion following his death, all doubts as to the legitimacy of the relic had been laid to rest. The body of the Municipal Chairman had been identified at last, named, and quickly buried, and his secrets buried with him. Nirmal's assailant was in prison now: he had not worked alone. Some group of seasoned politicians had put him up to it. Politics! The word was foul to Meena.

Let them investigate and prosecute, indict, condemn and execute, nothing changed, nothing was restored.

Crisis is tiring, I'm counting on that . . .

That was your great mistake, Meena thought. She held the letter up to catch the last of the light. How worn it was! The paper would never go brittle and snap at the folds. Already it was faintly discolored and supple from so much handling, the texture of flesh almost, limp from the dampness of her hands.

I do not know what the future holds, but I know that my past is . . .

It was hard to read in the ebbing light, but Meena wasn't reading now so much as prompting. She knew each word by heart. *I wait for the morning faithfully.* The note had been written on the night of the honorable retreat. *Tomorrow we shall see.* She trailed her finger over the ending slowly.

More in person when the time comes.

Love,

A. G. Mojtabai lived for several years in Iran and Pakistan, near the Indian border. Since returning to the United States, she has been librarian at the City College of New York, and taught Philosophy at Hunter College and Narrative Fiction at New York University.

Ms. Mojtabai is the author of two previous novels, *Mundome* and *The 400 Eels of Sigmund Freud*. Her third novel, *A Stopping Place*, was written during 1976–78, while the author was a Fellow of the Radcliffe Institute for Independent Study. She is currently Briggs-Copeland Lecturer on English at Harvard University.